UNDISCOVERED COUNTRY

UNDISCOVERED COUNTRY

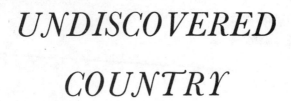

THE NEW ZEALAND STORIES OF
KATHERINE MANSFIELD

EDITED BY IAN A. GORDON

1724-1974

Longman
1724-1974

Longman Group Limited, London

Associated companies, branches and representatives
throughout the world

First published 1974

ISBN 0 582 50214/4

Set in Monotype Baskerville
and printed in Great Britain
by J. W. Arrowsmith Ltd., Bristol, England

Contents

facing reality

child's relationship with father

[1] The dates give the year of composition. My dating, in a few instances, differs from Murry's, but is based on Katherine Mansfield's notebooks.

CONTENTS

CONTENTS

Acknowledgement

Stories first published in *The Doves' Nest* (1923) and in any later publication, and quotations from the letters and journals of Katherine Mansfield, are reproduced by arrangement with The Society of Authors as the literary representative of the estate of Katherine Mansfield.

Introduction

The longer I live the more I turn to New Zealand. I thank God I was born in New Zealand, A young country is a real heritage, though it takes one time to recognise it. But New Zealand is in my very bones.[1]

Katherine Mansfield was born in Wellington on 14 October, 1888. Her father was a merchant, Harold—later Sir Harold—Beauchamp; her mother Annie Burnell (Dyer) Beauchamp. The new daughter was christened, after a grandmother, Kathleen Mansfield Beauchamp. The household included two older sisters, the grandmother, and two aunts, sisters of Mrs Beauchamp. Other relatives lived near the family house, set, at 11 Tinakori Road, in a good part of the small colonial capital, and Katherine spent her first years of childhood in the warm atmosphere of an extended, close-knit, and well-to-do family where servants swept, her father's firm delivered the groceries, the butcher and the Chinese greengrocer called at the kitchen door, the women busy all day with house and children, while Harold—the king-pin, the solitary male—made decisions in his office in the town. Below the house and the garden lay Thorndon Esplanade, and beyond that fashionable promenade the children could see from the dining-room window the sparkling waters, the breakwater, and the busy wharves of Wellington harbour, where the ferry took off for the five-mile journey to the holiday settlement of Day's Bay across the water; the sturdier *Penguin* steamed for the stormy waters of Cook Strait to sheltered Picton and the idyllic Marlborough Sounds; and every now and again an ocean liner cast off for the 12 000 mile journey to the far distant country that for every Victorian New Zealander was simply 'Home'. It was altogether a happy childhood, and it was to be, for Katherine as she grew to the age of five, in the most literal sense of the word, unforgettable.

[1] Personal statements by Katherine Mansfield appear in italics throughout. The sources are given in the notes.

Harold in 1893 moved his family—now increased by a fourth daughter—to the country township of Karori, four miles from town. There, amid cows and ducks, the family remained till 1898. A son was born in 1894, the idolised 'Chummie' (Leslie Heron Beauchamp). The girls went to the local school, and revelled in the rural surroundings that would one day become the setting for 'Prelude' and 'The Doll's House'. In 1898 the three older girls moved to Wellington Girls' College, and there—in the college magazine—the nine-year-old author had her first story printed. In the same year Harold became a director of the Bank of New Zealand and moved his family to town once again, this time to a magnificent house at 75 Tinakori Road, where the parents could dazzle their now adolescent youngsters with the splendours that were later to be recaptured in the opening of 'The Garden-Party': a marquee; masses of canna lilies; a band; cream puffs from Godber's, the best pastrycook in town. It was a signal for the next move for the girls—to Miss Swainson's private school in nearby Fitzherbert Terrace. Little boys were accepted and Chummie went too. There they remained for four years. In a class photograph of the period Miss Swainson's girls—and especially the Beauchamp girls and their Maori classmate, Maata Mahupuka—face the camera with sleek assurance, the world at their feet.

Harold was determined to do his best for his daughters. In 1903 they were sent, in the care of their aunt Belle, to Queen's College, Harley Street, London. Katherine plunged into French, German, the cello—and the school magazine. She filled notebooks with her prose sketches, and began on a novel entitled 'Juliet', inspired by a youthful love affair with a young New Zealand musician. She had turned seventeen. Mr and Mrs Beauchamp arrived in London in 1906 to collect the products of their London finishing school, and the whole family were back in New Zealand by the end of the year. The two elder girls settled down easily to the excitement of the Wellington social round. Katherine joined in too and, indeed, rather enjoyed herself—there are elderly Wellingtonians who remember her as a dancing partner, and she was later to write it all in 'Her First Ball'—but at home she sulked, and filled still more notebooks with poems, sketches, vignettes. She was a writer and for her the only place was London: certainly not this small colonial town, where youthful dreams were limited to a bush picnic, a ball at Government House or the Drill Hall, a good marriage. Neither her next appearances in print (organised by her father with the help of a local journalist) nor his tactical diversion (an extensive camping trip through the wilder parts of the North Island) bent her from her purpose. London was— the words are her own—*la seule chose*. Harold Beauchamp, baffled, capitulated. He made her an allowance and she took ship. She was in London by August 1908, complete with manuscripts and notebooks.

II

I am the little Colonial walking in the London garden patch—allowed to look, perhaps, but not to linger. If I lie on the grass they positively shout at me: 'Look at her, lying on our grass, pretending she lives here, pretending this is her garden, and that tall back of the house, with the windows open and the coloured curtains lifting, is her house. She is a stranger—an alien. She is nothing but a little girl sitting on the Tinakori hills and dreaming: "I went to London and married an Englishman, and we lived in a tall grave house, with red geraniums and white daisies in the garden at the back." '

For the nineteen-year-old author her newly won independence meant freedom to write and freedom to gain experience. The latter process was not pleasant. Within a year of her arrival in London she was pregnant, married, and not to the father of her child, had left her husband, and—in the retreat of a Bavarian village—had suffered a miscarriage. Her writing, nevertheless, proceeded with an already assured professionalism; she was making a misery of her personal life, but the very wretchedness of her situation was the material for a series of short stories which, after an appearance in a periodical, formed the basis of her first published volume, *In a German Pension*, 1911. The settings and the characters are German. The situations reflect Katherine's own lonely predicament in Bavaria. One story, 'A Birthday' (written after her return to London) stands apart. A German, Andreas Binzer, nervously awaits the birth of his son. The story radiates a warm family feeling, in striking contrast to the snarling ill-humour of the other stories in the volume. The only thing German in 'A Birthday' is the name of the central character. The setting is none other than 11 Tinakori Road, remembered—although Katherine had left that house in the storeman's dray for Karori at the age of five—in the sharpest of detail: the old 'suspension bridge' and the Princess Hotel—'the public-house at the corner'—on the way to town, the dining-room looking 'over the breakwater of the harbour' . . . it all came flooding back, and in this sensitively told story, written only three years after her departure from New Zealand, she firmly reunited herself with the unexciting colonial town and the middle-class family she had so petulantly bidden farewell to. It was to establish a pattern for the remainder of her life and writing.

In 1912 Katherine fell finally, and permanently, in love. John Middleton Murry, talented, and with literary ambitions, newly down from Oxford, met and captivated her. They lived together, unable to marry till 1918, when her first husband divorced her. The full story of their complex relationship lies beyond the scope of this introduction. Murry gave Katherine a centre. He provided her with a fine critical intelligence against which she could test her rapidly improving skill. When he became an editor of successive journals, he provided an outlet for her talent. Over the years with Murry she grew in stature. Her work became known in England, France and America and the two volumes published in her lifetime (*Bliss and Other Stories* and *The Garden-Party and Other Stories*) established a reputation that was firmly consolidated by the two volumes edited, after her death in 1923, by Murry and entitled *The Doves' Nest* and *Something Childish*. Later, by working over many hundreds of loose sheets of her manuscripts and old diaries, he then established for her a second reputation in those volumes he (not Katherine) entitled the *Journal* and the *Scrapbook*. She owed him much and during her lifetime she freely acknowledged it.

And yet, between these two people so much in love with each other, there were reticences. Each preserved large areas jealously marked private. The 1914–18 War and the illness of Katherine's later years kept them apart for long periods, he in England, she in the South of France. Even in the early days of their relationship, they could sometimes live at different addresses, not infrequently with the Channel in between. They kept their finances strictly separate, banking in different banks. Resources were pooled for common expenses; beyond that, money was formally lent backwards and forwards—and repayment rigidly exacted. Neither trusted the other completely. Murry, till he arranged her papers after her death, did not know that, increasingly, Katherine had come to regard herself as an exile—'a stranger—an alien'—'allowed to look, perhaps, but not to linger'. It was obvious enough in the stories: more and more, in spite of the brilliance of stories with an English or a European setting, her themes came to 'linger' on New Zealand. Into that area of her mind and heart, Murry had no entry.

It has always been recognised that some of her best stories are based on her Wellington memories. The full extent of her commitment has been obscured by the sheer mechanics of publishing a writer whose work is done in the short story form. The two collections she edited herself, *Bliss* and *The Garden-Party*, are made up of work of various dates of composition, settings ranging over England, the Continent and New Zealand. She assembled both collections simply from what she had available that was fit and ready for publication in volume form. After her death, four more collections of her work were published. The choice and the manner of presentation in each was determined by Murry. He did a series of successive garnerings from her manuscripts, resulting in *The Doves' Nest* in 1923, *Something Childish* in 1924, the *Journal* in 1927, and the *Scrapbook* in 1939. Many of the manuscripts are now in the Turnbull Library in Wellington, and a careful examination of these shows that the editorial choice for each collection was quite haphazard. Apart from the fragmentary diary entries (which find their way into the so-called *Journal*) there was no rationale in Murry's arrangement. Later editions of all her collections have not altered the random order; they are simple reprints. The reader and critic of the final *Collected Stories* (which is itself no more than a gathering of simple reprints of the original single volumes) is faced with a series of brilliant single achievements, on which he must impose what unity he can.

Unity there was, and this present collection, by reprinting in a re-arranged order Katherine's 'New Zealand' stories and sketches, is an attempt to underline those themes that dominated her life as a mature artist. By presenting only the New

Zealand stories, some masterpieces—notably 'Life of Ma Parker' and 'The Daughters of the Late Colonel'—find no place. The loss is offset by a cohesion that Katherine might herself have imposed had she lived to organise the final arrangement of her work. Her mind was working in that direction. In one of her notebooks (begun in August 1920) she writes that she must 'really get down to my novel *Karori*'. The present collection is probably as close as we shall ever come to *Karori*. It is a family chronicle, seen from the point of view of a child growing up, and told with sophisticated technique. In these stories and sketches, the family name changes; the personal names change too. But we are clearly reading the chronicle of one family, lovingly remembered, memories of 'real' experience merging imperceptibly with the fiction of a creative imagination, the whole distanced by time and space, and unified by the selecting eye of a great prose artist.

III

I want to write recollections of my own country. Yes, I want to write about my own country till I simply exhaust my store. Not only because it is a 'sacred debt' that I pay to my country because my brother and I were born there, but also because in my thoughts I range with him over the remembered places. I am never far away from them. I long to renew them in writing.

Ah, the people—the people we loved there—of them, too, I want to write. Another 'debt of love'. Oh, I want for one moment to make our undiscovered country leap into the eyes of the Old World. It must be mysterious, as though floating. It must take the breath. It must be 'one of those islands' . . . I shall tell everything, even of how the laundry-basket squeaked at 75.

Katherine in the 1911 story, 'A Birthday', had come to terms with her adolescent self. She could now recollect with pleasure —and with advantages—what she had left behind. Two stories, published in 1912, show further use of New Zealand themes. 'The Woman at the Store' is a violent tale of the colonial backblocks conjured up by a memory of the camping journey of 1907; 'The Little Girl' is a tender narrative of a father and a small daughter who finally come to understand each other. In 'New Dresses', of the same date, the whole family play their part. There are, in the next year or so, further New Zealand stories, but interspersed with much else.

What determined the final direction of her writing was the arrival in early 1915 of Chummie, on his way to join the army. He spent his leave with Katherine, and brother and sister spent hours in Katherine's little 'top room' in London, luxuriating in childhood memories. For Katherine the floodgates opened, and she began a series of sketches and reminiscences. Two, 'The Wind Blows' and 'The Apple Tree', appeared towards the end of the year. By October Chummie was dead, killed in a training accident.

The death of her brother was traumatic to Katherine. She fled from Murry, who was powerless to console her. Devastated by grief, and yet utterly professional, she completed in the South of France by early 1916 a long story, 'The Aloe', on the Karori years of the family. It was later revised and re-named 'Prelude'. Thereafter, at intervals in the few years that were left to her, the great, and the lesser, New Zealand stories occupy more and more of the private room of her mind. They did not emerge immediately. The 1917 stories are mainly sketches and she offered few for publication. 1918 saw 'Sun and Moon' and 'A Married Man's Story' and the following year some short pieces. It was not till 1920 that she was able to settle down and see clearly how to complete the task she had set herself and for the remainder of her writing life (she ceased in mid-1922) she was working with concentrated fury: 'The Stranger', 'Sixpence', 'An Ideal Family', 'Her First Ball', 'The Voyage', 'At the Bay', 'The Garden-Party', 'The Doll's House', 'Weak Heart', 'Taking the Veil', 'The Fly', 'Six Years After', and many lesser—some of them not so much lesser as unfinished —stories sped from her pen; all of them segments of the family chronicle, much of it her most enduring work. When she ceased writing after 'The Fly', 'Six Years After' and 'The Canary' (all elegies for her dead brother) she had fully repaid her sacred debt. Both as a writer and as a human being she had simply exhausted her store.

IV

Father at the last was wonderfully dear to me. I mean to be held and kissed and called my precious child was almost too much—to feel someone's arms round me and someone saying, 'Get better, you little wonder. You're your Mother over again'. It's not being called a wonder. It's having love present, close, warm, to be felt and returned.

To uncover an artist's source material offers no explanation of the artistry. Reading Katherine's New Zealand stories raises an immediate question: what was she doing in these stories? She was, first, reconstituting in literary form a Victorian New Zealand middle-class family and the inter-relationship of its members. It is what the English novel had been doing for a couple of centuries. But she was a creative writer of fiction, not a documenting sociologist. She was, specifically, not painting a picture of *her* family. Both critics and biographers have been led astray by a too-ready and facile identification of her characters and the real-life figures that lay behind them. This kind of assumption belittles her achievement and falsifies some of the important people in her life. Even when she appears to be no more than 'remembering'—witness the sketch called (though the actual title was probably provided by Murry) 'A Recollection of Childhood'—she is creating much more than she is remembering. It is a 'recollection' of a baby sister, Gwen, who died in childhood. One has only to remind oneself that, at the time of Gwen's death, Katherine had just passed her second birthday, to see that the 'Recollection', with its rounded and sharply-realised characterisation and its so authentic dialogue, is pure imaginative creation of a high order.

Almost all of the stories are envisaged from the point of view of a girl growing up, the child Kezia in the 'Burnell' group, the adolescent Laura in the 'Sheridan' group. This central figure (seeing eye and focus of the narrative) has, of course, much of Katherine herself. But Kezia-Laura is not quite the Katherine (whom all called Kass) of the 'real' family. Katherine organised her material as a family chronicle, seen through the eyes of one of the younger girls, the four 'real' sisters variously drawn on for the three—sometimes two—sisters of the stories, the narrative focus shifting between the youngest and the second youngest.

If one must be chary of reading too much of the detail of the stories as authentic reminiscences, one must also avoid leaning too heavily on the stories—or any isolated element in them—for biographical information. A. Alpers in his biography falls on occasion into this fallacy, most notably in his portrayal of Harold Beauchamp, whom he accuses of the 'blackest sins', of which he 'repented' after Katherine's death. There is no question that the central figure of her stories—the Binzer–Burnell–Sheridan–Hammond–Neave–Boss father-figure—owes much to Harold Beauchamp. But Alpers has fallen victim to a widely held legend, of Beauchamp as a wicked banker and Katherine as a starving artist. Nothing could be further from the truth. Her unpublished diaries and minutely kept accounts (as a banker's daughter she was a great keeper of accounts) reveal that her father supported her with an ever-increasing allowance, without a break, for her entire life. In her later years (not counting many gifts, and bills silently paid by the London manager of the Bank of New Zealand) her private allowance was £300 a year, an agreeable cushion in the 1920s. The baffled father and the ambitious and discontented nineteen-year-old girl of 1908—as is clear from unpublished letters and their later re-unions—quietly re-established the warm relationship of earlier years.

Everything in the stories is unquestionably based on experience. Katherine wrote of nothing that she had not herself experienced. But it is always experience transmuted. The children in 'Prelude' and 'At the Bay' live the happy world of fantasy she had known as a child. The girls in 'Kezia and Tui' reflect her friendship in Miss Swainson's school with her Maori class-mate Maata. The Laura–Laurie pair, with the twinned names, mirrors her close relationship with her brother Chummie. The boy hero of 'The Scholarship', who wins an award that will take him away from his 'darling little town' to Europe ('and God knows—if he'd ever see it again') echoes Katherine's own relief (and also her private fears) when her father gave her a kind of 'scholarship' that made possible the final departure from New Zealand. Sometimes she will even blend experience from her later life with earlier memories. 'Cassandra' is a 'Sheridan' story. But the heroine, Cassandra, is now grown up, married, and appeals to her mother for consolation when she thinks her husband has betrayed her. A temporary distrust of Murry provided one part of the story; her New Zealand 'Garden-

Party' family provided the other. And Katherine was scholar enough to indicate the assumption of adult burdens by a mere shift in name: the innocent Kass has become Cassandra, the classical forecaster of doom.

Katherine's final achievement in her New Zealand stories was to create, in sharply-realistic and contemporary prose, a romantic dream-world. New Zealand becomes an Arcadian country—'it must', she wrote in one of her notebooks, 'be mysterious, as though floating'. The material was the landscape of houses and gardens in remembered streets, rural Karori, the harbour, the trips to the Sounds, the sea and the beaches. The people ('Ah the people—the people we loved there') are idealised, happy, encapsulated in a world that never was, like the figures in one of Katherine's best-loved poems, Keats' *Ode On A Grecian Urn*.

When she stepped outside that pastoral world, in the final group of stories I have called 'Scenes from Colonial Life', she loses touch: she can only reproduce what she overheard or read in the more sensational pages of the local newspaper. What could a girl of her background know of Millie or Ole Underwood or the Woman in the Store, she with her fastidious distaste for the smell of cooking mutton chops, 'commercial travellers and second-class, N.Z.'? This was, arguably, a more' real' New Zealand than Katherine Mansfield's. In the years of her growing up, New Zealand was publicly attempting to 'leap into the eyes of the Old World', by offering its particular version of a new world in the political acts of Richard John Seddon and the writings of William Pember Reeves. Katherine Mansfield's alternative offer was the 'undiscovered country', a landscape of the mind, a pastoral dream with a higher reality of its own.

V

I have a passion for technique. I have a passion for making the thing into a whole if you know what I mean. Out of technique is born real style, I believe. There are no short cuts.

I choose not only the length of every sentence, but even the sound of every sentence. I choose the rise and fall of every paragraph to fit her, and to fit her on that day and at that very moment. After I'd written it I read it aloud—numbers of times—just as one would play over *a musical composition—trying to get it nearer and nearer to the expression—until it fitted her.*

I want to write a kind of long elegy . . . perhaps not in poetry. Nor perhaps in prose. Almost certainly in a kind of special prose.

Katherine's ultimate achievement was to create a new kind of fiction in a new kind of prose. In her early work there is plenty of sharply observed character, accurately rendered dialogue, neat story-line. But the author is always on the outside, observing and reporting. The beginnings of a new method first appear in 'The Little Governess', written in 1915. It was not, however, until she set herself down in early 1916 to write the first version of 'Prelude' that she finally broke through to a new structure and a new technique, which are the hallmarks of all her later work. There was clearly nothing in her New Zealand memories by themselves that could have made her the finished artist she now became. It was simply that having found her theme, she found her manner.

The structure of Katherine's stories after 1915 abandons the somewhat mechanical progression of events of her earlier work. She herself called the new structure 'the Prelude method—it just unfolds and opens'. The stories are organic and not mechanical in structure, multi-cellular like living tissue. 'Prelude' has twelve such 'cells', as has 'At the Bay'. 'The Stranger' has two. Other stories have a single-cell structure. 'The Prelude method' was flexible. Some cells contain brisk narrative (Pat killing the duck in 'Prelude'; the breakfast scene in 'At the Bay'); in others action slows to passive absorption (Kezia in the old house in 'Prelude'); or to static inactivity, the central character of the cell lost in the mind's recesses (Linda Burnell 'dreaming the morning away' in 'At the Bay'); sometimes the central 'character' of a cell is not a person but a landscape, a seascape, a gardenscape, but all very much part of the 'story'. There is little 'plot', in the traditional sense, but as each cell 'unfolds and opens' the reader is brought in to share the life of the family.

The reader is brought in. How does she achieve this feat of a shared experience? Partly, it is brought about because Katherine herself in her New Zealand stories was able to share in every experience she recorded. 'I've *been* this man, *been* this woman', she wrote Murry after completing 'The Stranger', 'I've stood for hours on the Auckland wharf. I've been out in the stream waiting to be berthed—I've been a seagull hovering at the stern and a hotel porter whistling through his teeth. It isn't as if one sits and watches the spectacle. That would be thrilling enough, God knows. But one *is* the spectacle for the time'.

For Katherine, to *be* the spectacle required only her own power of sympathetic recall. To induce her reader to *be* the spectacle was a different matter. It required an originality of technique and a use of prose that is her major contribution to the craft of fiction. It is done at different levels. At one end of the scale, entire passages are interior monologues, the events seen or felt from the point of view of one or other of the characters. The reader is placed 'inside' the character, as in the recorded reverie of Linda in 'At the Bay' or in the double and over-lapping thought-processes of husband and wife in 'The Stranger'. The technique can be extremely subtle—after three paragraphs of description, Kezia in the seventh section of 'At the Bay' makes her first spoken entry with a question 'What are you looking at, my grandma?' Kezia has, in fact, been present throughout, the whole prior 'description' of beach landscape having been seen—and recorded—through her eyes. The reader has from the first line been placed 'inside' Kezia's mind, and he is well prepared for her spoken entry because she has been 'in' the scene from the beginning. Technical feats of this degree of virtuosity are regular in the developed Mansfield stories.

Her virtuosity extends down the scale, from the entire shape and structure of a story, through all its components, right down to the level of sentence and phrase. Everything is carefully planned, and carried off brilliantly. One of her most skilful stylistic and structural devices is to switch (within the sentence) from the 'voice' of the narrator to the overheard 'voice' of one of her characters:

The grandmother's lap was full and Linda Burnell could not possibly have held *a lump of a child* on hers for any distance. ['Prelude']

'Bring me some fresh blotting-paper', he said sternly, 'and look sharp about it.' And while *the old dog* padded away . . . ['The Fly']

He scarcely troubled to clasp her, and they moved away so gently, *it was more like walking than dancing.* ['Her First Ball']
Finally he flung his overcoat on to the bedside. *At last the fool was gone.* ['The Stranger']
In each of the above passages, the words I have italicised each indicate a shift in 'voice' from that of the narrator to that of Linda, the Boss, Leila, and Hammond. Each character has been brought directly 'inside' a sentence that began as neutral and externalised narrative.

Katherine wrote many of her stories in a 'kind of special prose', which draws on the stratagems of poetry, notably an unobtrusive—but powerful—use of symbolism: the dying of the bedroom fire in the final pages of 'The Stranger'; the balloonings of Ma Parker's apron (but only by an 'icy wind'); the counterpointed 'gold' and 'white' imagery of the opening of 'An Ideal Family', announcing its theme of youth and age; the over-riding symbol that extends even to the title in 'The Aloe' and 'The Fly'; the blue/gold symbolism in the early pages of 'The Garden-Party', which gives way at the tragic end of the story to a collocation of dark/smoky/flicker/shadow/black. There is nothing in the best writing of Katherine Mansfield that is not planned and executed with consummate skill. She is one of the most professional writers in the language and her writing can stand up to the most rigorous analysis, well beyond the limits of the present introductory essay.

In this edition, the New Zealand stories are reprinted from the various collections made during her lifetime and after her death. The date of composition is noted after each story. They are presented, however, not in order of composition, but in the order of the inner events of the family's history. The chronology is the chronology of the family. Earlier and later work is thus presented side by side, and the reader must be prepared for stylistic variation. It must be emphasised it is not the intention of this book to be either an anthology of show pieces or a demonstration of the progress of an artist. What is here presented is a reorganisation of Katherine's entire 'New Zealand' writing, finished and unfinished, edited in a sequence, which will, I hope, reinforce and illuminate the themes and preoccupations that sustain the underlying unity of her work.

PART ONE

Spring: *the Burnells*

Enna Blake

My literary career began with short-story writing in New Zealand. I was nine years old when my first attempt was published.

'Oh, mother, it is still raining, and you say I can't go out.' It was a girl who spoke; she looked about ten. She was standing in a well-furnished room, and was looking out of a large bay window. 'No, Enna, dear,' said her mother, 'you have a little cold, and I don't want it made worse.' Just then the gong rang for luncheon, and they went into the dining-room. In the midst of this meal the maid came in with the letters; there was one for Enna and one for Mrs. Blake. As it had stopped raining after lunch, they all went outside, where Enna seated herself in a shady nook and began to read her letter. It was a note from Lucy Brown, to ask her and her mother to spend a few weeks holiday with her at her home at Torquay. Enna was delighted, and ran to ask her mother.

And so it happened that next morning they got into the train that bore them to Torquay. When Enna was tired of looking out of the window she lay back in her seat and knew nothing more until she heard the porter shout 'Torquay'. Lucy was on the platform to welcome them. 'I am so glad you have come,' she said, 'mother thought your music might prevent you.' They had a pleasant drive to Sunny Glen; it was nine o'clock at night when they reached it, and so they were told to go to bed at once, which Enna willingly did.

The next day was very fine. Mrs. Brown proposed that they should go ferning. So soon after breakfast they started. 'It seems just the day for enjoying one's self,' said Lucy, as they climbed the hill. 'Yes,' Enna answered, 'to-day here is much nicer than in London.' At about twelve o'clock the

3

two girls sat on a log and ate their dinners. 'I should think it would be very nice to get some moss,' Enna said; so off they trudged. The girls spent a very happy day, and got a great many nice ferns and some beautiful moss. And that night Enna said she thought it was the nicest day she had ever spent in the country. The next day was very wet, so they had to stay indoors, but they made cakes, scones, ginger-nuts, and other dainties for a party she meant to have the day after next. At about eight o'clock that night a box came directed to Lucy, in her uncle's hand. On opening it she found a darling little kitten; it was pure white except for a black spot on its neck. Lucy was delighted, and played with it all the rest of the evening.

The third day of Enna's stay was very pleasant. The girls went for a ride in the morning, and visited some girl friends of Lucy's in the afternoon. When they had had tea a gentleman came to see Mrs. Brown and amused them for the rest of the evening. And, indeed, the weeks flew by too quickly, but when the holidays did come to an end, Enna thought it was the happiest holiday she had ever had.

KATHLEEN BEAUCHAMP, aged 9 years.

(1898)

An Unfinished Memory

*I begin to think of an unfinished memory which has been with me
for years. It is a very good story if only I can tell it right, and it is
called* Lena. *It plays in New Zealand and would go in the book.
If only I can get right down to it.*

*Dear Brother, as I jot these notes, I am speaking to you. To
whom did I always write when I kept those huge complaining
diaries? Was it to myself? But now as I write these words and talk
of getting down to the New Zealand atmosphere, I see you opposite
to me, I see your thoughtful, shining eyes. Yes, it is to you. We were
travelling—sitting opposite to each other and moving very fast. Ah,
my darling, how have I kept away from this tremendous joy? Each
time I take up my pen you are with me. You are mine. You are my
playfellow, my brother, and we shall range all over our country
together. It is with you that I see, and that is why I see so clearly.
That is a great mystery. My brother, I have doubted these last few
days. I have been in dreadful places. I have felt that I could not
come through to you. But now, quite suddenly, the mists are rising,
and I see and I know you are near me. You are more vividly with me
now this moment than if you were alive and I were writing to you
from a short distance away. As you speak my name, the name you
call me by that I love so—'Katie!'—your lip lifts in a smile—you
believe in me, you know I am here. Oh, Chummie! put your arms
round me. I was going to write: Let us shut out everybody. But no,
it is not that. Only we shall 'look on' at them together. My brother,
you know, with all my desire, my will is weak. To do things—even
to write absolutely for myself and by myself—is awfully hard for me.
God knows why, when my desire is so strong. But just as it was
always our delight to sit together—you remember?—and to talk of
the old days, down to the last detail—the last feeling—looking at*

5

each other and by our eyes expressing when speech ended how
intimately we understood each other—so now, my dear one, we shall do
that again. You know how unhappy I have been lately. I almost felt:
Perhaps 'the new man' will not live. Perhaps I am not yet risen . . .
But now I do not doubt. It is the idea (it has always been there, but
never as it is with me to-night) that I do not write alone. That in
every word I write and every place I visit I carry you with me.
Indeed, that might be the motto of my book. There are daisies on the
table and a red flower, like a poppy, shines through. Of daisies I will
write. Of the dark. Of the wind—and the sun and the mists. Of the
wharves. Ah! of all that you loved and that I too love and feel.
To-night it is made plain. However often I write and rewrite I shall
not really falter, dearest, and the book shall be written and ready.

(1916)

A Recollection
of Childhood

*Things happened so simply then, without preparation and without any
shock. They let me go into my mother's room (I remember standing
on tiptoe and using both hands to turn the big white china door-handle)
and there lay my mother in bed with her arms along the sheet, and
there sat my grandmother before the fire with a baby in a flannel
across her knees. My mother paid no attention to me at all. Perhaps
she was asleep, for my grandmother nodded and said in a voice
scarcely above a whisper, 'Come and see your little sister.' I tiptoed to
her voice across the room, and she parted the flannel, and I saw a
little round head with a tuft of goldy hair on it and a big face with
eyes shut—white as snow. 'Is it alive?' I asked. 'Of course,' said
grandmother. 'Look at her holding my finger.' And—yes, a hand,
scarcely bigger than my doll's, in a frilled sleeve, was wound round
her finger. 'Do you like her?' said my grandmother. 'Yes. Is she
going to play with the doll's house?' 'By-and-by,' said the grandmother, and I felt very pleased. Mrs. Heywood had just given us the
doll's house. It was a beautiful one with a verandah and a balcony
and a door that opened and shut and two chimneys. I wanted badly
to show it to someone else.*

'Her name is Gwen', said the grandmother. 'Kiss her.'

*I bent down and kissed the little goldy tuft. But she took no
notice. She lay quite still with her eyes shut.*

'Now go and kiss mother,' said the grandmother.

*But mother did not want to kiss me. Very languid, leaning against
the pillows, she was eating some sago. The sun shone through the
windows and winked on the brass knobs on the big bed.*

*After that grandmother came into the nursery with Gwen, and sat
in front of the nursery fire in the rocking chair with her. Meg and
Tadpole were away staying with Aunt Harriet, and they had gone*

7

before the new doll's house arrived, so that was why I so longed to have somebody to show it to. I had gone all through it myself, from the kitchen to the dining-room, up into the bedrooms with the doll's lamp on the table, heaps and heaps of times.

'When will she play with it?' I asked grandmother.

'By-and-by, darling.'

It was spring. Our garden was full of big white lilies. I used to run out and sniff them and come in again with my nose all yellow.

'Can't she go out?'

At last, one very fine day, she was wrapped in the warm shawl and grandmother carried her into the cherry orchard, and walked up and down under the falling cherry flowers. Grandmother wore a grey dress with white pansies on it. The doctor's carriage was waiting at the door, and the doctor's little dog, Jackie, rushed at me and snapped at my bare legs. When we went back to the nursery and the shawl was taken away, little white petals like feathers fell out of the folds. But Gwen did not look, even then. She lay in grandmother's arms, her eyes just open to show a line of blue, her face very white, and the one tuft of goldy hair standing up on her head.

All day, all night grandmother's arms were full. I had no lap to climb into, no pillow to rest against. All belonged to Gwen. But Gwen did not notice this; she never put up her hand to play with the silver brooch that was a half-moon with five little owls sitting on it; she never pulled grandmother's watch from her bodice and opened the back by herself to see grandfather's hair; she never buried her head close to smell the lavender water, or took up grandmother's spectacle case and wondered at its being really silver. She just lay still and let herself be rocked.

Down in the kitchen one day old Mrs. McElvie came to the door and asked Bridget about the poor little mite, and Bridget said, 'Kep' alive on bullock's blood hotted in a saucer over a candle.' After that I felt frightened of Gwen, and I decided that even when she did play with the doll's house I would not let her go upstairs into the bedroom —only downstairs, and then only when I saw she could look.

Late one evening I sat by the fire on my little carpet hassock and grandmother rocked, singing the song she used to sing to me, but more gently. Suddenly she stopped and I looked up. Gwen opened her eyes and turned her little round head to the fire and looked and looked at it and then—turned her eyes up to the face bending over her. I saw her tiny body stretch out and her hands flew up, and 'Ah! Ah! Ah!' called the grandmother.

8

Bridget dressed me next morning. When I went into the nursery I sniffed. A big vase of the white lilies was standing on the table. Grandmother sat in her chair to one side with Gwen in her lap, and a funny little man with his head in a black bag was standing behind a box of china eggs.

'Now!' he said, and I saw my grandmother's face change as she bent over little Gwen.

'Thank you,' said the man, coming out of the bag. The picture was hung over the nursery fire. I thought it looked very nice. The doll's house was in it—verandah and balcony and all. Gran held me up to kiss my little sister.

(1916)

A Bad Idea

Something's happened to me—something bad. And I don't know what to do about it. I don't see any way out for the life of me. The worst of it is, I can't get this thing into focus—if you know what I mean. I just feel in a muddle—in the hell of a muddle. It ought to be plain to anyone that I'm not the kind of man to get mixed up in a thing like this. I'm not one of your actor Johnnies, or a chap in a book. I'm—well I knew what I was all right until yesterday. But now—I feel helpless, yes, that's the word, helpless. Here I sit, chucking stones at the sea like a child that's missed its mother. And everybody else has cut along home hours ago and tea's over and it's getting on for time to light the lamp. I shall have to go home too, sooner or later. I see that, of course. In fact, would you believe it? at this very moment I wish I was there in spite of everything? What's she doing? My wife, I mean. Has she cleared away? Or has she stayed there staring at the table with the plates pushed back? My God! when I think that I could howl like a dog—if you know what I mean . . . .

I should have realized it was all U.P. this morning when she didn't get up for breakfast. I did, in a way. But I couldn't face it. I had the feeling that if I said nothing special and just treated it as one of her bad headache days and went off to the office, by the time I got back this evening the whole affair would have blown over somehow. No, that wasn't it. I felt a bit like I do now, 'helpless'. What was I to do? Just go on. That was all I could think of. So I took her up a cup of tea and a couple of slices of thin bread and butter as per usual on her headache days. The blind was still down. She was lying on her back. I think she had a wet handkerchief on her forehead. I'm not sure, for I couldn't look at her. It was a beastly feeling. And she said in a weak kind of voice, 'Put the jug on the table, will you?' I put it down. I said, 'Can I do anything?' And she said, 'No. I'll be all right in half an hour.' But her voice, you know! It did for me. I barged out as quick as I could, snatched my hat and stick from the hall-stand and dashed off for the tram.

Here's a queer thing—you needn't believe me if you don't want to—the moment I got out of the house I forgot that about my wife. It was a splendid morning, soft, with the sun making silver ducks on the sea. The kind of morning when you know it's going to keep hot and fine all day. Even the tram bell sounded different, and the little school kids crammed between people's knees had bunches of flowers. I don't know—I can't understand why—I just felt happy, but happy in a way I'd never been before, happy to beat the band! That wind that had been so strong the night before was still blowing a bit. It felt like her—the other—touching me. Yes, it did. Brought it back, every bit of it. If I told you how it took me, you'd say I was mad. I felt reckless—didn't care if I was late for the office or not and I wanted to do every one a kindness. I helped the little kids out of the tram. One little chap dropped his cap, and when I picked it up for him and said, 'Here, sonny!' . . . well, it was all I could do not to make a fool of myself.

At the office it was just the same. It seemed to me I'd never known the fellows at the office before. When old Fisher came over to my desk and put down a couple of giant sweet peas as per usual with his 'Beat 'em, old man, beat 'em!'—I didn't feel annoyed. I didn't care that he was riddled with conceit about his garden. I just looked at them and I said quietly, 'Yes, you've done it this time.' He didn't know what to make of it. Came back in about five minutes and asked me if I had a headache.

And so it went on all day. In the evening I dashed home with the home-going crowd, pushed open the gate, saw the hall-door open as it always is and sat down on the little chair just inside to take off my boots. My slippers were there, of course. This seemed to me a good sign. I put my boots into the rack in the cupboard under the stairs, changed my office coat and made for the kitchen. I knew my wife was there. Wait a bit. The only thing I couldn't manage was my whistling as per usual, 'I often lie awake and think, What a dreadful thing is work. . . .' I had a try, but nothing came of it. Well, I opened the kitchen door and said, 'Hullo! How's everybody?' But as soon as I'd said that—even before—I knew the worst had happened. She was standing at the table beating the salad dressing. And when she

11

looked up and gave a kind of smile and said 'Hullo!' you could
have knocked me down! My wife looked dreadful—there's no
other word for it. She must have been crying all day. She'd
put some white flour stuff on her face to take away the marks—
but it only made her look worse. She must have seen I spotted
something, for she caught up the cup of cream and poured some
into the salad bowl—like she always does, you know, so
quick, so neat, in her own way—and began beating again. I
said, 'Is your head better?' But she didn't seem to hear. She
said, 'Are you going to water the garden before or after supper?'
What could I say? I said, 'After', and went off to the dining-
room, opened the evening paper and sat by the open window—
well, hiding behind that paper, I suppose.

I shall never forget sitting there. People passing by, going
down the road, sounded so peaceful. And a man passed with
some cows. I—I envied him. My wife came in and out. Then
she called me to supper and we sat down. I suppose we ate some
cold meat and salad. I don't remember. We must have. But
neither of us spoke. It's like a dream now. Then she got up,
changed the plates, and went to the larder for the pudding. Do
you know what the pudding was? Well, of course, it wouldn't
mean anything to you. It was my favourite—the kind she only
made me on special occasions—honeycomb cream. . . .

(1921)

A Birthday

Andreas Binzer woke slowly. He turned over on the narrow bed and stretched himself—yawned—opening his mouth as widely as possible and bringing his teeth together afterwards with a sharp 'click'. The sound of that click fascinated him; he repeated it quickly several times, with a snapping movement of the jaws. What teeth! he thought. Sound as a bell, every man jack of them. Never had one out, never had one stopped. That comes of no tomfoolery in eating, and a good regular brushing night and morning. He raised himself on his left elbow and waved his right arm over the side of the bed to feel for the chair where he put his watch and chain overnight. No chair was there—of course, he'd forgotten, there wasn't a chair in this wretched spare room. Had to put the confounded thing under his pillow. 'Half-past eight, Sunday, breakfast at nine—time for the bath'—his brain ticked to the watch. He sprang out of bed and went over to the window. The venetian blind was broken, hung fan-shaped over the upper pane. . . . 'That blind must be mended. I'll get the office boy to drop in and fix it on his way home to-morrow—he's a good hand at blinds. Give him two-pence and he'll do it as well as a carpenter. . . . Anna could do it herself if she was all right. So would I, for the matter of that, but I don't like to trust myself on rickety step-ladders.' He looked up at the sky: it shone, strangely white, unflecked with cloud; he looked down at the row of garden strips and back yards. The fence of these gardens was built along the edge of a gully, spanned by an iron suspension bridge, and the people had a wretched habit of throwing their empty tins over the fence into the gully. Just like them, of course! Andreas started counting the tins, and decided, viciously, to write a letter to the papers about it and sign it—sign it in full.

The servant girl came out of their back door into the yard carrying his boots. She threw one down on the ground, thrust

13

her hand into the other, and stared at it, sucking in her cheeks. Suddenly she bent forward, spat on the toecap, and started polishing with a brush rooted out of her apron pocket. . . . 'Slut of a girl! Heaven knows what infectious disease may be breeding now in that boot. Anna must get rid of that girl—even if she has to do without one for a bit—as soon as she's up and about again. The way she chucked one boot down and then spat upon the other! She didn't care whose boots she'd got hold of. *She* had no false notions of the respect due to the master of the house.' He turned away from the window and switched his bath towel from the wash-stand rail, sick at heart. 'I'm too sensitive for a man—that's what's the matter with me. Have been from the beginning, and will be to the end.'

There was a gentle knock at the door and his mother came in. She closed the door after her and leant against it. Andreas noticed that her cap was crooked, and a long tail of hair hung over her shoulder. He went forward and kissed her.

'Good morning, mother; how's Anna?'

The old woman spoke quickly, clasping and unclasping her hands.

'Andreas, please go to Doctor Erb as soon as you are dressed.'

'Why,' he said, 'is she bad?'

Frau Binzer nodded, and Andreas, watching her, saw her face suddenly change; a fine network of wrinkles seemed to pull over it from under the skin surface.

'Sit down on the bed a moment,' he said. 'Been up all night?'

'Yes. No, I won't sit down, I must go back to her. Anna has been in pain all night. She wouldn't have you disturbed before because she said you looked so run down yesterday. You told her you had caught a cold and been very worried.'

Straightway Andreas felt that he was being accused.

'Well, she made me tell her, worried it out of me; you know the way she does.'

Again Frau Binzer nodded.

'Oh yes, I know. She says, is your cold better, and there's a warm undervest for you in the left-hand corner of the big drawer.'

Quite automatically Andreas cleared his throat twice.

'Yes,' he answered. 'Tell her my throat certainly feels looser. I suppose I'd better not disturb her?'

'No, and besides, *time*, Andreas.'

'I'll be ready in five minutes.'

They went into the passage. As Frau Binzer opened the door of the front bedroom, a long wail came from the room.

That shocked and terrified Andreas. He dashed into the bathroom, turned on both taps as far as they would go, cleaned his teeth and pared his nails while the water was running.

'Frightful business, frightful business,' he heard himself whispering. 'And I can't understand it. It isn't as though it were her first—it's her third. Old Schäfer told me, yesterday, his wife simply "dropped" her fourth. Anna ought to have had a qualified nurse. Mother gives way to her. Mother spoils her. I wonder what she meant by saying I'd worried Anna yesterday. Nice remark to make to a husband at a time like this. Unstrung, I suppose—and my sensitiveness again.'

When he went into the kitchen for his boots, the servant girl was bent over the stove, cooking breakfast. 'Breathing into that, now, I suppose,' thought Andreas, and was very short with the servant girl. She did not notice. She was full of terrified joy and importance in the goings-on upstairs. She felt she was learning the secrets of life with every breath she drew. Had laid the table that morning saying, 'Boy,' as she put down the first dish, 'Girl', as she placed the second—it had worked out with the saltspoon to 'Boy'. 'For two pins I'd tell the master that, to comfort him, like,' she decided. But the master gave her no opening.

'Put an extra cup and saucer on the table,' he said; 'the doctor may want some coffee.'

'The doctor, sir?' The servant girl whipped a spoon out of a pan, and spilt two drops of grease on the stove. 'Shall I fry something extra?' But the master had gone, slamming the door after him. He walked down the street—there was nobody about at all—dead and alive this place on a Sunday morning. As he crossed the suspension bridge a strong stench of fennel and decayed refuse streamed from the gully, and again Andreas began concocting a letter. He turned into the main road. The shutters were still up before the shops. Scraps of newspaper, hay and fruit skins strewed the pavement; the gutters were choked with the leavings of Saturday night. Two dogs sprawled in the middle of the road, scuffling and biting. Only the public-house at the corner was open; a young barman slopped water over the doorstep.

Fastidiously, his lips curling, Andreas picked his way through the water. 'Extraordinary how I am noticing things this morning. It's partly the effect of Sunday. I loathe a Sunday when Anna's tied by the leg and the children are away. On Sunday a man has the right to expect his family. Everything here's filthy, the whole place might be down with the plague, and will be, too, if this street's not swept away. I'd like to have a hand on the government ropes.' He braced his shoulders. 'Now for this doctor.'

'Doctor Erb is at breakfast,' the maid informed him. She showed him into the waiting-room, a dark and musty place, with some ferns under a glass-case by the window. 'He says he won't be a minute, please, sir, and there is a paper on the table.'

'Unhealthy hole,' thought Binzer, walking over to the window and drumming his fingers on the glass fern-shade. 'At breakfast, is he? That's the mistake I made: turning out early on an empty stomach.'

A milk cart rattled down the street, the driver standing at the back, cracking a whip; he wore an immense geranium flower stuck in the lapel of his coat. Firm as a rock he stood, bending back a little in the swaying cart. Andreas craned his neck to watch him all the way down the road, even after he had gone, listening for the sharp sound of those rattling cans.

'H'm, not much wrong with him,' he reflected. 'Wouldn't mind a taste of that life myself. Up early, work all over by eleven o'clock, nothing to do but loaf about all day until milking time.' Which he knew was an exaggeration, but he wanted to pity himself.

The maid opened the door, and stood aside for Doctor Erb. Andreas wheeled round; the two men shook hands.

'Well, Binzer,' said the doctor jovially, brushing some crumbs from a pearl-coloured waistcoat, 'son and heir becoming importunate?'

Up went Binzer's spirits with a bound. Son and heir, by Jove! He was glad to have to deal with a man again. And a sane fellow this, who came across this sort of thing every day of the week.

'That's about the measure of it, Doctor,' he answered, smiling and picking up his hat. 'Mother dragged me out of bed this morning with imperative orders to bring you along.'

'Gig will be round in a minute. Drive back with me, won't you? Extraordinary, sultry day; you're as red as a beetroot already.'

Andreas affected to laugh. The doctor had one annoying habit—imagined he had the right to poke fun at everybody simply because he was a doctor. 'The man's riddled with conceit, like all these professionals,' Andreas decided.

'What sort of night did Frau Binzer have?' asked the doctor. 'Ah, here's the gig. Tell me on the way up. Sit as near the middle as you can, will you, Binzer? Your weight tilts it over a bit one side—that's the worst of you successful business men.'

'Two stone heavier than I, if he's a pound,' thought Andreas. 'The man may be all right in his profession—but heaven preserve me.'

'Off you go, my beauty.' Doctor Erb flicked the little brown mare. 'Did your wife get any sleep last night?'

'No; I don't think she did,' answered Andreas shortly. 'To tell you the truth, I'm not satisfied that she hasn't a nurse.'

'Oh, your mother's worth a dozen nurses,' cried the doctor, with immense gusto. 'To tell you the truth, I'm not keen on nurses—too raw—raw as rump-steak. They wrestle for a baby as though they were wrestling with Death for the body of Patroclus.... Ever seen that picture by an English artist. Leighton? Wonderful thing—full of sinew!'

'There he goes again,' thought Andreas, 'airing off his knowledge to make a fool of me.'

'Now your mother—she's firm—she's capable. Does what she's told with a fund of sympathy. Look at these shops we're passing—they're festering sores. How on earth this government can tolerate—'

'They're not so bad—sound enough—only want a coat of paint.'

The doctor whistled a little tune and flicked the mare again.

'Well, I hope the young shaver won't give his mother too much trouble,' he said. 'Here we are.'

A skinny little boy, who had been sliding up and down the back seat of the gig, sprang out and held the horse's head. Andreas went straight into the dining-room and left the servant girl to take the doctor upstairs. He sat down, poured out some coffee, and bit through half a roll before helping himself to fish. Then he noticed there was no hot plate for the fish—the whole house was at sixes and sevens. He rang the bell, but the servant girl came in with a tray holding a bowl of soup and a hot plate.

'I've been keeping them on the stove,' she simpered.

'Ah, thanks, that's very kind of you.' As he swallowed the soup his heart warmed to this fool of a girl.

'Oh, it's a good thing Doctor Erb has come,' volunteered the servant girl, who was bursting for want of sympathy.

'H'm, h'm,' said Andreas.

She waited a moment, expectantly, rolling her eyes, then in full loathing of mankind went back to the kitchen and vowed herself to sterility.

Andreas cleared the soup bowl, and cleared the fish. As he ate, the room slowly darkened. A faint wind sprang up and beat the tree branches against the window. The dining-room looked over the breakwater of the harbour, and the sea swung heavily in rolling waves. Wind crept round the house, moaning drearily.

'We're in for a storm. That means I'm boxed up here all day. Well, there's one blessing; it'll clear the air.' He heard the servant girl rushing importantly round the house, slamming windows. Then he caught a glimpse of her in the garden, un-pegging tea towels from the line across the lawn. She was a worker, there was no doubt about that. He took up a book, and wheeled his arm-chair over to the window. But it was useless. Too dark to read; he didn't believe in straining his eyes, and gas at ten o'clock in the morning seemed absurd. So he slipped down in the chair, leaned his elbows on the padded arms and gave himself up, for once, to idle dreaming. 'A boy? Yes, it was bound to be a boy this time. . . .' 'What's your family, Binzer?' 'Oh, I've two girls and a boy!' A very nice little number. Of course he was the last man to have a favourite child, but a man needed a son. 'I'm working up the business for my son! Binzer & Son! It would mean living very tight for the next ten years, cutting expenses as fine as possible; and then—'

A tremendous gust of wind sprang upon the house, seized it, shook it, dropped, only to grip the more tightly. The waves swelled up along the breakwater and were whipped with broken foam. Over the white sky flew tattered streamers of grey cloud.

Andreas felt quite relieved to hear Doctor Erb coming down the stairs; he got up and lit the gas.

'Mind if I smoke in here?' asked Doctor Erb, lighting a cigarette before Andreas had time to answer. 'You don't smoke, do you? No time to indulge in pernicious little habits!'

'How is she now?' asked Andreas, loathing the man.

'Oh, well as can be expected, poor little soul. She begged me to come down and have a look at you. Said she knew you were worrying.' With laughing eyes the doctor looked at the break-fast-table. 'Managed to peck a bit, I see, eh?'

'Hoo-wih!' shouted the wind, shaking the window-sashes.

'Pity—this weather,' said Doctor Erb.

'Yes, it gets on Anna's nerves, and it's just nerve she wants.'

'Eh, what's that?' retorted the doctor. 'Nerve! Man alive! She's got twice the nerve of you and me rolled into one. Nerve! she's nothing but nerve. A woman who works as she does about the house and has three children in four years thrown in with the dusting, so to speak!'

He pitched his half-smoked cigarette into the fire-place and frowned at the window.

'Now *he's* accusing me,' thought Andreas. 'That's the second time this morning—first mother and now this man taking advantage of my sensitiveness.' He could not trust himself to speak, and rang the bell for the servant girl.

'Clear away the breakfast things,' he ordered. 'I can't have them messing about on the table till dinner!'

'Don't be hard on the girl,' coaxed Doctor Erb. 'She's got twice the work to do to-day.'

At that Binzer's anger blazed out.

'I'll trouble you, Doctor, not to interfere between me and my servants!' And he felt a fool at the same moment for not saying 'servant.'

Doctor Erb was not perturbed. He shook his head, thrust his hands into his pockets, and began balancing himself on toe and heel.

'You're jagged by the weather,' he said wryly, 'nothing else. A great pity—this storm. You know climate has an immense effect upon birth. A fine day perks a woman—gives her heart for her business. Good weather is as necessary to a confinement as it is to a washing day. Not bad—that last remark of mine—for a professional fossil, eh?'

Andreas made no reply.

19

'Well, I'll be getting back to my patient. Why don't you take a walk, and clear your head? That's the idea for you.'

'No,' he answered, 'I won't do that; it's too rough.'

He went back to his chair by the window. While the servant girl cleared away he pretended to read . . . then his dreams! It seemed years since he had had the time to himself to dream like that—he never had a breathing space. Saddled with work all day, and couldn't shake it off in the evening like other men. Besides, Anna was interested—they talked of practically nothing else together. Excellent mother she'd make for a boy; she had a grip of things.

Church bells started ringing through the windy air, now sounding as though from very far away, then again as though all the churches in the town had been suddenly transplanted into their street. They stirred something in him, those bells, something vague and tender. Just about that time Anna would call him from the hall. 'Andreas, come and have your coat brushed. I'm ready.' Then off they would go, she hanging on his arm, and looking up at him. She certainly was a little thing. He remembered once saying when they were engaged, 'Just as high as my heart,' and she had jumped on to a stool and pulled his head down, laughing. A kid in those days, younger than her children in nature, brighter, more 'go' and 'spirit' in her. The way she'd run down the road to meet him after business! And the way she laughed when they were looking for a house. By Jove! that laugh of hers! At the memory he grinned, then grew suddenly grave. Marriage certainly changed a woman far more than it did a man. Talk about sobering down. She had lost all her go in two months! Well, once this boy business was over she'd get stronger. He began to plan a little trip for them. He'd take her away and they'd loaf about together somewhere. After all, dash it, they were young still. She'd got into a groove; he'd have to force her out of it, that's all.

He got up and went into the drawing-room, carefully shut the door and took Anna's photograph from the top of the piano. She wore a white dress with a big bow of some soft stuff under the chin, and stood, a little stiffly, holding a sheaf of artificial poppies and corn in her hands. Delicate she looked even then; her masses of hair gave her that look. She seemed to droop under the heavy braids of it, and yet she was smiling. Andreas caught his breath sharply. She was his wife—that girl.

20

Posh! it had only been taken four years ago. He held it close to him, bent forward and kissed it. Then rubbed the glass with the back of his hand. At that moment, fainter than he had heard in the passage, more terrifying, Andreas heard again that wailing cry. The wind caught it up in mocking echo, blew it over the house-tops, down the street, far away from him. He flung out his arms, 'I'm so damnably helpless,' he said, and then, to the picture, 'Perhaps it's not as bad as it sounds; perhaps it is just my sensitiveness.' In the half-light of the drawing-room the smile seemed to deepen in Anna's portrait, and to become secret, even cruel. 'No,' he reflected, 'that smile is not at all her happiest expression—it was a mistake to let her have it taken smiling like that. She doesn't look like my wife—like the mother of my son.' Yes, that was it, she did not look like the mother of a son who was going to be a partner in the firm. The picture got on his nerves; he held it in different lights, looked at it from a distance, sideways, spent, it seemed to Andreas afterwards, a whole lifetime trying to fit it in. The more he played with it the deeper grew his dislike of it. Thrice he carried it over to the fire-place and decided to chuck it behind the Japanese umbrella in the grate; then he thought it absurd to waste an expensive frame. There was no good in beating about the bush. Anna looked like a stranger—abnormal, a freak—it might be a picture taken just before or after death.

Suddenly he realised that the wind had dropped, that the whole house was still, terribly still. Cold and pale, with a disgusting feeling that spiders were creeping up his spine and across his face, he stood in the centre of the drawing-room, hearing Doctor Erb's footsteps descending the stairs.

He saw Doctor Erb come into the room; the room seemed to change into a great glass bowl that spun round, and Doctor Erb seemed to swim through this glass bowl towards him, like a goldfish in a pearl-coloured waistcoat.

'My beloved wife has passed away!' He wanted to shout it out before the doctor spoke.

'Well, she's hooked a boy this time!' said Doctor Erb. Andreas staggered forward.

'Look out. Keep on your pins,' said Doctor Erb, catching Binzer's arm, and murmuring, as he felt it, 'Flabby as butter.'

A glow spread all over Andreas. He was exultant.

21

'Well, by God! Nobody can accuse *me* of not knowing what suffering is,' he said.

(1911)

How Pearl Button was Kidnapped

Pearl Button swung on the little gate in front of the House of Boxes. It was the early afternoon of a sunshiny day with little winds playing hide-and-seek in it. They blew Pearl Button's pinafore frill into her mouth, and they blew the street dust all over the House of Boxes. Pearl watched it—like a cloud—like when mother peppered her fish and the top of the pepper-pot came off. She swung on the little gate, all alone, and she sang a small song. Two big women came walking down the street. One was dressed in red and the other was dressed in yellow and green. They had pink handkerchiefs over their heads, and both of them carried a big flax basket of ferns. They had no shoes and stockings on, and they came walking along, slowly, because they were so fat, and talking to each other and always smiling. Pearl stopped swinging, and when they saw her they stopped walking. They looked and looked at her and then they talked to each other, waving their arms and clapping their hands together. Pearl began to laugh.

The two women came up to her, keeping close to the hedge and looking in a frightened way towards the House of Boxes.

'Hallo, little girl!' said one.

Pearl said, 'Hallo!'

'You all alone by yourself?'

Pearl nodded.

'Where's your mother?'

'In the kitching, ironing-because-it's-Tuesday.'

The women smiled at her and Pearl smiled back. 'Oh,' she said, 'haven't you got very white teeth indeed! Do it again.'

The dark women laughed, and again they talked to each

other with funny words and wavings of the hands. 'What's your name?' they asked her.

'Pearl Button.'

'You coming with us, Pearl Button? We got beautiful things to show you,' whispered one of the women. So Pearl got down from the gate and she slipped out into the road. And she walked between the two dark women down the windy road, taking little running steps to keep up, and wondering what they had in their House of Boxes.

They walked a long way. 'You tired?' asked one of the women, bending down to Pearl. Pearl shook her head. They walked much further. 'You not tired?' asked the other woman. And Pearl shook her head again, but tears shook from her eyes at the same time and her lips trembled. One of the women gave over her flax basket of ferns and caught Pearl Button up in her arms, and walked with Pearl Button's head against her shoulder and her dusty little legs danging. She was softer than a bed and she had a nice smell—a smell that made you bury your head and breathe and breathe it. . . .

They set Pearl Button down in a log room full of other people the same colour as they were—and all these people came close to her and looked at her, nodding and laughing and throwing up their eyes. The woman who had carried Pearl took off her hair ribbon and shook her curls loose. There was a cry from the other women, and they crowded close and some of them ran a finger through Pearl's yellow curls, very gently, and one of them, a young one, lifted all Pearl's hair and kissed the back of her little white neck. Pearl felt shy but happy at the same time. There were some men on the floor, smoking, with rugs and feather mats round their shoulders. One of them made a funny face at her and he pulled a great big peach out of his pocket and set it on the floor, and flicked it with his finger as though it were a marble. It rolled right over to her. Pearl picked it up. 'Please can I eat it?' she asked. At that they all laughed and clapped their hands, and the man with the funny face made another at her and pulled a pear out of his pocket and sent it bobbling over the floor. Pearl laughed. The women sat on the floor and Pearl sat down too. The floor was very dusty. She carefully pulled up her pinafore and dress and sat on her petticoat as she had been taught to sit in dusty places, and she ate the fruit, the juice running all down her front.

24

'Oh!' she said in a very frightened voice to one of the women, 'I've spilt all the juice!'

'That doesn't matter at all,' said the woman, patting her cheek. A man came into the room with a long whip in his hand. He shouted something. They all got up, shouting, laughing, wrapping themselves up in rugs and blankets and feather mats. Pearl was carried again, this time into a great cart, and she sat on the lap of one of her women with the driver beside her. It was a green cart with a red pony and a black pony. It went very fast out of the town. The driver stood up and waved the whip round his head. Pearl peered over the shoulder of her woman. Other carts were behind like a procession. She waved at them. Then the country came. First fields of short grass with sheep on them and little bushes of white flowers and pink briar rose baskets—then big trees on both sides of the road—and nothing to be seen except big trees. Pearl tried to look through them but it was quite dark. Birds were singing. She nestled closer in the big lap. The woman was warm as a cat, and she moved up and down when she breathed, just like purring. Pearl played with a green ornament round her neck, and the woman took the little hand and kissed each of her fingers and then turned it over and kissed the dimples. Pearl had never been happy like this before. On the top of a big hill they stopped. The driving man turned to Pearl and said, 'Look, look!' and pointed with his whip.

And down at the bottom of the hill was something perfectly different—a great big piece of blue water was creeping over the land. She screamed and clutched at the big woman. 'What is it, what is it?'

'Why,' said the woman, 'it's the sea.'

'Will it hurt us—is it coming?'

'Ai-e, no, it doesn't come to us. It's very beautiful. You look again.'

Pearl looked. 'You're sure it can't come,' she said.

'Ai-e, no. It stays in its place,' said the big woman. Waves with white tops came leaping over the blue. Pearl watched them break on a long piece of land covered with garden-path shells. They drove round a corner.

There were some little houses down close to the sea, with wood fences round them and gardens inside. They comforted her. Pink and red and blue washing hung over the fences, and as they came near more people came out, and five yellow dogs with long thin tails. All the people were fat and laughing, with little naked babies holding on to them or rolling about in the gardens like puppies. Pearl was lifted down and taken into a tiny house with only one room and a veranda. There was a girl there with two pieces of black hair down to her feet. She was setting the dinner on the floor. 'It *is* a funny place,' said Pearl, watching the pretty girl while the woman unbuttoned her little drawers for her. She was very hungry. She ate meat and vegetables and fruit and the woman gave her milk out of a green cup. And it was quite silent except for the sea outside and the laughs of the two women watching her. 'Haven't you got any Houses of Boxes?' she said. 'Don't you all live in a row? Don't the men go to offices? Aren't there any nasty things?'

They took off her shoes and stockings, her pinafore and dress. She walked about in her petticoat and then she walked outside with the grass pushing between her toes. The two women came out with different sorts of baskets. They took her hands. Over a little paddock, through a fence, and then on warm sand with brown grass in it they went down to the sea. Pearl held back when the sand grew wet, but the women coaxed, 'Nothing to hurt, very beautiful. You come.' They dug in the sand and found some shells which they threw into the baskets. The sand was wet as mud pies. Pearl forgot her fright and began digging too. She got hot and wet and suddenly over her feet broke a little line of foam. 'Oo, oo!' she shrieked, dabbling with her feet. 'Lovely, lovely!' She paddled in the shallow water. It was warm. She made a cup of her hands and caught some of it. But it stopped being blue in her hands. She was so excited that she rushed over to her woman and flung her little thin arms round the woman's neck, hugging her, kissing. . . .

Suddenly the girl gave a frightful scream. The woman raised herself and Pearl slipped down on the sand and looked towards the land. Little men in blue coats—little blue men came running, running towards her with shouts and whistlings—a crowd of little blue men to carry her back to the House of Boxes.

(1912)

26

About Pat

In the days of our childhood we lived in a great old rambling house planted lonesomely in the midst of huge gardens, orchards and paddocks. We had few toys, but—far better—plenty of good strong mud and a flight of concrete steps that grew hot in the heat of the sun and became dreams of ovens.

The feeling of making a mud pie with all due seriousness, is one of the most delicious feelings that we experience; you sit with your mixture in the doll's saucepan, or if it is soup, in the doll's wash-hand basin, and stir and stir, and thicken and 'whip', and become more deliciously grimy each minute; whilst the sense of utter wickedness you have if it happens to be on clean pinafore days thrills me to this hour.

Well I remember one occasion when we made pies with real flour, stole some water from the dish by the dog's kennel, baked them and ate them.

Very soon after, three crushed, subdued little girls wended their way quietly up to bed, and the blind was pulled down.

At that period our old Irish gardener was our hero. His name was Patrick Sheehan. On Sunday he wore gloves with real 'kid backs', and a tie-pin made out of a boar's tusk. Every morning I went across to the feed-room where he cleaned father's boots, and always at a certain stage of the proceedings, I would say, 'Oh please, Pat, don't!' He invariably replied that 'nothing else at all gave them such a fine gloss'. He used to hoist me up on to the table, and recount long tales of the Dukes of Ireland whom he had seen and even conversed with. We were most proud of our gardener having rubbed shoulders with Ireland's aristocracy, and in the evening when Pat was at tea in the kitchen we would steal out and beg him to show us the manners of the people in Ireland. Standing in a row, hand in hand, we would watch while Pat put some salt on his knife, tapped it off with his fork, the little finger of his right hand well curled, in a manner which seemed to us ingenious enough for the first Lords of the land.

Pat was never very fond of me. I am afraid he did not think my character at all desirable. I professed no joy in having a bird in a cage; and one day committed the unpardonable offence of picking a pumpkin flower. He never recovered from the shock occasioned by that last act of barbarism. I can see him now, whenever I came near, nodding his head and saying, 'Well now to think! It might have become the finest vegetable of the season, and given us food for weeks.'

Pat's birthdays occurred with alarming frequency. We always gave him the same presents—three sticks of Juno tobacco and three cakes of hoky-poky. The presentation took place in the back-yard, and he sang us a wonderful Irish song, of which we never guessed any more than the phrase, 'I threw up me hat'. It seemed to be the one definite remark throughout.

He considered it a duty to propose to each cook who came to the house, making them the offer of himself, the gloves with the 'kid backs', and the boar-tusk tie-pin whenever the occasion demanded. They never by any chance accepted him, and I am sure that he never expected them to do so.

Every afternoon he used to brush his old brown bowler hat, harness the mare and start for town, and every evening when he had come home it was my delight to wait till he had un-harnessed the mare, then to be lifted on to her back, and start at a jogging trot through the big white gates, down the quiet road and into the paddock. There I waited until Pat came swinging along with the milk pails.

On those late evenings he had wonderful stories to tell of a little old man no bigger than his thumb with a hat as high as the barbed-wire fence, who in the night crept out of the creek, climbed up the blue-gum tree, picked some leaves from the topmost branches, and then crept down again.

'You see,' Pat would say, his dear weather-beaten face as grave as possible, 'it's from blue gums that you get eucalyptus, and the old man suffered from cold, living in such dampness.'

On those evenings, too, I had my first lessons in the mysterious art of milking, but try as I would I could never obtain more than a teacupful. On several occasions the ignominy of this reduced me to tears, but Pat would say, 'You see, she's such a keen old cow is Daisy. Having had children of her own, she knows how much you ought to have, and how much more would give you indigestion.' I was always much comforted. Pat had a wonderfully young heart. He entered into our pleasures with as much zest as we did ourselves. I played a game which had no end and no beginning, but was called 'Beyond the Blue Mountains'. The scene was generally placed near the rhubarb beds, and Pat officiated as the villain, the hero, and even the villainess, with unfailing charm.

Sometimes, to make it more real, we had lunch together, sitting on the wheel-barrow turned upside down, and sharing the slice of German sausage and a bath-bun with loaf sugar on it.

On Sunday mornings Pat, in the full glory of a clean shirt and corduroy trousers, took us for a walk in the great pine plantation.

He, childishly, used to collect gum and carry it in a corner of his handkerchief. For years afterwards I believed that those trees just grew for the old witches of the woods, who used their needles in making the big, big umbrella over our heads, and all the dresses of the flowers, basting their nice, fine, blue-sky calico with the gum thoughtfully provided for them. . . .

When we left that house in the country and went to live in town, Pat left us to try his luck in the goldfields. We parted with bitter tears. He presented each of my sisters with a gold-finch and me with a pair of white china vases cheerfully embroidered with forget-me-nots and pink roses. His parting advice to us was to look after ourselves in this world and never to pick the flowers out of the vegetable garden because we liked the colour.

From that day to this I have never heard of him.

(1905)

Prelude

recollection a rural surroundings

reflects her life as a child full of fantasy

*I try to make family life
so gorgeous—not hatred
and cold linoleum—but
warmth and hydrangeas.*

I

There was not an inch of room for Lottie and Kezia in the buggy. When Pat swung them on top of the luggage they wobbled; the grandmother's lap was full and Linda Burnell could not possibly have held a lump of a child on hers for any distance. Isabel, very superior, was perched beside the new handy-man on the driver's seat. Holdalls, bags and boxes were piled upon the floor. 'These are absolute necessities that I will not let out of my sight for one instant,' said Linda Burnell, her voice trembling with fatigue and excitement.

Lottie and Kezia stood on the patch of lawn just inside the gate all ready for the fray in their coats with brass anchor buttons and little round caps with battleship ribbons. Hand in hand, they stared with round solemn eyes, first at the absolute necessities and then at their mother.

'We shall simply have to leave them. That is all. We shall simply have to cast them off,' said Linda Burnell. A strange little laugh flew from her lips; she leaned back against the buttoned leather cushions and shut her eyes, her lips trembling with laughter. Happily at that moment Mrs. Samuel Josephs, who had been watching the scene from behind her drawing-room blind, waddled down the garden path.

'Why nod leave the chudren with be for the afterdoon, Brs. Burnell? They could go on the dray with the storeban when he comes in the eveding. Those thigs on the path have to go, dod't they?'

30

'Yes, everything outside the house is supposed to go,' said Linda Burnell, and she waved a white hand at the tables and chairs standing on their heads on the front lawn. How absurd they looked! Either they ought to be the other way up, or Lottie and Kezia ought to stand on their heads, too. And she longed to say: 'Stand on your heads, children, and wait for the storeman.' It seemed to her that would be so exquisitely funny that she could not attend to Mrs. Samuel Josephs.

The fat creaking body leaned across the gate, and the big jelly of a face smiled. 'Dod't you worry, Brs. Burnell. Loddie and Kezia can have tea with by chudren in the dursery, and I'll see theb on the dray afterwards.'

The grandmother considered. 'Yes, it really is quite the best plan. We are very obliged to you, Mrs. Samuel Josephs. Children, say "thank you" to Mrs. Samuel Josephs.'

Two subdued chirrups: 'Thank you, Mrs. Samuel Josephs.'

'And be good little girls, and—come closer—' they advanced, 'don't forget to tell Mrs. Samuel Josephs when you want to . . .'

'No, granma.'

'Dod't worry, Brs. Burnell.'

At the last moment Kezia let go Lottie's hand and darted towards the buggy.

'I want to kiss my granma good-bye again.'

But she was too late. The buggy rolled off up the road, Isabel bursting with pride, her nose turned up at all the world, Linda Burnell prostrated, and the grandmother rummaging among the very curious oddments she had had put in her black silk reticule at the last moment, for something to give her daughter. The buggy twinkled away in the sunlight and fine golden dust up the hill and over. Kezia bit her lip, but Lottie, carefully finding her handkerchief first, set up a wail.

'Mother! Granma!'

Mrs. Samuel Josephs, like a huge warm black silk tea-cosy, enveloped her.

'It's all right, by dear. Be a brave child. You come and blay in the dursery!'

She put her arm round weeping Lottie and led her away. Kezia followed, making a face at Mrs. Samuel Josephs' placket, which was undone as usual, with two long pink corset laces hanging out of it. . . .

Lottie's weeping died down as she mounted the stairs, but

the sight of her at the nursery door with swollen eyes and a blob of a nose gave great satisfaction to the S. J.s, who sat on two benches before a long table covered with American cloth and set out with immense plates of bread and dripping and two brown jugs that faintly steamed.

'Hullo! You've been crying!'

'Ooh! Your eyes have gone right in.'

'Doesn't her nose look funny.'

'You're all red-and-patchy.'

Lottie was quite a success. She felt it and swelled, smiling timidly.

'Go and sid by Zaidee, ducky,' said Mrs. Samuel Josephs, 'and Kezia, you sid ad the end by Boses.'

Moses grinned and gave her a nip as she sat down; but she pretended not to notice. She did hate boys.

'Which will you have?' asked Stanley, leaning across the table very politely, and smiling at her. 'Which will you have to begin with—strawberries and cream or bread and dripping?'

'Strawberries and cream, please,' said she.

'Ah-h-h-h.' How they all laughed and beat the table with their teaspoons. Wasn't that a take-in! Wasn't it now! Didn't he fox her! Good old Stan!

'Ma! She thought it was real.'

Even Mrs. Samuel Josephs, pouring out the milk and water, could not help smiling. 'You bustn't tease theb on their last day,' she wheezed.

But Kezia bit a big piece out of her bread and dripping, and then stood the piece up on her plate. With the bite out it made a dear little sort of a gate. Pooh! She didn't care! A tear rolled down her cheek, but she wasn't crying. She couldn't have cried in front of those awful Samuel Josephs. She sat with her head bent, and as the tear dripped slowly down, she caught it with a neat little whisk of her tongue and ate it before any of them had seen.

II

After tea Kezia wandered back to their own house. Slowly she walked up the back steps, and through the scullery into the kitchen. Nothing was left in it but a lump of gritty yellow soap in one corner of the kitchen window-sill and a piece of flannel stained with a blue bag in another. The fire-place was choked up with rubbish. She poked among it but found nothing except a hair-tidy with a heart painted on it that had belonged to the servant girl. Even that she left lying, and she trailed through the narrow passage into the drawing-room. The Venetian blind was pulled down but not drawn close. Long pencil rays of sunlight shone through and the wavy shadow of a bush outside danced on the gold lines. Now it was still, now it began to flutter again, and now it came almost as far as her feet. Zoom! Zoom! a blue-bottle knocked against the ceiling; the carpet-tacks had little bits of red fluff sticking to them.

The dining-room window had a square of coloured glass at each corner. One was blue and one was yellow. Kezia bent down to have one more look at a blue lawn with blue arum lilies growing at the gate, and then at a yellow lawn with yellow lilies and a yellow fence. As she looked a little Chinese Lottie came out on to the lawn and began to dust the tables and chairs with a corner of her pinafore. Was that really Lottie? Kezia was not quite sure until she had looked through the ordinary window.

Upstairs in her father's and mother's room she found a pill box black and shiny outside and red in, holding a blob of cotton wool.

'I could keep a bird's egg in that,' she decided.

In the servant girl's room there was a stay-button stuck in a crack of the floor, and in another crack some beads and a long needle. She knew there was nothing in her grandmother's room; she had watched her pack. She went over to the window and leaned against it, pressing her hands against the pane.

Kezia liked to stand so before the window. She liked the feeling of the cold shining glass against her hot palms, and she liked to watch the funny white tops that came on her fingers when she pressed them hard against the pane. As she stood there, the day flickered out and dark came. With the dark crept the wind snuffling and howling. The windows of the empty house shook, a creaking came from the walls and floors, a piece of loose iron on the roof banged forlornly. Kezia was suddenly quite, quite still, with wide open eyes and knees pressed to-gether. She was frightened. She wanted to call Lottie and to

33

go on calling all the while she ran downstairs and out of the house. But IT was just behind her, waiting at the door, at the head of the stairs, at the bottom of the stairs, hiding in the passage, ready to dart out at the back door. But Lottie was at the back door, too.

'Kezia!' she called cheerfully. 'The storeman's here. Everything is on the dray and three horses, Kezia. Mrs. Samuel Josephs has given us a big shawl to wear round us, and she says to button up your coat. She won't come out because of asthma.' Lottie was very important.

'Now then, you kids,' called the storeman. He hooked his big thumbs under their arms and up they swung. Lottie arranged the shawl 'most beautifully' and the storeman tucked up their feet in a piece of old blanket.

'Lift up. Easy does it.'

They might have been a couple of young ponies. The storeman felt over the cords holding his load, unhooked the brake-chain from the wheel, and whistling, he swung up beside them.

'Keep close to me,' said Lottie, 'because otherwise you pull the shawl away from my side, Kezia.'

But Kezia edged up to the storeman. He towered beside her big as a giant and he smelled of nuts and new wooden boxes.

III

It was the first time that Lottie and Kezia had ever been out so late. Everything looked different—the painted wooden houses far smaller than they did by day, the gardens far bigger and wider. Bright stars speckled the sky and the moon hung over the harbour dabbling the waves with gold. They could see the lighthouse shining on Quarantine Island, and the green lights on the old coal hulks.

'There comes the Picton boat,' said the storeman, pointing to a little steamer all hung with bright beads.

But when they reached the top of the hill and began to go down the other side the harbour disappeared, and although they were still in the town they were quite lost. Other carts rattled past. Everybody knew the storeman.

'Night, Fred.'

'Night O,' he shouted.

Kezia liked very much to hear him. Whenever a cart appeared in the distance she looked up and waited for his voice. He was an old friend; and she and her grandmother had often been to his place to buy grapes. The storeman lived alone in a cottage that had a glasshouse against one wall built by himself. All the glasshouse was spanned and arched over with one beautiful vine. He took her brown basket from her, lined it with three large leaves, and then he felt in his belt for a little horn knife, reached up and snapped off a big blue cluster and laid it on the leaves so tenderly that Kezia held her breath to watch. He was a very big man. He wore brown velvet trousers, and he had a long brown beard. But he never wore a collar, not even on Sunday. The back of his neck was burnt bright red.

'Where are we now?' Every few minutes one of the children asked him the question.

'Why, this is Hawk Street, or Charlotte Crescent.'

'Of course it is,' Lottie pricked up her ears at the last name; she always felt that Charlotte Crescent belonged specially to her. Very few people had streets with the same name as theirs.

'Look, Kezia, there is Charlotte Crescent. Doesn't it look different?' Now everything familiar was left behind. Now the big dray rattled into unknown country, along new roads with high clay banks on either side, up steep, steep hills, down into bushy valleys, through wide shallow rivers. Further and further. Lottie's head wagged; she drooped, she slipped half into Kezia's lap and lay there. But Kezia could not open her eyes wide enough. The wind blew and she shivered; but her cheeks and ears burned.

'Do stars ever blow about?' she asked.

'Not to notice,' said the storeman.

'We've got a nuncle and a naunt living near our new house,' said Kezia. 'They have got two children, Pip, the eldest is called, and the youngest's name is Rags. He's got a ram. He has to feed it with a nenamuel teapot and a glove top over the spout. He's going to show us. What is the difference between a ram and a sheep?'

'Well, a ram has horns and runs for you.'

Kezia considered. 'I don't want to see it frightfully,' she said. 'I hate rushing animals like dogs and parrots. I often dream that animals rush at me—even camels—and while they are rushing, their heads swell e-enormous.'

The storeman said nothing. Kezia peered up at him, screwing up her eyes. Then she put her finger out and stroked his sleeve; it felt hairy. 'Are we near?' she asked.

'Not far off, now,' answered the storeman. 'Getting tired?'

'Well, I'm not an atom bit sleepy,' said Kezia. 'But my eyes keep curling up in such a funny sort of way.' She gave a long sigh, and to stop her eyes from curling she shut them. . . . When she opened them again they were clanking through a drive that cut through the garden like a whip-lash, looping suddenly an island of green, and behind the island, but out of sight until you came upon it, was the house. It was long and low built, with a pillared veranda and balcony all the way round. The soft white bulk of it lay stretched upon the green garden like a sleeping beast. And now one and now another of the windows leaped into light. Someone was walking through the empty rooms carrying a lamp. From the window downstairs the light of a fire flickered. A strange beautiful excitement seemed to stream from the house in quivering ripples.

'Where are we?' said Lottie, sitting up. Her reefer cap was all on one side and on her cheek there was the print of an anchor button she had pressed against while sleeping. Tenderly the storeman lifted her, set her cap straight, and pulled down her crumpled clothes. She stood blinking on the lowest veranda step watching Kezia, who seemed to come flying through the air to her feet.

'Ooh!' cried Kezia, flinging up her arms. The grandmother came out of the dark hall carrying a little lamp. She was smiling.

'You found your way in the dark?' said she.

'Perfectly well.'

But Lottie staggered on the lowest veranda step like a bird fallen out of the nest. If she stood still for a moment she fell asleep; if she leaned against anything her eyes closed. She could not walk another step.

'Kezia,' said the grandmother, 'can I trust you to carry the lamp?'

'Yes, my granma.'

The old woman bent down and gave the bright breathing thing into her hands and then she caught up drunken Lottie. 'This way.'

Through a square hall filled with bales and hundreds of parrots (but the parrots were only on the wall-paper) down a narrow passage where the parrots persisted in flying past Kezia with her lamp.

'Be very quiet,' warned the grandmother, putting down Lottie and opening the dining-room door. 'Poor little mother has got such a headache.'

Linda Burnell, in a long cane chair, with her feet on a hassock and a plaid over her knees, lay before a crackling fire. Burnell and Beryl sat at the table in the middle of the room eating a dish of fried chops and drinking tea out of a brown china teapot. Over the back of her mother's chair leaned Isabel. She had a comb in her fingers and in a gentle absorbed fashion she was combing the curls from her mother's forehead. Outside the pool of lamp and firelight the room stretched dark and bare to the hollow windows.

'Are those the children?' But Linda did not really care; she did not even open her eyes to see.

'Put down the lamp, Kezia,' said Aunt Beryl, 'or we shall have the house on fire before we are out of the packing cases. More tea, Stanley?'

'Well, you might just give me five-eighths of a cup,' said Burnell, leaning across the table. 'Have another chop, Beryl. Tip-top meat, isn't it? Not too lean and not too fat.' He turned to his wife. 'You're sure you won't change your mind, Linda darling?'

'The very thought of it is enough.' She raised one eyebrow in the way she had. The grandmother brought the children bread and milk and they sat up to table, flushed and sleepy behind the wavy steam.

'I had meat for my supper,' said Isabel, still combing gently. 'I had a whole chop for my supper, the bone and all and Worcester sauce. Didn't I, father?'

'Oh, don't boast, Isabel,' said Aunt Beryl.

Isabel looked astounded. 'I wasn't boasting, was I, Mummy? I never thought of boasting. I thought they would like to know. I only meant to tell them.'

'Very well. That's enough,' said Burnell. He pushed back

37

his plate, took a tooth-pick out of his pocket and began picking his strong white teeth.

'You might see that Fred has a bite of something in the kitchen before he goes, will you, mother?'

'Yes, Stanley.' The old woman turned to go.

'Oh, hold on half a jiffy. I suppose nobody knows where my slippers were put? I suppose I shall not be able to get at them for a month or two—what?'

'Yes,' came from Linda. 'In the top of the canvas holdall marked "urgent necessities."'

'Well, you might get them for me, will you, mother?'

'Yes, Stanley.'

Burnell got up, stretched himself, and going over to the fire he turned his back to it and lifted up his coat tails.

'By Jove, this is a pretty pickle. Eh, Beryl?'

Beryl, sipping tea, her elbows on the table, smiled over the cup at him. She wore an unfamiliar pink pinafore; the sleeves of her blouse were rolled up to her shoulders showing her lovely freckled arms, and she had let her hair fall down her back in a long pigtail.

'How long do you think it will take to get straight—couple of weeks—eh?' he chaffed.

'Good heavens, no' said Beryl airily. 'The worst is over already. The servant girl and I have simply slaved all day, and ever since mother came she has worked like a horse, too. We have never sat down for a moment. We have had a day.'

Stanley scented a rebuke.

'Well, I suppose you did not expect me to rush away from the office and nail carpets—did you?'

'Certainly not,' laughed Beryl. She put down her cup and ran out of the dining-room.

'What the hell does she expect us to do?' asked Stanley. 'Sit down and fan herself with a palm-leaf fan while I have a gang of professionals to do the job? By Jove, if she can't do a hand's turn occasionally without shouting about it in return for . . .'

And he gloomed as the chops began to fight the tea in his sensitive stomach. But Linda put up a hand and dragged him down to the side of her long chair.

'This is a wretched time for you, old boy,' she said. Her cheeks were very white, but she smiled and curled her fingers into the big red hand she held. Burnell became quiet. Suddenly

38

he began to whistle 'Pure as a lily, joyous and free'—a good sign.

'Think you're going to like it?' he asked.

'I don't want to tell you, but I think I ought to, mother,' said Isabel. 'Kezia is drinking tea out of Aunt Beryl's cup.'

IV

They were taken off to bed by the grandmother. She went first with a candle; the stairs rang to their climbing feet. Isabel and Lottie lay in a room to themselves, Kezia curled in her grandmother's soft bed.

'Aren't there going to be any sheets, my granma?'

'No, not to-night.'

'It's tickly,' said Kezia, 'but it's like Indians.' She dragged her grandmother down to her and kissed her under the chin. 'Come to bed soon and be my Indian brave.'

'What a silly you are,' said the old woman, tucking her in as she loved to be tucked.

'Aren't you going to leave me a candle?'

'No. Sh—h. Go to sleep.'

'Well, can I have the door left open?'

She rolled herself up into a round but she did not go to sleep. From all over the house came the sound of steps. The house itself creaked and popped. Loud whispering voices came from downstairs. Once she heard Aunt Beryl's rush of high laughter, and once she heard a loud trumpeting from Burnell blowing his nose. Outside the window hundreds of black cats with yellow eyes sat in the sky watching her—but she was not frightened. Lottie was saying to Isabel:

'I'm going to say my prayers in bed to-night.'

'No, you can't, Lottie.' Isabel was very firm. 'God only excuses you saying your prayers in bed if you've got a temperature.' So Lottie yielded:

> 'Gentle Jesus meek anmile,
> Look pon a little chile.
> Pity me, simple Lizzie,
> Suffer me to come to thee.'

39

And then they lay down back to back, their little behinds just touching, and fell asleep.

Standing in a pool of moonlight Beryl Fairfield undressed herself. She was tired, but she pretended to be more tired than she really was—letting her clothes fall, pushing back with a languid gesture her warm, heavy hair.

'Oh, how tired I am—very tired.'

She shut her eyes a moment, but her lips smiled. Her breath rose and fell in her breast like two fanning wings. The window was wide open; it was warm, and somewhere out there in the garden a young man, dark and slender, with mocking eyes, tip-toed among the bushes, and gathered the flowers into a big bouquet, and slipped under her window and held it up to her. She saw herself bending forward. He thrust his head among the bright waxy flowers, sly and laughing. 'No, no,' said Beryl. She turned from the window and dropped her nightgown over her head.

'How frightfully unreasonable Stanley is sometimes,' she thought, buttoning. And then, as she lay down, there came the old thought, the cruel thought—ah, if only she had money of her own.

A young man, immensely rich, has just arrived from England. He meets her quite by chance. . . . The new governor is un-married. . . . There is a ball at Government house. . . . Who is that exquisite creature in *eau-de-nil* satin? Beryl Fair-field. . . .

'The thing that pleases me,' said Stanley, leaning against the side of the bed and giving himself a good scratch on his shoulders and back before turning in, 'is that I've got the place dirt cheap, Linda. I was talking about it to little Wally Bell to-day and he said he simply could not understand why they had accepted my figure. You see land about here is bound to become more and more valuable . . . in about ten years' time . . . of course we shall have to go very slow and cut down expenses as fine as possible. Not asleep—are you?'

'No, dear. I've heard every word,' said Linda.

He sprang into bed, leaned over her and blew out the candle.

'Good night, Mr. Business Man,' said she, and she took hold of his head by the ears and gave him a quick kiss. Her faint far-away voice seemed to come from a deep well.

'Good night, darling.' He slipped his arm under her neck and drew her to him.

'Yes, clasp me,' said the faint voice from the deep well.

Pat the handy-man sprawled in his little room behind the kitchen. His sponge-bag, coat and trousers hung from the door-peg like a hanged man. From the edge of the blanket his twisted toes protruded, and on the floor beside him there was an empty cane bird-cage. He looked like a comic picture.

'Honk, honk,' came from the servant girl. She had adenoids.

Last to go to bed was the grandmother.

'What. Not asleep yet?'

'No, I'm waiting for you,' said Kezia. The old woman sighed and lay down beside her. Kezia thrust her head under her grandmother's arm and gave a little squeak. But the old woman only pressed her faintly, and sighed again, took out her teeth, and put them in a glass of water beside her on the floor.

In the garden some tiny owls, perched on the branches of a lace-bark tree, called: 'More pork; more pork.' And far away in the bush there sounded a harsh rapid chatter: 'Ha-ha-ha . . . Ha-ha-ha.'

V

Dawn came sharp and chill with red clouds on a faint green sky and drops of water on every leaf and blade. A breeze blew over the garden, dropping dew and dropping petals, shivered over the drenched paddocks, and was lost in the sombre bush. In the sky some tiny stars floated for a moment and then they were gone—they were dissolved like bubbles. And plain to be heard in the early quiet was the sound of the creek in the paddock running over the brown stones, running in and out of the sandy hollows, hiding under clumps of dark berry bushes, spilling into a swamp of yellow water flowers and cresses.

And then at the first beam of sun the birds began. Big cheeky birds, starlings and mynahs, whistled on the lawns, the little birds, the goldfinches and linnets and fan-tails, flicked from bough to bough. A lovely kingfisher perched on the paddock fence preening his rich beauty, and a *tui* sang his three notes and laughed and sang them again.

'How loud the birds are,' said Linda in her dream. She was walking with her father through a green paddock sprinkled with daisies. Suddenly he bent down and parted the grasses and showed her a tiny ball of fluff just at her feet. 'Oh, papa, the darling.' She made a cup of her hands and caught the tiny bird and stroked its head with her finger. It was quite tame. But a funny thing happened. As she stroked it began to swell, it ruffled and pouched, it grew bigger and bigger and its round eyes seemed to smile knowingly at her. Now her arms were hardly wide enough to hold it and she dropped it into her apron. It had become a baby with a big naked head and a gaping bird-mouth, opening and shutting. Her father broke into a loud clattering laugh and she woke to see Burnell standing by the windows rattling the Venetian blind up to the very top.

'Hullo,' he said. 'Didn't wake you, did I? Nothing much wrong with the weather this morning.'

He was enormously pleased. Weather like this set a final seal on his bargain. He felt, somehow, that he had bought the lovely day, too—got it chucked in dirt cheap with the house and ground. He dashed off to his bath and Linda turned over and raised herself on one elbow to see the room by daylight. All the furniture had found a place—all the old paraphernalia, as she expressed it. Even the photographs were on the mantelpiece and the medicine bottles on the shelf above the washstand. Her clothes lay across a chair—her outdoor things, a purple cape and a round hat with a plume in it. Looking at them she wished that she was going away from this house, too. And she saw herself driving away from them all in a little buggy, driving away from everybody and not even waving.

Back came Stanley girt with a towel, glowing and slapping his thighs. He pitched the wet towel on top of her hat and cape and standing firm in the exact centre of a square of sunlight he began to do his exercises. Deep breathing, bending and squatting like a frog and shooting out his legs. He was so delighted with his firm, obedient body that he hit himself on the chest and gave a loud 'Ah'. But this amazing vigour seemed to set him worlds away from Linda. She lay on the white tumbled bed and watched him as if from the clouds.

'Oh, damn! Oh, blast!' said Stanley, who had butted into a crisp white shirt only to find that some idiot had fastened the neck-band and he was caught. He stalked over to Linda waving his arms.

'You look like a big fat turkey,' said she.

'Fat. I like that,' said Stanley. 'I haven't a square inch of fat on me. Feel that.'

'It's rock—it's iron,' mocked she.

'You'd be surprised,' said Stanley, as though this were intensely interesting, 'at the number of chaps at the club who have got a corporation. Young chaps, you know—men of my age.' He began parting his bushy ginger hair, his blue eyes fixed and round in the glass, his knees bent, because the dressing-table was always—confound it—a bit too low for him. 'Little Wally Bell, for instance,' and he straightened, describing upon himself an enormous curve with the hairbrush. 'I must say I've a perfect horror . . .'

'My dear, don't worry. You'll never be fat. You are far too energetic.'

'Yes, yes, I suppose that's true,' said he, comforted for the hundredth time, and taking a pearl penknife out of his pocket he began to pare his nails.

'Breakfast, Stanley,' Beryl was at the door. 'Oh Linda, mother says you are not to get up yet.' She popped her head in at the door. She had a big piece of syringa stuck through her hair.

'Everything we left on the veranda last night is simply sopping this morning. You should see poor dear mother wringing out the tables and the chairs. However, there is no harm done—' this with the faintest glance at Stanley.

'Have you told Pat to have the buggy round in time? It's a good six and a half miles to the office.'

'I can imagine what this early start for the office will be like,' thought Linda. 'It will be very high pressure indeed.'

'Pat, Pat.' She heard the servant girl calling. But Pat was evidently hard to find; the silly voice went baa—baaing through the garden.

Linda did not rest again until the final slam of the front door told her that Stanley was really gone.

Later she heard her children playing in the garden. Lottie's stolid, compact little voice cried: 'Ke—zia. Isa—bel.' She was

43

always getting lost or losing people only to find them again, to her great surprise, round the next tree or the next corner. 'Oh, there you are after all.' They had been turned out after breakfast and told not to come back to the house until they were called. Isabel wheeled a neat pramload of prim dolls and Lottie was allowed for a great treat to walk beside her holding the doll's parasol over the face of the wax one.

'Where are you going to, Kezia?' asked Isabel, who longed to find some light and menial duty that Kezia might perform and so be roped in under her government.

'Oh, just away,' said Kezia. . . .

Then she did not hear them any more. What a glare there was in the room. She hated blinds pulled up to the top at any time, but in the morning it was intolerable. She turned over to the wall and idly, with one finger, she traced a poppy on the wall-paper with a leaf and a stem and a fat bursting bud. In the quiet, and under her tracing finger, the poppy seemed to come alive. She could feel the sticky, silky petals, the stem, hairy like a gooseberry skin, the rough leaf and the tight glazed bud. Things had a habit of coming alive like that. Not only large substantial things like furniture but curtains and the patterns of stuffs and the fringes of quilts and cushions. How often she had seen the tassel fringe of her quilt change into a funny procession of dancers with priests attending. . . . For there were some tassels that did not dance at all but walked stately, bent forward as if praying or chanting. How often the medicine bottles had turned into a row of little men with brown top-hats on; and the washstand jug had a way of sitting in the basin like a fat bird in a round nest.

'I dreamed about birds last night,' thought Linda. What was it? She had forgotten. But the strangest part of this coming alive of things was what they did. They listened, they seemed to swell out with some mysterious important content, and when they were full she felt that they smiled. But it was not for her, only, their sly secret smile; they were members of a secret society and they smiled among themselves. Sometimes, when she had fallen asleep in the daytime, she woke and could not lift a finger, could not even turn her eyes to left or right because THEY were there; sometimes when she went out of a room and left it empty, she knew as she clicked the door to that THEY were filling it. And there were times in the evenings when she was upstairs, perhaps, and everybody else was down, when she could hardly escape from them. Then she could not hurry, she could not hum a tune; if she tried to say ever so carelessly— 'Bother that old thimble'—THEY were not deceived. THEY knew how frightened she was; THEY saw how she turned her head away as she passed the mirror. What Linda always felt was that THEY wanted something of her, and she knew that if she gave herself up and was quiet, more than quiet, silent, motionless, something would really happen.

'It's very quiet now,' she thought. She opened her eyes wide, and she heard the silence spinning its soft endless web. How lightly she breathed; she scarcely had to breathe at all.

Yes, everything had come alive down to the minutest, tiniest particle, and she did not feel her bed, she floated, held up in the air. Only she seemed to be listening with her wide open watchful eyes, waiting for someone to come who just did not come, watching for something to happen that just did not happen.

VI

In the kitchen at the long deal table under the two windows old Mrs. Fairfield was washing the breakfast dishes. The kitchen window looked out on to a big grass patch that led down to the vegetable garden and the rhubarb beds. On one side the grass patch was bordered by the scullery and wash-house and over this whitewashed lean-to there grew a knotted vine. She had noticed yesterday that a few tiny corkscrew tendrils had come right through some cracks in the scullery ceiling and all the windows of the lean-to had a thick frill of ruffled green.

'I am very fond of a grape vine,' declared Mrs. Fairfield, 'but I do not think that the grapes will ripen here. It takes Australian sun.' And she remembered how Beryl when she was a baby had been picking some white grapes from the vine on the back veranda of their Tasmanian house and she had been stung on the leg by a huge red ant. She saw Beryl in a little plaid dress with red ribbon tie-ups on the shoulders screaming so dreadfully that half the street rushed in. And how the child's leg had swelled! 'T—t—t—t!' Mrs. Fairfield caught her breath remembering. 'Poor child, how terrifying it was.' And she set her lips tight and went over to the stove for some more hot water. The water frothed up in the big soapy bowl with pink and blue bubbles on top of the foam. Old Mrs. Fairfield's arms were bare to the elbow and stained a bright pink. She wore a grey foulard dress patterned with large purple pansies, a white linen apron and a high cap shaped like a jelly mould of white muslin. At her throat there was a silver crescent moon with five little owls seated on it, and round her neck she wore a watch-guard made of black beads.

It was hard to believe that she had not been in that kitchen for years; she was so much a part of it. She put the crocks away with a sure, precise touch, moving leisurely and ample from the stove to the dresser, looking into the pantry and the larder as though there were not an unfamiliar corner. When she had finished, everything in the kitchen had become part of a series of patterns. She stood in the middle of the room wiping her hands on a check cloth; a smile beamed on her lips; she thought it looked very nice, very satisfactory.

'Mother! Mother! Are you there?' called Beryl.

'Yes, dear. Do you want me?'

'No. I'm coming,' and Beryl rushed in, very flushed, dragging with her two big pictures.

'Mother, whatever can I do with these awful hideous Chinese paintings that Chung Wah gave Stanley when he went bankrupt? It's absurd to say that they are valuable, because they were hanging in Chung Wah's fruit shop for months before. I can't make out why Stanley wants them kept. I'm sure he thinks them just as hideous as we do, but it's because of the frames,' she said spitefully. 'I suppose he thinks the frames might fetch something some day or other.'

'Why don't you hang them in the passage?' suggested Mrs. Fairfield; 'they would not be much seen there.'

'I can't. There is no room. I've hung all the photographs of his office there before and after building, and the signed photos of his business friends, and that awful enlargement of Isabel lying on the mat in her singlet.' Her angry glance swept the placid kitchen. 'I know what I'll do. I'll hang them here. I will tell Stanley they got a little damp in the moving so I have put them in here for the time being.'

She dragged a chair forward, jumped on it, took a hammer and a big nail out of her pinafore pocket and banged away.

'There! That is enough! Hand me the picture, mother.'

'One moment, child.' Her mother was wiping over the carved ebony frame.

'Oh, mother, really you need not dust them. It would take years to dust all those little holes.' And she frowned at the top of her mother's head and bit her lip with impatience. Mother's deliberate way of doing things was simply maddening. It was old age, she supposed, loftily.

At last the two pictures were hung side by side. She jumped off the chair, stowing away the little hammer.

'They don't look so bad there, do they?' said she. 'And at any rate nobody need gaze at them except Pat and the servant girl —have I got a spider's web on my face, mother? I've been poking into that cupboard under the stairs and now something keeps tickling my nose.'

But before Mrs. Fairfield had time to look Beryl had turned away. Someone tapped on the window: Linda was there, nodding and smiling. They heard the latch of the scullery door lift and she came in. She had no hat on; her hair stood upon her head in curling rings and she was wrapped up in an old cashmere shawl.

'I'm so hungry,' said Linda: 'where can I get something to eat, mother? This is the first time I've been in the kitchen. It says "mother" all over; everything is in pairs.'

'I will make you some tea,' said Mrs. Fairfield, spreading a clean napkin over a corner of the table, 'and Beryl can have a cup with you.'

'Beryl, do you want half my gingerbread?' Linda waved the knife at her. 'Beryl, do you like the house now that we are here?'

'Oh yes, I like the house immensely and the garden is beautiful, but it feels very far away from everything to me. I can't imagine people coming out from town to see us in that dreadful jolting bus, and I am sure there is not anyone here to come and call. Of course it does not matter to you because—'

'But there's the buggy,' said Linda. 'Pat can drive you into town whenever you like.'

That was a consolation, certainly, but there was something at the back of Beryl's mind, something she did not even put into words for herself.

47

'Oh, well, at any rate it won't kill us,' she said dryly, putting down her empty cup and standing up and stretching. 'I am going to hang curtains.' And she ran away singing:

> 'How many thousand birds I see
> That sing aloud from every tree . . .'

'. . . birds I see That sing aloud from every tree. . . .' But when she reached the dining-room she stopped singing, her face changed; it became gloomy and sullen.

'One may as well rot here as anywhere else,' she muttered savagely, digging the stiff brass safety-pins into the red serge curtains.

The two left in the kitchen were quiet for a little. Linda leaned her cheek on her fingers and watched her mother. She thought her mother looked wonderfully beautiful with her back to the leafy window. There was something comforting in the sight of her that Linda felt she could never do without. She needed the sweet smell of her flesh, and the soft feel of her cheeks and her arms and shoulders still softer. She loved the way her hair curled, silver at her forehead, lighter at her neck, and bright brown still in the big coil under the muslin cap. Exquisite were her mother's hands, and the two rings she wore seemed to melt into her creamy skin. And she was always so fresh, so delicious. The old woman could bear nothing but linen next to her body and she bathed in cold water winter and summer.

'Isn't there anything for me to do?' asked Linda.

'No, darling. I wish you would go into the garden and give an eye to your children; but that I know you will not do.'

'Of course I will, but you know Isabel is much more grown up than any of us.'

'Yes, but Kezia is not,' said Mrs. Fairfield.

'Oh, Kezia has been tossed by a bull hours ago,' said Linda, winding herself up in her shawl again.

But no, Kezia had seen a bull through a hole in a knot of wood in the paling that separated the tennis lawn from the paddock. But she had not liked the bull frightfully, so she had walked away back through the orchard, up the grassy slope, along the path by the lace-bark tree and so into the spread tangled garden. She did not believe that she would ever not get lost in this garden. Twice she had found her way back to the big iron gates they had driven through the night before, and then had turned to walk up the drive that led to the house, but there were so many little paths on either side. On one side they all led into a tangle of tall dark trees and strange bushes with flat velvet leaves and feathery cream flowers that buzzed with flies when you shook them—this was the frightening side, and no garden at all. The little paths were here wet and clayey with tree roots spanned across them like the marks of big fowls' feet.

But on the other side of the drive there was a high box border and the paths had box edges and all of them led into a deeper and deeper tangle of flowers. The camellias were in bloom, white and crimson and pink and white striped with flashing leaves. You could not see a leaf on the syringa bushes for the white clusters. The roses were in flower—gentlemen's button-hole roses, little white ones, but far too full of insects to hold under anyone's nose, pink monthly roses with a ring of fallen petals round the bushes, cabbage roses on thick stalks, moss roses, always in bud, pink smooth beauties opening curl on curl, red ones so dark they seemed to turn black as they fell, and a certain exquisite cream kind with a slender red stem and bright scarlet leaves.

There were clumps of fairy bells, and all kinds of geraniums, and there were little trees of verbena and bluish lavender bushes and a bed of pelargoniums with velvet eyes and leaves like moths' wings. There was a bed of nothing but mignonette and another of nothing but pansies—borders of double and single daisies and all kinds of little tufty plants she had never seen before.

The red-hot pokers were taller than she; the Japanese sunflowers grew in a tiny jungle. She sat down on one of the box borders. By pressing hard at first it made a nice seat. But how dusty it was inside! Kezia bent down to look and sneezed and rubbed her nose.

And then she found herself at the top of the rolling grassy slope that led down to the orchard. . . . She looked down at the slope a moment; then she lay down on her back, gave a squeak and rolled over and over into the thick flowery orchard grass. As she lay waiting for things to stop spinning, she decided to go up to the house and ask the servant girl for an empty matchbox. She wanted to make a surprise for the grandmother. . . .

49

First she would put a leaf inside with a big violet lying on it, then she would put a very small white picotee, perhaps, on each side of the violet, and then she would sprinkle some lavender on the top, but not to cover their heads.

She often made these surprises for the grandmother, and they were always most successful.

'Do you want a match, my granny?'

'Why, yes, child, I believe a match is just what I'm looking for.'

The grandmother slowly opened the box and came upon the picture inside.

'Good gracious, child! How you astonished me!'

'I can make her one every day here,' she thought, scrambling up the grass on her slippery shoes.

But on her way back to the house she came to that island that lay in the middle of the drive, dividing the drive into two arms that met in front of the house. The island was made of grass banked up high. Nothing grew on the top except one huge plant with thick, grey-green, thorny leaves, and out of the middle there sprang up a tall stout stem. Some of the leaves of the plant were so old that they curled up in the air no longer; they turned back, they were split and broken; some of them lay flat and withered on the ground.

Whatever could it be? She had never seen anything like it before. She stood and stared. And then she saw her mother coming down the path.

'Mother, what is it?' asked Kezia.

Linda looked up at the fat swelling plant with its cruel leaves and fleshy stem. High above them, as though becalmed in the air, and yet holding so fast to the earth it grew from, it might have had claws instead of roots. The curving leaves seemed to be hiding something; the blind stem cut into the air as if no wind could ever shake it.

'That is an aloe, Kezia,' said her mother.

'Does it ever have any flowers?'

'Yes, Kezia,' and Linda smiled down at her, and half shut her eyes. 'Once every hundred years.'

VII

On his way home from the office Stanley Burnell stopped the buggy at the Bodega, got out and bought a large bottle of oysters. At the Chinaman's shop next door he bought a pineapple in the pink of condition, and noticing a basket of fresh black cherries he told John to put him in a pound of those as well. The oysters and the pine he stowed away in the box under the front seat, but the cherries he kept in his hand.

Pat, the handy-man, leapt off the box and tucked him up again in the brown rug.

'Lift yer feet, Mr. Burnell, while I give yer a fold under,' said he.

'Right! Right! First-rate!' said Stanley. 'You can make straight for home now.'

Pat gave the grey mare a touch and the buggy sprang forward.

'I believe this man is a first-rate chap,' thought Stanley. He liked the look of him sitting up there in his neat brown coat and brown bowler. He liked the way Pat had tucked him in, and he liked his eyes. There was nothing servile about him—and if there was one thing he hated more than another it was servility. And he looked as if he was pleased with his job—happy and contented already.

The grey mare went very well; Burnell was impatient to be out of the town. He wanted to be home. Ah, it was splendid to live in the country—to get right out of that hole of a town once the office was closed; and this drive in the fresh warm air, knowing all the while that his own house was at the other end, with its garden and paddocks, its three tip-top cows and enough fowls and ducks to keep them in poultry, was splendid too.

As they left the town finally and bowled away up the deserted road his heart beat hard for joy. He rooted in the bag and began to eat the cherries, three or four at a time, chucking the stones over the side of the buggy. They were delicious, so plump and cold, without a spot or a bruise on them.

Look at those two, now—black one side and white the other —perfect! A perfect little pair of Siamese twins. And he stuck them in his button-hole. . . . By Jove, he wouldn't mind giving that chap up there a handful—but no, better not. Better wait until he had been with him a bit longer.

He began to plan what he would do with his Saturday afternoons and his Sundays. He wouldn't go to the club for lunch on Saturday. No, cut away from the office as soon as possible, and get them to give him a couple of slices of cold meat and half a lettuce when he got home. And then he'd get a few chaps out from town to play tennis in the afternoon. Not too many —three at most. Beryl was a good player, too.... He stretched out his right arm and slowly bent it, feeling the muscle. . . . A bath, a good rub-down, a cigar on the veranda after dinner. . . .

On Sunday morning they would go to church—children and all. Which reminded him that he must hire a pew, in the sun if possible and well forward so as to be out of the draught from the door. In fancy he heard himself intoning extremely well: 'When thou didst overcome the *Sharp*ness of Death Thou didst open the *King*dom of Heaven to *all* Believers.' And he saw the neat brass-edged card on the corner of the pew—Mr. Stanley Burnell and family. . . . The rest of the day he'd loaf about with Linda. . . . Now they were walking about the garden; she was on his arm, and he was explaining to her at length what he intended doing at the office the week following. He heard her saying: 'My dear, I think that is most wise. . . .' Talking things over with Linda was a wonderful help even though they were apt to drift away from the point.

Hang it all! They weren't getting along very fast. Pat had put the brake on again. Ugh! What a brute of a thing it was. He could feel it in the pit of his stomach.

A sort of panic overtook Burnell whenever he approached near home. Before he was well inside the gate he would shout to anyone within sight: 'Is everything all right?' And then he did not believe it was until he heard Linda say: 'Hullo! Are you home again?' That was the worst of living in the country —it took the deuce of a long time to get back. . . . But now they weren't far off. They were on the top of the last hill; it was a gentle slope all the way now and not more than half a mile.

Pat trailed the whip over the mare's back and he coaxed her: 'Goop now. Goop now.'

It wanted a few minutes to sunset. Everything stood motionless bathed in bright, metallic light and from the paddocks on either side there streamed the milky scent of ripe grass. The iron gates were open. They dashed through and up the drive and round the island, stopping at the exact middle of the veranda.

'Did she satisfy yer, sir?' said Pat, getting off the box and grinning at his master.

'Very well indeed, Pat,' said Stanley.

Linda came out of the glass door; her voice rang in the shadowy quiet. 'Hullo! Are you home again?'

At the sound of her his heart beat so hard that he could hardly stop himself dashing up the steps and catching her in his arms.

'Yes, I'm home again. Is everything all right?'

Pat began to lead the buggy round to the side gate that opened into the courtyard.

'Here, half a moment,' said Burnell. 'Hand me those two parcels.' And he said to Linda, 'I've brought you back a bottle of oysters and a pineapple,' as though he had brought her back all the harvest of the earth.

They went into the hall; Linda carried the oysters in one hand and the pineapple in the other. Burnell shut the glass door, threw his hat down, put his arms round her and strained her to him, kissing the top of her head, her ears, her lips, her eyes.

'Oh, dear! Oh, dear!' said she. 'Wait a moment. Let me put down these silly things,' and she put the bottle of oysters and the pine on a little carved chair. 'What have you got in your button-hole—cherries?' She took them out and hung them over his ear.

'Don't do that, darling. They are for you.'

So she took them off his ear again. 'You don't mind if I save them. They'd spoil my appetite for dinner. Come and see your children. They are having tea.'

The lamp was lighted on the nursery table. Mrs. Fairfield was cutting and spreading bread and butter. The three little girls sat up to table wearing large bibs embroidered with their names. They wiped their mouths as their father came in ready to be kissed. The windows were open; a jar of wild flowers stood on the mantelpiece, and the lamp made a big soft bubble of light on the ceiling.

'You seem pretty snug, mother,' said Burnell, blinking at the light. Isabel and Lottie sat one on either side of the table, Kezia at the bottom—the place at the top was empty.

'That's where my boy ought to sit,' thought Stanley. He

tightened his arm round Linda's shoulder. By God, he was a perfect fool to feel as happy as this!

'We are, Stanley. We are very snug,' said Mrs. Fairfield, cutting Kezia's bread into fingers.

'Like it better than town—eh, children?' asked Burnell.

'Oh, yes,' said the three little girls, and Isabel added as an after-thought: 'Thank you very much indeed, father dear.'

'Come upstairs,' said Linda. 'I'll bring your slippers.'

But the stairs were too narrow for them to go up arm in arm. It was quite dark in the room. He heard her ring tapping on the marble mantelpiece as she felt for the matches.

'I've got some, darling. I'll light the candles.'

But instead he came up behind her and again he put his arms round her and pressed her head into his shoulder.

'I'm so confoundedly happy,' he said.

'Are you?' She turned and put her hands on his breast and looked up at him.

'I don't know what has come over me,' he protested.

It was quite dark outside now and heavy dew was falling. When Linda shut the window the cold dew touched her finger tips. Far away a dog barked. 'I believe there is going to be a moon,' she said.

At the words, and with the cold wet dew on her fingers, she felt as though the moon had risen—that she was being strangely discovered in a flood of cold light. She shivered; she came away from the window and sat down upon the box ottoman beside Stanley.

·   ·   ·   ·   ·   ·

In the dining-room, by the flicker of a wood fire, Beryl sat on a hassock playing the guitar. She had bathed and changed all her clothes. Now she wore a white muslin dress with black spots on it and in her hair she had pinned a black silk rose.

> Nature has gone to her rest, love,
>   See, we are alone.
> Give me your hand to press, love,
>   Lightly within my own.

She played and sang half to herself, for she was watching herself playing and singing. The firelight gleamed on her shoes, on the ruddy belly of the guitar, and on her white fingers. . . .

'If I were outside the window and looked in and saw myself I really would be rather struck,' thought she. Still more softly she played the accompaniment—not singing now but listening.

'. . . The first time that I ever saw you, little girl—oh, you had no idea that you were not alone—you were sitting with your little feet upon a hassock, playing the guitar. God, I can never forget. . . .' Beryl flung up her head and began to sing again:

'Even the moon is aweary . . .'

But there came a loud bang at the door. The servant girl's crimson face popped through.

'Please, Miss Beryl, I've got to come and lay.'

'Certainly, Alice,' said Beryl, in a voice of ice. She put the guitar in a corner. Alice lunged in with a heavy black iron tray.

'Well, I have had a job with that oving', said she. 'I can't get nothing to brown.'

'Really!' said Beryl.

But no, she could not stand that fool of a girl. She ran into the dark drawing-room and began walking up and down. . . . Oh, she was restless, restless. There was a mirror over the mantel. She leaned her arms along and looked at her pale shadow in it. How beautiful she looked, but there was nobody to see, nobody.

'Why must you suffer so?' said the face in the mirror. 'You were not made for suffering. . . . Smile!'

Beryl smiled, and really her smile *was* so adorable that she smiled again—but this time because she could not help it.

VIII

'Good morning, Mrs. Jones.'

'Oh, good morning, Mrs. Smith. I'm so glad to see you. Have you brought your children?'

'Yes, I've brought both my twins. I have had another baby since I saw you last, but she came so suddenly that I haven't had time to make her any clothes yet. So I left her. . . . How is your husband?'

'Oh, he is very well, thank you. At least he had an awful cold but Queen Victoria—she's my godmother, you know—sent him a case of pine-apples and that cured it im—mediately. Is that your new servant?'

'Yes, her name's Gwen. I've only had her two days. Oh, Gwen, this is my friend, Mrs. Smith.'

'Good morning, Mrs. Smith. Dinner won't be ready for about ten minutes.'

'I don't think you ought to introduce me to the servant. I think I ought to just begin talking to her.'

'Well, she's more of a lady-help than a servant and you do introduce lady-helps, I know, because Mrs. Samuel Josephs had one.'

'Oh, well, it doesn't matter,' said the servant carelessly, beating up a chocolate custard with half a broken clothes peg. The dinner was baking beautifully on a concrete step. She began to lay the cloth on a pink garden seat. In front of each person she put two geranium leaf plates, a pine needle fork and a twig knife. There were three daisy heads on a laurel leaf for poached eggs, some slices of fuchsia petal cold beef, some lovely little rissoles made of earth and water and dandelion seeds, and the chocolate custard which she had decided to serve in the pawa shell she had cooked it in.

'You needn't trouble about my children,' said Mrs. Smith graciously. 'If you'll just take this bottle and fill it at the tap—I mean at the dairy.'

'Oh, all right,' said Gwen, and she whispered to Mrs. Jones: 'Shall I go and ask Alice for a little bit of real milk?'

But someone called from the front of the house and the luncheon party melted away, leaving the charming table, leaving the rissoles and the poached eggs to the ants and to an old snail who pushed his quivering horns over the edge of the garden seat and began to nibble a geranium plate.

'Come round to the front, children. Pip and Rags have come.'

The Trout boys were the cousins Kezia had mentioned to the storeman. They lived about a mile away in a house called Monkey Tree Cottage. Pip was tall for his age, with lank black hair and a white face, but Rags was very small and so thin that when he was undressed his shoulder blades stuck out like two little wings. They had a mongrel dog with pale blue eyes and a

56

long tail turned up at the end who followed them everywhere; he was called Snooker. They spent half their time combing and brushing Snooker and dosing him with various awful mixtures concocted by Pip, and kept secretly by him in a broken jug covered with an old kettle lid. Even faithful little Rags was not allowed to know the full secret of these mixtures. . . . Take some carbolic tooth powder and a pinch of sulphur powdered up fine, and perhaps a bit of starch to stiffen up Snooker's coat. . . . But that was not all; Rags privately thought that the rest was gun-powder. . . . And he never was allowed to help with the mixing because of the danger. . . . 'Why, if a spot of this flew in your eye, you would be blinded for life,' Pip would say, stirring the mixture with an iron spoon. 'And there's always the chance —just the chance, mind you—of it exploding if you whack it hard enough . . . . Two spoons of this in a kerosene tin will be enough to kill thousands of fleas.' But Snooker spent all his spare time biting and snuffling, and he stank abominably.

'It's because he is such a grand fighting dog,' Pip would say. 'All fighting dogs smell.'

The Trout boys had often spent the day with the Burnells in town, but now that they lived in this fine house and boncer garden they were inclined to be very friendly. Besides, both of them liked playing with girls—Pip, because he could fox them so, and because Lottie was so easily frightened, and Rags for a shameful reason. He adored dolls. How he would look at a doll as it lay asleep, speaking in a whisper and smiling timidly, and what a treat it was to him to be allowed to hold one. . . .

'Curve your arms round her. Don't keep them stiff like that. You'll drop her,' Isabel would say sternly.

Now they were standing on the veranda and holding back Snooker, who wanted to go into the house but wasn't allowed to because Aunt Linda hated decent dogs.

'We came over in the bus with mum,' they said, 'and we're going to spend the afternoon with you. We brought over a batch of our gingerbread for Aunt Linda. Our Minnie made it. It's all over nuts.'

'I skinned the almonds,' said Pip. 'I just stuck my hand into a saucepan of boiling water and grabbed them out and gave them a kind of pinch and the nuts flew out of the skins, some of them as high as the ceiling. Didn't they, Rags?'

Rags nodded. 'When they make cakes at our place,' said

57

Pip, 'we always stay in the kitchen, Rags and me, and I get the bowl and he gets the spoon and the egg-beater. Sponge cake's best. It's all frothy stuff, then.'

He ran down the veranda steps to the lawn, planted his hands on the grass, bent forward, and just did not stand on his head.

'That lawn's all bumpy,' he said. 'You have to have a flat place for standing on your head. I can walk round the monkey tree on my head at our place. Can't I, Rags?'

'Nearly,' said Rags faintly.

'Stand on your head on the veranda. That's quite flat,' said Kezia.

'No, smarty,' said Pip. 'You have to do it on something soft. Because if you give a jerk and fall over, something in your neck goes click, and it breaks off. Dad told me.'

'Oh, do let's play something,' said Kezia.

'Very well,' said Isabel quickly. 'we'll play hospitals. I will be the nurse and Pip can be the doctor and you and Lottie and Rags can be the sick people.'

Lottie didn't want to play that, because last time Pip had squeezed something down her throat and it hurt awfully.

'Pooh,' scoffed Pip. 'It was only the juice out of a bit of mandarin peel.'

'Well, let's play ladies,' said Isabel. 'Pip can be the father and you can be all our dear little children.'

'I hate playing ladies,' said Kezia. 'You always make us go to church hand in hand and come home and go to bed.'

Suddenly Pip took a filthy handkerchief out of his pocket. 'Snooker! Here, sir,' he called. But Snooker, as usual, tried to sneak away, his tail between his legs. Pip leapt on top of him, and pressed him between his knees.

'Keep his head firm, Rags,' he said, and he tied the handkerchief round Snooker's head with a funny knot sticking up at the top.

'Whatever is that for?' asked Lottie.

'It's to train his ears to grow more close to his head—see?' said Pip. 'All fighting dogs have ears that lie back. But Snooker's ears are a bit too soft.'

'I know,' said Kezia. 'They are always turning inside out. I hate that.'

Snooker lay down, made one feeble effort with his paw to get the handkerchief off, but finding he could not, trailed after the children, shivering with misery.

IX

Pat came swinging along; in his hand he held a little tomahawk that winked in the sun.

'Come with me,' he said to the children, 'and I'll show
you how the kings of Ireland chop the head off a duck.'

They drew back—they didn't believe him, and besides, the
Trout boys had never seen Pat before.

'Come on now,' he coaxed, smiling and holding out his
hand to Kezia.

'Is it a real duck's head? One from the paddock?'

'It is,' said Pat. She put her hand in his hard dry one, and
he stuck the tomahawk in his belt and held out the other to
Rags. He loved little children.

'I'd better keep hold of Snooker's head if there's going to be
any blood about,' said Pip, 'because the sight of blood makes
him awfully wild.' He ran ahead dragging Snooker by the
handkerchief.

'Do you think we ought to go?' whispered Isabel. 'We
haven't asked or anything. Have we?'

At the bottom of the orchard a gate was set in the paling
fence. On the other side a steep bank led down to a bridge
that spanned the creek, and once up the bank on the other side
you were on the fringe of the paddocks. A little old stable in
the first paddock had been turned into a fowl-house. The fowls
had strayed far away across the paddock down to a dumping
ground in a hollow, but the ducks kept close to that part of the
creek that flowed under the bridge.

Tall bushes overhung the stream with red leaves and yellow
flowers and clusters of blackberries. At some places the stream
was wide and shallow, but at others it tumbled into deep little
pools with foam at the edges and quivering bubbles. It was in
these pools that the big white ducks had made themselves at
home, swimming and guzzling along the weedy banks.

Up and down they swam, preening their dazzling breasts, and
other ducks with the same dazzling breasts and yellow bills
swam upside down with them.

'There is the little Irish navy,' said Pat, 'and look at the
old admiral there with the green neck and the grand little flag-
staff on his tail.'

He pulled a handful of grain from his pocket and began to

walk towards the fowl-house, lazy, his straw hat with the broken crown pulled over his eyes.

'Lid. Lid—lid—lid—lid—' he called.

'Qua. Qua—qua—qua—qua—' answered the ducks, making for land, and flapping and scrambling up the bank they streamed after him in a long waddling line. He coaxed them, pretending to throw the grain, shaking it in his hands and calling to them until they swept round him in a white ring.

From far away the fowls heard the clamour and they too came running across the paddock, their heads thrust forward, their wings spread, turning in their feet in the silly way fowls run and scolding as they came.

Then Pat scattered the grain and the greedy ducks began to gobble. Quickly he stooped, seized two, one under each arm, and strode across to the children. Their darting heads and round eyes frightened the children—all except Pip.

'Come on, sillies,' he cried, 'they can't bite. They haven't any teeth. They've only got those two little holes in their beaks for breathing through.'

'Will you hold one while I finish with the other?' asked Pat. Pip let go of Snooker. 'Won't I? Won't I? Give us one. I don't mind how much he kicks.'

He nearly sobbed with delight when Pat gave the white lump into his arms.

There was an old stump beside the door of the fowl-house. Pat grabbed the duck by the legs, laid it flat across the stump, and almost at the same moment down came the little tomahawk and the duck's head flew off the stump. Up the blood spurted over the white feathers and over his hand.

When the children saw the blood they were frightened no longer. They crowded round him and began to scream. Even Isabel leaped about crying: 'The blood! The blood!' Pip forgot all about his duck. He simply threw it away from him and shouted, 'I saw it. I saw it,' and jumped round the wood block.

Rags, with cheeks as white as paper, ran up to the little head, put out a finger as if he wanted to touch it, shrank back again and then again put out a finger. He was shivering all over.

Even Lottie, frightened little Lottie, began to laugh and pointed at the duck and shrieked: 'Look, Kezia, look.'

'Watch it!' shouted Pat. He put down the body and it began to waddle—with only a long spurt of blood where the head had been; it began to pad away without a sound towards the steep bank that led to the stream. . . . That was the crowning wonder.

'Do you see that? Do you see that?' yelled Pip. He ran among the little girls tugging at their pinafores.

'It's like a little engine. It's like a funny little railway engine,' squealed Isabel.

But Kezia suddenly rushed at Pat and flung her arms round his legs and butted her head as hard as she could against his knees.

'Put head back! Put head back!' she screamed.

When he stooped to move her she would not let go or take her head away. She held on as hard as she could and sobbed: 'Head back! Head back!' until it sounded like a loud strange hiccup.

'It's stopped. It's tumbled over. It's dead,' said Pip.

Pat dragged Kezia up into his arms. Her sun-bonnet had fallen back, but she would not let him look at her face. No, she pressed her face into a bone in his shoulder and clasped her arms round his neck.

The children stopped screaming as suddenly as they had begun. They stood round the dead duck. Rags was not frightened of the head any more. He knelt down and stroked it now.

'I don't think the head is quite dead yet,' he said. 'Do you think it would keep alive if I gave it something to drink?'

But Pip got very cross: 'Bah! You baby.' He whistled to Snooker and went off.

When Isabel went up to Lottie, Lottie snatched away.

'What are you always touching me for, Isabel?'

'There now,' said Pat to Kezia. 'There's the grand little girl.'

She put up her hands and touched his ears. She felt something. Slowly she raised her quivering face and looked. Pat wore little round gold ear-rings. She never knew that men wore ear-rings. She was very much surprised.

'Do they come on and off?' she asked huskily.

X

Up in the house, in the warm tidy kitchen, Alice, the servant girl, was getting the afternoon tea. She was 'dressed'. She had on a black stuff dress that smelt under the arms, a white apron like a large sheet of paper, and a lace bow pinned on to her hair with two jetty pins. Also her comfortable carpet slippers were changed for a pair of black leather ones that pinched her corn on her little toe something dreadful. . . .

It was warm in the kitchen. A blow-fly buzzed, a fan of whity steam came out of the kettle, and the lid kept up a rattling jig as the water bubbled. The clock ticked in the warm air, slow and deliberate, like the click of an old woman's knitting needle, and sometimes—for no reason at all, for there wasn't any breeze—the blind swung out and back, tapping the window.

Alice was making water-cress sandwiches. She had a lump of butter on the table, a barracouta loaf, and the cresses tumbled in a white cloth.

But propped against the butter dish there was a dirty, greasy little book, half unstitched, with curled edges, and while she mashed the butter she read:

'To dream of black-beetles drawing a hearse is bad. Signifies death of one you hold near or dear, either father, husband, brother, son, or intended. If beetles crawl backwards as you watch them it means death from fire or from great height such as flight of stairs, scaffolding, etc.

'Spiders. To dream of spiders creeping over you is good. Signifies large sum of money in near future. Should party be in family way an easy confinement may be expected. But care should be taken in sixth month to avoid eating of probable present of shellfish. . . .'

'How many thousand birds I see.'

Oh, life. There was Miss Beryl. Alice dropped the knife and slipped the *Dream Book* under the butter dish. But she hadn't time to hide it quite, for Beryl ran into the kitchen and up to the table, and the first thing her eye lighted on were those greasy edges. Alice saw Miss Beryl's meaning little smile and the way she raised her eyebrows and screwed up her eyes as though she were not quite sure what that could be. She decided to answer if Miss Beryl should ask her: 'Nothing as belongs to you, Miss.' But she knew Miss Beryl would not ask her.

Alice was a mild creature in reality, but she had the most marvellous retorts ready for questions that she knew would never be put to her. The composing of them and the turning of them over and over in her mind comforted her just as much as if they'd been expressed. Really, they kept her alive in places where she'd been that chivvied she'd been afraid to go to bed at night with a box of matches on the chair in case she bit the tops off in her sleep, as you might say.

'Oh, Alice,' said Miss Beryl. 'There's one extra to tea, so heat a plate of yesterday's scones, please. And put on the Victoria sandwich as well as the coffee cake. And don't forget to put little doyleys under the plates—will you? You did yesterday, you know, and the tea looked so ugly and common. And, Alice, don't put that dreadful old pink and green cosy on the afternoon teapot again. That is only for the mornings. Really, I think it ought to be kept for the kitchen—it's so shabby and quite smelly. Put on the Japanese one. You quite understand, don't you?'

Miss Beryl had finished.

'That sing aloud from every tree . . .'

she sang as she left the kitchen, very pleased with her firm handling of Alice.

Oh, Alice was wild. She wasn't one to mind being told, but there was something in the way Miss Beryl had of speaking to her that she couldn't stand. Oh, that she couldn't. It made her curl up inside, as you might say, and she fair trembled. But what Alice really hated Miss Beryl for was that she made her feel low. She talked to Alice in a special voice as though she wasn't quite all there; and she never lost her temper with her—never. Even when Alice dropped anything or forgot anything important Miss Beryl seemed to have expected it to happen.

'If you please, Mrs. Burnell,' said an imaginary Alice, as she buttered the scones, 'I'd rather not take my orders from Miss Beryl. I may be only a common servant girl as doesn't know how to play the guitar, but . . .'

This last thrust pleased her so much that she quite recovered her temper.

'The only thing to do,' she heard, as she opened the dining-room door, 'is to cut the sleeves out entirely and just have a broad band of black velvet over the shoulders instead. . . .'

XI

The white duck did not look as if it had ever had a head when Alice placed it in front of Stanley Burnell that night. It lay, in beautifully basted resignation, on a blue dish—its legs tied together with a piece of string and a wreath of little balls of stuffing round it.

It was hard to say which of the two, Alice or the duck, looked the better basted; they were both such a rich colour and they both had the same air of gloss and strain. But Alice was fiery red and the duck a Spanish mahogany.

Burnell ran his eye along the edge of the carving knife. He prided himself very much upon his carving, upon making a first-class job of it. He hated seeing a woman carve; they were always too slow and they never seemed to care what the meat looked like afterwards. Now he did; he took a real pride in cutting delicate shaves of cold beef, little wads of mutton, just the right thickness, and in dividing a chicken or a duck with nice precision. . . .

'Is this the first of the home products?' he asked, knowing perfectly well that it was.

'Yes, the butcher did not come. We have found out that he only calls twice a week.'

But there was no need to apologise. It was a superb bird. It wasn't meat at all, but a kind of very superior jelly. 'My father would say,' said Burnell, 'this must have been one of those birds whose mother played to it in infancy upon the German flute. And the sweet strains of the dulcet instrument acted with such effect upon the infant mind . . . Have some more, Beryl? You and I are the only ones in this house with a real feeling for food. I'm perfectly willing to state, in a court of law, if necessary, that I love good food.'

Tea was served in the drawing-room, and Beryl, who for some reason had been very charming to Stanley ever since he came home, suggested a game of crib. They sat at a little table near one of the open windows. Mrs. Fairfield disappeared, and Linda lay in a rocking-chair, her arms above her head, rocking to and fro.

'You don't want the light—do you, Linda?' said Beryl. She moved the tall lamp so that she sat under its soft light.

How remote they looked, those two, from where Linda sat and rocked. The green table, the polished cards, Stanley's big hands and Beryl's tiny ones, all seemed to be part of one mysterious movement. Stanley himself, big and solid, in his dark suit, took his ease, and Beryl tossed her bright head and pouted. Round her throat she wore an unfamiliar velvet ribbon. It changed her, somehow—altered the shape of her face—but it was charming, Linda decided. The room smelled of lilies; there were two big jars of arums in the fire-place.

'Fifteen two—fifteen four—and a pair is six and a run of three is nine,' said Stanley, so deliberately, he might have been counting sheep.

'I've nothing but two pairs,' said Beryl, exaggerating her woe because she knew how he loved winning.

The cribbage pegs were like two little people going up the road together, turning round the sharp corner, and coming down the road again. They were pursuing each other. They did not so much want to get ahead as to keep near enough to talk—to keep near, perhaps that was all.

But no, there was always one who was impatient and hopped away as the other came up, and would not listen. Perhaps the white peg was frightened of the red one, or perhaps he was cruel and would not give the red one a chance to speak. . . .

In the front of her dress Beryl wore a bunch of pansies, and once when the little pegs were side by side, she bent over and the pansies dropped out and covered them.

'What a shame,' said she, picking up the pansies. 'Just as they had a chance to fly into each other's arms.'

'Farewell, my girl,' laughed Stanley, and away the red peg hopped.

The drawing-room was long and narrow with glass doors that gave on to the veranda. It had a cream paper with a pattern of gilt roses, and the furniture, which had belonged to old Mrs. Fairfield, was dark and plain. A little piano stood against the wall with yellow pleated silk let into the carved front. Above it hung an oil painting by Beryl of a large cluster of surprised-looking clematis. Each flower was the size of a small saucer, with a centre like an astonished eye fringed in black. But the room was not finished yet. Stanley had set his heart on a chesterfield and two decent chairs. Linda liked it best as it was. . . .

Two big moths flew in through the window and round and round the circle of lamplight.

'Fly away before it is too late. Fly out again.'

Round and round they flew; they seemed to bring the silence and the moonlight in with them on their silent wings. . . .

'I've two kings,' said Stanley. 'Any good?'

'Quite good,' said Beryl.

Linda stopped rocking and got up. Stanley looked across. 'Anything the matter, darling?'

'No, nothing. I'm going to find mother.'

She went out of the room and standing at the foot of the stairs she called, but her mother's voice answered her from the veranda.

The moon that Lottie and Kezia had seen from the store-man's wagon was full, and the house, the garden, the old woman and Linda—all were bathed in dazzling light.

'I have been looking at the aloe,' said Mrs. Fairfield. 'I believe it is going to flower this year. Look at the top there. Are those buds, or is it only an effect of light?'

As they stood on the steps, the high grassy bank on which the aloe rested rose up like a wave, and the aloe seemed to ride upon it like a ship with the oars lifted. Bright moonlight hung upon the lifted oars like water, and on the green wave glittered the dew.

'Do you feel it, too,' said Linda, and she spoke to her mother with the special voice that women use at night to each other as though they spoke in their sleep or from some hollow cave— 'Don't you feel that it is coming towards us?'

She dreamed that she was caught up out of the cold water into the ship with the lifted oars and the budding mast. Now the oars fell striking quickly, quickly. They rowed far away over the top of the garden trees, the paddocks and the dark bush beyond. Ah, she heard herself cry: 'Faster! Faster!' to those who were rowing.

How much more real this dream was than that they should go back to the house where the sleeping children lay and where Stanley and Beryl played cribbage.

'I believe those are buds,' said she. 'Let us go down into the garden, mother. I like that aloe. I like it more than anything here. And I am sure I shall remember it long after I've forgotten all the other things.'

She put her hand on her mother's arm and they walked down the steps, round the island and on to the main drive that led to the front gates.

Looking at it from below she could see the long sharp thorns that edged the aloe leaves, and at the sight of them her heart grew hard. . . . She particularly liked the long sharp thorns. . . . Nobody would dare to come near the ship or to follow after.

'Not even my Newfoundland dog,' thought she, 'that I'm so fond of in the daytime.'

For she really was fond of him; she loved and admired and respected him tremendously. Oh, better than anyone else in the world. She knew him through and through. He was the soul of truth and decency, and for all his practical experience he was awfully simple, easily pleased and easily hurt. . . .

If only he wouldn't jump at her so, and bark so loudly, and watch her with such eager, loving eyes. He was too strong for her; she had always hated things that rushed at her, from a child. There were times when he was frightening—really frightening. When she just had not screamed at the top of her voice: 'You are killing me.' And at those times she had longed to say the most coarse, hateful things. . . .

'You know I'm very delicate. You know as well as I do that my heart is affected, and the doctor has told you I may die any moment. I have had three great lumps of children already. . . .'

Yes, yes, it was true. Linda snatched her hand from mother's arm. For all her love and respect and admiration she hated him. And how tender he always was after times like those, how submissive, how thoughtful. He would do anything for her; he longed to serve her. . . . Linda heard herself saying in a weak voice:

'Stanley, would you light a candle?'

And she heard his joyful voice answer: 'Of course I will, my darling.' And he leapt out of bed as though he were going to leap at the moon for her.

It had never been so plain to her as it was at this moment. There were all her feelings for him, sharp and defined, one as

67

true as the other. And there was this other, this hatred, just as real as the rest. She could have done her feelings up in little packets and given them to Stanley. She longed to hand him that last one, for a surprise. She could see his eyes as he opened that. . . .

She hugged her folded arms and began to laugh silently. How absurd life was—it was laughable, simply laughable. And why this mania of hers to keep alive at all? For it really was a mania, she thought, mocking and laughing.

'What am I guarding myself for so preciously? I shall go on having children and Stanley will go on making money and the children and the gardens will grow bigger and bigger, with whole fleets of aloes in them for me to choose from.'

She had been walking with her head bent, looking at nothing. Now she looked up and about her. They were standing by the red and white camellia trees. Beautiful were the rich dark leaves spangled with light and the round flowers that perch among them like red and white birds. Linda pulled a piece of verbena and crumpled it, and held her hands to her mother.

'Delicious,' said the old woman. 'Are you cold, child? Are you trembling? Yes, your hands are cold. We had better go back to the house.'

'What have you been thinking about?' said Linda. 'Tell me.'

'I haven't really been thinking of anything. I wondered as we passed the orchard what the fruit trees were like and whether we should be able make much jam this autumn. There are splendid healthy currant bushes in the vegetable garden. I noticed them to-day. I should like to see those pantry shelves thoroughly well stocked with our own jam. . . .'

XII

'My darling Nan,

Don't think me a piggy wig because I haven't written before. I haven't had a moment, dear, and even now I feel so exhausted that I can hardly hold a pen.

Well, the dreadful deed is done. We have actually left the giddy whirl of town, and I can't see how we shall ever go back again, for my brother-in-law has bought this house "lock, stock and barrel," to use his own words.

In a way, of course, it is an awful relief, for he has been threatening to take a place in the country ever since I've lived with them—and I must say the house and garden are awfully nice—a million times better than that awful cubby-hole in town.

But buried, my dear. Buried isn't the word.

We have got neighbours, but they are only farmers—big louts of boys who seem to be milking all day, and two dreadful females with rabbit teeth who brought us some scones when we were moving and said they would be pleased to help. But my sister who lives a mile away doesn't know a soul here, so I am sure we never shall. It's pretty certain nobody will ever come out from town to see us, because though there is a bus it's an awful old rattling thing with black leather sides that any decent person would rather die than ride in for six miles.

Such is life. It's a sad ending for poor little B. I'll get to be a most awful frump in a year or two and come and see you in a mackintosh and a sailor hat tied on with a white china silk motor veil. So pretty.

Stanley says that now we are settled—for after the most awful week of my life we really are settled—he is going to bring out a couple of men from the club on Saturday afternoons for tennis. In fact, two are promised as a great treat to-day. But, my dear, if you could see Stanley's men from the club . . . rather fattish, the type who look frightfully indecent without waistcoats—always with toes that turn in rather—so conspicuous when you are walking about a court in white shoes. And they are pulling up their trousers every minute—don't you know—and whacking at imaginary things with their rackets.

I used to play with them at the club last summer, and I am sure you will know the type when I tell you that after I'd been there about three times they all called me Miss Beryl. It's a weary world. Of course mother simply loves the place, but then I suppose when I am mother's age I shall be content to sit in the sun and shell peas into a basin. But I'm not—not—not.

What Linda thinks about the whole affair, per usual, I haven't the slightest idea. Mysterious as ever. . . .

My dear, you know that white satin dress of mine. I have taken the sleeves out entirely, put bands of black velvet across the shoulders and two big red poppies off my dear sister's *chapeau*. It is a great success, though when I shall wear it I do not know.'

Beryl sat writing this letter at a little table in her room. In a way, of course, it was all perfectly true, but in another way it was all the greatest rubbish and she didn't believe a word of it. No, that wasn't true. She felt all those things, but she didn't really feel them like that.

It was her other self who had written that letter. It not only bored, it rather disgusted her real self.

'Flippant and silly,' said her real self. Yet she knew that she'd send it and she'd always write that kind of twaddle to Nan Pym. In fact, it was a very mild example of the kind of letter she generally wrote.

Beryl leaned her elbows on the table and read it through again. The voice of the lettter seemed to come up to her from the page. It was faint already, like a voice heard over the telephone, high, gushing, with something bitter in the sound. Oh, she detested it to-day.

'You've always got so much animation,' said Nan Pym. 'That's why men are so keen on you.' And she had added, rather mournfully, for men were not at all keen on Nan, who was a solid kind of girl, with fat hips and a high colour—'I can't understand how you can keep it up. But it is your nature, I suppose.'

What rot. What nonsense. It wasn't her nature at all. Good heavens, if she had ever been her real self with Nan Pym, Nannie would have jumped out of the window with surprise. . . . My dear, you know that white satin of mine. . . . Beryl slammed the letter-case to.

She jumped up and half unconsciously, half consciously she drifted over to the looking-glass.

There stood a slim girl in white—a white serge skirt, a white silk blouse, and a leather belt drawn in very tightly at her tiny waist.

Her face was heart-shaped, wide at the brows and with a pointed chin—but not too pointed. Her eyes, her eyes were perhaps her best feature; they were such a strange uncommon colour—greeny blue with little gold points in them.

70

She had fine black eyebrows and long lashes—so long, that
when they lay on her cheeks you positively caught the light in
them, someone or other had told her.

Her mouth was rather large. Too large? No, not really.
Her underlip protruded a little; she had a way of sucking
it in that somebody else had told her was awfully fasci-
nating.

Her nose was her least satisfactory feature. Not that it was
really ugly. But it was not half as fine as Linda's. Linda really
had a perfect little nose. Hers spread rather—not badly. And
in all probability she exaggerated the spreadiness of it just
because it was her nose, and she was so awfully critical of
herself. She pinched it with a thumb and first finger and made
a little face. . . .

Lovely, lovely hair. And such a mass of it. It had the colour
of fresh fallen leaves, brown and red with a glint of yellow.
When she did it in a long plait she felt it on her backbone like a
long snake. She loved to feel the weight of it dragging her head
back, and she loved to feel it loose, covering her bare arms.
'Yes, my dear, there is no doubt about it, you really are a
lovely little thing.'

At the words her bosom lifted; she took a long breath of
delight, half closing her eyes.

But even as she looked the smile faded from her lips and
eyes. Oh, God, there she was, back again, playing the same old
game. False—false as ever. False as when she'd written to Nan
Pym. False even when she was alone with herself, now.

What had that creature in the glass to do with her, and why
was she staring? She dropped down to one side of her bed
and buried her face in her arms.

'Oh,' she cried, 'I am so miserable—so frightfully miserable.
I know that I'm silly and spiteful and vain; I'm always acting a
part. I'm never my real self for a moment.' And plainly,
plainly, she saw her false self running up and down the stairs,
laughing a special trilling laugh if they had visitors, standing
under the lamp if a man came to dinner, so that he should see
the light on her hair, pouting and pretending to be a little girl
when she was asked to play the guitar. Why? She even kept it
up for Stanley's benefit. Only last night when he was reading
the paper her false self had stood beside him and leaned
against his shoulder on purpose. Hadn't she put her hand over

71

his, pointing out something so that he should see how white her hand was beside his brown one.

How despicable! Despicable! Her heart was cold with rage. 'It's marvellous how you keep it up,' said she to the false self. But then it was only because she was so miserable—so miserable. If she had been happy and leading her own life, her false life would cease to be. She saw the real Beryl—a shadow . . . a shadow. Faint and unsubstantial she shone. What was there of her except the radiance? And for what tiny moments she was really she. Beryl could almost remember every one of them. At those times she had felt: 'Life is rich and mysterious and good, and I am rich and mysterious and good, too.' Shall I ever be that Beryl for ever? Shall I? How can I? And was there ever a time when I did not have a false self? . . . But just as she had got that far she heard the sound of little steps running along the passage; the door handle rattled. Kezia came in.

'Aunt Beryl, mother says will you please come down? Father is home with a man and lunch is ready.'

Botheration! How she had crumpled her skirt, kneeling in that idiotic way.

'Very well, Kezia.' She went over to the dressing table and powdered her nose.

Kezia crossed too, and unscrewed a little pot of cream and sniffed it. Under her arm she carried a very dirty calico cat.

When Aunt Beryl ran out of the room she sat the cat up on the dressing-table and stuck the top of the cream jar over its ear.

'Now look at yourself,' said she sternly.

The calico cat was so overcome by the sight that it toppled over backwards and bumped and bumped on to the floor. And the top of the cream jar flew through the air and rolled like a penny in a round on the linoleum—and did not break.

But for Kezia it had broken the moment it flew through the air, and she picked it up, hot all over, and put it back on the dressing-table.

Then she tiptoed away, far too quickly and airily. . . .

(1915–1917)

The Doll's House

recollection of rural surroundings

When dear old Mrs. Hay went back to town after staying with
the Burnells she sent the children a doll's house. It was so big
that the carter and Pat carried it into the courtyard, and there
it stayed, propped up on two wooden boxes beside the feed-
room door. No harm could come to it; it was summer. And
perhaps the smell of paint would have gone off by the time it
had to be taken in. For, really, the smell of paint coming from
that doll's house ('Sweet of old Mrs. Hay, of course; most sweet
and generous!')—but the smell of paint was quite enough to
make anyone seriously ill, in Aunt Beryl's opinion. Even before
the sacking was taken off. And when it was. . .

There stood the doll's house, a dark, oily, spinach green,
picked out with bright yellow. Its two solid little chimneys,
glued on to the roof, were painted red and white, and the door,
gleaming with yellow varnish, was like a little slab of toffee.
Four windows, real windows, were divided into panes by a
broad streak of green. There was actually a tiny porch, too,
painted yellow, with big lumps of congealed paint hanging
along the edge.

But perfect, perfect little house! Who could possibly mind
the smell? It was part of the joy, part of the newness.

'Open it quickly, someone!'

The hook at the side was stuck fast. Pat prised it open with
his penknife, and the whole house front swung back, and—
there you were, gazing at one and the same moment into the
drawing-room and dining-room, the kitchen and two bedrooms.
That is the way for a house to open! Why don't all houses open
like that? How much more exciting than peering through the
slit of a door into a mean little hall with a hat-stand and two

73

umbrellas! That is—isn't it?—what you long to know about a house when you put your hand on the knocker. Perhaps it is the way God opens houses at the dead of night when He is taking a quiet turn with an angel. . . .

'Oh-oh!' The Burnell children sounded as though they were in despair. It was too marvellous; it was too much for them. They had never seen anything like it in their lives. All the rooms were papered. There were pictures on the walls, painted on the paper, with gold frames complete. Red carpet covered all the floors except the kitchen; red plush chairs in the drawing-room, green in the dining-room; tables, beds with real bedclothes, a cradle, a stove, a dresser with tiny plates and one big jug. But what Kezia liked more than anything, what she liked frightfully, was the lamp. It stood in the middle of the dining-room table, an exquisite little amber lamp with a white globe. It was even filled all ready for lighting, though, of course, you couldn't light it. But there was something inside that looked like oil and moved when you shook it.

The father and mother dolls, who sprawled very stiff as though they had fainted in the drawing-room, and their two little children asleep upstairs were really too big for the doll's house. They didn't look as though they belonged. But the lamp was perfect. It seemed to smile at Kezia, to say, 'I live here.' The lamp was real.

The Burnell children could hardly walk to school fast enough the next morning. They burned to tell everybody, to describe, to—well—to boast about their doll's house before the school-bell rang.

'I'm to tell,' said Isabel, 'because I'm the eldest. And you two can join in after. But I'm to tell first.'

There was nothing to answer. Isabel was bossy, but she was always right, and Lottie and Kezia knew too well the powers that went with being eldest. They brushed through the thick buttercups at the road edge and said nothing.

'And I'm to choose who's to come and see it first. Mother said I might.'

For it had been arranged that while the doll's house stood in the courtyard they might ask the girls at school, two at a time, to come and look. Not to stay to tea, of course, or to come traipsing through the house. But just to stand quietly in the courtyard while Isabel pointed out the beauties, and Lottie and Kezia looked pleased. . . .

But hurry as they might, by the time they had reached the tarred palings of the boys' playground the bell had begun to jangle. They only just had time to whip off their hats and fall into line before the roll was called. Never mind. Isabel tried to make up for it by looking very important and mysterious and by whispering behind her hand to the girls near her, 'Got something to tell you at playtime.'

Playtime came and Isabel was surrounded. The girls of her class nearly fought to put their arms round her, to walk away with her, to beam flatteringly, to be her special friend. She held quite a court under the huge pine trees at the side of the playground. Nudging, giggling together, the little girls pressed up close. And the only two who stayed outside the ring were the two who were always outside, the little Kelveys. They knew better than to come anywhere near the Burnells.

For the fact was, the school the Burnell children went to was not at all the kind of place their parents would have chosen if there had been any choice. But there was none. It was the only school for miles. And the consequence was all the children of the neighbourhood, the Judge's little girls, the doctor's daughters, the store-keeper's children, the milkman's, were forced to mix together. Not to speak of there being an equal number of rude, rough little boys as well. But the line had to be drawn somewhere. It was drawn at the Kelveys. Many of the children, including the Burnells, were not allowed even to speak to them. They walked past the Kelveys with their heads in the air, and as they set the fashion in all matters of behaviour, the Kelveys were shunned by everybody. Even the teacher had a special voice for them, and a special smile for the other children when Lil Kelvey came up to her desk with a bunch of dreadfully common-looking flowers.

They were the daughters of a spry, hard-working little washerwoman, who went about from house to house by the day. This was awful enough. But where was Mr. Kelvey? Nobody knew for certain. But everybody said he was in prison. So they were the daughters of a washerwoman and a gaolbird. Very nice company for other people's children! And they looked it. Why Mrs. Kelvey made them so conspicuous was hard to understand. The truth was they were dressed in 'bits' given to her by the people for whom she worked. Lil, for instance, who was a stout, plain child, with big freckles, came to school in a dress made from a green art-serge tablecloth of the Burnells', with red plush sleeves from the Logans' curtains. Her hat, perched on top of her high forehead, was a grown-up woman's hat, once the property of Miss Lecky, the postmistress. It was turned up at the back and trimmed with a large scarlet quill. What a little guy she looked! It was impossible not to laugh. And her little sister, our Else, wore a long white dress, rather like a nightgown, and a pair of little boy's boots. But whatever our Else wore she would have looked strange. She was a tiny wishbone of a child, with cropped hair and enormous solemn eyes—a little white owl. Nobody had ever seen her smile; she scarcely ever spoke. She went through life holding on to Lil, with a piece of Lil's skirt screwed up in her hand. Where Lil went, our Else followed. In the playground, on the road going to and from school, there was Lil marching in front and our Else holding on behind. Only when she wanted anything, or when she was out of breath, our Else gave Lil a tug, a twitch, and Lil stopped and turned round. The Kelveys never failed to understand each other.

Now they hovered at the edge; you couldn't stop them listening. When the little girls turned round and sneered, Lil, as usual, gave her silly, shamefaced smile, but our Else only looked.

And Isabel's voice, so very proud, went on telling. The carpet made a great sensation, but so did the beds with real bedclothes, and the stove with an oven door.

When she finished Kezia broke in. 'You've forgotten the lamp, Isabel.'

'Oh yes,' said Isabel, 'and there's a teeny little lamp, all made of yellow glass, with a white globe that stands on the dining-room table. You couldn't tell it from a real one.'

'The lamp's best of all,' cried Kezia. She thought Isabel wasn't making half enough of the little lamp. But nobody paid any attention. Isabel was choosing the two who were to come back with them that afternoon and see it. She chose Emmie Cole and Lena Logan. But when the others knew they were all to have a chance, they couldn't be nice enough to Isabel. One by one they put their arms round Isabel's waist and walked her off. They had something to whisper to her, a secret. 'Isabel's *my* friend.'

76

Only the little Kelveys moved away forgotten; there was nothing more for them to hear.

Days passed, and as more children saw the doll's house, the fame of it spread. It became the one subject, the rage. The one question was, 'Have you seen Burnells' doll's house? Oh, ain't it lovely!' 'Haven't you seen it? Oh, I say!'

Even the dinner hour was given up to talking about it. The little girls sat under the pines eating their thick mutton sandwiches and big slabs of johnny cake spread with butter. While always, as near as they could get, sat the Kelveys, our Else holding on to Lil, listening too, while they chewed their jam sandwiches out of a newspaper soaked with large red blobs.

'Mother,' said Kezia, 'can't I ask the Kelveys just once?'

'Certainly not, Kezia.'

'But why not?'

'Run away, Kezia; you know quite well why not.'

At last everybody had seen it except them. On that day the subject rather flagged. It was the dinner hour. The children stood together under the pine trees, and suddenly, as they looked at the Kelveys eating out of their paper, always by themselves, always listening, they wanted to be horrid to them. Emmie Cole started the whisper.

'Lil Kelvey's going to be a servant when she grows up.'

'O-oh, how awful!' said Isabel Burnell, and she made eyes at Emmie.

Emmie swallowed in a very meaning way and nodded to Isabel as she'd seen her mother do on those occasions.

'It's true—it's true—it's true,' she said.

Then Lena Logan's little eyes snapped. 'Shall I ask her?' she whispered.

'Bet you don't,' said Jessie May.

'Pooh, I'm not frightened,' said Lena. Suddenly she gave a little squeal and danced in front of the other girls. 'Watch! Watch me! Watch me now!' said Lena. And sliding, gliding, dragging one foot, giggling behind her hand, Lena went over to the Kelveys.

Lil looked up from her dinner. She wrapped the rest quickly away. Our Else stopped chewing. What was coming now?

77

'Is it true you're going to be a servant when you grow up, Lil Kelvey?' shrilled Lena.

Dead silence. But instead of answering, Lil only gave her silly, shamefaced smile. She didn't seem to mind the question at all. What a sell for Lena! The girls began to titter.

Lena couldn't stand that. She put her hands on her hips; she shot forward. 'Yah, yer father's in prison!' she hissed spitefully.

This was such a marvellous thing to have said that the little girls rushed away in a body, deeply, deeply excited, wild with joy. Someone found a long rope, and they began skipping. And never did they skip so high, run in and out so fast, or do such daring things as on that morning.

In the afternoon Pat called for the Burnell children with the buggy and they drove home. There were visitors. Isabel and Lottie, who liked visitors, went upstairs to change their pinafores. But Kezia thieved out at the back. Nobody was about; she began to swing on the big white gates of the courtyard. Presently, looking along the road, she saw two little dots. They grew bigger, they were coming towards her. Now she could see that one was in front and one close behind. Now she could see that they were the Kelveys. Kezia stopped swinging. She slipped off the gate as if she was going to run away. Then she hesitated. The Kelveys came nearer, and beside them walked their shadows, very long, stretching right across the road with their heads in the buttercups. Kezia clambered back on the gate; she had made up her mind; she swung out.

'Hullo,' she said to the passing Kelveys.

They were so astounded that they stopped. Lil gave her silly smile. Our Else stared.

'You can come and see our doll's house if you want to,' said Kezia, and she dragged one toe on the ground. But at that Lil turned red and shook her head quickly.

'Why not?' asked Kezia.

Lil gasped, then she said, 'Your ma told our ma you wasn't to speak to us.'

'Oh, well,' said Kezia. She didn't know what to reply. 'It doesn't matter. You can come and see our doll's house all the same. Come on. Nobody's looking.'

But Lil shook her head still harder.

'Don't you want to?' asked Kezia.

Suddenly there was a twitch, a tug at Lil's skirt. She turned round. Our Else was looking at her with big, imploring eyes; she was frowning; she wanted to go. For a moment Lil looked at our Else very doubtfully. But then our Else twitched her skirt again. She started forward. Kezia led the way. Like two little stray cats they followed across the courtyard to where the doll's house stood.

'There it is,' said Kezia.

There was a pause. Lil breathed loudly, almost snorted; our Else was still as stone.

'I'll open it for you,' said Kezia kindly. She undid the hook and they looked inside.

'There's the drawing-room and the dining-room, and that's the—'

'Kezia!'

Oh, what a start they gave!

'Kezia!'

It was Aunt Beryl's voice. They turned round. At the back door stood Aunt Beryl, staring as if she couldn't believe what she saw.

'How dare you ask the little Kelveys into the courtyard!' said her cold, furious voice. 'You know as well as I do, you're not allowed to talk to them. Run away, children, run away at once. And don't come back again,' said Aunt Beryl. And she stepped into the yard and shooed them out as if they were chickens.

'Off you go immediately!' she called, cold and proud.

They did not need telling twice. Burning with shame, shrinking together, Lil huddling along like her mother, our Else dazed, somehow they crossed the big courtyard and squeezed through the white gate.

'Wicked, disobedient little girl!' said Aunt Beryl bitterly to Kezia, and she slammed the doll's house to.

The afternoon had been awful. A letter had come from Willie Brent, a terrifying, threatening letter, saying if she did not meet him that evening in Pulman's Bush, he'd come to the front door and ask the reason why! But now that she had frightened those little rats of Kelveys and given Kezia a good scolding, her heart felt lighter. That ghastly pressure was gone. She went back to the house humming.

When the Kelveys were well out of sight of Burnells', they

sat down to rest on a big red drainpipe by the side of the road. Lil's cheeks were still burning; she took off the hat with the quill and held it on her knee. Dreamily they looked over the hay paddocks, past the creek, to the group of wattles where Logan's cows stood waiting to be milked. What were their thoughts?

Presently our Else nudged up close to her sister. But now she had forgotten the cross lady. She put out a finger and stoked her sister's quill; she smiled her rare smile.

'I seen the little lamp,' she said softly.

Then both were silent once more.

(1921)

New Dresses

Mrs. Carsfield and her mother sat at the dining-room table putting the finishing touches to some green cashmere dresses. They were to be worn by the two Misses Carsfield at church on the following day, with applegreen sashes, and straw hats with ribbon tails. Mrs. Carsfield had set her heart on it, and this being a late night for Henry, who was attending a meeting of the Political League, she and the old mother had the dining-room to themselves and could make 'a peaceful litter' as she expressed it. The red cloth was taken off the table—where stood the wedding-present sewing-machine, a brown work-basket, the 'material', and some torn fashion journals. Mrs. Carsfield worked the machine, slowly, for she feared the green thread would give out, and had a sort of tired hope that it might last longer if she was careful to use a little at a time; the old woman sat in a rocking-chair, her skirt turned back, and her felt-slippered feet on a hassock, tying the machine threads and stitching some narrow lace on the necks and cuffs. The gas jet flickered. Now and again the old woman glanced up at the jet and said, 'There's water in the pipe, Anne, that's what's the matter,' then was silent, to say again a moment later, 'There must be water in that pipe, Anne,' and again, with quite a burst of energy, '*Now* there is—I'm *certain* of it.'

Anne frowned at the sewing-machine. 'The way mother *harps* on things—it gets frightfully on my nerves,' she thought. 'And always when there's no earthly opportunity to better a thing. . . . I suppose it's old age—but most aggravating.' Aloud she said: 'Mother, I'm having a really substantial hem in this dress of Rose's—the child has got so leggy lately. And don't put any lace on Helen's cuffs; it will make a distinction, and besides she's so careless about rubbing her hands on anything grubby.'

'Oh, there's plenty,' said the old woman. 'I'll put it a little higher up.' And she wondered why Anne had such a down on

81

Helen—Henry was just the same. They seemed to want to hurt Helen's feelings—the distinction was merely an excuse.

'Well,' said Mrs. Carsfield, 'you didn't see Helen's clothes when I took them off to-night. Black from head to foot after a week. And when I compared them before her eyes with Rose's she merely shrugged, you know that habit she's got, and began stuttering. I really shall have to see Dr. Malcolm about her stuttering, if only to give her a good fright. I believe it's merely an affectation she's picked up at school—that she can help it.'

'Anne, you know she's always stuttered. You did just the same when you were her age, she's highly strung.' The old woman took off her spectacles, breathed on them, and rubbed them with a corner of her sewing apron.

'Well, the last thing in the world to do her any good is to let her imagine *that*,' answered Anne, shaking out one of the green frocks and pricking at the pleats with her needle. 'She is treated exactly like Rose, and the Boy hasn't a nerve. Did you see him when I put him on the rocking-horse to-day, for the first time? He simply gurgled with joy. He's more the image of his father every day.'

'Yes, he certainly is a thorough Carsfield,' assented the old woman, nodding her head.

'Now that's another thing about Helen,' said Anne. 'The peculiar way she treats Boy, staring at him and frightening him as she does. You remember when he was a baby how she used to take away his bottle to see what he would do? Rose is perfect with the child—but Helen . . .'

The old woman put down her work on the table. A little silence fell, and through the silence the loud ticking of the dining-room clock. She wanted to speak her mind to Anne once and for all about the way she and Henry were treating Helen, ruining the child, but the ticking noise distracted her. She could not think of the words and sat there stupidly, her brain going *tick*, *tick* to the dining-room clock.

'How loudly that clock ticks,' was all she said.

'Oh, there's mother—off the subject again—giving me no help or encouragement,' thought Anne. She glanced at the clock.

'Mother, if you've finished that frock, would you go into the kitchen and heat up some coffee and perhaps cut a plate of ham. Henry will be in directly. I'm practically through with this second frock by myself.' She held it up for inspection. 'Aren't they charming? They ought to last the children a good two years, and then I expect they'll do for school—lengthened, and perhaps dyed.'

'I'm glad we decided on the more expensive material,' said the old woman.

Left alone in the dining-room Anne's frown deepened and her mouth drooped—a sharp line showed from nose to chin. She breathed deeply and pushed back her hair. There seemed to be no air in the room, she felt stuffed up, and it seemed so useless to be tiring herself out with fine sewing for Helen. One never got through with children and never had any gratitude from them—except Rose—who was exceptional. Another sign of old age in mother was her absurd point of view about Helen and her 'touchiness' on the subject. There was one thing, Mrs. Carsfield said to herself. She was determined to keep Helen apart from Boy. He had all his father's sensitiveness to unsympathetic influences. A blessing that the girls were at school all day!

At last the dresses were finished and folded over the back of the chair. She carried the sewing-machine over to the bookshelves, spread the tablecloth, and went over to the window. The blind was up, she could see the garden quite plainly: there must be a moon about. And then she caught sight of something shining on the garden seat. A book, yes, it must be a book, left there to get soaked through by the dew. She went out into the hall, put on her goloshes, gathered up her skirt, and ran into the garden. Yes, it was a book. She picked it up carefully. Damp already—and the cover bulging. She shrugged her shoulders in the way that her little daughter had caught from her. In the shadowy garden that smelled of grass and rose leaves Anne's heart hardened. Then the gate clicked and she saw Henry striding up the front path.

'Henry!' she called.

'Hullo,' he cried, 'what on earth are you doing down there.... Moon-gazing, Anne?' She ran forward and kissed him.

'Oh, look at this book,' she said. 'Helen's been leaving it about again. My dear, how you smell of cigars!'

Said Henry: 'You've got to smoke a decent cigar when you're with these other chaps. Looks so bad if you don't.

But come inside, Anne; you haven't got anything on. Let the book go hang! You're cold, my dear, you're shivering.' He put his arm round her shoulder. 'See the moon over there, by the chimney? Fine night. By Jove! I had the fellows roaring to-night—I made a colossal joke. One of them said: "Life is a game of cards," and I, without thinking, just straight out . . .' Henry paused by the door and held up a finger. 'I said . . . well, I've forgotten the exact words, but they shouted, my dear, simply shouted. No, I'll remember what I said in bed to-night; you know I always do.'

'I'll take this book into the kitchen to dry on the stove-rack,' said Anne, and she thought, as she banged the pages, 'Henry has been drinking beer again, that means indigestion to-morrow. No use mentioning Helen to-night.'

When Henry had finished the supper he lay back in the chair, picking his teeth, and patted his knee for Anne to come and sit there.

'Hullo,' he said, jumping her up and down, 'what's the green fandangles on the chair back? What have you and mother been up to, eh?'

Said Anne airily, casting a most careless glance at the green dresses, 'Only some frocks for the children. Remnants for Sunday.'

The old woman put the plate and cup and saucer together, then lighted a candle.

'I think I'll go to bed,' she said cheerfully.

'Oh, dear me, how unwise of mother,' thought Anne. 'She makes Henry suspect by going away like that, as she always does if there's any unpleasantness brewing.'

'No, don't go to bed yet, mother,' cried Henry jovially. 'Let's have a look at the things.' She passed him over the dresses, faintly smiling. Henry rubbed them through his fingers.

'So these are the remnants, are they, Anne? Don't feel much like the Sunday trousers my mother used to make me out of an ironing blanket. How much did you pay for this a yard, Anne?'

Anne took the dresses from him and played with a button of his waistcoat.

'Forget the exact price, darling. Mother and I rather skimped them, even though they were so cheap. What can

great big men bother about clothes . . .? Was Lumley there
to-night?'

'Yes, he says their kid was a bit bandy-legged at just the
same age as Boy. He told me of a new kind of chair for children
that the draper had just got in—makes them sit with their
legs straight. By the way, have you got this month's draper's
bill?'

She had been waiting for that—had known it was coming.
She slipped off his knee and yawned.

'Oh, dear me,' she said, 'I think I'll follow mother. Bed's
the place for me.' She stared at Henry vacantly. 'Bill—bill
did you say, dear? Oh, I'll look it out in the morning.'

'No, Anne, hold on.' Henry got up and went over to the
cupboard where the bill file was kept. 'To-morrow's no good
—because it's Sunday. I want to get that account off my chest
before I turn in. Sit down there—in the rocking-chair—you
needn't stand!'

She dropped into the chair and began humming, all the while
her thoughts coldly busy and her eyes fixed on her husband's
broad back as he bent over the cupboard door. He dawdled
over finding the file.

'He's keeping me in suspense on purpose,' she thought.
'We can afford it—otherwise why should I do it? I know
our income and our expenditure. I'm not a fool. They're a
hell upon earth every month, these bills.' And she thought
of her bed upstairs, yearned for it, imagining she had never
felt so tired in her life.

'Here we are!' said Henry. He slammed the file on to the
table.

'Draw up your chair. . . .'

'Clayton: Seven yards green cashmere at five shillings a
yard—thirty-five shillings.' He read the item twice—then
folded the sheet over and bent towards Anne. He was flushed
and his breath smelt of beer. She knew exactly how he took
things in that mood, and she raised her eyebrows and nodded.

'Do you mean to tell me,' stormed Henry, 'that lot over there
cost thirty-five shillings—that stuff you've been mucking up for
the children. Good God! Anybody would think you'd married a
millionaire. You could buy your mother a trousseau with that
money. You're making yourself a laughing-stock for the whole
town. How do you think I can buy Boy a chair or anything else

—if you chuck away my earnings like that? Time and again
you impress upon me the impossibility of keeping Helen decent;
and then you go decking her out the next moment in thirty-five
shillings' worth of green cashmere. . . .'

On and on stormed the voice.

'He'll have calmed down in the morning, when the beer's
worked off,' thought Anne, and later, as she toiled up to bed,
'When he sees how they'll last, he'll understand. . . .'

A brilliant Sunday morning. Henry and Anne, quite recon-
ciled, sitting in the dining-room waiting for church time to the
tune of Carsfield junior, who steadily thumped the shelf of his
high chair with a gravy spoon given him from the breakfast
table by his father.

'That beggar's got muscle,' said Henry proudly. 'I've timed
him by my watch. He's kept that up for five minutes without
stopping.'

'Extraordinary,' said Anne, buttoning her gloves. 'I think
he's had that spoon almost long enough now, dear, don't you?
I'm so afraid of him putting it into his mouth.'

'Oh, I've got an eye on him.' Henry stood over his small
son. 'Go it, old man. Tell mother boys like to kick up a row.'

Anne kept silence. At any rate, it would keep his eye off the
children when they came down in those cashmeres. She was
still wondering if she had drummed into their minds often
enough the supreme importance of being careful and of taking
them off immediately after church before dinner, and why
Helen was fidgety when she was pulled about at all, when the
door opened and the old woman ushered them in, complete to
the straw hats with ribbon tails.

She could not help thrilling, they looked so very superior—
Rose carrying her prayer-book in a white case embroidered
with a pink woollen cross. But she feigned indifference immediately and the lateness of the hour. Not a word more on the
subject from Henry, even with the thirty-five shillings' worth
walking hand in hand before him all the way to church. Anne
decided that was really generous and noble of him. She
looked up at him, walking with the shoulders thrown back. How
fine he looked in that long black coat with the white silk tie just
showing! And the children looked worthy of him. She squeezed
his hand in church, conveying by that silent pressure 'It was for

your sake I made the dresses; of course, you can't understand that, but *really*, Henry.' And she fully believed it.

On their way home the Carsfield family met Doctor Malcolm out walking with a black dog carrying his stick in its mouth. Doctor Malcolm stopped and asked after Boy so intelligently that Henry invited him to dinner.

'Come and pick a bone with us and see Boy for yourself,' he said. And Doctor Malcolm accepted. He walked beside Henry and shouted over his shoulder, 'Helen, keep an eye on *my* boy baby, will you, and see he doesn't swallow that walking-stick. Because, if he does, a tree will grow right out of his mouth or it will go to his tail and make it so stiff that a wag will knock you into kingdom come!'

'Oh, Doctor Malcolm!' laughed Helen, stooping over the dog. 'Come along, doggie, give it up, there's a good boy!'

'Helen, your dress!' warned Anne.

'Yes, indeed,' said Doctor Malcolm. 'They are looking top-notchers to-day—the two young ladies.'

'Well, it really *is* Rose's colour,' said Anne. 'Her complexion is so much more vivid than Helen's.'

Rose blushed. Doctor Malcolm's eyes twinkled, and he kept a tight rein on himself from saying she looked like a tomato in a lettuce salad.

'That child wants taking down a peg,' he decided. 'Give me Helen every time. She'll come to her own yet and lead them just the dance they need.'

Boy was having his midday sleep when they arrived home, and Doctor Malcolm begged that Helen might show him round the garden. Henry, repenting already of his generosity, gladly assented, and Anne went into the kitchen to interview the servant girl.

'Mumma, let me come too and taste the gravy,' begged Rose.

'Huh!' muttered Doctor Malcolm. 'Good riddance.'

He established himself on the garden bench—put up his feet and took off his hat to give the sun 'a chance of growing a second crop,' he told Helen.

She asked soberly: 'Doctor Malcolm, do you really like my dress?'

'Of course I do, my lady. Don't you?'

'Oh yes, I'd like to be born and die in it. But it was such a fuss—tryings on, you know, and pullings, and "don'ts." I believe mother would kill me if it got hurt. I even knelt on my petticoat all through church because of dust on the hassock.'

'Bad as that?' asked Doctor Malcolm, rolling his eyes at Helen.

'Oh, *far* worse,' said the child, then burst into laughter and shouted 'Hellish!' dancing over the lawn.

'Take care, they'll hear you, Helen.'

'Oh, booh! It's just dirty old cashmere—serve them right. They can't see me if they're not here to see and so it doesn't matter. It's only with them I feel funny.'

'Haven't you got to remove your finery before dinner?'

'No, because you're here.'

'Oh my prophetic soul!' groaned Doctor Malcolm.

Coffee was served in the garden. The servant girl brought out some cane chairs and a rug for Boy. The children were told to go away and play.

'Leave off worrying Doctor Malcolm, Helen,' said Henry. 'You mustn't be a plague to people who are not members of your own family.' Helen pouted and dragged over to the swing for comfort. She swung high, and thought Doctor Malcolm was a most beautiful man—and wondered if his dog had finished the plate of bones in the back yard. Decided to go and see. Slower she swung, then took a flying leap; her tight skirt caught on a nail—there was a sharp, tearing sound— quickly she glanced at the others—they had not noticed— and then at the frock—at a hole big enough to stick her hand through. She felt neither frightened nor sorry. 'I'll go and change it,' she thought.

'Helen, where are you going to?' called Anne.

'Into the house for a book.'

The old woman noticed that the child held her skirt in a peculiar way. Her petticoat string must have come untied. But she made no remark. Once in the bedroom Helen unbuttoned the frock, slipped out of it, and wondered what to do next. Hide it somewhere—she glanced all round the room— there was nowhere safe from them. Except the top of the cupboard—but even standing on a chair she could not throw so high—it fell back on top of her every time—the horrid, hateful thing. Then her eyes lighted on her school satchel hanging on the end of the bedpost. Wrap it in her school pinafore—put it in the bottom of the bag with the pencil case on top. They'd never look there. She returned to the garden in the every-day dress—but forgot about the book.

'A-ah,' said Anne, smiling ironically. 'What a new leaf for Doctor Malcolm's benefit! Look, mother, Helen has changed without being told to.'

'Come here, dear, and be done up properly.' She whispered to Helen: 'Where did you leave your dress?'

'Left it on the side of the bed. *Where* I took it off,' sang Helen.

Doctor Malcolm was talking to Henry of the advantages derived from public school education for the sons of commercial men, but he had his eye on the scene and, watching Helen, he smelt a rat—smelt a Hamelin tribe of them.

Confusion and consternation reigned. One of the green cashmeres had disappeared—spirited off the face of the earth—during the time that Helen took it off and the children's tea.

'Show me the exact spot,' scolded Mrs. Carsfield for the twentieth time. 'Helen, tell the truth.'

'Mumma, I *swear* I left it on the floor.'

'Well, it's no good swearing if it's not there. It can't have been stolen!'

'I did see a very funny-looking man in a white cap walking up and down the road and staring in the windows as I came up to change.' Sharply Anne eyed her daughter.

'Now,' she said, 'I k*now* you are telling lies.'

She turned to the old woman, in her voice something of pride and joyous satisfaction. 'You hear, mother—this cock-and-bull story?'

When they were near the end of the bed Helen blushed and turned away from them. And now and again she wanted to shout 'I tore it, I tore it,' and she fancied she had said it and seen their faces, just as sometimes in bed she dreamed she had got up and dressed. But as the evening wore on she grew quite careless—glad only of one thing—people had to go to sleep at night. Viciously she stared at the sun shining through the window space and making a pattern of the curtain on the bare nursery floor. And then she looked at Rose, painting a text at the nursery table with a whole egg-cup full of water to herself. . . .

Henry visited their bedroom the last thing. She heard him come creaking into their room and hid under the bedclothes. But Rose betrayed her.

'Helen's not asleep,' piped Rose.

Henry sat by the bedside pulling his moustache.

'If it were not Sunday, Helen, I would whip you. As it is, and I must be at the office early to-morrow, I shall give you a sound smacking after tea in the evening. . . . Do you hear me?'

She grunted.

'You love your father and mother, don't you?'

No answer.

Rose gave Helen a dig with her foot.

'Well,' said Henry, sighing deeply, 'I suppose you love Jesus?'

'Rose has scratched my leg with her toe-nail,' answered Helen.

Henry strode out of the room and flung himself on to his own bed with his outdoor boots on the starched bolster, Anne noticed, but he was too overcome for her to venture a protest. The old woman was in the bedroom, too, idly combing the hairs from Anne's brush. Henry told them the story, and was gratified to observe Anne's tears.

'It *is* Rose's turn for her toe-nails after the bath next Saturday,' commented the old woman.

In the middle of the night Henry dug his elbow into Mrs. Carsfield.

'I've got an idea,' he said. 'Malcolm's at the bottom of this.'

'No . . . how . . . why . . . where . . . bottom of what?'

'Those damned green dresses.'

'Wouldn't be surprised,' she managed to articulate, thinking 'imagine his rage if I woke *him* up to tell him an idiotic thing like that!'

'Is Mrs. Carsfield at home?' asked Doctor Malcolm.

'No, sir, she's out visiting,' answered the servant girl.

'Is Mr. Carsfield anywhere about?'

'Oh no, sir, he's never home midday.'

'Show me into the drawing-room.'

The servant girl opened the drawing-room door, cocked her eye at the doctor's bag. She wished he would leave it in the hall—even if she could only *feel* the outside without opening it. . . . But the doctor kept it in his hand.

The old woman sat in the drawing-room, a roll of knitting on her lap. Her head had fallen back—her mouth was open—she was asleep and quietly snoring. She started up at the sound of the doctor's footsteps and straightened her cap.

'Oh, Doctor—you *did* take me by surprise. I was dreaming that Henry had bought Anne five little canaries. Please sit down!'

'No, thanks. I just popped in on the chance of catching you alone. . . . You see this bag?'

The old woman nodded.

'Now, are you any good at opening bags?'

'Well, my husband was a great traveller and once I spent a whole night in a railway train.'

'Well, have a go at opening this one.'

The old woman knelt on the floor—her fingers trembled.

'There's nothing startling inside?' she asked.

'Well, it won't bite exactly,' said Doctor Malcolm.

The catch sprang open—the bag yawned like a toothless mouth, and she saw, folded in its depths—green cashmere—with narrow lace on the neck and sleeves.

'Fancy that!' said the old woman mildly. 'May I take it out, Doctor?' She professed neither astonishment nor pleasure —and Malcolm felt disappointed.

'Helen's dress,' he said, and bending towards her, raised his voice. 'That young spark's Sunday rig-out.'

'I'm not deaf, Doctor,' answered the old woman. 'Yes, I thought it looked like it. I told Anne only this morning it was bound to turn up somewhere.' She shook the crumpled frock and looked it over. 'Things always do if you give them time; I've noticed that so often—it's such a blessing.'

'You know Lindsay—the postman? Gastric ulcers—called there this morning. . . . Saw this brought in by Lena, who'd got it from Helen on her way to school. Said the kid fished it out of her satchel rolled in a pinafore, and said her mother had told her to give it away because it did not fit her. When I saw the tear I understood yesterday's "new leaf", as Mrs. Carsfield put it. Was up to the dodge in a jiffy. Got the dress—bought some stuff at Clayton's and made my sister Bertha sew it while I had dinner. I knew what would be happening this end of the line—and I knew you'd see Helen through for the sake of getting one in at Henry.'

'How thoughtful of you, Doctor!' said the old woman. 'I'll tell Anne I found it under my dolman.'

'Yes, that's your ticket,' said Doctor Malcolm.

'But, of course, Helen would have forgotten the whipping by to-morrow morning and I'd promised her a new doll. . . .' The old woman spoke regretfully.

Doctor Malcolm snapped his bag together. 'It's no good talking to the old bird,' he thought, 'she doesn't take in half I say. Don't seem to have got any forrader than doing Helen out of a doll.'

(1911)

Evening

*'Do you remember, Katie?' I hear his voice in the trees and flowers,
in scents and light and shadow. Have people, apart from these
far-away people, ever existed for me? Or have they always failed me
and faded because I denied them reality? Supposing I were to die as I
sit at this table, playing with my Indian paper-knife, what would
be the difference? No difference at all. Then why don't I commit
suicide? Because I feel I have a duty to perform to the lovely time
when we were both alive. I want to write about it, and he wanted
me to. We talked it over in my little top room in London. I said: I
will just put on the front page: To my brother, Leslie Heron
Beauchamp. Very well: it shall be done.*

*They are walking up and down the garden in Acacia Road. It is
dusky; the Michaelmas daisies are bright as feathers. From the old
fruit-tree at the bottom of the garden—the slender tree rather like
a poplar—there falls a little round pear, hard as a stone.*

*'Did you hear that, Katie! Can you find it? By Jove—that
familiar sound.'*

*Their hands move over the thin moist grass. He picks it up, and,
unconsciously, as of old, polishes it on his handkerchief.*

*'Do you remember the enormous number of pears there used to be
on that old tree?'*

'Down by the violet bed.'

*'And how after there'd been a Southerly Buster we used to go out
with clothes baskets to pick them up?'*

*'And how while we stooped they went on falling, bouncing on our
backs and heads?'*

*'And how far they used to be scattered, ever so far, under the
violet leaves, down the steps, right down to the lily-lawn? We used
to find them trodden in the grass. And how soon the ants got to them.*

I can see now that little round hole with a sort of fringe of brown pepper round it.'

'Do you know that I've never seen pears like them since?'

'They were so bright, canary yellow—and small. And the peel was so thin and the pips jet—jet black. First you pulled out the little stem and sucked it. It was faintly sour, and then you ate them always from the top—core and all.'

'The pips were delicious.'

'Do you remember sitting on the pink garden seat?'

'I shall never forget that pink garden seat. It is the only garden seat for me. Where is it now? Do you think we shall be allowed to sit on it in Heaven?'

'It always wobbled a bit and there were usually the marks of a snail on it.'

'Sitting on that seat, swinging our legs and eating the pears—'

'But isn't it extraordinary how deep our happiness was—how positive—deep, shining, warm. I remember the way we used to look at each other and smile—do you?—sharing a secret. . . . What was it?'

'I think it was the family feeling—we were almost like one child. I always see us walking about together, looking at things together with the same eyes, discussing. . . . I felt that again—just now—when we looked for the pear in the grass. I remembered ruffling the violet leaves with you—Oh, that garden!'

'Do you remember that some of the pears we found used to have little teeth marks in them?'

'Yes.'

'Who bit them?'

'It was always a mystery.'

He puts his arm round her. They pace up and down. And the round moon shines over the pear tree, and the ivy walls of the garden glitter like metal. The air smells chill . . . heavy . . . very cold.

'We shall go back there one day—when it's all over.'

'We'll go back together.'

'And find everything—'

'Everything!'

She leans against his shoulder. The moonlight deepens. Now they are facing the back of the house. A square of light shows in the window.

'Give me your hand. You know I shall always be a stranger here.'

'Yes, darling, I know.'

'Walk up and down once more and then we'll go in.'

94

'*It's so curious—my absolute confidence that I'll come back. I feel it's as certain as this pear.*'

'*I feel that too.*'

'*I couldn't not come back. You know that feeling. It's awfully mysterious.*'

The shadows on the grass are long and strange; a puff of strange wind whispers in the ivy and the old moon touches them with silver.

She shivers.

'*You're cold.*'

'*Dreadfully cold.*'

He puts his arm round her. Suddenly he kisses her—

'*Good-bye, darling.*'

'*Ah, why do you say that!*'

'*Darling, good-bye . . . good-bye!*'

(1915)

The
Apple-Tree

There were two orchards belonging to the old house. One, that we called the 'wild' orchard, lay beyond the vegetable garden; it was planted with bitter cherries and damsons and transparent yellow plums. For some reason it lay under a cloud; we never played there, we did not even trouble to pick up the fallen fruit; and there, every Monday morning, to the round open space in the middle, the servant girl and the washer-woman carried the wet linen—grandmother's nightdresses, father's striped shirts, the hired man's cotton trousers and the servant girl's 'dreadfully vulgar' salmon-pink flannelette drawers jigged and slapped in horrid familiarity.

But the other orchard, far away and hidden from the house, lay at the foot of a little hill and stretched right over to the edge of the paddocks—to the clumps of wattles bobbing yellow in the bright sun and the blue gums with their streaming sickle-shaped leaves. There, under the fruit trees, the grass grew so thick and coarse that it tangled and knotted in your shoes as you walked, and even on the hottest day it was damp to touch when you stopped and parted it this way and that, looking for windfalls— the apples marked with a bird's beak, the big bruised pears, the quinces, so good to eat with a pinch of salt, but so delicious to smell that you could not bite for sniffing. . . .

One year the orchard had its Forbidden Tree. It was an apple-tree discovered by father and a friend during an after-dinner prowl one Sunday afternoon.

'Great Scott!' said the friend, lighting upon it with every appearance of admiring astonishment: 'Isn't that a——?' And a rich, splendid name settled like an unknown bird on the tree.

'Yes, I believe it is,' said father lightly. He knew nothing whatever about the names of fruit trees.

'Great Scott!' said the friend again: 'They're wonderful apples. Nothing like 'em—and you're going to have a tip-top crop. Marvellous apples! You can't beat 'em!'

'No, they're very fine—very fine,' said father carelessly, but looking upon the tree with new and lively interest.

'They're rare—they're very rare. Hardly ever see 'em in England nowadays,' said the visitor and set a seal on father's delight. For father was a self-made man and the price he had to pay for everything was so huge and so painful that nothing rang so sweet to him as to hear his purchase praised. He was young and sensitive still. He still wondered whether in the deepest sense he got his money's worth. He still had hours when he walked up and down in the moonlight half deciding to 'chuck this confounded rushing to the office every day—and clear out—clear out once and for all.' And now to discover that he'd a valuable apple-tree thrown in with the orchard—an apple-tree that this Johnny from England positively envied!

'Don't touch that tree! Do you hear me, children?' said he, bland and firm; and when the guest had gone, with quite another voice and manner:

'If I catch either of you touching those apples you shall not only go to bed—you shall each have a good sound whipping.' Which merely added to its magnificence.

Every Sunday morning after church father, with Bogey and me tailing after, walked through the flower garden, down the violet path, past the lace-bark tree, past the white rose and syringa bushes, and down the hill to the orchard. The apple-tree —like the Virgin Mary—seemed to have been miraculously warned of its high honour, standing apart from its fellows, bending a little under its clusters, fluttering its polished leaves, important and exquisite before father's awful eye. His heart swelled to the sight—we knew his heart swelled. He put his hands behind his back and screwed up his eyes in the way he had. There it stood—the accidental thing—the thing that no one had been aware of when the hard bargain was driven. It hadn't been counted in, hadn't in a way been paid for. If the house had been burned to the ground at that time it would have meant less to him than the destruction of his tree. And how we played up to him, Bogey and I—Bogey with his scratched knees pressed together, his hands behind his back, too, and a round cap on his head with 'H.M.S. Thunderbolt' printed across it.

The apples turned from pale green to yellow; then they had deep pink stripes painted on them, and then the pink melted all over the yellow, reddened, and spread into a fine clear crimson.

At last the day came when father took out of his waistcoat pocket a little pearl pen-knife. He reached up. Very slowly and very carefully he picked two apples growing on a bough.

'By Jove! They're warm.' cried father in amazement. 'They're wonderful apples! Tip-top! Marvellous!' he echoed. He rolled them over in his hands.

'Look at that!' he said. 'Not a spot—not a blemish!' And he walked through the orchard with Bogey and me stumbling after, to a tree-stump under the wattles. We sat, one on either side of father. He laid one apple down, opened the pearl pen-knife and neatly and beautifully cut the other in half.

'By Jove! Look at that!' he exclaimed.

'Father!' we cried, dutiful but really enthusiastic, too. For the lovely red colour had bitten right through the white flesh of the apple; it was pink to the shiny black pips lying so justly in their scaly pods. It looked as though the apple had been dipped in wine.

'Never seen *that* before,' said father. 'You won't find an apple like that in a hurry!' He put it to his nose and pronounced an unfamiliar word. 'Bouquet! What a bouquet!' And then he handed to Bogey one half, to me the other.

'Don't *bolt* it!' said he. It was agony to give even so much away. I knew it, while I took mine humbly and humbly Bogey took his.

Then he divided the second with the same neat beautiful little cut of the pearl knife.

I kept my eyes on Bogey. Together we took a bite. Our mouths were full of a floury stuff, a hard, faintly bitter skin—a horrible taste of something dry. . . .

'Well?' asked father, very jovial. He had cut his two halves into quarters and was taking out the little pods. 'Well?'

Bogey and I stared at each other, chewing desperately. In that second of chewing and swallowing a long silent conversation passed between us—and a strange meaning smile. We swallowed. We edged near father, just touching him.

'Perfect!' we lied. 'Perfect—father! Simply lovely!'

But it was no use. Father spat his out and never went near the apple-tree again.

(1915)

about a father & daughter who
finally come to understand eachother

The Little Girl

*Don't think I underestimate the
enormous power parents can have. I
don't. It's staggering, it's titanic.
After all, they are real giants when
we are only table high and they act
accordingly . . . we have to find the
gift in it. We can't afford to
waste such an expenditure of
feeling; we have to learn from
it—and we* do*, I most deeply
believe, come to be thankful for it.*

To the little girl he was a figure to be feared and avoided.
Every morning before going to business he came into the nursery and gave her a perfunctory kiss, to which she responded
with 'Good-bye, father.' And oh, the glad sense of relief when
she heard the noise of the buggy growing fainter and fainter
down the long road!

In the evening, leaning over the banisters at his home-
coming, she heard his loud voice in the hall. 'Bring my tea into
the smoking-room. . . . Hasn't the paper come yet? Have they
taken it into the kitchen again? Mother, go and see if my
paper's out there—and bring me my slippers.'

'Kezia,' mother would call to her, 'if you're a good girl
you can come down and take off father's boots.' Slowly the
girl would slip down the stairs, holding tightly to the banisters
with one hand—more slowly still, across the hall, and push
open the smoking-room door.

100

By that time he had his spectacles on and looked at her over them in a way that was terrifying to the little girl.

'Well, Kezia, get a move on and pull off these boots and take them outside. Been a good girl to-day?'

'I d-d-don't know, father.'

'You d-d-don't know? If you stutter like that mother will have to take you to the doctor.'

She never stuttered with other people—had quite given it up —but only with father, because then she was trying so hard to say the words properly.

'What's the matter? What are you looking so wretched about? Mother, I wish you would teach this child not to appear on the brink of suicide. . . . Here, Kezia, carry my teacup back to the table—carefully; your hands jog like an old lady's. And try to keep your handkerchief in your pocket, *not* up your sleeve.'

'Y-y-yes, father.'

On Sundays she sat in the same pew with him in church, listening while he sang in a loud, clear voice, watching while he made little notes during the sermon with the stump of a blue pencil on the back of an envelope—his eyes narrowed to a slit—one hand beating a silent tattoo on the pew ledge. He said his prayers so loudly she was certain God heard him above the clergyman.

He was so big—his hands and his neck, especially his mouth when he yawned. Thinking about him alone in the nursery was like thinking about a giant.

On Sunday afternoons grandmother sent her down to the drawing-room, dressed in her brown velvet, to have a 'nice talk with father and mother.' But the little girl always found mother reading *The Sketch* and father stretched out on the couch, his handkerchief on his face, his feet propped on one of the best sofa pillows, and so soundly sleeping that he snored.

She, perched on the piano-stool, gravely watched him until he woke and stretched, and asked the time—then looked at her.

'Don't stare so, Kezia. You look like a little brown owl.'

One day, when she was kept indoors with a cold, the grand-mother told her that father's birthday was next week, and suggested she should make him a pin-cushion for a present out of a beautiful piece of yellow silk.

Laboriously, with a double cotton, the little girl stitched three sides. But what to fill it with? That was the question. The grandmother was out in the garden, and she wandered into mother's bedroom to look for 'scraps.' On the bed-table she discovered a great many sheets of fine paper, gathered them up, shredded them into tiny pieces, and stuffed her case, then sewed up the fourth side.

That night there was a hue and cry over the house. Father's great speech for the Port Authority had been lost. Rooms were ransacked—servants questioned. Finally mother came into the nursery.

'Kezia, I suppose you didn't see some papers on a table in our room?'

'Oh yes,' she said. 'I tore them up for my s'prise.'

'*What!*' screamed mother. 'Come straight down to the dining-room this instant.'

And she was dragged down to where father was pacing to and fro, hands behind his back.

'Well?' he said sharply.

Mother explained.

He stopped and stared in a stupefied manner at the child.

'Did you do that?'

'N-n-no,' she whispered.

'Mother, go up to the nursery and fetch down the damned thing—see that the child's put to bed this instant.'

Crying too much to explain, she lay in the shadowed room watching the evening light sift through the venetian blinds and trace a sad little pattern on the floor.

Then father came into the room with a ruler in his hands.

'I am going to whip you for this,' he said.

'Oh, no, no!' she screamed, cowering down under the bedclothes.

He pulled them aside.

'Sit up,' he commanded, 'and hold out your hands. You must be taught once and for all not to touch what does not belong to you.'

'But it was for your b-b-birthday.'

Down came the ruler on her little, pink palms.

Hours later, when the grandmother had wrapped her in a shawl and rocked her in the rocking-chair, the child cuddled close to her soft body.

'What did Jesus make fathers for?' she sobbed.

'Here's a clean hanky, darling, with some of my lavender water on it. Go to sleep, pet; you'll forget all about it in the morning. I tried to explain to father, but he was too upset to listen to-night.'

But the child never forgot. Next time she saw him she whipped both hands behind her back, and a red colour flew into her cheeks.

The Macdonalds lived in the next-door house. Five children there were. Looking through a hole in the vegetable garden fence the little girl saw them playing 'tag' in the evening. The father with the baby Mac on his shoulders, two little girls hanging on to his coat tails, ran round and round the flower beds, shaking with laughter. Once she saw the boys turn the hose on him—*turn the hose on him*—and he made a great grab at them, tickling them until they got hiccoughs.

Then it was she decided there were different sorts of fathers.

Suddenly, one day, mother became ill, and she and grandmother drove into town in a closed carriage.

The little girl was left alone in the house with Alice, the 'general.' That was all right in the daytime, but while Alice was putting her to bed she grew suddenly afraid.

'What'll I do if I have nightmare?' she asked. 'I *often* have nightmare, and then grannie takes me into her bed—I can't stay in the dark—it all gets 'whispery.' . . . What'll I do if I do?'

'You just go to sleep, child,' said Alice, pulling off her socks and whacking them against the bedrail, 'and don't you holler out and wake your poor pa.'

But the same old nightmare came—the butcher with a knife and a rope who grew nearer and nearer, smiling that dreadful smile, while she could not move, could only stand still, crying out, 'Grandma, grandma!' She woke shivering, to see father beside her bed, a candle in his hand.

'What's the matter?' he said.

'Oh, a butcher—a knife—I want grannie.' He blew out the candle, bent down and caught up the child in his arms, carrying her along the passage to the big bedroom. A newspaper was on the bed—a half-smoked cigar balanced against his reading-lamp. He pitched the paper on the floor, threw the cigar into the fire-place, then carefully tucked up the child.

103

He lay down beside her. Half asleep still, still with the butcher's smile all about her, it seemed she crept close to him, snuggled her head under his arm, held tightly to his pyjama jacket.

Then the dark did not matter; she lay still.

'Here, rub your feet against my legs and get them warm,' said father.

Tired out, he slept before the little girl. A funny feeling came over her. Poor father! Not so big, after all—and with no one to look after him . . . . He was harder than the grandmother, but it was a nice hardness . . . . And every day he had to work and was too tired to be a Mr. Macdonald . . . . She had torn up all his beautiful writing . . . . She stirred suddenly, and sighed.

'What's the matter?' asked father. 'Another dream?'

'Oh,' said the little girl, 'my head's on your heart; I can hear it going. What a big heart you've got, father dear.'

(1912)

That Woman

Sitting astride the bow window ledge, smelling the heliotrope—
or was it the sea?—half of Kezia was in the garden and half of
her in the room.

'Have you put down the Harcourts?'

'Yes, Mrs. Phil and Mrs. Charlie.'

'And the Fields?'

'Mrs. *and* the Misses Field.'

'And Rose Conway?'

'Yes, and that Melbourne girl staying with her.'

'Old Mrs. Grady?'

'Do you think—necessary?'

'My dear, she does so love a good cackle'

'Oh, but that way she has of dipping everything in her tea!
Iced chocolate cake and the ends of her feather boa dipped in
tea. . . .'

'How marvellously that ribbon has lasted, Harrie! Marvellously!'

That was Aunt Beryl's voice. She, Aunt Harrie and Mother
sat at the round table with big shallow teacups in front of
them.

In the dusky light, in their white puffed-up muslin blouses
with wing sleeves, they were three birds at the edge of a lily
pond. Beyond them the shadowy room melted into the shadow;
the gold picture frames were traced upon the air; the cut-glass
door-knob glittered; a song—a white butterfly with wings
outspread—clung to the ebony piano.

Aunt Harrie's plaintive, singing tones: 'It's very faded,
really, if you look into it. I don't think it can possibly stand
another ironing.'

'If I were rich,' said Aunt Beryl, 'with real money to spend—
not save' . . .

'What about—what about asking that Gibbs woman?'

'Linda!'

'How can you suggest such a thing!'

'Well, why not? She needn't come. But it must be so horrid not to be asked anywhere!'

'But, good heavens, whose fault is it? Who could ask her?'

'She's nobody but herself to blame.'

'She's simply flown in people's faces.'

'And it must be so particularly dreadful for Mr. Gibbs.'

'But Harrie, dear, he's dead.'

'Of course, Linda, that's just it. He must feel so helpless, looking down.'

Kezia heard her mother say: 'I never thought of that. Yes, that might be . . . very maddening!'

Aunt Beryl's cool little voice gushed up and overflowed: 'It's really nothing to laugh at, Linda. There are some things one really must draw the line at.'

(1916)

At the Bay

— happy world a fantasy as a child.

*I shall tackle something different—
a long story: At the Bay, with
more difficult relationships. That's
the whole problem.*

*It took me nearly a month to
'recover' from At the Bay. I
made at least three false starts. But
I could not get away from the
sound of the sea, and Beryl
fanning her hair at the window.
These things would not die down.*

I

Very early morning. The sun was not yet risen, and the whole
of Crescent Bay was hidden under a white sea-mist. The big
bush-covered hills at the back were smothered. You could not
see where they ended and the paddocks and bungalows began.
The sandy road was gone and the paddocks and bungalows
the other side of it; there were no white dunes covered with
reddish grass beyond them; there was nothing to mark which
was beach and where was the sea. A heavy dew had fallen.
The grass was blue. Big drops hung on the bushes and just did
not fall; the silvery, fluffy toi-toi was limp on its long stalks,
and all the marigolds and the pinks in the bungalow gardens
were bowed to the earth with wetness. Drenched were the cold
fuchsias, round pearls of dew lay on the flat nasturtium leaves.
It looked as though the sea had beaten up softly in the darkness, as though one immense wave had come rippling, rippling
—how far? Perhaps if you had waked up in the middle of the

107

night you might have seen a big fish flicking in at the window and gone again. . . .

Ah-Aah! sounded the sleepy sea. And from the bush there came the sound of little streams flowing, quickly, lightly, slipping between the smooth stones, gushing into ferny basins and out again; and there was the splashing of big drops on large leaves, and something else—what was it?—a faint stirring and shaking, the snapping of a twig and then such silence that it seemed someone was listening.

Round the corner of Crescent Bay, between the piled-up masses of broken rock, a flock of sheep came pattering. They were huddled together, a small, tossing, woolly mass, and their thin, stick-like legs trotted along quickly as if the cold and the quiet had frightened them. Behind them an old sheep-dog, his soaking paws covered with sand, ran along with his nose to the ground, but carelessly, as if thinking of something else. And then in the rocky gateway the shepherd himself appeared. He was a lean, upright old man, in a frieze coat that was covered with a web of tiny drops, velvet trousers tied under the knee, and a wideawake with a folded blue handkerchief round the brim. One hand was crammed into his belt, the other grasped a beautifully smooth yellow stick. And as he walked, taking his time, he kept up a very soft light whistling, an airy, far-away fluting that sounded mournful and tender. The old dog cut an ancient caper or two and then drew up sharp, ashamed of his levity, and walked a few dignified paces by his master's side. The sheep ran forward in little pattering rushes; they began to bleat, and ghostly flocks and herds answered them from under the sea. 'Baa! Baaa!' For a time they seemed to be always on the same piece of ground. There ahead was stretched the sandy road with shallow puddles; the same soaking bushes showed on either side the same shadowy palings. Then something immense came into view; an enormous shock-haired giant with his arms stretched out. It was the big gum tree outside Mrs. Stubbs's shop, and as they passed by there was a strong whiff of eucalyptus. And now big spots of light gleamed in the mist. The shepherd stopped whistling; he rubbed his red nose and wet beard on his wet sleeve and, screwing up his eyes, glanced in the direction of the sea. The sun was rising. It was marvellous how quickly the mist thinned, sped away, dissolved from the shallow plain, rolled up from the bush and was gone as if in a hurry to escape; big twists and curls jostled and shouldered each other as the silvery beams broadened. The far-away sky—a bright, pure blue—was reflected in the puddles, and the drops, swimming along the telegraph poles, flashed into points of light. Now the leaping, glittering sea was so bright it made one's eyes ache to look at it. The shepherd drew a pipe, the bowl as small as an acorn, out of his breast-pocket, fumbled for a chunk of speckled tobacco, pared off a few shavings and stuffed the bowl. He was a grave, fine-looking old man. As he lit up and the blue smoke wreathed his head, the dog, watching, looked proud of him.

'Baa! Baaa!' The sheep spread out into a fan. They were just clear of the summer colony before the first sleeper turned over and lifted a drowsy head; their cry sounded in the dreams of little children . . . who lifted their arms to drag down, to cuddle the darling little woolly lambs of sleep. Then the first inhabitant appeared; it was the Burnells' cat Florrie, sitting on the gatepost, far too early as usual, looking for their milk-girl. When she saw the old sheep-dog she sprang up quickly, arched her back, drew in her tabby head, and seemed to give a little fastidious shiver. 'Ugh! What a coarse, revolting creature!' said Florrie. But the old sheep-dog, not looking up, waggled past, flinging out his legs from side to side. Only one of his ears twitched to prove that he saw, and thought her a silly young female.

The breeze of morning lifted in the bush and the smell of leaves and wet black earth mingled with the sharp smell of the sea. Myriads of birds were singing. A goldfinch flew over the shepherd's head and, perching on the tiptop of a spray, it turned to the sun, ruffling its small breast feathers. And now they had passed the fisherman's hut, passed the charred-looking little *whare* where Leila the milk-girl lived with her old Gran. The sheep strayed over a yellow swamp and Wag, the sheep-dog, padded after, rounded them up and headed them for the steeper, narrower rocky pass that led out of Crescent Bay and towards Daylight Cove. 'Baa! Baaa!' Faint the cry came as they rocked along the fast-drying road. The shepherd put away his pipe, dropping it into his breast-pocket so that the little bowl hung over. And straightway the soft airy whistling began again. Wag ran out along a ledge of rock after something that smelled, and ran back again disgusted. Then pushing, nudging, hurrying, the sheep rounded the bend and the shepherd followed after out of sight.

II

A few moments later the back door of one of the bungalows opened, and a figure in a broad-striped bathing-suit flung down the paddock, cleared the stile, rushed through the tussock grass into the hollow, staggered up the sandy hillock, and raced for dear life over the big porous stones, over the cold, wet pebbles, on to the hard sand that gleamed like oil. Splish-Splosh! Splish-Splosh! The water bubbled round his legs as Stanley Burnell waded out exulting. First man in as usual! He'd beaten them all again. And he swooped down to souse his head and neck.

'Hail, brother! All hail, Thou Mighty One!' A velvety bass voice came booming over the water.

Great Scott! Damnation take it! Stanley lifted up to see a dark head bobbing far out and an arm lifted. It was Jonathan Trout—there before him! 'Glorious morning!' sang the voice.

'Yes, very fine!' said Stanley briefly. Why the dickens didn't the fellow stick to his part of the sea? Why should he come barging over to this exact spot? Stanley gave a kick, a lunge and struck out, swimming overarm. But Jonathan was a match for him. Up he came, his black hair sleek on his forehead, his short beard sleek.

'I had an extraordinary dream last night!' he shouted.

What was the matter with the man? This mania for conversation irritated Stanley beyond words. And it was always the same—always some piffle about a dream he'd had, or some cranky idea he'd got hold of, or some rot he'd been reading. Stanley turned over on his back and kicked with his legs till he was a living water-spout. But even then . . . 'I dreamed I was hanging over a terrifically high cliff, shouting to someone below.' You would be! thought Stanley. He could stick no more of it. He stopped splashing. 'Look here, Trout,' he said, 'I'm in rather a hurry this morning.'

'You're WHAT?' Jonathan was so surprised—or pretended to be—that he sank under the water, then reappeared again blowing.

'All I mean is,' said Stanley, 'I've no time to—to—to fool about. I want to get this over. I'm in a hurry. I've work to do this morning—see?'

Jonathan was gone before Stanley had finished. 'Pass, friend!' said the bass voice gently, and he slid away through the water with scarcely a ripple. . . . But curse the fellow! He'd ruined Stanley's bathe. What an unpractical idiot the man was! Stanley struck out to sea again, and then as quickly swam in again, and away he rushed up the beach. He felt cheated.

Jonathan stayed a little longer in the water. He floated, gently moving his hands like fins, and letting the sea rock his long, skinny body. It was curious, but in spite of everything he was fond of Stanley Burnell. True, he had a fiendish desire to tease him sometimes, to poke fun at him, but at bottom he was sorry for the fellow. There was something pathetic in his determination to make a job of everything. You couldn't help feeling he'd be caught out one day, and then what an almighty cropper he'd come! At that moment an immense wave lifted Jonathan, rode past him, and broke along the beach with a joyful sound. What a beauty! And now there came another. That was the way to live—carelessly, recklessly, spending one-self. He got on to his feet and began to wade towards the shore, pressing his toes into the firm, wrinkled sand. To take things easy, not to fight against the ebb and flow of life, but to give way to it—that was what was needed. It was this tension that was all wrong. To live—to live! And the perfect morning, so fresh and fair, basking in the light, as though laughing at its own beauty, seemed to whisper, 'Why not?'

But now he was out of the water Jonathan turned blue with cold. He ached all over; it was as though someone was wring-ing the blood out of him. And stalking up the beach, shivering, all his muscles tight, he too felt his bathe was spoilt. He'd stayed in too long.

III

Beryl was alone in the living-room when Stanley appeared, wearing a blue serge suit, a stiff collar and a spotted tie. He looked almost uncannily clean and brushed; he was going to town for the day. Dropping into his chair, he pulled out his watch and put it beside his plate.

'I've just got twenty-five minutes,' he said. 'You might go and see if the porridge is ready, Beryl?'

'Mother's just gone for it,' said Beryl. She sat down at the table and poured out his tea.

'Thanks!' Stanley took a sip. 'Hallo!' he said in an astonished voice, 'you've forgotten the sugar.'

'Oh, sorry!' But even then Beryl didn't help him; she pushed the basin across. What did this mean? As Stanley helped himself his blue eyes widened; they seemed to quiver. He shot a quick glance at his sister-in-law and leaned back.

'Nothing wrong, is there?' he asked carelessly, fingering his collar.

Beryl's head was bent; she turned her plate in her fingers.

'Nothing,' said her light voice. Then she too looked up, and smiled at Stanley. 'Why should there be?'

'O-oh! No reason at all as far as I know. I thought you seemed rather—'

At that moment the door opened and the three little girls appeared, each carrying a porridge plate. They were dressed alike in blue jerseys and knickers; their brown legs were bare, and each had her hair plaited and pinned up in what was called a horse's tail. Behind them came Mrs. Fairfield with the tray.

'Carefully, children,' she warned. But they were taking the very greatest care. They loved being allowed to carry things. 'Have you said good-morning to your father?'

'Yes, grandma.' They settled themselves on the bench opposite Stanley and Beryl.

'Good morning, Stanley!' Old Mrs. Fairfield gave him his plate.

'Morning, mother! How's the boy?'

'Splendid! He only woke up once last night. What a perfect morning!' The old woman paused, her hand on the loaf of bread, to gaze out of the open door into the garden. The sea sounded. Through the wide-open window streamed the sun on to the yellow varnished walls and bare floor. Everything on the table flashed and glittered. In the middle there was an old salad bowl filled with yellow and red nasturtiums. She smiled, and a look of deep content shone in her eyes.

'You might *cut* me a slice of that bread, mother,' said Stanley. 'I've only twelve and a half minutes before the coach passes. Has anyone given my shoes to the servant girl?'

'Yes, they're ready for you.' Mrs. Fairfield was quite unruffled.

'Oh, Kezia! Why are you such a messy child!' cried Beryl despairingly.

'Me, Aunt Beryl?' Kezia stared at her. What had she done now? She had only dug a river down the middle of her porridge, filled it, and was eating the banks away. But she did that every single morning, and no one had said a word up till now.

'Why can't you eat your food properly like Isabel and Lottie?' How unfair grown-ups are!

'But Lottie always makes a floating island, don't you, Lottie?'

'I don't,' said Isabel smartly. 'I just sprinkle mine with sugar and put on the milk and finish it. Only babies play with their food.'

Stanley pushed back his chair and got up.

'Would you get me those shoes, mother? And, Beryl, if you've finished, I wish you'd cut down to the gate and stop the coach. Run in to your mother, Isabel, and ask her where my bowler hat's been put. Wait a minute—have you children been playing with my stick?'

'No, father!'

'But I put it here,' Stanley began to bluster. 'I remember distinctly putting it in this corner. Now, who's had it? There's no time to lose. Look sharp! The stick's got to be found.'

Even Alice, the servant girl, was drawn into the chase. 'You haven't been using it to poke the kitchen fire with by any chance?'

Stanley dashed into the bedroom where Linda was lying. 'Most extraordinary thing. I can't keep a single possession to myself. They've made away with my stick, now!'

'Stick, dear? What stick?' Linda's vagueness on these occasions could not be real, Stanley decided. Would nobody sympathise with him?

'Coach! Coach, Stanley!' Beryl's voice cried from the gate.

Stanley waved his arm to Linda. 'No time to say good-bye!' he cried. And he meant that as a punishment to her.

He snatched his bowler hat, dashed out of the house, and swung down the garden path. Yes, the coach was there waiting, and Beryl, leaning over the open gate, was laughing up at somebody or other just as if nothing had happened. The heartlessness of women! The way they took it for granted it was your job to slave away for them while they didn't even take the trouble to see that your walking-stick wasn't lost. Kelly trailed his whip across the horses.

'Good-bye, Stanley,' called Beryl, sweetly and gaily. It was easy enough to say good-bye! And there she stood, idle, shading her eyes with her hand. The worst of it was Stanley had to shout good-bye too, for the sake of appearances. Then he saw her turn, give a little skip and run back to the house. She was glad to be rid of him!

Yes, she was thankful. Into the living-room she ran and called 'He's gone!' Linda cried from her room: 'Beryl! Has Stanley gone?' Old Mrs. Fairfield appeared, carrying the boy in his little flannel coatee.

'Gone?'

'Gone!'

Oh, the relief, the difference it made to have the man out of the house. Their very voices were changed as they called to one another; they sounded warm and loving and as if they shared a secret. Beryl went over to the table. 'Have another cup of tea, mother. It's still hot.' She wanted, somehow, to celebrate the fact that they could do what they liked now. There was no man to disturb them; the whole perfect day was theirs.

'No, thank you, child', said old Mrs. Fairfield, but the way at that moment she tossed the boy up and said 'a-goos-a-goos-a-ga!' to him meant that she felt the same. The little girls ran into the paddock like chickens let out of a coop.

Even Alice, the servant girl, washing up the dishes in the kitchen, caught the infection and used the precious tank water in a perfectly reckless fashion.

'Oh, these men!' said she, and she plunged the teapot into the bowl and held it under the water even after it had stopped bubbling, as if it too was a man and drowning was too good for them.

114

IV

'Wait for me, Isa-bel! Kezia, wait for me!'

There was poor little Lottie, left behind again, because she found it so fearfully hard to get over the stile by herself. When she stood on the first step her knees began to wobble; she grasped the post. Then you had to put one leg over. But which leg? She never could decide. And when she did finally put one leg over with a sort of stamp of despair—then the feeling was awful. She was half in the paddock still and half in the tussock grass. She clutched the post desperately and lifted up her voice. 'Wait for me!'

'No, don't you wait for her, Kezia!' said Isabel. 'She's such a little silly. She's always making a fuss. Come on!' And she tugged Kezia's jersey. 'You can use my bucket if you come with me,' she said kindly. 'It's bigger than yours.' But Kezia couldn't leave Lottie all by herself. She ran back to her. By this time Lottie was very red in the face and breathing heavily.

'Here, put your other foot over,' said Kezia.

'Where?'

Lottie looked down at Kezia as if from a mountain height.

'Here where my hand is.' Kezia patted the place.

'Oh, *there* do you mean?' Lottie gave a deep sigh and put the second foot over.

'Now—sort of turn round and sit down and slide,' said Kezia.

'But there's nothing to sit down *on*, Kezia,' said Lottie.

She managed it at last, and once it was over she shook herself and began to beam.

'I'm getting better at climbing over stiles, aren't I, Kezia?'

Lottie's was a very hopeful nature.

The pink and the blue sunbonnet followed Isabel's bright red sunbonnet up that sliding, slipping hill. At the top they paused to decide where to go and to have a good stare at who was there already. Seen from behind, standing against the sky-line, gesticulating largely with their spades, they looked like minute puzzled explorers.

The whole family of Samuel Josephs was there already with their lady-help, who sat on a camp-stool and kept order with a whistle that she wore tied round her neck, and a small cane with which she directed operations. The Samuel Josephs never played by themselves or managed their own game. If they did, it ended in the boys pouring water down the girls' necks or the girls trying to put little black crabs into the boys' pockets. So Mrs. S. J. and the poor lady-help drew up what she called a 'brogramme' every morning to keep them 'abused and out of bischief.' It was all competitions or races or round games. Everything began with a piercing blast of the lady-help's whistle and ended with another. There were even prizes—large, rather dirty paper parcels which the lady-help with a sour little smile drew out of a bulging string kit. The Samuel Josephs fought fearfully for the prizes and cheated and pinched one another's arms—they were all expert pinchers. The only time the Burnell children ever played with them Kezia had got a prize, and when she undid three bits of paper she found a very small rusty button-hook. She couldn't understand why they made such a fuss. . . .

But they never played with the Samuel Josephs now or even went to their parties. The Samuel Josephs were always giving children's parties at the Bay and there was always the same food. A big washhand basin of very brown fruit salad, buns cut into four and a washhand jug full of something the lady-help called 'Limmonadear.' And you went away in the evening with half the frill torn off your frock or something spilled all down the front of your openwork pinafore, leaving the Samuel Josephs leaping like savages on their lawn. No! They were too awful.

On the other side of the beach, close down to the water, two little boys, their knickers rolled up, twinkled like spiders. One was digging, the other pattered in and out of the water, filling a small bucket. They were the Trout boys, Pip and Rags. But Pip was so busy digging and Rags was so busy helping that they didn't see their little cousins until they were quite close.

'Look!' said Pip. 'Look what I've discovered.' And he showed them an old, wet, squashed-looking boot. The three little girls stared.

'Whatever are you going to do with it?' asked Kezia.

'Keep it, of course!' Pip was very scornful. 'It's a find—see?'

Yes, Kezia, saw that. All the same . . .

'There's lots of things buried in the sand,' explained Pip. 'They get chucked up from wrecks. Treasure. Why—you might find—'

'But why does Rags have to keep on pouring water in?' asked Lottie.

'Oh, that's to moisten it,' said Pip, 'to make the work a bit easier. Keep it up, Rags.'

And good little Rags ran up and down, pouring in the water that turned brown like cocoa.

'Here, shall I show you what I found yesterday?' said Pip mysteriously, and he stuck his spade into the sand. 'Promise not to tell.'

They promised.

'Say, cross my heart straight dinkum.'

The little girls said it.

Pip took something out of his pocket, rubbed it a long time on the front of his jersey, then breathed on it and rubbed it again.

'Now turn round!' he ordered.

They turned round.

'All look the same way! Keep still! Now!'

And his hand opened; he held up to the light something that flashed, that winked, that was a most lovely green.

'It's a nemeral,' said Pip solemnly.

'Is it really, Pip?' Even Isabel was impressed.

The lovely green thing seemed to dance in Pip's fingers. Aunt Beryl had a nemeral in a ring, but it was a very small one. This one was as big as a star and far more beautiful.

V

As the morning lengthened whole parties appeared over the sand-hills and came down on the beach to bathe. It was understood that at eleven o'clock the women and children of the summer colony had the sea to themselves. First the women undressed, pulled on their bathing dresses and covered their heads in hideous caps like sponge-bags; then the children were unbuttoned. The beach was strewn with little heaps of clothes and shoes; the big summer hats, with stones on them to keep them from blowing away, looked like immense shells. It was strange that even the sea seemed to sound differently when all those leaping, laughing figures ran into the waves. Old Mrs.

Fairfield, in a lilac cotton dress and a black hat tied under the chin, gathered her little brood and got them ready. The little Trout boys whipped their shirts over their heads, and away the five sped, while their grandma sat with one hand in her knitting-bag ready to draw out the ball of wool when she was satisfied they were safely in.

The firm compact little girls were not half so brave as the tender, delicate-looking little boys. Pips and Rags, shivering, crouching down, slapping the water, never hesitated. But Isabel, who could swim twelve strokes, and Kezia, who could nearly swim eight, only followed on the strict understanding they were not to be splashed. As for Lottie, she didn't follow at all. She liked to be left to go in her own way, please. And that way was to sit down at the edge of the water, her legs straight, her knees pressed together, and to make vague motions with her arms as if she expected to be wafted out to sea. But when a bigger wave than usual, an old whiskery one, came lolloping along in her direction, she scrambled to her feet with a face of horror and flew up the beach again.

'Here, mother, keep these for me, will you?'

Two rings and a thin gold chain were dropped into Mrs. Fairfield's lap.

'Yes, dear. But aren't you going to bathe here?'

'No-o,' Beryl drawled. She sounded vague. 'I'm undressing further along. I'm going to bathe with Mrs. Harry Kember.'

'Very well.' But Mrs. Fairfield's lips set. She disapproved of Mrs. Harry Kember. Beryl knew it.

Poor old mother, she smiled, as she skimmed over the stones. Poor old mother! Old! Oh, what joy, what bliss it was to be young . . . .

'You look very pleased,' said Mrs. Harry Kember. She sat hunched up on the stones, her arms round her knees, smoking.

'It's such a lovely day,' said Beryl, smiling down at her.

'Oh, my *dear*!' Mrs. Harry Kember's voice sounded as though she knew better than that. But then her voice always sounded as though she knew something more about you than you did yourself. She was a long, strange-looking woman with narrow hands and feet. Her face, too, was long and narrow and exhausted-looking; even her fair curled fringe looked burnt out and withered. She was the only woman at the Bay

118

who smoked, and she smoked incessantly, keeping the cigarette between her lips while she talked, and only taking it out when the ash was so long you could not understand why it did not fall. When she was not playing bridge—she played bridge every day of her life—she spent her time lying in the full glare of the sun. She could stand any amount of it; she never had enough. All the same, it did not seem to warm her. Parched, withered, cold, she lay stretched on the stones like a piece of tossed-up driftwood. The women at the Bay thought she was very, very fast. Her lack of vanity, her slang, the way she treated men as though she was one of them, and the fact that she didn't care twopence about her house and called the servant Gladys 'Glad-eyes,' was disgraceful. Standing on the veranda steps Mrs. Kember would call in her indifferent, tired voice, 'I say, Glad-eyes, you might heave me a handkerchief if I've got one, will you?' And Glad-eyes, a red bow in her hair instead of a cap, and white shoes, came running with an impudent smile. It was an absolute scandal! True, she had no children, and her husband . . . Here the voices were always raised; they became fervent. How can he have married her? How can he, how can he? It must have been money, of course, but even then!

Mrs. Kember's husband was at least ten years younger than she was, and so incredibly handsome that he looked like a mask or a most perfect illustration in an American novel rather than a man. Black hair, dark blue eyes, red lips, a slow sleepy smile, a fine tennis player, a perfect dancer, and with it all a mystery. Harry Kember was like a man walking in his sleep. Men couldn't stand him, they couldn't get a word out of the chap; he ignored his wife just as she ignored him. How did he live? Of course there were stories, but such stories! They simply couldn't be told. The women he'd been seen with, the places he'd been seen in . . . but nothing was ever certain, nothing definite. Some of the women at the Bay privately thought he'd commit a murder one day. Yes, even while they talked to Mrs Kember and took in the awful concoction she was wearing, they saw her, stretched as she lay on the beach; but cold, bloody, and still with a cigarette stuck in the corner of her mouth.

Mrs. Kember rose, yawned, unsnapped her belt buckle, and tugged at the tape of her blouse. And Beryl stepped out of her skirt and shed her jersey, and stood up in her short white petticoat, and her camisole with ribbon bows on the shoulders.

'Mercy on us,' said Mrs. Harry Kember, 'what a little beauty you are!'

'Don't!' said Beryl softly; but, drawing off one stocking and then the other, she felt a little beauty.

'My dear—why not?' said Mrs. Harry Kember, stamping on her own petticoat. Really—her underclothes! A pair of blue cotton knickers and a linen bodice that reminded one somehow of a pillow-case. . . . 'And you don't wear stays, do you?' She touched Beryl's waist, and Beryl sprang away with a small affected cry. Then 'Never!' she said firmly.

'Lucky little creature,' sighed Mrs. Kember, unfastening her own.

Beryl turned her back and began the complicated movements of someone who is trying to take off her clothes and to pull on her bathing-dress all at one and the same time.

'Oh, my dear—don't mind me,' said Mrs. Harry Kember. 'Why be shy? I shan't eat you. I shan't be shocked like those other ninnies.' And she gave her strange neighing laugh and grimaced at the other women.

But Beryl was shy. She never undressed in front of anybody. Was that silly? Mrs. Harry Kember made her feel it was silly, even something to be ashamed of. Why be shy indeed! She glanced quickly at her friend standing so boldly in her torn chemise and lighting a fresh cigarette; and a quick, bold, evil feeling started up in her breast. Laughing recklessly, she drew on the limp, sandy-feeling bathing-dress that was not quite dry and fastened the twisted buttons.

'That's better,' said Mrs. Harry Kember. They began to go down the beach together. 'Really, it's a sin for you to wear clothes, my dear. Somebody's got to tell you some day.'

The water was quite warm. It was that marvellous transparent blue, flecked with silver, but the sand at the bottom looked gold; when you kicked with your toes there rose a little puff of gold-dust. Now the waves just reached her breast. Beryl stood, her arms outstretched, gazing out, and as each wave came she gave the slightest little jump, so that it seemed it was the wave which lifted her so gently.

'I believe in pretty girls having a good time,' said Mrs. Harry Kember. 'Why not? Don't you make a mistake, my dear. Enjoy yourself.' And suddenly she turned turtle, dis-

appeared, and swam away quickly, quickly, like a rat. Then she
flicked round and began swimming back. She was going
to say something else. Beryl felt that she was being poisoned
by this cold woman, but she longed to hear. But oh, how
strange, how horrible! As Mrs. Harry Kember came up close
she looked, in her black waterproof bathing-cap, with her
sleepy face lifted above the water, just her chin touching, like
a horrible caricature of her husband.

VI

In a steamer chair, under a manuka tree that grew in the
middle of the front grass patch, Linda Burnell dreamed the
morning away. She did nothing. She looked up at the dark,
close, dry leaves of the manuka, at the chinks of blue between,
and now and again a tiny yellowish flower dropped on her.
Pretty—yes, if you held one of those flowers on the palm of
your hand and looked at it closely, it was an exquisite small
thing. Each pale yellow petal shone as if each was the careful
work of a loving hand. The tiny tongue in the centre gave it
the shape of a bell. And when you turned it over the outside
was a deep bronze colour. But as soon as they flowered, they
fell and were scattered. You brushed them off your frock as you
talked; the horrid little things got caught in one's hair. Why,
then, flower at all? Who takes the trouble—or the joy—to make
all these things that are wasted, wasted . . . . It was uncanny.

On the grass beside her, lying between two pillows, was the
boy. Sound asleep he lay, his head turned away from his
mother. His fine dark hair looked more like a shadow than like
real hair, but his ear was a bright, deep coral. Linda clasped
her hands above her head and crossed her feet. It was very
pleasant to know that all these bungalows were empty, that
everybody was down on the beach, out of sight, out of hearing.
She had the garden to herself; she was alone.

Dazzling white the picotees shone; the golden-eyed marigolds glittered; the nasturtiums wreathed the veranda poles
in green and gold flame. If only one had time to look at these
flowers long enough, time to get over the sense of novelty and
strangeness, time to know them! But as soon as one paused to

part the petals, to discover the under-side of the leaf, along came Life and one was swept away. And, lying in her cane chair, Linda felt so light; she felt like a leaf. Along came Life like a wind and she was seized and shaken; she had to go. Oh dear, would it always be so? Was there no escape?

. . . Now she sat on the veranda of their Tasmanian home, leaning against her father's knee. And he promised, 'As soon as you and I are old enough, Linny, we'll cut off somewhere, we'll escape. Two boys together. I have a fancy I'd like to sail up a river in China.' Linda saw that river, very wide, covered with little rafts and boats. She saw the yellow hats of the boatmen and she heard their high, thin voices as they called . . .

'Yes, papa.'

But just then a very broad young man with bright ginger hair walked slowly past their house, and slowly, solemnly even, uncovered. Linda's father pulled her ear teasingly, in the way he had.

'Linny's beau,' he whispered.

'Oh, papa, fancy being married to Stanley Burnell!'

Well, she was married to him. And what was more she loved him. Not the Stanley whom everyone saw, not the everyday one; but a timid, sensitive, innocent Stanley who knelt down every night to say his prayers, and who longed to be good. Stanley was simple. If he believed in people—as he believed in her, for instance—it was with his whole heart. He could not be disloyal; he could not tell a lie. And how terribly he suffered if he thought anyone—she—was not being dead straight, dead sincere with him! 'This is too subtle for me!' He flung out the words, but his open, quivering, distraught look was like the look of a trapped beast.

But the trouble was—here Linda felt almost inclined to laugh, though heaven knows it was no laughing matter—she saw *her* Stanley so seldom. There were glimpses, moments, breathing spaces of calm, but all the rest of the time it was like living in a house that couldn't be cured of the habit of catching fire, or a ship that got wrecked every day. And it was always Stanley who was in the thick of the danger. Her whole time was spent in rescuing him, and restoring him, and calming him down, and listening to his story. And what was left of her time was spent in the dread of having children.

Linda frowned; she sat up quickly in her steamer chair and clasped her ankles. Yes, that was her real grudge against life; that was what she could not understand. That was the question she asked and asked, and listened in vain for the answer. It was all very well to say it was the common lot of women to bear children. It wasn't true. She, for one, could prove that wrong. She was broken, made weak, her courage was gone, through child-bearing. And what made it doubly hard to bear was, she did not love her children. It was useless pretending. Even if she had had the strength she never would have nursed and played with the little girls. No, it was as though a cold breath had chilled her through and through on each of those awful journeys; she had no warmth left to give them. As to the boy —well, thank heaven, mother had taken him; he was mother's, or Beryl's, or anybody's who wanted him. She had hardly held him in her arms. She was so indifferent about him, that as he lay there . . . Linda glanced down.

The boy had turned over. He lay facing her, and he was no longer asleep. His dark-blue, baby eyes were open; he looked as though he was peeping at his mother. And suddenly his face dimpled; it broke into a wide, toothless smile, a perfect beam, no less.

'I'm here!' that happy smile seemed to say. 'Why don't you like me?'

There was something so quaint, so unexpected about that smile that Linda smiled herself. But she checked herself and said to the boy coldly, 'I don't like babies.'

'Don't like babies?' The boy couldn't believe her. 'Don't like *me*?' He waved his arms foolishly at his mother.

Linda dropped off her chair on to the grass.

'Why do you keep on smiling?' she said severely. 'If you knew what I was thinking about, you wouldn't.'

But he only squeezed up his eyes, slyly, and rolled his head on the pillow. He didn't believe a word she said.

'We know all about that!' smiled the boy.

Linda was so astonished at the confidence of this little creature. . . . Ah no, be sincere. That was not what she felt; it was something far different, it was something so new, so . . . The tears danced in her eyes; she breathed in a small whisper to the boy, 'Hallo, my funny!'

But by now the boy had forgotten his mother. He was

serious again. Something pink, something soft waved in front
of him. He made a grab at it and it immediately disappeared.
But when he lay back, another, like the first, appeared. This
time he determined to catch it. He made a tremendous effort
and rolled right over.

VII

The tide was out; the beach was deserted; lazily flopped
the warm sea. The sun beat down, beat down hot and fiery on
the fine sand, baking the grey and blue and black and white-
veined pebbles. It sucked up the little drop of water that lay in
the hollow of the curved shells; it bleached the pink convolvulus
that threaded through and through the sand-hills. Nothing
seemed to move but the small sand-hoppers. Pit-pit-pit!
They were never still.

Over there on the weed-hung rocks that looked at low tide
like shaggy beasts come down to the water to drink, the sunlight seemed to spin like a silver coin dropped into each of the
small rock pools. They danced, they quivered, and minute
ripples laved the porous shores. Looking down, bending over,
each pool was like a lake with pink and blue houses clustered
on the shores; and oh! the vast mountainous country behind
those houses—the ravines, the passes, the dangerous creeks
and fearful tracks that led to the water's edge. Underneath
waved the sea-forest—pink thread-like trees, velvet anemones,
and orange berry-spotted weeds. Now a stone on the bottom
moved, rocked, and there was a glimpse of a black feeler;
now a thread-like creature wavered by and was lost. Something
was happening to the pink, waving trees; they were changing
to a cold moonlight blue. And now there sounded the faintest
'plop.' Who made that sound? What was going on down there?
And how strong, how damp the seaweed smelt in the hot
sun. . . .

The green blinds were drawn in the bungalows of the
summer colony. Over the verandas, prone on the paddock,
flung over the fences, there were exhausted-looking bathing-
dresses and rough striped towels. Each back window seemed to
have a pair of sand-shoes on the sill and some lumps of rock or a

bucket or a collection of pawa shells. The bush quivered in a haze of heat; the sandy road was empty except for the Trouts' dog Snooker, who lay stretched in the very middle of it. His blue eye was turned up, his legs stuck out stiffly, and he gave an occasional desperate sounding puff, as much as to say he had decided to make an end of it and was only waiting for some kind cart to come along.

'What are you looking at, my grandma? Why do you keep stopping and sort of staring at the wall?'

Kezia and her grandmother were taking their siesta together. The little girl, wearing only her short drawers and her under-bodice, her arms and legs bare, lay on one of the puffed-up pillows of her grandma's bed, and the old woman, in a white ruffled dressing-gown, sat in a rocker at the window, with a long piece of pink knitting in her lap. This room that they shared, like the other rooms of the bungalow, was of light varnished wood and the floor was bare. The furniture was of the shabbiest, the simplest. The dressing-table, for instance, was a packing-case in a sprigged muslin petticoat, and the mirror above was very strange; it was as though a little piece of forked lightning was imprisoned in it. On the table there stood a jar of sea-pinks, pressed so tightly together they looked more like a velvet pin-cushion, and a special shell which Kezia had given her grandma for a pin-tray, and another even more special which she had thought would make a very nice place for a watch to curl up in.

'Tell me, grandma,' said Kezia.

The old woman sighed, whipped the wool twice round her thumb, and drew the bone needle through. She was casting on.

'I was thinking of your Uncle William, darling,' she said quietly.

'My Australian Uncle William?' said Kezia. She had another.

'Yes, of course.'

'The one I never saw?'

'That was the one.'

'Well, what happened to him?' Kezia knew perfectly well, but she wanted to be told again.

'He went to the mines, and he got sunstroke there and died,' said old Mrs. Fairfield.

Kezia blinked and considered the picture again. . . . A little

125

man fallen over like a tin soldier by the side of a big black
hole.

'Does it make you sad to think about him, grandma?'
She hated her grandma to be sad.

It was the old woman's turn to consider. Did it make her
sad? To look back, back. To stare down the years, as Kezia
had seen her doing. To look after *them* as a woman does, long
after *they* were out of sight. Did it make her sad? No, life
was like that.

'No, Kezia.'

'But why?' asked Kezia. She lifted one bare arm and
began to draw things in the air. 'Why did Uncle William
have to die? He wasn't old.'

Mrs. Fairfield began counting the stitches in threes. 'It
just happened,' she said in an absorbed voice.

'Does everybody have to die?' asked Kezia.

'Everybody!'

'*Me?*' Kezia sounded fearfully incredulous.

'Some day, my darling.'

'But, grandma.' Kezia waved her left leg and waggled the
toes. They felt sandy. 'What if I just won't?'

The old woman sighed again and drew a long thread from
the ball.

'We're not asked, Kezia,' she said sadly. 'It happens to
all of us sooner or later.'

Kezia lay still thinking this over. She didn't want to die.
It meant she would have to leave here, leave everywhere, for
ever, leave—leave her grandma. She rolled over quickly.

'Grandma,' she said in a startled voice.

'What, my pet!'

'*You're* not to die.' Kezia was very decided.

'Ah, Kezia'—her grandma looked up and smiled and shook
her head—'don't let's talk about it.'

'But you're not to. You couldn't leave me. You couldn't
not be there.' This was awful. 'Promise me you won't ever
do it, grandma,' pleaded Kezia.

The old woman went on knitting.

'Promise me! Say never!'

But still her grandma was silent.

Kezia rolled off the bed; she couldn't bear it any longer, and
lightly she leapt on to her grandma's knees, clasped her hands

round the old woman's throat and began kissing her, under the chin, behind the ear, and blowing down her neck.

'Say never . . . say never . . . say never—' she gasped between the kisses. And then she began, very softly and lightly, to tickle her grandma.

'Kezia!' The old woman dropped her knitting. She swung back in the rocker. She began to tickle Kezia. 'Say never, say never, say never,' gurgled Kezia, while they lay there laughing in each other's arms. 'Come, that's enough, my squirrel! That's enough, my wild pony!' said old Mrs. Fairfield, setting her cap straight. 'Pick up my knitting.'

Both of them had forgotten what the 'never' was about.

VIII

The sun was still full on the garden when the back door of the Burnells' shut with a bang and a very gay figure walked down the path to the gate. It was Alice, the servant girl, dressed for her afternoon out. She wore a white cotton dress with such large red spots on it, and so many that they made you shudder, white shoes and a leghorn turned up under the brim with poppies. Of course she wore gloves, white ones, stained at the fastenings with iron-mould, and in one hand she carried a very dashed-looking sunshade which she referred to as her *perishall*.

Beryl, sitting in the window, fanning her freshly washed hair, thought she had never seen such a guy. If Alice had only blacked her face with a piece of cork before she started out the picture would have been complete. And where did a girl like that go to in a place like this? The heart-shaped Fijian fan beat scornfully at that lovely bright mane. She supposed Alice had picked up some horrible common larrikin and they'd go off into the bush together. Pity to make herself so conspicuous; they'd have hard work to hide with Alice in that rig-out.

But no, Beryl was unfair. Alice was going to tea with Mrs. Stubbs, who'd sent her an 'invite' by the little boy who called for orders. She had taken ever such a liking to Mrs. Stubbs ever since the first time she went to the shop to get something for her mosquitoes.

'Dear heart!' Mrs. Stubbs had clapped her hand to her side. 'I never seen anyone so eaten. You might have been attacked by canningbals.'

Alice did wish there'd been a bit of life on the road though. Made her feel so queer, having nobody behind her. Made her feel all weak in the spine. She couldn't believe that someone wasn't watching her. And yet it was silly to turn round; it gave you away. She pulled up her gloves, hummed to herself and said to the distant gum tree, 'Shan't be long now.' But that was hardly company.

Mrs. Stubbs's shop was perched on a little hillock just off the road. It had two big windows for eyes, a broad veranda for a hat, and the sign on the roof, scrawled MRS. STUBBS'S was like a little card stuck rakishly in the hat crown.

On the veranda there hung a long string of bathing-dresses, clinging together as though they'd just been rescued from the sea rather than waiting to go in, and beside them there hung a cluster of sand-shoes so extraordinarily mixed that to get at one pair you had to tear apart and forcibly separate at least fifty. Even then it was the rarest thing to find the left that belonged to the right. So many people had lost patience and gone off with one shoe that fitted and one that was a little too big. ... Mrs. Stubbs prided herself on keeping something of everything. The two windows, arranged in the form of precarious pyramids, were crammed so tight, piled so high, that it seemed only a conjuror could prevent them from toppling over. In the left-hand corner of one window, glued to the pane by four gelatine lozenges, there was—and there had been from time immemorial—a notice:

> LOST! HANSOME GOLE BROOCH
> SOLID GOLD
> ON OR NEAR BEACH
> REWARD OFFERED

Alice pressed open the door. The bell jangled, the red serge curtains parted, and Mrs. Stubbs appeared. With her broad smile and the long bacon knife in her hand she looked like a friendly brigand. Alice was welcomed so warmly that she found it quite difficult to keep up her 'manners.' They consisted of persistent little coughs and hems, pulls at her gloves, tweaks at her skirt, and a curious difficulty in seeing what was set before her or understanding what was said.

Tea was laid on the parlour table—ham, sardines, a whole pound of butter, and such a large johnny cake that it looked like an advertisement for somebody's baking powder. But the Primus stove roared so loudly that it was useless to try to talk above it. Alice sat down on the edge of a basket-chair while Mrs. Stubbs pumped the stove still higher. Suddenly Mrs. Stubbs whipped the cushion off a chair and disclosed a large brown paper parcel.

'I've just had some new photers taken, my dear,' she shouted cheerfully to Alice. 'Tell me what you think of them.'

In a very dainty, refined way Alice wet her finger and put the tissue back from the first one. Life! How many there were! There were three dozzing at least. And she held hers up to the light.

Mrs. Stubbs sat in an arm-chair, leaning very much to one side. There was a look of mild astonishment on her large face, and well there might be. For though the arm-chair stood on a carpet, to the left of it, miraculously skirting the carpet border, there was a dashing waterfall. On her right stood a Grecian pillar with a giant fern tree on either side of it, and in the background towered a gaunt mountain, pale with snow.

'It is a nice style, isn't it?' shouted Mrs. Stubbs; and Alice had just screamed 'Sweetly' when the roaring of the Primus stove died down, fizzled out, ceased, and she said 'Pretty' in a silence that was frightening.

'Draw up your chair, my dear,' said Mrs. Stubbs, beginning to pour out. 'Yes,' she said thoughtfully, as she handed the tea, 'but I don't care about the size. I'm having an enlargemint. All very well for Christmas cards, but I never was the one for small photers myself. You get no comfort out of them. To say the truth, I find them dis'eartening.'

Alice quite saw what she meant.

'Size,' said Mrs. Stubbs. 'Give me size. That was what my poor dear husband was always saying. He couldn't stand anything small. Gave him the creeps. And, strange as it may seem, my dear'—here Mrs. Stubbs creaked and seemed to expand herself at the memory—'it was dropsy that carried him off at the larst. Many's the time they drawn one and a half pints from 'im at the 'ospital. . . . It seemed like a judgmint.'

Alice burned to know exactly what it was that was drawn from him. She ventured, 'I suppose it was water.'

But Mrs. Stubbs fixed Alice with her eyes and replied meaningly, 'It was *liquid*, my dear.'

Liquid! Alice jumped away from the word like a cat and came back to it, nosing and wary.

'That's 'im!' said Mrs. Stubbs, and she pointed dramatically to the life-size head and shoulders of a burly man with a dead white rose in the button-hole of his coat that made you think of a curl of cold mutton fat. Just below, in silver letters on a red cardboard ground, were the words, 'Be not afraid, it is I.'

'It's ever such a fine face,' said Alice faintly.

The pale-blue bow on the top of Mrs. Stubbs's fair frizzy hair quivered. She arched her plump neck. What a neck she had! It was bright pink where it began and then it changed to warm apricot, and that faded to the colour of a brown egg and then to a deep creamy.

'All the same, my dear,' she said surprisingly, 'freedom's best!' Her soft, fat chuckle sounded like a purr. 'Freedom's best,' said Mrs. Stubbs again.

Freedom! Alice gave a loud, silly little titter. She felt awkward. Her mind flew back to her own kitching. Ever so queer! She wanted to be back in it again.

IX

A strange company assembled in the Burnells' washhouse after tea. Round the table there sat a bull, a rooster, a donkey that kept forgetting it was a donkey, a sheep and a bee. The washhouse was the perfect place for such a meeting because they could make as much noise as they liked and nobody ever interrupted. It was a small tin shed standing apart from the bungalow. Against the wall there was a deep trough and in the corner a copper with a basket of clothes-pegs on top of it. The little window, spun over with cobwebs, had a piece of candle and a mouse-trap on the dusty sill. There were clothes-lines criss-crossed overhead and, hanging from a peg on the wall, a very big, a huge, rusty horseshoe. The table was in the middle with a form at either side.

'You can't be a bee, Kezia. A bee's not an animal. It's a ninseck.'

'Oh, but I do want to be a bee frightfully,' wailed Kezia. . . . A tiny bee, all yellow-furry, with striped legs. She drew her legs up under her and leaned over the table. She felt she was a bee.

'A ninsek must be an animal,' she said stoutly. 'It makes a noise. It's not like a fish.'

'I'm a bull, I'm a bull!' cried Pip. And he gave such a tremendous bellow—how did he make that noise?—that Lottie looked quite alarmed.

'I'll be a sheep,' said little Rags. 'A whole lot of sheep went past this morning.'

'How do you know?'

'Dad heard them. Baa!' He sounded like the little lamb that trots behind and seems to wait to be carried.

'Cock-a-doodle-do!' shrilled Isabel. With her red cheeks and bright eyes she looked like a rooster.

'What'll I be?' Lottie asked everybody, and she sat there smiling, waiting for them to decide for her. It had to be an easy one.

'Be a donkey, Lottie.' It was Kezia's suggestion. 'Hee-haw! You can't forget that.'

'Hee-haw!' said Lottie solemnly. 'When do I have to say it?'

'I'll explain, I'll explain,' said the bull. It was he who had the cards. He waved them round his head. 'All be quiet! All listen!' And he waited for them. 'Look here, Lottie.' He turned up a card. 'It's got two spots on it—see? Now, if you put that card in the middle and somebody else has one with two spots as well, you say 'Hee-haw,' and the card's yours.'

'Mine?' Lottie was round-eyed. 'To keep?'

'No, silly. Just for the game, see? Just while we're playing.' The bull was very cross with her.

'Oh, Lottie, you *are* a little silly,' said the proud rooster.

Lottie looked at both of them. Then she hung her head; her lip quivered. 'I don't not want to play,' she whispered. The others glanced at one another like conspirators. All of them knew what that meant. She would go away and be discovered somewhere standing with her pinny thrown over

131

her head, in a corner, or against a wall, or even behind a chair.

'Yes, you *do*, Lottie. It's quite easy,' said Kezia.

And Isabel, repentant, said exactly like a grown-up, 'Watch *me* Lottie, and you'll soon learn.'

'Cheer up, Lot,' said Pip. 'There, I know what I'll do. I'll give you the first one. It's mine, really, but I'll give it to you. Here you are.' And he slammed the card down in front of Lottie.

Lottie revived at that. But now she was in another difficulty. 'I haven't got a hanky,' she said; 'I want one badly, too.'

'Here, Lottie, you can use mine.' Rags dipped into his sailor blouse and brought up a very wet-looking one, knotted together. 'Be very careful,' he warned her. 'Only use that corner. Don't undo it. I've got a little star-fish inside I'm going to try and tame.'

'Oh, come on, you girls,' said the bull. 'And mind—you're not to look at your cards. You've got to keep your hands under the table till I say "Go." '

Smack went the cards round the table. They tried with all their might to see, but Pip was too quick for them. It was very exciting, sitting there in the washhouse; it was all they could do not to burst into a little chorus of animals before Pip had finished dealing.

'Now, Lottie, you begin.'

Timidly Lottie stretched out a hand, took the top card off her pack, had a good look at it—it was plain she was counting the spots—and put it down.

'No, Lottie, you can't do that. You mustn't look first. You must turn it the other way over.'

'But then everybody will see it the same time as me,' said Lottie.

The game proceeded. Mooe-ooo-er! The bull was terrible. He charged over the table and seemed to eat the cards up.

Bss-ss! said the bee.

Cock-a-doodle-do! Isabel stood up in her excitement and moved her elbows like wings.

Baa! Little Rags put down the King of Diamonds and Lottie put down the one they called the King of Spain. She had hardly any cards left.

'Why don't you call out, Lottie?'

'I've forgotten what I am,' said the donkey woefully.

'Well, change! Be a dog instead! Bow-wow!'

'Oh yes. That's *much* easier.' Lottie smiled again. But when she and Kezia both had one Kezia waited on purpose. The others made signs to Lottie and pointed. Lottie turned very red; she looked bewildered, and at last she said, "Hee-haw! Ke-zia.'

'Ss! Wait a minute!' They were in the very thick of it when the bull stopped them, holding up his hand. 'What's that? What's that noise?'

'What noise? What do you mean?' asked the rooster.

'Ss! Shut up! Listen!' They were mouse-still. 'I thought I heard a—a sort of knocking,' said the bull.

'What was it like?' asked the sheep faintly.

No answer.

The bee gave a shudder. 'Whatever did we shut the door for?' she said softly. Oh, why, why had they shut the door?

While they were playing, the day had faded; the gorgeous sunset had blazed and died. And now the quick dark came racing over the sea, over the sand-hills, up the paddock. You were frightened to look in the corners of the washhouse, and yet you had to look with all your might. And somewhere, far away, grandma was lighting a lamp. The blinds were being pulled down; the kitchen fire leapt in the tins on the mantlepiece.

'It would be awful now,' said the bull, 'if a spider was to fall from the ceiling on to the table, wouldn't it?'

'Spiders don't fall from ceilings.'

'Yes, they do. Our Min told us she'd seen a spider as big as a saucer, with long hairs on it like a gooseberry."

Quickly all the little heads were jerked up; all the little bodies drew together, pressed together.

'Why doesn't somebody come and call us?' cried the rooster.

Oh, those grown-ups, laughing and snug, sitting in the lamp-light, drinking out of cups! They'd forgotten about them. No, not really forgotten. That was what their smile meant. They had decided to leave them there all by themselves.

Suddenly Lottie gave such a piercing scream that all of them jumped off the forms, all of them screamed too. 'A face—a face looking!' shrieked Lottie.

It was true, it was real. Pressed against the window was a pale face, black eyes, a black beard.

'Grandma! Mother! Somebody!'

But they had not got to the door, tumbling over one another, before it opened for Uncle Jonathan. He had come to take the little boys home.

X

He had meant to be there before, but in the front garden he had come upon Linda walking up and down the grass, stopping to pick off a dead pink or give a top-heavy carnation something to lean against, or to take a deep breath of something, and then walking on again, with her little air of remoteness. Over her white frock she wore a yellow, pink-fringed shawl from the Chinaman's shop.

'Hallo, Jonathan!' called Linda. And Jonathan whipped off his shabby panama, pressed it against his breast, dropped on one knee, and kissed Linda's hand.

'Greeting, my Fair One! Greeting, my Celestial Peach Blossom!' boomed the bass voice gently. 'Where are the other noble dames?'

"Beryl's out playing bridge and mother's giving the boy his bath. . . . Have you come to borrow something?'

The Trouts were for ever running out of things and sending across to the Burnells' at the last moment.

But Jonathan only answered, 'A little love, a little kindness'; and he walked by his sister-in-law's side.

Linda dropped into Beryl's hammock under the manuka tree and Jonathan stretched himself on the grass beside her, pulled a long stalk and began chewing it. They knew each other well. The voices of children cried from the other gardens. A fisherman's light cart shook along the sandy road, and from far away they heard a dog barking; it was muffled as though the dog had its head in a sack. If you listened you could just hear the soft swish of the sea at full tide sweeping the pebbles. The sun was sinking.

'And so you go back to the office on Monday, do you, Jonathan?' asked Linda.

'On Monday the cage door opens and clangs to upon the victim for another eleven months and a week,' answered Jonathan.

134

Linda swung a little. 'It must be awful,' she said slowly.

'Would ye have me laugh, my fair sister? Would ye have me weep?'

Linda was so accustomed to Jonathan's way of talking that she paid no attention to it.

'I suppose,' she said vaguely, 'one gets used to it. One gets used to anything.'

'Does one? Hum!' The 'Hum' was so deep it seemed to boom from underneath the ground. 'I wonder how it's done,' brooded Jonathan; 'I've never managed it.'

Looking at him as he lay there, Linda thought again how attractive he was. It was strange to think that he was only an ordinary clerk, that Stanley earned twice as much money as he. What was the matter with Jonathan? He had no ambition; she supposed that was it. And yet one felt he was gifted, exceptional. He was passionately fond of music; every spare penny he had went on books. He was always full of new ideas, schemes, plans. But nothing came of it all. The new fire blazed in Jonathan; you almost heard it roaring softly as he explained, described and dilated on the new thing; but a moment later it had fallen in and there was nothing but ashes, and Jonathan went about with a look like hunger in his black eyes. At these times he exaggerated his absurd manner of speaking, and he sang in church—he was the leader of the choir—with such fearful dramatic intensity that the meanest hymn put on an unholy splendour.

'It seems to me just as imbecile, just as infernal, to have to go to the office on Monday,' said Jonathan, 'as it always has done and always will do. To spend all the best years of one's life sitting on a stool from nine to five, scratching in somebody's ledger! It's a queer use to make of one's . . . one and only life, isn't it? Or do I fondly dream?' He rolled over on the grass and looked up at Linda. 'Tell me, what is the difference between my life and that of an ordinary prisoner. The only difference I can see is that I put myself in jail and nobody's ever going to let me out. That's a more intolerable situation than the other. For if I'd been—pushed in, against my will— kicking, even—once the door was locked, or at any rate in five years or so, I might have accepted the fact and begun to take an interest in the flight of flies or counting the warder's steps along the passage with particular attention to variations of tread and so on. But as it is, I'm like an insect that's flown into a room of its own accord. I dash against the walls, dash against the windows, flop against the ceiling, do everything on God's earth, in fact, except fly out again. And all the while I'm thinking, like that moth, or that butterfly, or whatever it is, 'The shortness of life! The shortness of life!' I've only one night or one day, and there's this vast dangerous garden, waiting out there, undiscovered, unexplored.'

'But, if you feel like that, why—' began Linda quickly.

'*Ah!*' cried Jonathan. And that 'Ah!' was somehow almost exultant. 'There you have me. Why? Why indeed? There's the maddening, mysterious question. Why don't I fly out again? There's the window or the door or whatever it was I came in by. It's not hopelessly shut—is it? Why don't I find it and be off? Answer me that, little sister.' But he gave her no time to answer.

'I'm exactly like that insect again. For some reason'— Jonathan paused between the words—'it's not allowed, it's forbidden, it's against the insect law, to stop banging and flop-ping and crawling up the pane even for an instant. Why don't I leave the office? Why don't I seriously consider, this moment, for instance, what it is that prevents me leaving? It's not as though I'm tremendously tied. I've two boys to provide for, but, after all, they're boys. I could cut off to sea, or get a job up-country, or—' Suddenly he smiled at Linda and said in a changed voice, as if he were confiding a secret, 'Weak . . . weak. No stamina. No anchor. No guiding principle, let us call it.' But then the dark velvety voice rolled out:

> Would ye hear the story
> How it unfolds itself . . .

and they were silent.

The sun had set. In the western sky there were great masses of crushed-up rose-coloured clouds. Broad beams of light shone through the clouds and beyond them as if they would cover the whole sky. Overhead the blue faded; it turned a pale gold, and the bush outlined against it gleamed dark and brilliant like metal. Sometimes when those beams of light show in the sky they are very awful. They remind you that up there sits Jehovah, the jealous God, the Almighty, Whose eye is upon you, ever watchful, never weary. You remember that at

His coming the whole earth will shake into one ruined grave-
yard; the cold, bright angels will drive you this way and that,
and there will be no time to explain what could be explained so
simply. . . . But to-night it seemed to Linda there was something infinitely joyful and loving in those silver beams. And
now no sound came from the sea. It breathed softly as if it
would draw that tender, joyful beauty into its own bosom.

'It's all wrong, it's all wrong,' came the shadowy voice of
Jonathan. 'It's not the scene, it's not the setting for . . . three
stools, three desks, three inkpots and a wire blind.'

Linda knew that he would never change, but she said, 'Is it
too late, even now?'

'I'm old—I'm old,' intoned Jonathan. He bent towards her,
he passed his hand over his head. 'Look!' His black hair
was speckled all over with silver, like the breast plumage of a
black fowl.

Linda was surprised. She had no idea that he was grey.
And yet, as he stood up beside her and sighed and stretched,
she saw him, for the first time, not resolute, not gallant, not
careless, but touched already with age. He looked very tall
on the darkening grass, and the thought crossed her mind,
'He is like a weed.'

Jonathan stooped again and kissed her fingers.

'Heaven reward thy sweet patience, lady mine,' he murmured. 'I must go seek those heirs to my fame and fortune. . . .'
He was gone.

XI

Light shone in the windows of the bungalow. Two square
patches of gold fell upon the pinks and the peaked marigolds.
Florrie, the cat, came out on to the veranda and sat on the top
step, her white paws close together, her tail curled round. She
looked content, as though she had been waiting for this
moment all day.

'Thank goodness, it's getting late,' said Florrie. 'Thank
goodness, the long day is over.' Her greengage eyes opened.

Presently there sounded the rumble of the coach, the crack
of Kelly's whip. It came near enough for one to hear the voices

of the men from town, talking loudly together. It stopped at the Burnells' gate.

Stanley was half-way up the path before he saw Linda. 'Is that you, darling?'

'Yes, Stanley.'

He leapt across the flower-bed and seized her in his arms. She was enfolded in that familiar, eager, strong embrace.

'Forgive me, darling, forgive me,' stammered Stanley, and he put his hand under her chin and lifted her face to him.

'Forgive you?' smiled Linda. 'But whatever for?'

'Good God! You can't have forgotten,' cried Stanley Burnell. 'I've thought of nothing else all day. I've had the hell of a day. I made up my mind to dash out and telegraph, and then I thought the wire mightn't reach you before I did. I've been in tortures, Linda.'

'But, Stanley,' said Linda, 'what must I forgive you for?'

'Linda!'—Stanley was very hurt—'didn't you realise— you must have realised—I went away without saying good-bye to you this morning? I can't imagine how I can have done such a thing. My confounded temper, of course. But—well—' and he sighed and took her in his arms again—'I've suffered for it enough to-day.'

'What's that you've got in your hand?' asked Linda. 'New gloves? Let me see.'

'Oh, just a cheap pair of wash-leather ones,' said Stanley humbly. 'I noticed Bell was wearing some in the coach this morning, so, as I was passing the shop, I dashed in and got myself a pair. What are you smiling at? You don't think it was wrong of me, do you?'

'On the *con*-trary, darling,' said Linda, 'I think it was most sensible.'

She pulled one of the large, pale gloves on her own fingers and looked at her hand, turning it this way and that. She was still smiling.

Stanley wanted to say, 'I was thinking of you the whole time I bought them.' It was true, but for some reason he couldn't say it. 'Let's go in,' said he.

XII

Why does one feel so different at night? Why is it so exciting
to be awake when everybody else is asleep? Late—it is very
late! And yet every moment you feel more and more wakeful,
as though you were slowly, almost with every breath, waking
up into a new, wonderful, far more thrilling and exciting
world than the daylight one. And what is this queer sensation
that you're a conspirator? Lightly, stealthily you move about
your room. You take something off the dressing-table and
put it down again without a sound. And everything, even the
bedpost, knows you, responds, shares your secret. . . .

You're not very fond of your room by day. You never
think about it. You're in and out, the door opens and slams,
the cupboard creaks. You sit down on the side of your bed,
change your shoes and dash out again. A dive down to the
glass, two pins in your hair, powder your nose and off again.
But now—it's suddenly dear to you. It's a darling little funny
room. It's yours. Oh, what a joy it is to own things! Mine
—my own!

'My very own for ever?'

'Yes.' Their lips met.

No, of course, that had nothing to do with it. That was all
nonsense and rubbish. But, in spite of herself, Beryl saw so
plainly two people standing in the middle of her room. Her
arms were round his neck; he held her. And now he whispered
'My beauty, my little beauty!' She jumped off her bed, ran
over to the window and kneeled on the window-seat, with her
elbows on the sill. But the beautiful night, the garden, every
bush, every leaf, even the white palings, even the stars, were
conspirators too. So bright was the moon that the flowers were
bright as by day; the shadow of the nasturtiums, exquisite lily-
like leaves and wide-open flowers, lay across the silvery veranda.
The manuka tree, bent by the southerly winds, was like a bird
on one leg stretching out a wing.

But when Beryl looked at the bush, it seemed to her the bush
was sad.

'We are dumb trees, reaching up in the night, imploring we
know not what,' said the sorrowful bush.

It is true when you are by yourself and you think about life,
it is always sad. All that excitement and so on has a way of

suddenly leaving you, and it's as though, in the silence, some-body called your name and you heard your name for the first time. 'Beryl!'

'Yes, I'm here. I'm Beryl. Who wants me?'

'Beryl!'

'Let me come.'

It is lonely living by oneself. Of course, there are relations, friends, heaps of them; but that's not what she means. She wants someone who will find the Beryl they none of them know, who will expect her to be that Beryl always. She wants a lover.

'Take me away from all these other people, my love. Let us go far away. Let us live our life, all new, all ours, from the very beginning. Let us make our fire. Let us sit down to eat together. Let us have long talks at night.'

And the thought was almost, 'Save me, my love. Save me!'

... 'Oh, go on! Don't be a prude, my dear. You enjoy yourself while you're young. That's my advice.' And a high rush of silly laughter joined Mrs. Harry Kember's loud, indifferent neigh.

You see, it's so frightfully difficult when you've nobody. You're so at the mercy of things. You can't just be rude. And you've always this horror of seeming inexperienced and stuffy like the other ninnies at the Bay. And—and it's fasci-nating to know you've power over people. Yes, that is fasci-nating. . . .

Oh why, oh why doesn't 'he' come soon?

If I go on living here, thought Beryl, anything may happen to me.

'But how do you know he is coming at all?' mocked a small voice within her.

But Beryl dismissed it. She couldn't be left. Other people, perhaps, but not she. It wasn't possible to think that Beryl Fairfield never married, that lovely fascinating girl.

'Do you remember Beryl Fairfield?'

'Remember her! As if I could forget her! It was one summer at the Bay that I saw her. She was standing on the beach in a blue'—no, pink—'muslin frock, holding on a big cream'—no, black—'straw hat. But it's years ago now.'

'She's as lovely as ever, more so if anything.'

Beryl smiled, bit her lip, and gazed over the garden. As she gazed, she saw somebody, a man, leave the road, step along the paddock beside their palings as if he was coming straight towards her. Her heart beat. Who was it? Who could it be? It couldn't be a burglar, certainly not a burglar, for he was smoking and he strolled lightly. Beryl's heart leapt; it seemed to turn right over and then to stop. She recognised him.

'Good evening, Miss Beryl,' said the voice softly.

'Good evening.'

'Won't you come for a little walk?' it drawled.

Come for a walk—at that time of night! 'I couldn't. Everybody's in bed. Everybody's asleep.'

'Oh,' said the voice lightly, and a whiff of sweet smoke reached her. 'What does everybody matter? Do come! It's such a fine night. There's not a soul about.'

Beryl shook her head. But already something stirred in her, something reared its head.

The voice said, 'Frightened?' It mocked, 'Poor little girl!'

'Not in the least,' said she. As she spoke that weak thing within her seemed to uncoil, to grow suddenly tremendously strong; she longed to go!

And just as if this was quite understood by the other, the voice said, gently and softly, but finally, 'Come along!'

Beryl stepped over her low window, crossed the veranda, ran down the grass to the gate. He was there before her.

'That's right,' breathed the voice, and it teased, 'You're not frightened, are you? You're not frightened?'

She was; now she was here she was terrified and it seemed to her everything was different. The moonlight stared and glittered; the shadows were like bars of iron. Her hand was taken.

'Not in the least,' she said lightly. 'Why should I be?'

Her hand was pulled gently, tugged. She held back.

'No, I'm not coming any further,' said Beryl.

'Oh, rot!' Harry Kember didn't believe her. 'Come along! We'll just go as far as that fuchsia bush. Come along!'

The fuchsia bush was tall. It fell over the fence in a shower. There was a little pit of darkness beneath.

'No, really, I don't want to,' said Beryl.

For a moment Harry Kember didn't answer. Then he came close to her, turned to her, smiled and said quickly, 'Don't be silly! Don't be silly!'

His smile was something she'd never seen before. Was he drunk? That bright, blind, terrifying smile froze her with horror. What was she doing? How had she got here? The stern garden asked her as the gate pushed open, and quick as a cat Harry Kember came through and snatched her to him.

'Cold little devil! Cold little devil!' said the hateful voice.

But Beryl was strong. She slipped, ducked, wrenched free.

'You are vile, vile,' said she.

'Then why in God's name did you come?' stammered Harry Kember.

Nobody answered him.

A cloud, small, serene, floated across the moon. In that moment of darkness the sea sounded deep, troubled. Then the cloud sailed away, and the sound of the sea was a vague murmur, as though it waked out of a dark dream. All was still.

(1921)

Rose Eagle

It was wonderful how quickly Rose Eagle forgot the first four-teen years of her life. They were nothing but a dream, out of which she wakened to find herself sitting on her yellow tin box in the kitchen of her 'first place', with a queer shaking in her hands and knees and the hot blood burning and tightening her cheeks. She and the yellow tin box might have been washed throught the back door into Mrs. Taylor's kitchen on the last wave of a sea-storm—so forlorn and unfamiliar they appeared, and she turned her head from side to side as though she were sensing quiet and stillness for the first time. . . .

It was late in the afternoon of a hot December day. The sun shone through the drawn blind in long pencil rays of light, over the floor and the face of the dresser and a church calendar picture of a dreamy young Jesus with an armful of lambs; and facing her sat Mrs. Taylor, changing the baby who sprawled on her lap, waving his hands and blowing bubbles. Mrs. Taylor kept on talking to Rose in a vague singing voice. The clock on the mantelpiece ticked sharply and a tap in the scullery tip-tipped like stealthy footsteps.

'Yes, m'm,' said Rose Eagle, and 'No, m'm' to all that Mrs. Taylor said.

'You will share Reggie's room, Rose. Reggie is my oldest boy. He is four and he has just started school. And now that you have come I'll give up having baby at night—he keeps me awake so. You're used to babies?'

'Oh, yes, m'm!'

'I really do not feel well enough to tell you your duties today,' said Mrs. Taylor, languidly sticking safty-pins into the gurgling baby.

Rose Eagle got up and bent over Mrs. Taylor. 'Here,' she said 'give 'im to me', and as she straightened herself with the warm, fat lump in her arms, she felt frightened no longer. Baby

143

Taylor was to Rose Eagle the saucer of milk to the stray cat. The fact of acceptance proved resignation.

'My word! What 'air 'e's got!' said Rose Eagle, cuddling him. 'It's like black feathers.'

Mrs. Taylor rose with her hands to her head. Tall and thin in her lilac cotton dress, she pushed back from her forehead the heaping black hair, with eyes half-shut and quivering lips.

'My! you do look bad!' said Rose, relishing this performance. 'You go an' 'ave a lie down on your bed, m'm, an' I'll bring you a cup o' tea in a minute. I'll manage best ways I can.'

She followed her mistress out of the kitchen, along the little passage, into the best bedroom. 'Lie down! Take yer shoes off!' Mrs. Taylor submitted, sighing, and Rose Eagle tiptoed back into the kitchen.

This story seems to lack coherence and sharpness. That's the principal thing: it's not all sharp. It's like eating a bunch of grapes instead of a grape of caviare. . . . I have a pretty bad habit of spreading myself at times—of over-writing and under-stating. It's just carelessness.

(1916)

Aunt Fan

'Have you seen my cosmias, dear? Have you noticed my cosmias to-day? Really, even though they are mine I must say I've never seen so fine a show. Everybody remarks on them. People stop to stare. I think it's so marvellous of the children not to pick them now that they show over the fence. Those mauve ones! Did you ever see anything so delicate? Such an uncommon colour, too! And when I think all that beauty came out of one little threepenny packet from the D.I.C. . . .'

Frail as butterflies, the petals of the cosmias fluttered like wings in the gently breathing air. They were warm white, mauve, pale pink and lemon yellow. And, peeping through the delicate green, you could still see in the garden bed the little soiled seed packet stuck in a cleft of stick. Kezia remembered the day when she had watched Aunt Fan tear off a corner, shake the seed, like minute canary seed, than pat the fine earth over. And afterwards they had stood together, just as they were standing now, gazing at nothing, but seeing—just what they looked at this very minute. What was the difference really? It was too hard to understand. She said:

'They are most lovely, Aunt Fan.'

'Look at that bee, Kezia! Look at that great velvety fellow!'

They watched him. When he clung to a cosmia the flower leaned over, swung, quivered, it seemed to be teasing him, and when he flew away the petals moved as though they were laughing.

'But really I must go, Aunt Fan.'

'One moment, darling. I'll just get my kitchen scissors and snip off a dead head or two while you're here.' She was there and back again on the instant, and before Kezia realised what was happening, quickly, lavishly, Aunt Fan had begun cutting her finest largest flowers.

'Oh, Aunt Fan, what are you doing!' Kezia was horrified.

145

'Stop! I don't want one. Why will you always give everything away? We've millions and billions of flowers at home. The vases were only done yesterday. Oh, Aunt *Fan*!'

'Only these, Kezia, only this little selection for your own vase in your room.' She thrust them into Kezia's hand and squeezed the reluctant fingers.

'They flower all the better for being cut. You know that's true.'

Yes, that was comforting, Kezia smiled at an exquisite half-open bud, the petals springing from the centre like the feathers of a tiny shuttlecock.

'Well, goodbye, Aunt Fan.'

She turned, Aunt Fan took her in her arms, held her close, looked, just an instant, intently and gravely at her before she gave her a quick light kiss.

(1922)

146

A Man
and his Dog

To look at Mr. Potts one would have thought that there at least went someone who had nothing to boast about. He was a little, insignificant fellow with a crooked tie, a hat soo small for him and a coat too large. The brown canvas portfolio that he carried to and from the Post Office every day was not like a business man's portfolio. It was like a child's school satchel; it did up even with a round-eyed button. One imagined there were crumbs and an apple core inside. And then there was something funny about his boots, wasn't there? Through the laces his coloured socks peeped out. What the dickens had the chap done with the tongues? 'Fried 'em,' suggested the wit of the Chesney bus. Poor old Potts! 'More likely buried 'em in his garden.' Under his arm he clasped an umbrella. And in wet weather when he put it up he disappeared completely. He was not. He was a walking umbrella—no more—the umbrella became his shell.

Mr. Potts lived in a little bungalow on Chesney Flat. The bulge of the water tank to one side gave it a mournful air, like a little bungalow with the toothache. There was no garden. A path had been cut in the paddock turf from the gate to the front door, and two beds, one round, one oblong, had been cut in what was going to be the front lawn. Down that path went Potts every morning at half-past eight and was picked up by the Chesney bus; up that path walked Potts every evening while the great kettle of a bus droned on. In the late evening, when he crept as far as the gate, eager to smoke a pipe—he wasn't allowed to smoke any nearer to the house than that—so humble, so modest was his air, that the big, merrily shining stars seemed to wink at each other, to laugh, to say, 'Look at him! Let's throw something!'

147

When Potts got out of the tram at the Fire Station to change into the Chesney bus he saw that something was up. The car was there all right, but the driver was off his perch; he was flat on his face half under the engine, and the conductor, his cap off, sat on a step rolling a cigarette and looking dreamy. A little group of business men and a woman clerk or two stood staring at the empty car; there was something mournful, pitiful about the way it leaned to one side and shivered faintly when the driver shook something. It was like someone who'd had an accident and tries to say: 'Don't touch me! Don't come near me! Don't hurt me!'

But all this was so familiar—the cars had only been running to Chesney the last few months—that nobody said anything, nobody asked anything. They just waited on the off chance. In fact, two or three decided to walk it as Potts came up. But Potts didn't want to walk unless he had to. He was tired. He'd been up half the night rubbing his wife's chest—she had one of her mysterious pains—and helping the sleepy servant girl heat compresses and hot-water bottles and make tea. The window was blue and the roosters had started crowing before he lay down finally with feet like ice. And all this was familiar, too.

Standing at the edge of the pavement and now and again changing his brown canvas portfolio from one hand to the other Potts began to live over the night before. But it was vague, shadowy. He saw himself moving like a crab, down the passage to the cold kitchen and back again. The two candles quivered on the dark chest of drawers, and as he bent over his wife her big eyes suddenly flashed and she cried:

'I get no sympathy—no sympathy. You only do it because you have to. Don't contradict me. I can see you grudge doing it.'

Trying to soothe her only made matters worse. There had been an awful scene ending with her sitting up and saying solemnly with her hand raised: 'Never mind, it will not be for long now.' But the sound of these words frightened her so terribly that she flung back on the pillow and sobbed, 'Robert! Robert!' Robert was the name of the young man to whom she had been engaged years ago, before she met Potts. And Potts was very glad to hear him invoked. He had come to know that meant the crisis was over and she'd begin to quieten down. . . .

By this time Potts had wheeled round; he had walked across the pavement to the paling fence that ran beside. A piece of light grass pushed through the fence and some slender silky daisies. Suddenly he saw a bee alight on one of the daisies and the flower leaned over, swayed, shook, while the little bee clung and rocked. And as it flew away the petals fluttered as if joyfully. . . . Just for an instant Potts dropped into the world where this happened. He brought from it the timid smile with which he walked back to the car. But now everybody had disappeared except one young girl who stood beside the empty car reading.

At the tail of the procession came Potts in a cassock so much too large for him that it looked like a night-shirt and you felt that he ought to be carrying not a hymn and a prayer book but a candle. His voice was a very light plaintive tenor. It surprised everybody. It seemed to surprise him, too. But it was so plaintive that when he cried 'for the wings, for the wings of a dove,' the ladies in the congregation wanted to club together and buy him a pair.

Lino's nose quivered so pitifully, there was such a wistful, timid look in his eyes, that Potts' heart was wrung. But, of course, he would not show it. 'Well,' he said sternly, 'I suppose you'd better come home.' And he got up off the bench. Lino got up, too, but stood still, holding up a paw.
'But there's one thing,' said Potts, turning and facing him squarely, 'that we'd better be clear about before you do come. And it's this.' He pointed his finger at Lino, who started as though he expected to be shot. But he kept his bewildered wistful eyes upon his master. 'Stop this pretence of being a fighting dog,' said Potts more sternly than ever. 'You're not a fighting dog. You're a watch dog. That's what you are. Very well. Stick to it. But it's this infernal boasting I can't stand. It's that that gets me.'
In the moment's pause that followed while Lino and his master looked at each other it was curious how strong a resemblance was between them. Then Potts turned again and made for home.
And timidly, as though falling over his own paws, Lino followed after the humble little figure of his master. . . .

(1921)

Sixpence

Children are unaccountable little creatures. Why should a small
boy like Dicky, good as gold as a rule, sensitive, affectionate,
obedient, and marvellously sensible for his age, have moods
when, without the slightest warning, he suddenly went 'mad
dog,' as his sisters called it, and there was no doing anything
with him?

'Dicky, come here! Come here, sir, at once! Do you hear
your mother calling you? Dicky!'

But Dicky wouldn't come. Oh, he heard right enough. A
clear, ringing little laugh was his only reply. And away he
flew; hiding, running through the uncut hay on the lawn,
dashing past the woodshed, making a rush for the kitchen
garden, and there dodging, peering at his mother from behind
the mossy apple trunks, and leaping up and down like a wild
Indian.

It had begun at tea-time. While Dicky's mother and Mrs.
Spears, who was spending the afternoon with her, were quietly
sitting over their sewing in the drawing-room, this, according
to the servant girl, was what had happened at the children's
tea. They were eating their first bread and butter as nicely
and quietly as you please, and the servant girl had just poured
out the milk and water, when Dicky had suddenly seized the
bread plate, put it upside down on his head, and clutched the
bread knife.

'Look at me!' he shouted.

His startled sisters looked, and before the servant girl could
get there, the bread plate wobbled, slid, flew to the floor, and
broke into shivers. At this awful point the little girls lifted up
their voices and shrieked their loudest.

'Mother, come and look what he's done!'

'Dicky's broke a great big plate!'

'Come and stop him, mother!'

You can imagine how mother came flying. But she was too late. Dicky had leapt out of his chair, run through the french windows on to the veranda, and, well—there she stood—popping her thimble on and off, helpless. What could she do? She couldn't chase after the child. She couldn't stalk Dicky among the apples and damsons. That would be too undignified. It was more than annoying, it was exasperating. Especially as Mrs. Spears, Mrs. Spears of all people, whose two boys were so exemplary, was waiting for her in the drawing-room.

'Very well, Dicky,' she cried, 'I shall have to think of some way of punishing you.'

'I don't care,' sounded the high little voice, and again there came that ringing laugh. The child was quite beside himself. . . .

'Oh, Mrs. Spears, I don't know how to apologise for leaving you by yourself like this."

'It's quite all right, Mrs. Bendall,' said Mrs. Spears, in her soft, sugary voice, and raising her eyebrows in the way she had. She seemed to smile to herself as she stroked the gathers. 'These little things will happen from time to time. I only hope it was nothing serious.'

'It was Dicky,' said Mrs. Bendall, looking rather helplessly for her only fine needle. And she explained the whole affair to Mrs. Spears. 'And the worst of it is, I don't know how to cure him. Nothing when he's in that mood seems to have the slightest effect on him.'

Mrs. Spears opened her pale eyes. 'Not even a whipping?' said she.

But Mrs. Bendall, threading her needle, pursed up her lips. 'We never have whipped the children,' she said. 'The girls never seem to have needed it. And Dicky is such a baby, and the only boy. Somehow . . .'

'Oh, my dear,' said Mrs. Spears, and she laid her sewing down. 'I don't wonder Dicky has these little outbreaks. You don't mind my saying so? But I'm sure you make a great mistake in trying to bring up children without whipping them. Nothing really takes its place. And I speak from experience, my dear. I used to try gentler meaures'—Mrs. Spears drew in her breath with a little hissing sound—'soaping the boys' tongues, for instance, with yellow soap, or making them stand on the table for the whole of Saturday afternoon. But no, believe me,' said Mrs. Spears, 'there is nothing, there is nothing like handing them over to their father.'

Mrs. Bendall in her heart of hearts was dreadfully shocked to hear of that yellow soap. But Mrs. Spears seemed to take it so much for granted, that she did too.

'Their father,' she said. 'Then you don't whip them yourself?'

'Never.' Mrs. Spears seemed quite shocked at the idea. 'I don't think it's the mother's place to whip the children. It's the duty of the father. And, besides, he impresses them so much more.'

'Yes, I can imagine that,' said Mrs. Bendall faintly.

'Now my two boys,' Mrs. Spears smiled kindly, encouragingly, at Mrs. Bendall, 'would behave just like Dicky if they were not afraid to. As it is . . .'

'Oh, your boys are perfect little models,' cried Mrs. Bendall.

They were. Quieter, better-behaved little boys, in the presence of grown-ups, could not be found. In fact, Mrs. Spears' callers often made the remark that you never would have known that there was a child in the house. There wasn't—very often.

In the front hall, under a large picture of fat, cheery old monks fishing by the riverside, there was a thick, dark horse-whip that had belonged to Mr. Spears' father. And for some reason the boys preferred to play out of sight of this, behind the dog-kennel or in the tool-house, or round about the dust-bin.

'It's such a mistake,' sighed Mrs. Spears, breathing softly, as she folded her work, 'to be weak with children when they are little. It's such a sad mistake, and one so easy to make. It's so unfair to the child. That is what one has to remember. Now Dicky's little escapade this afternoon seemed to me as though he'd done it on purpose. It was the child's way of showing you that he needed a whipping.'

'Do you really think so?' Mrs. Bendall was a weak little thing, and this impressed her very much.

'I do; I feel sure of it. And a sharp reminder now and then,' cried Mrs. Spears in quite a professional manner, 'administered by the father, will save you so much trouble in the future. Believe me, my dear.' She put her dry, cold hand over Mrs. Bendall's.

'I shall speak to Edward the moment he comes in,' said Dicky's mother firmly.

The children had gone to bed before the garden gate banged, and Dicky's father staggered up the steep concrete steps carrying his bicycle. It had been a bad day at the office. He was hot, dusty, tired out.

But by this time Mrs. Bendall had become quite excited over the new plan, and she opened the door to him herself.

'Oh, Edward, I'm so thankful you have come home,' she cried.

'Why, what's happened?' Edward lowered the bicycle and took off his hat. A red angry pucker showed where the brim had pressed. 'What's up?'

'Come—come into the drawing-room,' said Mrs. Bendall, speaking very fast. 'I simply can't tell you how naughty Dicky has been. You have no idea—you can't have at the office all day—how a child of that age can behave. He's been simply dreadful. I have no control over him—none. I've tried everything, Edward, but it's all no use. The only thing to do,' she finished breathlessly, 'is to whip him—is for you to whip him, Edward.'

In the corner of the drawing-room there was a what-not, and on the top shelf stood a brown china bear with a painted tongue. It seemed in the shadow to be grinning at Dicky's father, to be saying, 'Hooray, this is what you've come home to!'

'But why on earth should I start whipping him?' said Edward, staring at the bear. 'We've never done it before.'

'Because,' said his wife, 'don't you see, it's the only thing to do. I can't control the child. . . .' Her words flew from her lips. They beat round him, beat round his tired head. 'We can't possibly afford a nurse. The servant girl has more than enough to do. And his naughtiness is beyond words. You don't understand, Edward; you can't, you're at the office all day.'

The bear poked out his tongue. The scolding voice went on Edward sank into a chair.

'What am I to beat him with?' he said weakly.

'Your slipper, of course,' said his wife. And she knelt down to untie his dusty shoes.

'Oh, Edward,' she wailed, 'you've still got your cycling clips on in the drawing-room. No, really—'

'Here, that's enough.' Edward nearly pushed her away.

'Give me that slipper.' He went up the stairs. He felt like a man in a dark net. And now he wanted to beat Dicky. Yes, damn it, he wanted to beat something. My God, what a life! The dust was still in his hot eyes, his arms felt heavy.

He pushed open the door of Dicky's slip of a room. Dicky was standing in the middle of the floor in his night-shirt. At the sight of him Edward's heart gave a warm throb of rage.

'Well, Dicky, you know what I've come for,' said Edward.

Dicky made no reply.

'I've come to give you a whipping.'

No answer.

'Lift up your night-shirt.'

At that Dicky looked up. He flushed a deep pink. 'Must I?' he whispered.

'Come on, now. Be quick about it,' said Edward, and, grasping the slipper, he gave Dicky three hard slaps.

'There, that'll teach you to behave properly to your mother.'

Dicky stood there, hanging his head.

'Look sharp and get into bed,' said his father.

Still he did not move. But a shaking voice said, 'I've not done my teeth yet, Daddy.'

'Eh, what's that?'

Dicky looked up. His lips were quivering, but his eyes were dry. He hadn't made a sound or shed a tear. Only he swallowed and said huskily, 'I haven't done my teeth, Daddy.'

But at the sight of that little face Edward turned, and, not knowing what he was doing, he bolted from the room, down the stairs, and out into the garden. Good God! What had he done? He strode along and hid in the shadow of the pear tree by the hedge. Whipped Dicky—whipped his little man with a slipper—and what the devil for? He didn't even know. Suddenly he barged into his room—and there was the little chap in his night-shirt. Dicky's father groaned and held on to the hedge. And he didn't cry. Never a tear. If only he'd cried or got angry. But that 'Daddy'! And again he heard the quivering whisper. Forgiving like that without a word. But he'd never forgive himself—never. Coward! Fool! Brute! And suddenly he remembered the time when Dicky had fallen off his knee and sprained his wrist while they were playing together. He hadn't cried then, either. And that was the little hero he had just whipped.

154

Something's got to be done about this, thought Edward. He strode back to the house, up the stairs, into Dicky's room. The little boy was lying in bed. In the half-light his dark head, with the square fringe, showed plain against the pale pillow. He was lying quite still, and even now he wasn't crying. Edward shut the door and leaned against it. What he wanted to do was to kneel down by Dicky's bed and cry himself and beg to be forgiven. But, of course, one can't do that sort of thing. He felt awkward, and his heart was wrung.

'Not asleep yet, Dicky?' he said lightly.

'No, Daddy.'

Edward came over and sat on his boy's bed, and Dicky looked at him through his long lashes.

'Nothing the matter, little chap, is there?' said Edward, half whispering.

'No-o, Daddy,' came from Dicky.

Edward put out his hand, and carefully he took Dicky's hot little paw.

'You—you mustn't think any more of what happened just now, little man,' he said huskily. 'See? That's all over now. That's forgotten. That's never going to happen again. See?'

'Yes, Daddy.'

'So the thing to do now is to buck up, little chap,' said Edward, 'and to smile.' And he tried himself an extraordinary trembling apology for a smile. 'To forget all about it—to— eh? Little man. . . . Old boy. . . .'

Dicky lay as before. This was terrible. Dicky's father sprang up and went over to the window. It was nearly dark in the garden. The servant girl had run out, and she was snatching, twitching some white clothes off the bushes and piling them over her arm. But in the boundless sky the evening star shone, and a big gum tree, black against the pale glow, moved its long leaves softly. All this he saw, while he felt in his trouser pocket for his money. Bringing it out, he chose a new sixpence and went back to Dicky.

'Here you are, little chap. Buy yourself something,' said Edward softly, laying the sixpence on Dicky's pillow.

But could even that—could even a whole sixpence—blot out what had been?

(1921)

155

The Skerritt
Girl

On her way back to the garden Susannah sat down on the hall chair for a minute to take a pebble out of her shoe. And she heard her mother say: 'No, I can't possibly do that. I can't possibly turn that dear good Mr. Taylor out of the house simply to make room for this Skerritt girl.'

It was a little difficult to explain the facts of the case to the Reverend Mr. Taylor, and Mrs. Downing hated having to do so. It seemed so unreasonable to ask him to turn out of the spare-room for the night for an unknown girl, when he was their regular guest, as it were, for the whole Synod, and so appreciative—poor lonely up-country man—of the spare-room double-bed. But there was nothing else to be done. In that extraordinary way men have, Harry, Mrs. Downing's husband, had rung up from the office to tell her that a Netta Skerritt had called on him that morning as she was passing through Wellington on her way to Nelson, and though neither of the Downings had ever seen her before, simply because her father and Harry Downing had known each other in the old days, Harry had immediately asked her to stay the night with them.

At that moment Susannah herself came in from the garden. She leaned her elbow on the round walnut table, crossed her legs, and cupped her burning cheeks in her hands.

'And you really won't mind Susannah's bed for the night, Mr. Taylor?' said Mrs. Downing anxiously, pouring him out a second cup of tea.

'Not at all, Mrs. Downing. I shall be as happy as a king,' said good cheerful Mr. Taylor.

But Susannah's eyes opened very wide. Her lips parted, she stared first at her mother, and then at Mr. Taylor's black coat, gleaming collar, and big yellow hands.

THE SKERRITT GIRL

'Is Mr. Taylor going to sleep in my bed, Mother?' said she, astounded.

'Yes, dear, but only for to-night,' said her mother absently, folding a piece of bread-and-butter. Mr. Taylor smiled his broad smile.

Susannah imagined him lying in her bed, his head tilted back, snoring like he snored on Sunday afternoons. How awful!

'With *me*?' she asked, horrified.

Mother flushed faintly, and Mr. Taylor gave a loud snort that might have been laughter.

'Don't be such a silly little girl, Susannah. Of course not. You are going to sleep in the spare room with Miss Skerritt.'

This was more mysterious still. Oh, dear, why were grown-ups like this? She had only run in for a piece of bread-and-butter; she wanted to get back to the garden. And here they were sitting in this dark room. It looked very dark, and the white cups shone on the walnut table like lilies in a lake, after the bright outside.

A moment later and there was nothing left of Netta Skerritt but a dint in the pillow and one long—much too long—blue-black hairpin gleaming on the pale carpet.

(1921)

Susannah

Of course there would have been no question of their going to the exhibition if Father had not had the tickets given to him. Little girls cannot expect to be given treats that cost extra money when only to feed them, buy them clothes, pay for their lessons and the house they live in takes their kind generous Father all day and every day working hard from morning till night—'except Saturday afternoons and Sundays,' said Susannah.

'Susannah!' Mother was very shocked. 'But do you know what would happen to your poor Father if he didn't have a holiday on Saturday afternoons and Sundays?'

'No,' said Susannah. She looked interested. 'What?'

'He would die,' said their Mother impressively.

'Would he?' said Susannah, opening her eyes. She seemed astounded, and Sylvia and Phyllis, who were four and five years older than she, chimed in with 'Of course' in a very superior tone. What a little silly-billy she was not to know that! They sounded so convinced and cheerful that their Mother felt a little shaken and hastened to change the subject. . . .

'So that is why,' she said a little vaguely, 'you must each thank Father separately before you go.'

'And then will he give us the money?' asked Phyllis.

'And then I shall ask him for whatever is necessary,' said their Mother firmly. She sighed suddenly and got up. 'Run along, children, and ask Miss Wade to dress you and get ready herself and then to come down to the dining-room. And now, Susannah, you are not to let go Miss Wade's hand from the moment you are through the gates until you are out again.'

'Well—what if I go on a horse?' inquired Susannah.

'Go on a horse—nonsense child! You're much too young for horses! Only big girls and boys can ride.'

158

'There're roosters for small children,' said Susannah, un-
daunted. 'I know, because Irene Heywood went on one and
when she got off she fell over.'

'All the more reason why you shouldn't go on,' said her
Mother.

But Susannah looked as though falling over had no terrors
for her. On the contrary.

About the exhibition, however, Sylvia and Phyllis knew as
little as Susannah. It was the first that had ever come to their
town. One morning, as Miss Wade, their lady help, rushed
them along to the Heywoods', whose governess they shared,
they had seen carts piled with great long planks of wood, sacks,
what looked like whole doors, and white flagstaffs, passing
through the wide gate of the Recreation Ground. And by
the time they were bowled home to their dinners there were
the beginnings of a high, thin fence, dotted with flagstaffs,
built all round the railings. From inside came a tremendous
noise of hammering, shouting, clanging; a little engine, hidden
away, went *Chuff-chuff-chuff. Chuff!* And round, woolly balls of
smoke were tossed over the palings.

First it was the day after the day after to-morrow, then plain
day after to-morrow, then to-morrow, and at last, the day
itself. When Susannah woke up in the morning there was a
little gold spot of sunlight watching her from the wall; it
looked as though it had been there for a long time, waiting to
remind her: 'It's to-day—you're going to-day—this afternoon. Here she is!'

(Second Version)

That afternoon they were allowed to cut jugs and basins out
of a draper's catalogue, and at tea-time they had real tea in the
doll's tea-set on the table. This was a very nice treat, indeed,
except that the doll's teapot wouldn't pour out even after you'd
poked a pin down the spout and blown into it.

But the next afternoon, which was Saturday, Father came
home in high feather. The front door banged so hard that the
whole house shook, and he shouted to Mother from the hall.

'Oh, how more than good of you, darling!' cried Mother,
'but how unnecessary too. Of course, they'll simply love it.
But to have spent all that money! You shouldn't have done it,
Daddy dear! They've totally forgotten all about it. And what

is this! Half a crown?' cried Mother. 'No! Two shillings, I see,' she corrected quickly, 'to spend as well. Children! Children! Come down, downstairs!'

Down they came, Phyllis and Sylvia leading, Susannah holding on. 'Do you know what Father's done?' And Mother held up her hand. What was she holding? Three cherry tickets and a green one. 'He's bought you tickets. You're to go to the circus, this very afternoon, all of you, with Miss Wade. What do you say to that?'

'Oh, Mummy! Lovely! Lovely!' cried Phyllis and Sylvia.

'Isn't it?' said Mother. 'Run upstairs. Run and ask Miss Wade to get you ready. Don't dawdle. Up you go! All of you.'

Away flew Phyllis and Sylvia, but still Susannah stayed where she was at the bottom of the stairs, hanging her head.

'Go along,' said Mother. And Father said sharply, 'What the devil's the matter with the child?'

Susannah's face quivered. 'I don't want to go,' she whispered.

'What! Don't want to go to the Exhibition! After Father's— You naughty, ungrateful child! Either you go to the Exhibition, Susannah, or you will be packed off to bed at once.'

Susannah's head bent low, lower still. All her little body bent forward. She looked as though she was going to bow down, to bow down to the ground, before her kind generous Father and beg for his forgiveness. . . .

(1920)

PART TWO

Summer: *the Sheridans*

Spring
in Tyrrell Street

On a fine spring morning, one of those delicious spotless mornings when one feels that celestial housemaids have been joyfully busy all through the night, Mrs. Quill locked the back door, the pantry window, and the front door, and set off for the railway station.

'Good-bye, wee house!' said she, as she shut the gate, and she felt the house heard and loved her. It was not quite empty. In her bedroom, in his cradle, Chi-chi lay sleeping his morning sleep. But the blind was down and he was so beautifully trained. She counted on him not waking up until she was back.

At that hour, all the little houses in Tyrrell Street basked in the radiant light; all the canaries, in *their* little houses hanging from the verandah poles, sang their shrillest. It was difficult to understand how the infants in perambulators who shared the verandahs with the canaries slept through the din. But they apparently did; no sound came from them. Up and down spanked the important-looking bright yellow butcher's cart, and in and out of the back gates went the baker's boy with his basket clamped to his back like a big shell.

It had rained in the night. There were still puddles—broken stars—on the road. But the pavement was beautifully dry. What a pleasure it was to walk on the nice clean pavement!

(1922)

Sisters

Just as they reached the gate, Agnes turned back.

'Where are you going now, my dear?' said Gertrude quickly.

'The sun's so boiling, I must have my parasol.'

'Oh, well, bring mine too, will you?' And Gertrude waited. In her pink dress, with one hand on the half-open gate, she felt like a picture. But, unfortunately, there was no one to see except the florid butcher spanking past in his yellow cart. Well, even a butcher is somebody, she thought, as Agnes came running back over the small blue gravel.

'Thanks! It is boiling. I had no idea.'

'Roasting—isn't it?' said Agnes.

And, putting up their parasols, off they sailed down the Avenue, on the way to the Misses Phipps to try on their new evening dresses. There they go, thought Gertrude, and there they go, thought Agnes,—the daughters of rich parents, young and attractive, one fair, one dark, one a soprano, one a contralto, with all the really thrilling things in life still to happen to them. And just then Major Trapp on his big chestnut horse turned into the Avenue, and dashing past saluted them; and they both bowed, charmingly, graciously like swans.

'He's out very early,' said Gertrude.

'Very!' came from Agnes.

'I've not got my hat too far forward, have I?' asked Gertrude anxiously.

'I don't think so,' answered wicked Agnes.

By great good fortune the tram was empty. The sisters had it all to themselves. Feeling grand, down they sat in one of the small wooden pens. The conductor blew his whistle, the driver banged his bell, the fat small horses started forward and away they swung. Merrily danced the pink bobbles on the fringes of the cotton blinds, and gaily the sunlight race under the arched roof.

164

'But what on earth am I to do with this?' cried Gertrude, gazing with exaggerated scorn and horror at the bouquet that old Mr. Phipps had cut and bound together so lovingly.

Agnes screwed up her eyes and smiled at the unearthly white and gold arum lily and the dove-blue columbines. 'I don't know,' said she. 'You can't possibly cart it about with you. It's like a barmaid's wedding bouquet.' And she laughed and put her hand to her glorious coil of thick hair.

Gertrude tossed it on to the floor, and kicked it under the seat. Just in time, as it happened.

(1921)

Saunders Lane

Our house in Tinakori Road stood far back from the road. It was a big, white-painted square house with a slender pillared verandah and balcony running all the way round it. In the front from the verandah edge the garden sloped away in terraces and flights of concrete steps— down—until you reached the stone wall covered with nasturtiums that had three gates let into it—the visitors' gate, the Tradesmen's gate, and a huge pair of old iron gates that were never used and clashed and clamoured when Bogey and I tried to swing on them.

Tinakori Road was not fashionable; it was very mixed. Of course there were some good houses in it, old ones, like ours for instance, hidden away in wildish gardens, and there was no doubt that land there would become extremely valuable, as Father said, if one bought enough and hung on.

It was high, it was healthy; the sun poured in all the windows all day long, and once we had a decent tramway service, as Father argued. . . .

But it was a little trying to have one's own washerwoman living next door who would persist in attempting to talk to Mother over the fence, and then, just beyond her 'hovel', as Mother called it, there lived an old man who burned leather in his back yard whenever the wind blew our way. And further along there lived an endless family of halfcastes who appeared to have planted their garden with empty jam tins and old sauce-pans and black iron kettles without lids. And then just opposite our house across the road there was a paling fence, and below the paling fence in a hollow, squeezed in almost under the fold of a huge gorse-covered hill, was Saunders Lane.

(1916)

Kezia and Tui

based on her friendship with a classmate

All that day school seemed unreal and silly to Kezia. Round and round, like a musical box with only one tune, went her mind on what had happened the evening before. Her head ached with trying to remember every little detail and every word. She did not want to remember—but somehow, she could not stop trying. She answered questions and made mistakes in her sums and recited 'How Horatius kept the Bridge' like a little girl in a dream. The day crawled by. 'That was the first time I've ever stood up to him,' she thought. 'I wonder if everything will be different now. We can't even pretend to like each other again.' Bottlenose! Bottlenose! She smiled again remembering the word, but at the same time she felt frightened. She had not seen her father that morning. The Grandmother told her that he had promised not to mention the subject again. 'But I didn't believe that,' thought Kezia. 'I wish it hadn't happened. No, I'm glad it has . . . I wish that he was dead—Oh, what Heaven that would be for us!' But she could not imagine that sort of person dying. She remembered suddenly the way he sucked in his moustache when he drank and the long hairs he had on his hands, and the noises he made when he had indigestion—No, that sort of person seemed too real to die. She worried the thought of him until she was furious with rage. 'How I detest him—detest him!' The class stood up to sing. Kezia shared a book with Tui.

> 'O forest, green and fair,
> O pine-trees waving high,
> How sweet their cool retreat,
> How full of rest!'

167

sang the little girls. Kezia looked out through the big bare windows to the wattle trees, their gold tassels nodding in the sunny air, and suddenly the sad tune and the trees moving so gently made her feel quite calm. She looked down at the withered sweet-pea that drooped from her blouse. She saw herself sitting on the Grandmother's lap and leaning against the Grandmother's bodice. That was what she wanted. To sit there and hear Grannie's watch ticking against her ear and bury her face in the soft warm place smelling of lavender and put up her hand and feel the five owls sitting on the moon.

Mrs. Fairfield was in the garden when she came home—stooping over the pansies. She had a little straw basket on her arm, half filled with flowers. Kezia went up to her and leant against her and played with her spectacle case.

'Sweetheart, listen,' she said. 'It's no good saying I'm sorry because I'm not. And I'm not ashamed either. It's no good trying to make me.' Her face grew hard. 'I *hate* that man and I won't pretend. But because you're more—' she hesitated, groping for the word, 'more *valuable* than he is, I won't behave like that again—not unless I absolutely feel I can't help it, Grannie.' She looked up and smiled. 'See?'

'I can't make you do what you don't want to, Kezia,' said Mrs. Fairfield.

'No,' said she. 'Nobody can, can they? Otherwise it wouldn't be any good wanting anything for your own self—would it? Aren't the pansies pretties, Grannie? I'd like to make pets of them.'

'I think they're rather like my little scaramouch in the face,' said Mrs. Fairfield, smiling and pulling Kezia's pink ear.

'Oh, thank goodness!' sighed Kezia. 'You're yourself again. We've made it up, haven't we? I can't bear being serious for a long time together. Oh my Grannie, I've got to be happy with you. When I go thinking of serious things I could poke out my tongue at myself.' She took Mrs. Fairfield's hand and stroked it. 'You do love me, don't you?'

'Of course, you silly billy.'

'We-ell,' laughed Kezia. 'That's the only real thing, isn't it?'

'There are two bits of cold pudding inside for you and Tui,' said Mrs. Fairfield. 'Run along and take it to her while I finish the ironing. I only came out while the iron was getting hot.'

'You won't be wretched if I leave you alone?' asked Kezia.

She danced into the house, found the pudding and danced over to the Beads'.

'Mrs. Bead! Tui! where are you?' she called, stepping over a saucepan, two big cabbages and Tui's hat and coat inside the kitchen door.

'We're upstairs. I'm washing my hair in the bathroom. Come up, darling,' cooed Tui. Kezia bounded up the stairs. Mrs. Bead in a pink flannel dressing-gown sat on the edge of the bath, and Tui stood in torn calico drawers, a towel round her shoulders and her head in a basin.

'Hallo, Mrs. Bead,' said Kezia. She buried her head in the Maori woman's neck and put her teeth in a roll of soft fat. Mrs. Bead pulled Kezia between her knees and had a good look at her.

'Well, Tui,' she said, 'you are a little fibber. Tui told me you'd had a fight with your father and he'd given you two black eyes.'

'I didn't—I didn't,' cried Tui, stamping. "No one is looking after me. Pour a jug of water on my head, Mummy. Oh, Kezia don't listen to her.'

'Pooh! it's nothing new,' said Kezia. 'You're always lying. I'll pour the water over your head.' She rolled up her sleeves and deluged Tui, who gave little moaning cries.

'I'm drowned, drowned, drowned,' she said, wringing out her long black hair.

'You have a lot of it,' said Kezia.

'Yes.' Tui twisted it round her head. 'But I shan't be content till it is down to my knees. Don't you think it would be nice to be able to wrap yourself up in your hair?'

'What funny ideas you have,' said Kezia, considering Tui. 'Mrs. Bead, don't you think Tui's getting awfully conceited?'

'Oh, not more than she ought to,' said Mrs. Bead, stretching herself and yawning. 'I believe in girls thinking about their appearance. Tui could do a lot with herself if she liked.'

'Well, she doesn't think about anything else, do you, Tui?'

'No, darling,' Tui smiled.

'Well, why should she?' remarked Mrs. Bead easily. 'She's not like you, Kezia. She hasn't got any brain for books, but she's real smart in making up complexion mixtures and she keeps her feet as neat as her hands.'

'When I grow up,' said Tui, 'I mean to be a terri-fic beauty.

Mother's going to take me to Sydney when I'm sixteen—but I mean to be the rage if I die for it. And then I'm going to marry a rich Englishman and have five little boys with beautiful blue eyes.'

'Well, you never know,' said Mrs. Bead. 'And if you turn out into a raging beauty, Tui, I'll take you to Sydney, sure. What a pity you couldn't come too, Kezia.'

'We'd make such an uncommon pair,' suggested Tui. Kezia shook her head.

'No, Grannie and I are going to live by ourselves when I grow up, and I'm going to make money out of flowers and vegetables and bees.'

'But don't you want to be rich?' cried Tui, 'and travel all over the world and have perfect clothes? Oh, dear, if I thought I was going to live all my life with Mummy in this piggy little house I believe I'd die of grief.'

'Yes, that's a good thing about you, Tui,' said Mrs. Bead. 'Though you're lazy like me, you want a lot to be lazy on; and you're quite right, dearie, quite right. I made a great mistake coming to a little town like this. But then I'd got sick of things and I had enough money to keep us, and once I got the furniture in here I seemed to lose heart, somehow. You ought to have ambition, Kezia, but I think you'll come on slower than Tui. You do keep skinny, don't you,' said Mrs. Bead. 'Why, Tui's got quite a figure beside you.'

'She hasn't got any front at all, Mummy,' gurgled Tui. 'Have you, chérie? Mummy, go downstairs and make us some cocoa, and I'll get dressed and come down to finish my hair at the fire.'

Mrs. Bead left the two little girls. They went into Tui's bedroom.

'Look!' said Tui. 'Doesn't it surprise you? Mummy and I fixed it yesterday.' The shabby untidy little room had changed to suit Tui's romantic mood. White muslin curtains made out of an old skirt of her mother's adorned the bed, and everywhere Kezia looked there were pink sateen bows. Over the looking-glass, on the back of the chair, on the gas bracket and the four black iron bed-poles.

'Why don't you put a bow on each of the knobs of the chest of drawers,' said Kezia, sarcastically, 'and round the washstand jug, too!'

170

'Oh!' Tui's face fell. 'Don't you like it, darling? We thought it was lovely. Mummy thought you'd think it fearfully artistic.'

'I think it looks awful,' said Kezia, 'and just like you. You're off your head lately, Tui Bead.'

'Really and truly you think so?' said Tui, making tragic eyes at herself in the looking-glass.

'Yes. Besides, if I were you, I would mend my drawers first,' she answered, scorning Tui's eyes.

'I wonder what makes you so hard, hard, hard. You're never nice to me now, Kezia.'

'Yes, I am. But you're so dotty. You seem to be getting all different.'

'Darling,' Tui put her arm round Kezia's waist, 'in my heart I'm just the same. Feel my hair. Do you think I've washed it successfully? Feel this bit. Is it silky?' Kezia gave it a pull.

'It's nearly as soft as you.'

'Come along downstairs, you kids,' called Mrs. Bead. 'And, Kezia, you can take a piece of my coconut cake to your Grandma. It hasn't riz at all and it's a little damp in the middle, but the ingredients are all the best quality.'

It was dark when she left the Beads'. She went home by the front way through their weedy garden and out of the gate into their own. Hawk Street was quiet. All over the sky there were little stars and the garden with its white flowers looked as though it were steeped in milk. The blinds were pulled down in their house but lamplight shone from the sitting-room and she knew her Father was there. But she did not care.

'What a lovely thing night is,' thought Kezia. 'I wish I could stay out here and watch it.' She bent her face over the spicy arum lilies and could not have enough of their scent. 'I shall *remember* just this moment,' decided the little girl. 'I shall always remember what I like and forget what I don't like.' How still and quiet it was! She could hear the dew dripping off the leaves. 'I wonder,' she thought, dreamy and grave, looking up at the stars, 'I wonder if there really *is* a God!'

(1916)

Maata

They did not fall like leaves—they fell like feathers—fluttering and floating from the trees that lined the road. Who was it used to say that every leaf you caught meant a happy month? Rhody, of course. She saw Rhody, the tall school girl, break from the 'crocodile' when they walked in the Park, and run after the leaves, with big, far too big gestures, as though she expected the whole tree to fall into her arms. Rhody used to keep the leaves in her Bible, and take them out and hold them up to the light and gaze at them in Scripture lessons. And she always said she knew each one apart. Well, if she said so—she did. Just like her.

The clock in the big Church struck five. But she did not hurry. Idle and happy she walked under the falling leaves. A sharp sweet scent was in the air, and a stronger, more wintry smell of damp earth. She could feel the mist on her eyelids and lips. The sensation of boundless strength and happiness flowed over her again. It was almost physical—her lungs felt like wings, she could fly away on a deep breath, light and strong.

'Oh, I am glad. Now I am myself again—now I am *quite safe*,' she said, like a little child that wakes in its bed after a nightmare. And she thought: 'If I could only remember always that under everything there is only this—that everything that is not this is on the surface and will not really matter in the end. What is life really? What is real and not real? Oh God!'

Came troubled sounds, familiar yet unreal, like the memory and the promise of sadness. They shook her heart. She did not want to listen. She could have listened for ever. Standing there in the dark she drifted away to that shadowy loneliness which sometimes seemed to her to be her only true life—the only changeless truth—the thing that she was never really certain was not reality after all. How extraordinary! She saw herself, all these last weeks, playing a part—being Maata—being herself,

carefully caring for things that after all didn't matter at all!
Why only that afternoon—a minute or two ago, she had believed
it all—and it was nothing, nothing.

(1915)

A Dream

Sometimes I glance up at the clock. Then I know I am expecting
Chummie. The bell peals. I run out on to the landing. I hear his hat
and stick thrown on to the hall-table. He runs up the stairs, three at a
time. 'Hullo, darling!' But I can't move—I can't move. He puts his
arm round me, holding me tightly, and we kiss—a long, firm, family
kiss. And the kiss means: We are of the same blood; we have
absolute confidence in each other; we love; all is well; nothing can
ever come between us.

We come into my room. He goes over to the glass. 'By Jove, I am
hot.' Yes, he is very hot. A deep childish colour shows in his cheeks,
his eyes are brilliant, his lips burn, he strokes the hair back from his
forehead with the palm of his hand. I pull the curtains together and
the room is shadowy. He flings himself down on the sommier and
lights a cigarette, and watches the smoke, rising so slowly.

'Is that better?' I ask.

'Perfect, darling—simply perfect. The light reminds me of . . .'

And then the dream is over and I begin working again.

(1919)

Sun
and Moon

*I dreamed a short story last night,
even down to its name, which was*
Sun and Moon. *It was very light.
I dreamed it all—about children . . .
I didn't dream that I read it. No, I
was in it, part of it, and it played
round invisible me. But the hero is
not more than 5. In my dream I saw a
supper table with the eyes of 5. It was
awfully queer—especially a plate of
half-melted ice-cream.*

In the afternoon the chairs came, a whole big cart full of little
gold ones with their legs in the air. And then the flowers came.
When you stared down from the balcony at the people carrying
them the flower pots looked like funny awfully nice hats
nodding up the path.

Moon thought they were hats. She said: 'Look. There's a
man wearing a palm on his head.' But she never knew the
difference between real things and not real ones.

There was nobody to look after Sun and Moon. Nurse was
helping Annie alter Mother's dress which was much-too-
long-and-tight-under-the-arms and Mother was running all
over the house and telephoning Father to be sure not to forget
things. She only had time to say: 'Out of my way, children!'

They kept out of her way—at any rate Sun did. He did so
hate being sent stumping back to the nursery. It didn't matter
about Moon. If she got tangled in people's legs they only threw

her up and shook her till she squeaked. But Sun was too heavy for that. He was so heavy that the fat man who came to dinner on Sundays used to say: 'Now, young man, let's try to lift you.' And then he'd put his thumbs under Sun's arms and groan and try and give it up at last saying: 'He's a perfect little ton of bricks!'

Nearly all the furniture was taken out of the dining-room. The big piano was put in a corner and then there came a row of flower pots and then there came the goldy chairs. That was for the concert. When Sun looked in a white-faced man sat at the piano—not playing, but banging at it and then looking inside. He had a bag of tools on the piano and he had stuck his hat on a statue against the wall. Sometimes he just started to play and then he jumped up again and looked inside. Sun hoped he wasn't the concert.

But of course the place to be in was the kitchen. There was a man helping in a cap like a blancmange, and their real cook, Minnie, was all red in the face and laughing. Not cross at all. She gave them each an almond finger and lifted them up on to the flour bin so that they could watch the wonderful things she and the man were making for supper. Cook brought in the things and he put them on dishes and trimmed them. Whole fishes, with their heads and eyes and tails still on, he sprinkled with red and green and yellow bits; he made squiggles all over the jellies, he stuck a collar on a ham and put a very thin sort of a fork in it; he dotted almonds and tiny round biscuits on the creams. And more and more things kept coming.

'Ah, but you haven't seen the ice pudding,' said Cook. 'Come along.' Why was she being so nice, thought Sun as she gave them each a hand. And they looked into the refrigerator.

Oh! Oh! Oh! It was a little house. It was a little pink house with white snow on the roof and green windows and a brown door and stuck in the door there was a nut for a handle.

When Sun saw the nut he felt quite tired and had to lean against Cook.

'Let me touch it. Just let me put my finger on the roof.' said Moon, dancing. She always wanted to touch all the food. Sun didn't.

'Now, my girl, look sharp with the table,' said Cook as the housemaid came in.

'It's a picture, Min,' said Nellie. 'Come along and have a look.' So they all went into the dining-room. Sun and Moon were almost frightened. They wouldn't go up to the table at first; they just stood at the door and made eyes at it.

It wasn't real night yet but the blinds were down in the dining-room and the lights turned on—and all the lights were red roses. Red ribbons and bunches of roses tied up the table at the corners. In the middle was a lake with rose petals floating on it.

'That's where the ice pudding is to be,' said Cook.

Two silver lions with wings had fruit on their backs and the salt-cellars were tiny birds drinking out of basins.

And all the winking glasses and shining plates and sparkling knives and forks—and all the food. And the little red table napkins made into roses. . . .

'Are people going to eat the food?' asked Sun.

'I should just think they are,' laughed Cook, laughing with Nellie. Moon laughed, too; she always did the same as other people. But Sun didn't want to laugh. Round and round he walked with his hands behind his back. Perhaps he never would have stopped if Nurse hadn't called suddenly: 'Now then, children. It's high time you were washed and dressed.' And they were marched off to the nursery.

While they were being unbuttoned Mother looked in with a white thing over her shoulders; she was rubbing stuff on her face.

'I'll ring for them when I want them, Nurse, and then they can just come down and be seen and go back again,' said she.

Sun was undressed first nearly to his skin, and dressed again in a white shirt with red and white daisies speckled on it, breeches with strings at the sides and braces that came over, white socks and red shoes.

'Now you're in your Russian costume,' said Nurse, flattening down his fringe.

'Am I?' said Sun.

'Yes. Sit quiet in that chair and watch your little sister.'

Moon took ages. When she had her socks put on she pretended to fall back on the bed and waved her legs at Nurse as she always did, and every time Nurse tried to make her curls with a finger and a wet brush she turned round and asked Nurse to show her the photo of her brooch or something like that. But at last she was finished too. Her dress stuck out, with fur on it, all white; there was even fluffy stuff on the legs of her drawers. Her shoes were white with big blobs on them.

'There you are, my lamb,' said Nurse. 'And you look like a sweet little cherub of a picture of a powder-puff.' Nurse rushed to the door. 'Ma'am, one moment.'

Mother came in again with half her hair down.

'Oh,' she cried. 'What a picture!'

'Isn't she,' said Nurse.

And Moon held out her skirts by the tips and dragged one of her feet. Sun didn't mind people not noticing him—much. . . .

After that they played clean, tidy games up at the table while Nurse stood at the door, and when the carriages began to come and the sound of laughter and voices and soft rustlings came from down below she whispered: 'Now then, children, stay where you are.' Moon kept jerking the tablecloth so that it all hung down her side and Sun hadn't any—and then she pretended she didn't do it on purpose.

At last the bell rang. Nurse pounced at them with the hair-brush, flattened his fringe, made her bow stand on end and joined their hands together.

'Down you go!' she whispered.

And down they went. Sun did feel silly holding Moon's hand like that but Moon seemed to like it. She swung her arm and the bell on her coral bracelet jingled.

At the drawing-room door stood Mother fanning herself with a black fan. The drawing-room was full of sweet-smelling, silky, rustling ladies and men in black with funny tails on their coats —like beetles. Father was among them, talking very loud, and rattling something in his pocket.

'What a picture!' cried the ladies. 'Oh, the ducks! Oh, the lambs! Oh, the sweets! Oh, the pets!'

All the people who couldn't get at Moon kissed Sun, and a skinny old lady with teeth that clicked said: 'Such a serious little poppet,' and rapped him on the head with something hard.

Sun looked to see if the same concert was there, but he was gone. Instead, a fat man with a pink head leaned over the piano talking to a girl who held a violin at her ear.

There was only one man that Sun really liked. He was a little grey man, with long grey whiskers, who walked about by himself. He came up to Sun and rolled his eyes in a very nice way and said: 'Hullo, my lad.' Then he went away. But soon he came back again and said: 'Fond of dogs?' Sun said: 'Yes.' But then he went away again, and though Sun looked for him everywhere he couldn't find him. He thought perhaps he'd gone outside to fetch in a puppy.

'Good night, my precious babies,' said Mother, folding them up in her bare arms. 'Fly up to your little nest.'

The Moon went and made a silly of herself again. She put up her arms in front of everybody and said: 'My Daddy must carry me.'

But they seemed to like it, and Daddy swooped down and picked her up as he always did.

Nurse was in such a hurry to get them to bed that she even interrupted Sun over his prayers and said: 'Get on with them, child, *do*.' And the moment after they were in bed and in the dark, except for the night-light in its little saucer.

'Are you asleep?' asked Moon.

'No,' said Sun. 'Are you?'

'No,' said Moon.

A long time after Sun woke up again. There was a loud, loud noise of clapping from downstairs, like when it rains. He heard Moon turn over.

'Moon, are you awake?'

'Yes, are you?'

'Yes. Well, let's go and look over the stairs.'

They had just got settled on the top step when the drawing-room door opened and they heard the party cross over the hall into the dining-room. Then that door was shut; there was a noise of 'pops' and laughing. Then that stopped and Sun saw them all walking round and round the lovely table with their hands behind their backs like he had done. . . . Round and round they walked, looking and staring. The man with the grey whiskers liked the little house best. When he saw the nut for a handle he rolled his eyes like he did before and said to Sun: 'Seen the nut?'

'Don't nod your head like that, Moon.'

'I'm not nodding. It's you.'

'It is not. I never nod my head.'

'O-oh, you do. You're nodding it now.'

'I'm not. I'm only showing you how not to do it.'

179

When they woke up again they could only hear Father's voice very loud, and Mother, laughing away. Father came out of the dining-room, bounded up the stairs, and nearly fell over them.

'Hullo!' he said. 'By Jove, Kitty, come and look at this.'

Mother came out. 'Oh, you naughty children,' said she from the hall.

'Let's have 'em down and give 'em a bone,' said Father. Sun had never seen him so jolly.

'No, certainly not,' said Mother.

'Oh, my Daddy, do! Do have us down,' said Moon.

'I'm hanged if I won't,' cried Father. 'I won't be bullied. Kitty—way there,' And he caught them up, one under each arm.

Sun thought Mother would have been dreadfully cross. But she wasn't. She kept on laughing at Father.

'Oh, you dreadful boy!' said she. But she didn't mean Sun.

'Come on, kiddies. Come and have some pickings,' said this jolly Father. But Moon stopped a minute.

'Mother—your dress is right off one side.'

'Is it?' said Mother. And Father said 'Yes' and pretended to bite her white shoulder, but she pushed him away.

And so they went back to the beautiful dining-room.

But—oh! oh! what had happened. The ribbons and the roses were all pulled untied. The little red table-napkins lay on the floor, all the shining plates were dirty and all the winking glasses. The lovely food that the man had trimmed was all thrown about, and there were bones and bits and fruit peels and shells everywhere. There was even a bottle lying down with stuff coming out of it on to the cloth and nobody stood it up again.

And the little pink house with the snow roof and the green windows was broken—broken—half melted away in the centre of the table.

'Come on, Sun,' said Father, pretending not to notice.

Moon lifted up her pyjama legs and shuffled up to the table and stood on a chair, squeaking away.

'Have a bit of this ice,' said Father, smashing in some more of the roof.

Mother took a little plate and held it for him; she put her other arm round his neck.

'Daddy! Daddy!' shrieked Moon. 'The little handle's left. The little nut. Kin I eat it?' And she reached across and picked it out of the door and scrunched it up, biting hard and blinking.

'Here, my lad,' said Father.

But Sun did not move from the door. Suddenly he put up his head and gave a loud wail.

'I think it's horrid—horrid—horrid!' he sobbed.

'There, you see!' said Mother. 'You see!'

'Off with you,' said Father, no longer jolly. 'This moment. Off you go.'

And wailing loudly, Sun stumped off to the nursery.

(1918)

The Wind Blows

Oh Chummie! put your arms
around me. I was going to write:
Let us shut out everybody. But no,
it is not that. Only we shall 'look
on' at them together . . . in every
word I write and every place I
visit I carry you with me. . . .Of
daisies I will write. Of the dark.
Of the wind—and the sun and the
mists. Of the wharves. Ah! of all
that you loved and that I too love
and feel.

Suddenly—dreadfully—she wakes up. What has happened? Something dreadful has happened. No—nothing has happened. It is only the wind shaking the house, rattling the windows, banging a piece of iron on the roof and making her bed tremble. Leaves flutter past the window, up and away; down in the avenue a whole newspaper wags in the air like a lost kite and falls, spiked on a pine tree. It is cold. Summer is over—it is autumn—everything is ugly. The carts rattle by, swinging from side to side; two Chinamen lollop along under their wooden yokes with the straining vegetable baskets—their pigtails and blue blouses fly out in the wind. A white dog on three legs yelps past the gate. It is all over! What is? Oh, everything! And she begins to plait her hair with shaking fingers, not daring to look in the glass. Mother is talking to grandmother in the hall.

'A perfect idiot! Imagine leaving anything out on the line in weather like this.... Now my best little Teneriffe-work teacloth is simply in ribbons. *What* is that extraordinary smell? It's the porridge burning. Oh, heavens—this wind!'

She has a music lesson at ten o'clock. At the thought the minor movement of the Beethoven begins to play in her head, the trills long and terrible like little rolling drums.... Marie Swainson runs into the garden next door to pick the 'chrysanths' before they are ruined. Her skirt flies up above her waist; she tries to beat it down, to tuck it between her legs while she stoops, but it is no use—up it flies. All the trees and bushes beat about her. She picks as quickly as she can, but she is quite distracted. She doesn't mind what she does—she pulls the plants up by the roots and bends and twists them, stamping her foot and swearing.

'For heaven's sake keep the front door shut! Go round to the back,' shouts someone. And then she hears Bogey:

'Mother, you're wanted on the telephone. Telephone, Mother. It's the butcher.'

How hideous life is—revolting, simply revolting.... And now her hat-elastic's snapped. Of course it would. She'll wear her old tam and slip out the back way. But Mother has seen.

'Matilda. Matilda. Come back im-me-diately! What on earth have you got on your head? It looks like a tea-cosy. And why have you got that mane of hair on your forehead?'

'I can't come back, Mother. I'll be late for my lesson.'

'Come back immediately!'

She won't. She won't. She hates Mother. 'Go to hell,' she shouts, running down the road.

In waves, in clouds, in big round whirls the dust comes stinging, and with it little bits of straw and chaff and manure. There is a loud roaring sound from the trees in the gardens, and standing at the bottom of the road outside Mr. Bullen's gate she can hear the sea sob: 'Ah!... Ah!... Ah-h!' But Mr. Bullen's drawing-room is as quiet as a cave. The windows are closed, the blinds half pulled, and she is not late. The-girl-before-her has just started playing MacDowell's 'To an Iceberg.' Mr. Bullen looks over at her and half smiles.

'Sit down,' he says. 'Sit over there in the sofa corner, little lady.'

How funny he is. He doesn't exactly laugh at you ... but there is just something ... Oh, how peaceful it is here. She likes this room. It smells of art serge and stale smoke and chrysanthemums . . . there is a big vase of them on the mantelpiece behind the pale photograph of Rubinstein . . . *à mon ami Robert Bullen*. . . . Over the black glittering piano hangs 'Solitude'—a dark tragic woman draped in white, sitting on a rock, her knees crossed, her chin on her hands.

'No, no!' says Mr. Bullen, and he leans over the other girl, puts his arms over her shoulders and plays the passage for her. The stupid—she's blushing! How ridiculous!

Now the-girl-before-her has gone; the front door slams. Mr. Bullen comes back and walks up and down, very softly, waiting for her. What an extraordinary thing. Her fingers tremble so that she can't undo the knot in the music satchel. It's the wind. . . . And her heart beats so hard she feels it must lift her blouse up and down. Mr. Bullen does not say a word. The shabby red piano seat is long enough for two people to sit side by side. Mr. Bullen sits down by her.

'Shall I begin with scales,' she asks, squeezing her hands together. 'I had some arpeggios, too.'

But he does not answer. She doesn't believe he even hears . . . and then suddenly his fresh hand with the ring on it reaches over and opens Beethoven.

'Let's have a little of the old master,' he says.

But why does he speak so kindly—so awfully kindly—and as though they had known each other for years and years and knew everything about each other.

He turns the page slowly. She watches his hand—it is a very nice hand and always looks as though it had just been washed.

'Here we are,' says Mr. Bullen.

Oh, that kind voice—Oh, that minor movement. Here comes the little drums. . . .

'Shall I take the repeat?'

'Yes, dear child.'

His voice is far, far too kind. The crotchets and quavers are dancing up and down the stave like little black boys on a fence. Why is he so . . . She will not cry—she has nothing to cry about. . . .

'What is it, dear child?'

Mr. Bullen takes her hands. His shoulder is there—just by her head. She leans on it ever so little, her cheek against the springy tweed.

'Life is so dreadful,' she murmurs, but she does not feel it's dreadful at all. He says something about 'waiting' and 'marking time' and 'that rare thing, a woman,' but she does not hear. It is so comfortable . . . for ever . . .

Suddenly the door opens and in pops Marie Swainson, hours before her time.

'Take the allegretto a little faster,' says Mr. Bullen, and gets up and begins to walk up and down again.

'Sit in the sofa corner, little lady,' he says to Marie.

The wind, the wind. It's frightening to be here in her room by herself. The bed, the mirror, the white jug and basin gleam like the sky outside. It's the bed that is frightening. There it lies, sound asleep. . . . Does Mother imagine for one moment that she is going to darn all those stockings knotted up on the quilt like a coil of snakes? She's not. No, Mother. I do not see why I should. . . . The wind—the wind! There's a funny smell of soot blowing down the chimney. Hasn't anyone written poems to the wind? . . . 'I bring fresh flowers to the leaves and showers.' . . . What nonsense.

'Is that you, Bogey?'

'Come for a walk round the esplanade, Matilda. I can't stand this any longer.'

'Right-o. I'll put on my ulster. Isn't it an awful day!' Bogey's ulster is just like hers. Hooking the collar she looks at herself in the glass. Her face is white, they have the same excited eyes and hot lips. Ah, they know those two in the glass. Good-bye, dears; we shall be back soon.

'This is better, isn't it?'

'Hook on,' says Bogey.

They cannot walk fast enough. Their heads bent, their legs just touching, they stride like one eager person through the town, down the asphalt zigzag where the fennel grows wild and on to the esplanade. It is dusky—just getting dusky. The wind is so strong that they have to fight their way through it, rocking like two old drunkards. All the poor little pahutu-kawas on the esplanade are bent to the ground.

'Come on! Come on! Let's get near.'

Over by the breakwater the sea is very high. They pull off their hats and her hair blows across her mouth, tasting of salt. The sea is so high that the waves do not break at all; they thump against the rough stone wall and suck up the weedy, dripping steps. A fine spray skims from the water right across the esplanade. They are covered with drops; the inside of her mouth tastes wet and cold.

Bogey's voice is breaking. When he speaks he rushes up and down the scale. It's funny—it makes you laugh—and yet it just suits the day. The wind carries their voices—away fly the sentences like little narrow ribbons.

'Quicker! Quicker!'

It is getting very dark. In the harbour the coal hulks show two lights—one high on a mast and one from the stern.

'Look, Bogey. Look over there.'

A big black steamer with a long loop of smoke streaming, with the portholes lighted, with lights everywhere, is putting out to sea. The wind does not stop her; she cuts through the waves, making for the open gate between the pointed rocks that leads to . . . It's the light that makes her look so awfully beautiful and mysterious. . . . *They* are on board leaning over the rail arm in arm.

'. . . Who are they?'

'. . . Brother and sister.'

'Look, Bogey, there's the town. Doesn't it look small? There's the post-office clock chiming for the last time. There's the esplanade where we walked that windy day. Do you remember? I cried at my music lesson that day—how many years ago! Good-bye, little island, good-bye. . . .'

Now the dark stretches a wing over the tumbling water. They can't see those two any more. Good-bye, good-bye. Don't forget. . . . But the ship is gone, now.

The wind—the wind.

(1915)

Love-
Lies-Bleeding

At half-past two the servant girl stumped along the narrow passage from the kitchen to the dining-room, thrust her head in at the door and shouted in her loud, impudent voice: 'Well, I'm off, Mrs. Eichelbaum. I'll be here to-morrow, Mrs. Eichelbaum.' Muffi waited until she heard the servant's steps crunch down the gravel path, heard the gate creak and slam, listened until those steps died away quite, and silence like a watchful spider began to spin its web over the little house. Everything changed. The white curtains bulged and blew out as though to the first breath of a mysterious breeze, blowing from nowhere; the dark furniture swelled with rich important life; all the plates on the sideboard, the pictures and ornaments, gleamed as though they shone through water; even the lilies, the faded lilies flung all over the green wall-paper, solemnly uncurled again, and she could hear the clock, ticking away, trotting away, galloping away . . . a rider with a dark plume round his hat riding on a white horse down a lonely road in the moonlight.

Stealthy as a little cat Muffi crept into the kitchen, up the stairs into their bedroom and the children's room, down again and into the study, to make sure that nobody was there, and then she came back to the dining-room and folded herself upon the shabby sofa before the window, her feet tucked under her, her hands shut in her lap.

The window of the dining -room looked out on to a paddock covered with long grass and ragged bushes. In one corner lay a heap of bricks, in another a load of timber was tumbled. Round three sides of the paddock there reared up three new houses, white, unsubstantial, puffed up in the air like half-

187

baked meringues. A fourth was being built; only the walls
and criss-cross beams showed. Everything that afternoon was
blurred with a thick sea mist, and somewhere in the paddock,
out of sight, a man was playing the cornet. He must have been
walking about while he played, for sometimes the notes sounded
loud and harsh, full of despair and threatening anger, sometimes they came from far away, bubbles of melancholy sound
floating on the swaying mist.

> Ta-ta-ta
> Tiddle-um tiddle-um
> Ta tiddley-um tum ta.

There was nobody to be seen and nothing to be heard except
that cornet and the tap of hammers in the hollow house.

'It's autumn,' thought Muffi. Her lips trembled, tasting the
mist and the cold air. 'Yes, it's autumn.'

Not that she felt sad. No, she merely responded, just as she
held up her face to the sun and wrapped herself together against
the rain. It was not Muffi's nature to rebel against anything.
Why should she? What good would it do? She accepted life
with cowlike female stupidity, as Max put it.

'And you are like all women,' he would sneer. 'You love
to make men believe that you are rarer beings, more delicately
attuned than they.... Nothing surprises me,' Max would
squeak in a mincing voice, flirting his fat hand, 'nothing
alarms me, I knew that it was going to rain, I knew that we
were going to miss the train, I knew that my children would
catch cold. I have my celestial messengers. But any man old
enough to shave himself knows that divine calm is simply
your lack of imagination, and that no woman ever feels
anything—once she is out of bed.'

The children loved their father when he began to talk like
that. He would walk up and down the room, holding up his
coat-tails for a skirt, laughing and jeering at women and at
their imbecile unbelievable vanity.... The children used to
sit at the table and bang with their fists and clap their hands
and jump up and down. 'Ah, Papa! Ah, my Papa! My darling
clever little Papa!' Rudi would cry; but Katerina, who was
eleven years old and quite a woman, realised that Papa really
meant Muffi when he tiptoed and squeaked, and therein lay her
joy.

Muffi smiled too, and when Rudi, quite overcome, would fling himself upon her, crying breathessly: 'Isn't it wonderful, my Papa?' she would answer: 'Yes, he is wonderful.' What did it matter?

> Ta-ta-ta
> Tiddle-um tiddle-um
> Ta tiddley-um tum ta

went the cornet. She had never heard it before. She hoped it was not going to be there every afternoon. Perhaps it was the sea mist that had brought it. What was the player like? He was an old man wearing a peaked cap and his grey beard was hung with a web of bright drops. She smiled; he stood before her, the cornet under his arm, wiping his face with a coloured handkerchief that smelt of tar. . . . Tell me, why do you play the cornet? . . . Now he was gone again, sitting perhaps behind the heap of timber, far away, and playing more forlornly than ever. . . .

She stirred and sighed and stretched herself.

'What am I going to do this afternoon?' thought Muffi. Every day she asked herself that question, and every day it ended in her doing just the same thing—nothing at all. In the winter she lay in front of the fire, staring at the bright dazzle; in summer she sat at the open window and watched the breeze skim through the long gleaming grass, and then those ragged bushes were covered with tiny cream flowers; and in autumn and winter she sat there too, only then the window was shut. Some days a sea mist covered everything, and other days the wild hooting south wind blew as if it meant to tear everything off the earth, tear everything up by the roots and send it spinning. She did not even think or dream. No, as she sat there, ever so faintly smiling, with something mocking in the way her eyelids lay upon her eyes, she looked like a person waiting for a train that she knew would not come, never would by any chance carry her away, did not even exist. . . .

During the afternoon the baker's boy came and left a loaf on the kitchen window sill. The round basket on his back always reminded her of a snail's shell. 'Here comes the snail,' she would say. Three times a week an awful butcher, a man so raw and red and willing to oblige that she always felt if he hadn't the pound and a half of steak she wanted he'd be quite willing to cut it off his own person and never notice the difference. . . . And very, very rarely, two shabby old nuns wheeling a perambulator knocked at the door and asked her if she had any scraps or bits of things for the orphan children at Lyall Bay. . . . No, she never had, but she liked very much seeing them at her door, smiling so gently, their hands tucked in their sleeves. They made her feel so small somehow, so like an orphan child herself. One of them always did the talking, and the other kept silent.

'You're not married, are you?' asked the talkative nun on one occasion.

'Oh, yes,' said Muffi.

'Glory be!' cried the old nun, and seemed positively to wring her hidden hands in horror.

'You've no children?' she asked, her old mouth falling open.

'Yes, I've a little boy of seven.'

'Mother of God!' cried the old nun, and that day they went away pushing the perambulator very slowly, as though it were heavy with the incredible news.

Any time after five o'clock the children came home from school. . . .

Five o'clock struck. Muffi got up from the sofa to put the kettle on for their tea. She was bending over the kitchen stove when someone tapped on the window. Rudi. Yes, there he was tapping on the window, smiling and nodding. Ah, the darling. He was home early. She flew to the back door and just had time to open it . . . to hold out her arms and in he tumbled.

'You're early. You darling. You're so beautifully early,' she stammered, kissing and hugging him. How wet and cold his cheeks were; and his fingers, even his fringe was damp. For a moment he could not speak. He might have been a little boy picked out of the sea, so breathless and exhausted was he. At last he swallowed twice and gave a final gasping sigh.

'I'm simply sopping from this mist,' he panted. 'Feel my cap, Muffi. Drenched!'

'Drenched,' said she, kneeling down to take off his reefer jacket.

'Oh, I'm still so out of breath,' he cried, stamping and wriggling his way out of the sleeves. 'I simply flew home.'

'Let me jump you on the table and take off your boots, my precious.'

190

'Oh, no!' He had got back his self-contained deliberate little voice. 'I can take off my own boots, Muffi, I always do.'

'Ah, no! Let me,' she pleaded. 'Just this once. Just for a treat.'

At that he threw back his head and looked at her, his eyes dancing.

'Well, you have got funny ideas of a treat.'

'Yes,' said she. 'I know I have. Awfully funny ideas. Now the other foot, old man.'

When she had finished, he sat on the table edge and swung his leg, pouting and frowning, and showing off just a tiny bit. He knew, as he sat there, that he was the most loved little boy in the world, the most admired, the most cherished. And Muffi let him know it. They were alone together so seldom; they could not afford to pretend, to waste a moment. He seemed to realise that. He said: 'Katerina will be home in a minute. I passed her on my way, dawdling along with that Lily Tar. I can't stand Lily Tar, Muffi. She's always got her arm round someone and she's always whispering.'

'Don't bother about her,' said Muffi, as much as to say: 'If Lily Tar dares to get in your way I shall see that she is destroyed instantly.' Lily Tar was gone. He looked down at his little red paws.

'My fingers are so stiff,' he said. 'I'll never be able to practise.'

'Sit down on the hassock here before the fire and give them a good warm.'

'It's very nice down here,' he decided after a moment. 'I love being down low and looking up at things—don't you? At people moving and the legs of chairs and tables and the shadows on the floor.' His voice tailed off, dreamy and absorbed. She let him be. She thought: 'He is getting back to himself after that horrible rowdy school.' But a moment later the front door slammed and Katerina came into the kitchen.

'Hullo!' said she, very airy. 'Why did you tear home so, Rudi? Lily and I could not help screaming at the way you were rushing along.'

'I heard you,' said Rudi. 'I knew you meant me to hear, didn't you?' At that she opened her big velvety eyes at him and laughed.

191

'What a baby you are!'

'But you did, didn't you?' he protested.

'Of course not,' she jeered. 'We were laughing at something quite different.'

'But you just said you were laughing at me, Katerina.'

'Oh, only in a way,' she drawled.

Rudi jumped up. 'Oh, Katerina,' he wailed, 'why do you tell such awful stories?'

Muffi's back was turned, so Katerina made a hideous face at him and sat down at the table. All the while she was eating her tea Katerina could not help smiling her strange little cat smile. The lids fell over her eyes as though she were basking before some mysterious warm secret that she would never share with a baby boy. When she helped herself to jam, holding the jam spoon high up in the air and letting the jam fall in red blobs on her bread, Rudi hated her so much he gave a great shudder of horror and pushed back his chair. Again she opened those big pansy velvet eyes and again the wide surprised stare.

'What is the matter, now?' asked Katerina.

But that was too much for Rudi. He couldn't understand it, no, he couldn't. 'Muffi, why does she do it? How can she?'

But Muffi gave barely a sign. 'Don't tease him so, Katerina!' she said. She poured some warm water into a basin and gave Rudi a thin shave of soap. And as he washed his hands he turned to her. . . .

(1917)

Sewing-Class

Why can't I change my hair-ribbon on Wednesday afternoon?
All the other girls are allowed to ; and it can't be because Mother
really thinks I shall lose my best one. I know a way to tie a
hair-ribbon so that it simply can't possibly come off, and she knows
I do because she taught me herself.

But 'No', says Mother. 'You may put on your threadwork
pinafore, but you may not put on your blue satin hair-ribbon.
Your ordinary brown velvet one is perfectly neat, suitable and
unobtrusive as it is. (Mother loves sentences like this.) I can't help
what all the other *girls do. Have you got your thimble?'*

'Yes, Mother, in my pocket.'
'Show it to me, dear.'
'I said, Mother, it was in my pocket.'
'Well, show it to me so that I can be perfectly sure.'
'Oh, Mother, why do *you treat me like a baby? You always*
seem to forget on purpose that I'm in my teens. None of the other
girls' Mothers. . . .'

Oh well, I'll take my blue satin hair ribbon in my pocket and
change when I get to school. It serves Mother right. I don't want to
deceive her, but she makes me deceive her, and she doesn't really care
a bit—she only wants to show her power.

It was Wednesday afternoon. I love Wednesday afternoons. I
simply adore them. We don't have any real school, only sewing
class and elocution in the drawing-room for the girls who take
private lessons. Everything is different on Wednesdays. Some of
the older ones even wear Japanese silk blouses, and we change into
our slippers and we all wash our hands at the lavatory basin in the
passage. The ink-pots are put away by the monitors, the desks
pushed against the wall. There is a long table down the middle of
the room with two big straw baskets on it. The chairs are arranged
in little groups. The windows are opened wide. Even the garden
outside—with its beaten paths and its flowery bushes tumbled and

193

*draggled because the little ones will root under them for their balls—
seems to change, to become real on Wednesdays. When we lift
our heads to thread our needles the fuchsia is lifting and the
camellias are white and red in the bright sun.*

*We are making cheap flannelette chemises for the Maori Mission.
They are as long as night-dresses, very full, with huge armholes and
a plain band round the neck—not even a lace edging. Those poor
Maoris! they can't all be as fat as these chemises. But Mrs. Wallis,
the Bishop's wife, said when she gave the newspaper pattern to the
headmistress, 'It is wiser to reckon on their being fat.' The
headmistress laughed very much and told Miss Burton, our class
mistress, but Miss Burton is very fat herself so she blushed
frightfully—of course, it was pure spite on the headmistress's part.
Skinny little thing! I know she thinks she has got a lovely slim
figure. You should see her pressing her little grey alpaca hips when
she is talking to the curate before Scripture lesson.*

*But even she is not the same on Wednesday afternoons. Her grey
alpaca dress is adorned with a black tulle bow. She wears a tall comb
in her hair, and when she's not inspecting the sewing she sits at the
end of the long table, her gold-rimmed eyeglasses hooked on her long
peaked nose that has such funny little red veins at the end of it, and
she reads Dickens aloud.*

*Our class-room is very big. The walls are free, so are the
window sashes and the doors; and all the girls sit in their little cane
chairs, their faces showing above a froth of cream flannelette; on their
heads their best hair-ribbons perch and quiver. Their hands lift and
fall as they sew those Maori Mission seams. Sometimes they sigh or
May Swainson sneezes. Ever since she had an operation on her nose
she is always sneezing. Or Madge Rothschild, who wears a glacé
silk petticoat, gets up and rustles to the table for her scissors or
some thread, or to ask if she has to turn down a selvedge.*

*But all the same it is quiet in the room, it is very quiet; and when
the headmistress reads Dickens aloud, there is something so
fascinating in her voice that I could listen for years and years. She
is reading* David Copperfield. *When there is a full-page
illustration she passes the book round for us to look. One by one
we put our sewing down. 'Quickly, girls! Don't dawdle over it!'*

*How funny! The headmistress herself is exactly like one of those
illustrations—so tiny, so spry. While she waits for the book to come
back she sits polishing her eyeglasses on a handkerchief that is tucked
between two hooks of her grey alpaca bodice. What does she remind*

194

me of? She reminds me of a bird and a donkey mixed. . . .
'Bring me that here to look at—will you, Katherine?'

(1916)

The Dressmaker

One great advantage in having your clothes made by Miss Phillips was that you had to go through the garden to get to the house. Perhaps it was the only advantage, for Miss Phillips was a strange, temperamental dressmaker with ever a surprise up her—no, indeed— in your own sleeve, for you. Sleeves were her weakness, her terror. I fancy she looked upon them as devils, to be wrestled with but never overcome. Now a body, once she had tried it on first in newspaper, then in unbleached calico and finally in the lining, she could make a very pretty fit to the figure. She liked to linger over her bodies, to stroke them, to revolve round them, hissing as was her wont, faintly. But the moment she dreaded came at last.

'Have you cut out the sleeve, Miss Phillips?'

'Yes, Miss. I 've—one moment, Miss. If you please!' And with a look half peevish half desperate, the strange funnel-shaped thing was held up for your arm to thrust into.

'The armhole is very tight, Miss Phillips.'

'They're wearing them very small this seasing, Miss.'

'But I can't get my hand near my head.'

'Near you read, Miss?' echoed Miss Phillips, as though it was the first time she had ever heard of this gymnastic feat being attempted. Finally, she repinned it and raised it on the shoulder.

'But now it's much too short, Miss Phillips. I wanted a lo—ong sleeve . . . I wanted a point over the hand.' Points over the hand always seemed to me, still seem to me, excessively romantic.

'Oh, Miss!' The tiny scissors then went 'sneep—sneep', like a bird on a cold morning, cut out a brown paper cuff and Miss Phillips pinned it on with fingers that trembled; while I frowned on the top of her head and even made faces at her in my rage. Her hair was so strange. It was grey, all in little tufts. It reminded you of a sheepskin hearthrug. And there were always threads, minute triangles of stuff, pieces of fluff sticking to it. It didn't want brushing, I thought, so much as a good sweeping and a shake out of the window.

In person Miss Phillips was extremely thin and squeezed in so tight that every breath creaked, and in moments of emotion she sounded like a ship at sea. She invariably wore the same black alpaca apron, fitted on her left breast—oh, how cruel, how sinister it looked to me! —with a tight little red plush heart pierced all over with needles and pins, and a malignant-looking safety-pin or two to stab deeper——

'If you please, Miss, while I unpin you . . .' Her small hard hands flew up, pinched, gripped like claws. She had a thin nose with just a dab of red on the tip as though some wicked child with a paint-brush had caught her sleeping.

'Thank you, Miss Phillips. And you'll let me have it on Saturday?'

'I'll send it for certain, Miss,' hissed Miss Phillips through a bristling mouthful of pins.

While I dressed in front of the long mirror that had spots at the side like frosted fingerprints, I loved to discover again that funny little room. In the corner by the fire-place stood the 'model' covered in red sateen. Its solidity ended at the hips in wire rings that reminded you of an egg-beater. But what a model it was! What shoulders, what a bosom—what curves, and no horrible arms to be clothed in sleeves, no head to be reached up to. It was Miss Phillips' God. It was also, I decided, a perfect lady. Thus and thus only do perfect ladies appear in the extreme privacy of her apartments. But above all it was god-like. I saw Miss Phillips alone, abstracted, lavishing her stuffs upon that imperturbable altar. Perhaps her failures even were to be excused. They were all part of a frenzy for sacrifice. . . .

(1922)

A Dance

Is Life going to be all like this? thought Laura. And she lay down in bed and put her arms round the pillow, and the pillow whispered: 'Yes, this is what Life is going to be like—only always more and more splendid—more and more marvellous!'

'But supposing,' said Laura, speaking very fast and with the greatest possible earnestness, 'supposing you were terrifically successful and were married to the person you adored, and you had every single thing you wanted,—and your first child was just born (that's supposed to be a marvellous moment, isn't it?), would you be really happier than you are now?'

They stared hard at each other a moment.

'I simply couldn't be.'

At his words Laura gave a beaming smile, a great sigh, and squeezed her brother's arm. 'Oh, what a relief!' she said. 'Neither could I—not possible.'

'Laura! Laurie! What are you doing up there? Come down at once. The N.'s have arrived!'

Laura stooped down and kissed her grandmother. 'You're by far the most beautiful girl in the rooms, my little precious!' she whispered.

As Grandma passed on, the Major and Laura suddenly turned round to catch her eye. She raised her eyebrows in a very childish astounded way, and sucked in her cheeks. The old woman actually blushed.

(1920)

Her First
Ball

Exactly when the ball began Leila would have found it hard to say. Perhaps her first real partner was the cab. It did not matter that she shared the cab with the Sheridan girls and their brother. She sat back in her own little corner of it, and the bolster on which her hand rested felt like the sleeve of an unknown young man's dress suit; and away they bowled, past waltzing lamp-posts and houses and fences and trees.

'Have you really never been to a ball before, Leila? But, my child, how too weird—' cried the Sheridan girls.

'Our nearest neighbour was fifteen miles,' said Leila softly, gently opening and shutting her fan.

Oh dear, how hard it was to be indifferent like the others! She tried not to smile too much; she tried not to care. But every single thing was so new and exciting . . . Meg's tuberoses, Jose's long loop of amber, Laura's little dark head, pushing above her white fur like a flower through snow. She would remember for ever. It even gave her a pang to see her cousin Laurie throw away the wisps of tissue paper he pulled from the fastenings of his new gloves. She would like to have kept those wisps as a keepsake, as a remembrance. Laurie leaned forward and put his hand on Laura's knee.

'Look here, darling,' he said. 'The third and the ninth as usual. Twig?'

Oh, how marvellous to have a brother! In her excitement Leila felt that if there had been time, if it hadn't been impossible, she couldn't have helped crying because she was an only child and no brother had ever said 'Twig?' to her; no sister would ever say, as Meg said to Jose that moment, 'I've never known your hair go up more successfully than it has to-night!'

But, of course, there was no time. They were at the drill hall already; there were cabs in front of them and cabs behind. The road was bright on either side with moving fan-like lights, and on the pavement gay couples seemed to float through the air; little satin shoes chased each other like birds.

'Hold on to me, Leila; you'll get lost,' said Laura.

'Come on, girls, let's make a dash for it,' said Laurie.

Leila put two fingers on Laura's pink velvet cloak, and they were somehow lifted past the big golden lantern, carried along the passage, and pushed into the little room marked 'Ladies.' Here the crowd was so great there was hardly space to take off their things; the noise was deafening. Two benches on either side were stacked high with wraps. Two old women in white aprons ran up and down tossing fresh armfuls. And everybody was pressing forward trying to get at the little dressing-table and mirror at the far end.

A great quivering jet of gas lighted the ladies' room. It couldn't wait; it was dancing already. When the door opened again and there came a burst of tuning from the drill hall, it leaped almost to the ceiling.

Dark girls, fair girls were patting their hair, tying ribbons again, tucking handkerchiefs down the fronts of their bodices, smoothing marble-white gloves. And because they were all laughing it seemed to Leila that they were all lovely.

'Aren't there any invisible hairpins?' cried a voice. 'How most extraordinary! I can't see a single invisible hairpin.'

'Powder my back, there's a darling,' cried someone else.

'But I must have a needle and cotton. I've torn simply miles and miles of the frill,' wailed a third.

Then, 'Pass them along, pass them along!' The straw basket of programmes was tossed from arm to arm. Darling little pink-and-silver programmes, with pink pencils and fluffy tassels. Leila's fingers shook as she took one out of the basket. She wanted to ask someone, 'Am I meant to have one too?' but she had just time to read: 'Waltz 3. *Two, Two in a Canoe*. Polka 4. *Making the Feathers Fly*,' when Meg cried, 'Ready, Leila?' and they pressed their way through the crush in the passage towards the big double doors of the drill hall.

Dancing had not begun yet, but the band had stopped tuning, and the noise was so great it seemed that when it did begin to play it would never be heard. Leila, pressing close to

Meg, looking over Meg's shoulder, felt that even the little quivering coloured flags strung across the ceiling were talking. She quite forgot to be shy; she forgot how in the middle of dressing she had sat down on the bed with one shoe off and one shoe on and begged her mother to ring up her cousins and say she couldn't go after all. And the rush of longing she had had to be sitting on the veranda of their forsaken up-country home, listening to the baby owls crying 'More pork' in the the moonlight, was changed to a rush of joy so sweet that it was hard to bear alone. She clutched her fan, and, gazing at the gleaming, golden floor, the azaleas, the lanterns, the stage at one end with its red carpet and gilt chairs and the band in a corner, she thought breathlessly, 'How heavenly; how simply heavenly!'

All the girls stood grouped together at one side of the doors, the men at the other, and the chaperones in dark dresses, smiling rather foolishly, walked with little careful steps over the polished floor towards the stage.

'This is my little country cousin Leila. Be nice to her. Find her partners; she's under my wing,' said Meg, going up to one girl after another.

Strange faces smiled at Leila—sweetly, vaguely. Strange voices answered, 'Of course, my dear.' But Leila felt the girls didn't really see her. They were looking towards the men. Why didn't the men begin? What were they waiting for? There they stood, smoothing their gloves, patting their glossy hair and smiling among themselves. Then, quite suddenly, as if they had only just made up their minds that that was what they had to do, the men came gliding over the parquet. There was a joyful flutter among the girls. A tall, fair man flew up to Meg, seized her programme, scribbled something; Meg passed him on to Leila. 'May I have the pleasure?' He ducked and smiled. There came a dark man wearing an eyeglass, then cousin Laurie with a friend, and Laura with a little freckled fellow whose tie was crooked. Then quite an old man—fat, with a big bald patch on his head—took her programme and murmured, 'Let me see, let me see!' And he was a long time comparing his programme, which looked black with names, with hers. It seemed to give him so much trouble that Leila was ashamed. 'Oh, please don't bother,' she said eagerly. But instead of replying the fat man wrote something, glanced at her again. 'Do I remember this bright little face?' he said softly. 'Is it known to me of yore?' At that moment the band began playing; the fat man disappeared. He was tossed away on a great wave of music that came flying over the gleaming floor, breaking the groups up into couples, scattering them, sending them spinning. . . .

Leila had learned to dance at boarding school. Every Saturday afternoon the boarders were hurried off to a little corrugated iron mission hall where Miss Eccles (of London) held her 'select' classes. But the difference between that dusty-smelling hall—with calico texts on the walls, the poor, terrified little woman in a brown velvet toque with rabbit's ears thumping the cold piano, Miss Eccles poking the girls' feet with her long white wand—and this, was so tremendous that Leila was sure if her partner didn't come and she had to listen to that marvellous music and to watch the others sliding, gliding over the golden floor, she would die at least, or faint, or lift her arms and fly out of one of those dark windows that showed the stars.

'Ours, I think—' Someone bowed, smiled, and offered her his arm; she hadn't to die after all. Someone's hand pressed her waist, and she floated away like a flower that is tossed into a pool.

'Quite a good floor, isn't it?' drawled a faint voice close to her ear.

'I think it's most beautifully slippery,' said Leila.

'Pardon!' The faint voice sounded surprised. Leila said it again. And there was a tiny pause before the voice echoed,

'Oh, quite!' and she was swung round again.

He steered so beautifully. That was the great difference between dancing with girls and men, Leila decided. Girls banged into each other and stamped on each other's feet; the girl who was gentleman always clutched you so.

The azaleas were separate flowers no longer; they were pink and white flags streaming by.

'Were you at the Bells' last week?' the voice came again. It sounded tired. Leila wondered whether she ought to ask him if he would like to stop.

'No, this is my first dance,' said she.

Her partner gave a little gasping laugh. 'Oh, I say,' he protested.

'Yes, it is really the first dance I've ever been to.' Leila was most fervent. It was such a relief to be able to tell somebody. 'You see, I've lived in the country all my life up till now. . . .'

At that moment the music stopped and they went to sit on two chairs against the wall. Leila tucked her pink satin feet under and fanned herself, while she blissfully watched the other couples passing and disappearing through the swing doors.

'Enjoying yourself, Leila?' asked Jose, nodding her golden head.

Laura passed and gave her the faintest little wink; it made Leila wonder for a moment whether she was quite grown up after all. Certainly her partner did not say very much. He coughed, tucked his handkerchief away, pulled down his waistcoat, took a minute thread off his sleeve. But it didn't matter. Almost immediately the band started and her second partner seemed to spring from the ceiling.

'Floor's not bad,' said the new voice. Did one always begin with the floor? And then, 'Were you at the Neaves' on Tuesday?' And again Leila explained. Perhaps it was a little strange that her partners were not more interested. For it was thrilling. Her first ball! She was only at the beginning of everything. It seemed to her that she had never known what the night was like before. Up till now it had been dark, silent, beautiful very often—oh yes—but mournful somehow. Solemn. And now it would never be like that again—it had opened dazzling bright.

'Care for an ice?' said her partner. And they went through the swing doors, down the passage, to the supper-room. Her cheeks burned, she was fearfully thirsty. How sweet the ices looked on little glass plates and how cold the frosted spoon was, iced too! And when they came back to the hall there was the fat man waiting for her by the door. It gave her quite a shock again to see how old he was; he ought to have been on the stage with the fathers and mothers. And when Leila compared him with her other partners he looked shabby. His waistcoat was creased, there was a button off his glove, his coat looked as if it was dusty with French chalk.

'Come along, little lady,' said the fat man. He scarcely troubled to clasp her, and they moved away so gently, it was more like walking than dancing. But he said not a word about the floor. 'Your first dance, isn't it?' he murmured.

'How *did* you know?'

'Ah,' said the fat man, 'that's what it is to be old!' He wheezed faintly as he steered her past an awkward couple. 'You see, I've been doing this kind of thing for the last thirty years.'

'Thirty years?' cried Leila. Twelve years before she was born!

'It hardly bears thinking about, does it?' said the fat man gloomily. Leila looked at his bald head, and she felt quite sorry for him.

'I think it's marvellous to be still going on,' she said kindly.

'Kind little lady,' said the fat man, and he pressed her a little closer and hummed a bar of the waltz. 'Of course,' he said, 'you can't hope to last anything like as long as that. No-o,' said the fat man, 'long before that you'll be sitting up there on the stage, looking on, in your nice black velvet. And these pretty arms will have turned into little short fat ones, and you'll beat time with such a different kind of fan—a black ebony one.' The fat man seemed to shudder. 'And you'll smile away like the poor old dears up there, and point to your daughter, and tell the elderly lady next to you how some dreadful man tried to kiss her at the club ball. And your heart will ache, ache'—the fat man squeezed her closer still, as if he really was sorry for that poor heart—'because no one wants to kiss you now. And you'll say how unpleasant these polished floors are to walk on, how dangerous they are. Eh, Mademoiselle Twinkletoes?' said the fat man softly.

Leila gave a light little laugh, but she did not feel like laughing. Was it—could it all be true? It sounded terribly true. Was this first ball only the beginning of her last ball, after all? At that the music seemed to change; it sounded sad, sad; it rose upon a great sigh. Oh, how quickly things changed! Why didn't happiness last for ever? For ever wasn't a bit too long.

'I want to stop,' she said in a breathless voice. The fat man led her to the door.

'No,' she said, 'I won't go outside. I won't sit down. I'll just stand here, thank you.' She leaned against the wall, tapping with her foot, pulling up her gloves and trying to smile. But deep inside her a little girl threw her pinafore over her head and sobbed. Why had he spoiled it all?

'I say, you know,' said the fat man, 'you mustn't take me seriously, little lady.'

'As if I should!' said Leila, tossing her small dark head and sucking her underlip. . . .

Again the couples paraded. The swing doors opened and shut. Now new music was given out by the bandmaster. But Leila didn't want to dance any more. She wanted to be home, or sitting on the veranda listening to those baby owls. When she looked through the dark windows at the stars they had long beams like wings. . . .

But presently a soft, melting, ravishing tune began, and a young man with curly hair bowed before her. She would have to dance, out of politeness, until she could find Meg. Very stiffly she walked into the middle; very haughtily she put her hand on his sleeve. But in one minute, in one turn, her feet glided, glided. The lights, the azaleas, the dresses, the pink faces, the velvet chairs, all became one beautiful flying wheel. And when her next partner bumped her into the fat man and he said, 'Par*don*,' she smiled at him more radiantly than ever. She didn't even recognise him again.

(1921)

The Sheridans

The light should fall on the figure of Mrs
Sheridan on her way home. Really I can
allow myself to write a great deal—to
describe it all—the baths, the avenue, the
people in the gardens, the Chinaman under
the tree in May Street. But in that case she
won't be conscious of these things. That's bad.
They must be seen and felt by her as she
wanders home. . . .I now remember . . . and
see that it must be written with love—real love.

It was late afternoon when Mrs. Sheridan, after having paid
Heaven knows how many calls, turned towards home.

'Thank Heaven, that's all over!' she sighed, as she clicked
the last gate to, and stuffed her little Chinese card-case into
her handbag.

But it was not all over. Although she hadn't the faintest
desire to remember her afternoon, her mind, evidently, was
determined she should not forget it. And so she walked along
seeing herself knocking at doors, crossing dim halls into large
pale drawing-rooms, hearing herself saying, 'No, she would
not have any tea, thank you. Yes, they were all splendidly
well. No, they had not seen it yet. The children were going
to-night. Yes, fancy, he had arrived. Young and good-looking
too! Quite an asset! Oh dear no! She was determined not to
allow any of her girls to marry. It was quite unnecessary now-
a-days, and such a risk!' And so on and so on.

'What nonsense calling is! What a waste of time! I have
never met a single woman yet who even pretended to like it.
Why keep it up then? Why not decide once and for all?
Mock-orange . . .' And Mrs. Sheridan woke out of her dream

206

to find herself standing under a beautiful mock-orange bush that grew against the white palings of old Mr. Phillips' garden. The little sponge-like fruits—flowers? which were they?—shone burning-bright in the late afternoon sun. 'They are like little worlds,' she thought, peering up through the large crumpled leaves; and she put out her hand and touched one gently. 'The feel of things is so strange, so different, one never seems to know a thing until one has felt it—at least that is true of flowers. Roses for instance,—who can smell a rose without kissing it? And pansies, little darlings they are! People don't pay half enough attention to pansies.' Now her glove was all brushed with yellow. But it didn't matter. She was glad, even. 'I wish you grew in my garden,' she said regretfully to the mock-orange bush, and she went on, thinking, 'I wonder why I love flowers so much. None of the children inherit it from me. Laura perhaps. But even then it's not the same. She's too young to feel as I do. I love flowers more than people, except my own family, of course. Take this afternoon, for instance. The only thing that really remains is that mock-orange. I mean, when I was standing under that bush, it was the only moment when I felt in touch with something. These things are very difficult to explain. But the fact remains I never feel that need of anybody—apart from Claude and the children. If the rest of the world was swept away to-morrow . . .'

Return again! Come—it was an agony to Mr. Sheridan to be late, or to know that others were late. It had always been so. Talking with his wife in the garden—the stillness, the lightness, the steps on the gravel—the dark trees, the flowers, the night-scented stocks—what happiness it was to walk with him there! What he said did not really matter so very much. But she felt she had him to herself in a way that no other occasion granted her. She felt *his ease*, and although he never looked at what she pointed out to him it did not matter. His 'very nice, dear!' was enough. He was always planning, always staring towards a future. . . . 'I should like later on.' But she—she did not care in the least; the present was all she loved and dwelt in. . . .

The excitement began first thing that morning by their father suddenly deciding that, after all, they could have champagne. What! Impossible! Mother was joking!

A fierce discussion had raged on this subject ever since the invitations were sent out, Father pooh-poohing—and refusing

207

to listen, and Mother, as usual siding with him when she was with him: ('Of course, darling: I quite agree') and siding with them when she was with them: ('Most unreasonable, I more than see the point'). So that by this time they had definitely given up hope of champagne, and had focussed all their attention on the hock cup instead. And now, for no reason whatever, with nobody saying a word to him—so like Father!—he had given in.

'It was just after Zaidee had brought in our morning tea. He was lying on his back, you know, staring at the ceiling. And suddenly he said: "I don't want the children to think I am a wet blanket about this dance affair. If it's going to make all that difference to them; if it's a question of the thing going with a swing or not going with a swing, then I'm inclined to let them have champagne. I'll call in and order it on my way to the Bank."'

'My dear! What did you say?'

'What could I say? I was overcome. I said: "That's very generous of you, Daddy dear", and I placed the entire plate of cut bread and butter on his chest. As a kind of sacrifice to the darling. I felt he deserved it, and he does so love those thin shaves of bread and butter.'

'Can't you see the plate,' cried Laurie, 'gently rising and falling on his pyjama jacket?'

They began to laugh, but it really was most thrilling. . . . Champagne did make all the difference—didn't it? Just the feeling it was there gave such a different . . . Oh, absolutely!

(1922)

208

By Moonlight

This isn't bad, but at the same time it's not good. It's too easy. I wish I could go back to N.Z. for a year.

Dinner was over. There was a whiff of Father's cigar from the hall, and then the door of the smoking-room shut, clicked. Mother went rustling to and fro, to and fro—to the dining-room door, speaking to Zaidee who was clearing away, giving Hans who was helping Zaidee his orders for to-morrow—to the music-room speaking to the girls.

'Francie darling, run upstairs and get me my cream feather boa, will you? My cream one. On the top of the tall wardrobe. Come here, child! How beautifully you have done your hair!'

'Really, dearest? It was simply thrown up. I was in such a hurry. . . .'

'How mysterious it is that if one really *tries* to get that effect. . . .'

'Yes, isn't it?'

There came a soft chain of sound from the music-room, as though Meg had flung a bright loop and snared the dreaming piano.

'We're going to try over Francie's new song,' said she. '*This Life is Weary.*'

'This Life is Weary!' cried Mother. 'Oh, dear, is it another tragic one? I can't understand why all these modern songs are so depressing. It seems so unnecessary. Why can't one for a change. . . .'

'Oh, but it's fascinating! said Meg. 'Listen!' And softly she played 'This Life is We-ary.' 'You can't say you like *Cupid at the Ferry* better than that?'

209

'I do,' said Mother. 'I like songs about primroses and cheerful normal birds and . . . and spring and so on.'

But Francie came floating down the stairs with the feather boa.

'It wasn't on the tall wardrobe, you little story,' said she, winding her Mother up in it. 'It was among your hats. And then you always pretend to be so tidy and unlike us.'

'If you don't speak to me with more respect,' said Mother, 'I shall go straight off and tell your Father. Thank you, darling child!'

Francie's little wooden heels tapped over the parquet floor of the music-room. 'Shut the door while we're practising will you,—please, Mother?'

The door shut and the piano seemed to have been waiting until it was alone with them, it burst out so passionately: 'This Life is Weary.'

Silence from the hall. Mother was still, her head bent, turning her rings. What was she thinking of? She looked up. The double doors on to the porch were open and the light in the glass lantern flickered faintly. Dreamily she went over to the hall-stand and picked something up. 'Why,' she murmured aloud, 'is there always one odd glove? Where does it come from?'

Down the passage, through the green-baize door that led to the kitchen regions, sailed Zaidee with her tray of trembling glass and winking silver and moon-white plates. And Hans followed with the finger-bowls, with the fruit-dishes and the plates piled with curls of tangerine peel and shavings of pineapple-outside.

The last tray was carried; the heavy baize door swung to with a 'whoof'. There came a faint ghostly chatter from the kitchen. Very far away it sounded.

Where was Laurie? He had gone straight off to his darkroom after dinner. She wouldn't disturb him—no! But all the same Laura slid off the landing window-sill, parted the embroidered velvet curtains that hid her so beautifully, and coming on to the stairs leaned her arms along the banisters. What was she to do?

'This Life is We-ary!
A Tear—a Sigh!
A Love that Change-es!'

210

sang Francie. And suddenly from that far-away kitchen there sounded a shrill little peal of laughter. . . .

How much bigger the house felt at night! thought Laura. All the lighted rooms and the passages that were dark and the cupboards and the front and back stairs. As to the cupboard under the stairs, Laura's eyes widened at the very thought of it. . . . She saw herself, suddenly, exploring it with a candle-end. There was the old croquet set, last year's goloshes, the shelf of dead lamps, and the buffalo horns tied up with ribbons. It was like exploring a cave.

Big—big and empty. No, not empty exactly, but awfully strange. For though the lights were up everywhere, through the open windows the darkness came flowing in from outside. It was the darkness that so gently breathed in the curtains, gathered in pools under the tables, and hid in the folds even of the coats down there in the hall. And the stairs! Stairs at night were utterly different to what they were by day, and people went up and down them quite differently. They were much more important, somehow; they might have led to anywhere.

But just as Laura thought that, she had an idea that some-one on the top landing was looking down at her. Someone had suddenly appeared from nowhere and with a brilliant round white face was staring! Oh, how awful! And it was shameful, too, to have such ideas at her age. She had decided the face was a Chinaman's before she had time to look up. What nonsense! It was the moon shining through the top landing window. And now there were moonbeam fingers on the banisters. Laura walked up the stairs slowly, but for some reason she tried not to make a sound, and looking down at her satin shoes, she pretended they were little birds tiptoeing up a dark branch.

'But now we're at the top of the tree,' she told them. And she stood with her head bent and her arms by her sides, waiting for someone. . . .

'It's only because people don't know she's here that they don't come,' thought Laura. 'She is wearing a white tulle dress with a black velvet sash—very nice! Charming! I say, Laurie, introduce me to your sister!' And someone came forward, stroking his white kid gloves.

Laura was so delighted she gave a little jump for joy, and

forgetting all about her resolve, she ran across the landing, down the passage, past the American bathroom and knocked at the darkroom door. . . .

(1921)

The
Garden-Party

*I am sitting in my own room thinking of Mother:
I want to cry. But my thoughts are beautiful and
full of gaiety. I think of our house, our garden,
us children—the lawn, the gate, and Mother
coming in. 'Children! Children!'*

*I thought of the Burnells, but no, I don't think
so. Much better, the Sheridans, the three girls and
the brother and the Father and Mother and so on.*

And after all the weather was ideal. They could not have had a
more perfect day for a garden-party if they had ordered it.
Windless, warm, the sky without a cloud. Only the blue was
veiled with a haze of light gold, as it is sometimes in early
summer. The gardener had been up since dawn, mowing the
lawns and sweeping them, until the grass and the dark flat
rosettes where the daisy plants had been seemed to shine. As for
the roses, you could not help feeling they understood that roses
are the only flowers that impress people at garden-parties;
the only flowers that everybody is certain of knowing. Hundreds, yes, literally hundreds, had come out in a single night;
the green bushes bowed down as though they had been visited
by archangels.

Breakfast was not yet over before the men came to put up
the marquee.

'Where do you want the marquee put, mother?'

'My dear child, it's no use asking me. I'm determined to
leave everying to you children this year. Forget I am your
mother. Treat me as an honoured guest.'

213

But Meg could not possible go and supervise the men. She had washed her hair before breakfast, and she sat drinking her coffee in a green turban, with a dark wet curl stamped on each cheek. Jose, the butterfly, always came down in a silk petticoat and a kimono jacket.

'You'll have to go, Laura; you're the artistic one.'

Away Laura flew, still holding her piece of bread-and-butter. It's so delicious to have an excuse for eating out of doors and, besides, she loved having to arrange things; she always felt she could do it so much better than anybody else.

Four men in their shirt-sleeves stood grouped together on the garden path. They carried staves covered with rolls of canvas and they had big tool-bags slung on their backs. They looked impressive. Laura wished now that she was not holding that piece of bread-and-butter, but there was nowhere to put it and she couldn't possibly throw it away. She blushed and tried to look severe and even a little bit short-sighted as she came up to them.

'Good morning,' she said, copying her mother's voice. But that sounded so fearfully affected that she was ashamed, and stammered like a little girl, 'Oh—er—have you come—is it about the marquee?'

'That's right, miss,' said the tallest of the men, a lanky, freckled fellow, and he shifted his tool-bag, knocked back his straw hat and smiled down at her. 'That's about it.'

His smile was so easy, so friendly, that Laura recovered. What nice eyes he had, small, but such a dark blue! And now she looked at the others, they were smiling, too. 'Cheer up, we won't bite,' their smile seemed to say. How very nice workmen were! And what a beautiful morning! She mustn't mention the morning; she must be business-like. The marquee.

'Well, what about the lily-lawn? Would that do?'

And she pointed to the lily-lawn with the hand that didn't hold the bread-and-butter. They turned, they stared in the direction. A little fat chap thrust out his underlip and the tall fellow frowned.

'I don't fancy it,' said he. 'Not conspicuous enough. You see, with a thing like a marquee'—and he turned to Laura in his easy way—'you want to put it somewhere where it'll give you a bang slap in the eye, if you follow me.'

Laura's upbringing made her wonder for a moment whether

it was quite respectful of a workman to talk to her of bangs slap
in the eye. But she did quite follow him.

'A corner of the tennis-court,' she suggested. 'But the
band's going to be in one corner.'

'H'm, going to have a band, are you?' said another of the
workmen. He was pale. He had a haggard look as his dark
eyes scanned the tennis-court. What was he thinking?

'Only a very small band,' said Laura gently. Perhaps he
wouldn't mind so much if the band was quite small. But the
tall fellow interrupted.

'Look here, miss, that's the place. Against those trees.
Over there. That'll do fine.'

Against the karakas. Then the karaka trees would be hidden.
And they were so lovely, with their broad, gleaming leaves,
and their clusters of yellow fruit. They were like trees you
imagined growing on a desert island, proud, solitary, lifting
their leaves and fruits to the sun in a kind of silent splendour.
Must they be hidden by a marquee?

They must. Already the men had shouldered their staves
and were making for the place. Only the tall fellow was left.
He bent down, pinched a sprig of lavender, put his thumb and
forefinger to his nose and snuffed up the smell. When Laura
saw that gesture she forgot all about the karakas in her wonder
at him caring for things like that—caring for the smell of
lavender. How many men that she knew would have done such
a thing? Oh, how extraordinarily nice workmen were, she
thought. Why couldn't she have workmen for friends rather
than the silly boys she danced with and who came to Sunday
night supper? She would get on much better with men like
these.

It's all the fault, she decided, as the tall fellow drew something on the back of an envelope, something that was to be
looped up or left to hang, of these absurd class distinctions.
Well, for her part, she didn't feel them. Not a bit, not an
atom. . . . And now there came the chock-chock of wooden
hammers. Someone whistled, someone sang out, 'Are you right
there matey?' 'Matey!' The friendliness of it, the—the— Just
to prove how happy she was, just to show the tall fellow how at
home she felt, and how she despised stupid conventions, Laura
took a big bite of her bread-and-butter as she stared at the
little drawing. She felt just like a work-girl.

'Laura, Laura, where are you? Telephone, Laura!' a voice cried from the house.

'Coming!' Away she skimmed, over the lawn, up the path, up the steps, across the veranda and into the porch. In the hall her father and Laurie were brushing their hats ready to go to the office.

'I say, Laura,' said Laurie very fast, 'you might just give a squiz at my coat before this afternoon. See if it wants pressing.'

'I will,' said she. Suddenly she couldn't stop herself. She ran at Laurie and gave him a small, quick squeeze. 'Oh, I do love parties, don't you?' gasped Laura.

'Ra-ther,' said Laurie's warm boyish voice, and he squeezed his sister too and gave her a gentle push. 'Dash off to the telephone, old girl.'

The telephone. 'Yes, yes; oh yes. Kitty? Good morning, dear. Come to lunch? Do, dear. Delighted, of course. It will only be a very scratch meal—just the sandwich crusts and broken meringue-shells and what's left over. Yes, isn't it a perfect morning? Your white? Oh, I certainly should. One moment—hold the line. Mother's calling.' And Laura sat back. 'What, mother? Can't hear.'

Mrs. Sheridan's voice floated down the stairs. 'Tell her to wear that sweet hat she had on last Sunday.'

'Mother says you're to wear that *sweet* hat you had on last Sunday. Good. One o'clock. Bye-bye.'

Laura put back the receiver, flung her arms over her head, took a deep breath, stretched and let them fall. 'Huh,' she sighed, and the moment after the sigh she sat up quickly. She was still, listening. All the doors in the house seemed to be open. The house was alive with soft, quick steps and running voices. The green baize door that led to the kitchen regions swung open and shut with a muffled thud. And now there came a long, chuckling absurd sound. It was the heavy piano being moved on its stiff castors. But the air! If you stopped to notice, was the air always like this? Little faint winds were playing chase in at the tops of the windows, out at the doors. And there were two tiny spots of sun, one on the inkpot, one on a silver photograph frame, playing too. Darling little spots. Especially the one on the inkpot lid. It was quite warm. A warm little silver star. She could have kissed it.

The front door bell pealed and there sounded the rustle of Sadie's print skirt on the stairs. A man's voice murmured; Sadie answered, careless, 'I'm sure I don't know. Wait. I'll ask Mrs. Sheridan.'

'What is it, Sadie?' Laura came into the hall.

'It's the florist, Miss Laura.'

It was, indeed. There, just inside the door, stood a wide, shallow tray full of pots of pink lilies. No other kind. Nothing but lilies—canna lilies, big pink flowers, wide open, radiant, almost frighteningly alive on bright crimson stems.

'O-oh, Sadie!' said Laura, and the sound was like a little moan. She crouched down as if to warm herself at that blaze of lilies; she felt they were in her fingers, on her lips, growing in her breast.

'It's some mistake,' she said faintly. 'Nobody ever ordered so many. Sadie, go and find mother.'

But at that moment Mrs. Sheridan joined them.

'It's quite right,' she said calmly. 'Yes, I ordered them. Aren't they lovely?' She pressed Laura's arm. 'I was passing the shop yesterday, and I saw them in the window. And I suddenly thought for once in my life I shall have enough canna lilies. The garden-party will be a good excuse.'

'But I thought you said you didn't mean to interfere,' said Laura. Sadie had gone. The florist's man was still outside at his van. She put her arm round her mother's neck and gently, very gently, she bit her mother's ear.

'My darling child, you wouldn't like a logical mother, would you? Don't do that. Here's the man.'

He carried more lilies still, another whole tray.

'Bank them up, just inside the door, on both sides of the porch, please,' said Mrs. Sheridan. 'Don't you agree, Laura?'

'Oh, I *do*, mother.'

In the drawing-room Meg, Jose and good little Hans had at last succeeded in moving the piano.

'Now, if we put this chesterfield against the wall and move everything out of the room except the chairs, don't you think?'

'Quite.'

'Hans, move these tables into the smoking-room, and bring a sweeper to take these marks off the carpet and—one moment, Hans—' Jose loved giving orders to the servants and they loved obeying her. She always made them feel they were

217

taking part in some drama. 'Tell mother and Miss Laura to come here at once.'

'Very good, Miss Jose.'

She turned to Meg. 'I want to hear what the piano sounds like, just in case I'm asked to sing this afternoon. Let's try over "This Life is Weary".'

Pom! Ta-ta-ta *Tee*-ta! The piano burst out so passionately that Jose's face changed. She clasped her hands. She looked mournfully and enigmatically at her mother and Laura as they came in.

> This Life is *Wee*-ary,
> A Tear—a Sigh.
> A Love that *Chan*-ges,
>   This Life is *Wee*-ary,
> A Tear—a Sigh.
> A Love that *Chan*-ges,
> And then . . . Good-bye!

But at the word 'Good-bye,' and although the piano sounded more desperate than ever, her face broke into a brilliant, dreadfully unsympathetic smile.

'Aren't I in good voice, mummy?' she beamed.

> This Life is *Wee*-ary,
> Hope comes to Die.
> A Dream—a *Wa*-kening.

But now Sadie interrupted them. 'What is it, Sadie?'

'If you please, m'm, cook says have you got the flags for the sandwiches?'

'The flags for the sandwiches, Sadie?' echoed Mrs. Sheridan dreamily. And the children knew by her face that she hadn't got them. 'Let me see.' And she said to Sadie firmly, 'Tell cook I'll let her have them in ten minutes.'

Sadie went.

'Now, Laura,' said her mother quickly, 'come with me into the smoking-room. I've got the names somewhere on the back of an envelope. You'll have to write them out for me. Meg, go upstairs this minute and take that wet thing off your head. Jose, run and finish dressing this instant. Do you hear me, children, or shall I have to tell your father when he comes home to-night? And—and, Jose, pacify cook if you do go into the kitchen, will you? I'm terrified of her this morning.'

218

The envelope was found at last behind the dining-room clock, though how it had got there Mrs. Sheridan could not imagine.

'One of you children must have stolen it out of my bag, because I remember vividly—cream-cheese and lemon-curd. Have you done that?'

'Yes.'

'Egg and—' Mrs. Sheridan held the envelope away from her. 'It looks like mice. It can't be mice, can it?'

'Olive, pet,' said Laura, looking over her shoulder.

'Yes, of course, olive. What a horrible combination it sounds. Egg and olive.'

They were finished at last, and Laura took them off to the kitchen. She found Jose there pacifying the cook, who did not look at all terrifying.

'I have never seen such exquisite sandwiches,' said Jose's rapturous voice. 'How many kinds did you say there were, cook? Fifteen?'

'Fifteen, Miss Jose.'

'Well, cook, I congratulate you.'

Cook swept up crusts with the long sandwich knife, and smiled broadly.

'Godber's has come,' announced Sadie, issuing out of the pantry. She had seen the man pass the window.

That meant the cream puffs had come. Godber's were famous for their cream puffs. Nobody ever thought of making them at home.

'Bring them in and put them on the table, my girl,' ordered cook.

Sadie brought them in and went back to the door. Of course Laura and Jose were far too grown-up to really care about such things. All the same, they couldn't help agreeing that the puffs looked very attractive. Very. Cook began arranging them, shaking off the extra icing sugar.

'Don't they carry one back to all one's parties?' said Laura.

'I suppose they do,' said practical Jose, who never liked to be carried back. 'They look beautifully light and feathery, I must say.'

'Have one each, my dears,' said cook in her comfortable voice. 'Yer ma won't know.'

Oh, impossible. Fancy cream puffs so soon after breakfast. The very idea made one shudder. All the same, two minutes later Jose and Laura were licking their fingers with that absorbed inward look that only comes from whipped cream.

'Let's go into the garden, out by the back way', suggested Laura. 'I want to see how the men are getting on with the marquee. They're such awfully nice men.'

But the back door was blocked by cook, Sadie, Godber's man and Hans.

Something had happened.

'Tuk-tuk-tuk,' clucked cook like an agitated hen. Sadie had her hand clapped to her cheek as though she had tooth-ache. Hans' face was screwed up in the effort to understand. Only Godber's man seemed to be enjoying himself; it was his story.

'What's the matter? What's happened?'

'There's been a horrible accident,' said cook. 'A man killed.'

'A man killed! Where? How? When?'

But Godber's man wasn't going to have his story snatched from under his very nose.

'Know those little cottages just below here, miss?' Know them? Of course she knew them. 'Well, there's a young chap living there, name of Scott, a carter. His horse shied at a traction-engine, corner of Hawke Street this morning, and he was thrown out on the back of his head. Killed.'

'Dead!' Laura stared at Godber's man.

'Dead when they picked him up,' said Godber's man with relish. 'They were taking the body home as I come up here. 'And he said to the cook, 'He's left a wife and five little ones.'

'Jose, come here.' Laura caught hold of her sister's sleeve and dragged her through the kitchen to the other side of the green baize door. There she paused and leaned against it. 'Jose!' she said, horrified, 'however are we going to stop everything?'

'Stop everything, Laura!' cried Jose in astonishment. 'What do you mean?'

'Stop the garden-party, of course.' Why did Jose pretend?

But Jose was still more amazed. 'Stop the garden-party? My dear Laura, don't be so absurd. Of course we can't do anything of the kind. Nobody expects us to. Don't be so extravagant,'

'But we can't possibly have a garden-party with a man dead just outside the front gate.'

That really was extravagant, for the little cottages were in a lane to themselves at the very bottom of a steep rise that led up to the house. A broad road ran between. True, they were far too near. They were the greatest possible eyesore and they had no right to be in that neighbourhood at all. They were little mean dwellings painted a chocolate brown. In the garden patches there was nothing but cabbage stalks, sick hens and tomato cans. The very smoke coming out of their chimneys was poverty-stricken. Little rags and shreds of smoke, so unlike the great silvery plumes that uncurled from the Sheridans' chimneys. Washerwomen lived in the lane and sweeps and a cobbler and a man whose house-front was studded all over with minute bird-cages. Children swarmed. When the Sheridans were little they were forbidden to set foot there because of the revolting language and of what they might catch. But since they were grown up Laura and Laurie on their prowls sometimes walked through. It was disgusting and sordid. They came out with a shudder. But still one must go everywhere; one must see everything. So through they went.

'And just think of what the band would sound like to that poor woman,' said Laura.

'Oh, Laura!' Jose began to be seriously annoyed. 'If you're going to stop a band playing every time someone has an accident, you'll lead a very strenuous life. I'm every bit as sorry about it as you. I feel just as sympathetic.' Her eyes hardened. She looked at her sister just as she used to when they were little and fighting together. 'You won't bring a drunken workman back to life by being sentimental,' she said softly.

'Drunk! Who said he was drunk?' Laura turned furiously on Jose. She said just as they had used to say on those occasions, 'I'm going straight up to tell mother.'

'Do, dear,' cooed Jose.

'Mother, can I come into your room?' Laura turned the big glass door-knob.

'Of course, child. Why, what's the matter? What's given you such a colour?' And Mrs. Sheridan turned round from her dressing-table. She was trying on a new hat.

221

'Mother, a man's been killed,' began Laura.

'*Not* in the garden?' interrupted her mother.

'No, no!'

'Oh, what a fright you gave me!' Mrs. Sheridan sighed with relief and took off the big hat and held it on her knees.

'But listen, mother,' said Laura. Breathless, half choking, she told the dreadful story. 'Of course, we can't have our party, can we?' she pleaded. 'The band and everybody arriving. They'd hear us, mother; they're nearly neighbours!'

To Laura's astonishment her mother behaved just like Jose; it was harder to bear because she seemed amused. She refused to take Laura seriously.

'But, my dear child, use your common sense. It's only by accident we've heard of it. If someone had died there normally —and I can't understand how they keep alive in those poky little holes—we should still be having our party, shouldn't we?'

Laura had to say 'yes' to that, but she felt it was all wrong. She sat down on her mother's sofa and pinched the cushion frill.

'Mother, isn't it really terribly heartless of us?' she asked.

'Darling!' Mrs. Sheridan got up and came over to her, carrying the hat. Before Laura could stop her she had popped it on. 'My child!' said her mother, 'the hat is yours. It's made for you. It's much too young for me. I have never seen you look such a picture. Look at yourself!' And she held up her hand-mirror.

'But, mother,' Laura began again. She couldn't look at herself; she turned aside.

This time Mrs. Sheridan lost patience just as Jose had done.

'You are being very absurd, Laura,' she said coldly. 'People like that don't expect sacrifices from us. And it's not very sympathetic to spoil everybody's enjoyment as you're doing now.'

'I don't understand,' said Laura, and she walked quickly out of the room into her own bedroom. There, quite by chance, the first thing she saw was this charming girl in the mirror, in her black hat trimmed with gold daisies and a long black velvet ribbon. Never had she imagined she could look like that. Is mother right? she thought. And now she hoped her mother was right. Am I being extravagant? Perhaps it was extravagant. Just for a moment she had another glimpse of that poor

222

woman and those little children and the body being carried into the house. But it all seemed blurred, unreal, like a picture in the newspaper. I'll remember it again after the party's over, she decided. And somehow that seemed quite the best plan. . . .

Lunch was over by half-past one. By half-past two they were all ready for the fray. The green-coated band had arrived and was established in a corner of the tennis-court.

'My dear!' trilled Kitty Maitland, 'aren't they too like frogs for words? You ought to have arranged them round the pond with the conductor in the middle on a leaf.'

Laurie arrived and hailed them on his way to dress. At the sight of him Laura remembered the accident again. She wanted to tell him. If Laurie agreed with the others, then it was bound to be all right. And she followed him into the hall.

'Laurie!'

'Hallo!' He was half-way upstairs, but when he turned round and saw Laura he suddenly puffed out his cheeks and goggled his eyes at her. 'My word, Laura! You do look stunning,' said Laurie. 'What an absolutely topping hat!'

Laura said faintly 'Is it?' and smiled up at Laurie and didn't tell him after all.

Soon after that people began coming in streams. The band struck up; the hired waiters ran from the house to the marquee. Wherever you looked there were couples strolling, bending to the flowers, greeting, moving on over the lawn. They were like bright birds that had alighted in the Sheridans' garden for this one afternoon, on their way to—where? Ah, what happiness it is to be with people who all are happy, to press hands, press cheeks, smile into eyes.

'Darling Laura, how well you look!'

'What a becoming hat, child!'

'Laura, you look quite Spanish. I've never seen you look so striking.'

And Laura, glowing, answered softly, 'Have you had tea? Won't you have an ice? The passion-fruit ices really are rather special.' She ran to her father and begged him: 'Daddy darling, can't the band have something to drink?'

And the perfect afternoon slowly ripened, slowly faded, slowly its petals closed.

'Never a more delightful garden-party . . .' 'The greatest success . . .' 'Quite the most . . .'

223

Laura helped her mother with the good-byes. They stood side by side in the porch till it was all over.

'All over, all over, thank heaven,' said Mrs. Sheridan. 'Round up the others, Laura. Let's go and have some fresh coffee. I'm exhausted. Yes, it's been very successful. But oh, these parties, these parties! Why will you children insist on giving parties!' And they all of them sat down in the deserted marquee.

'Have a sandwich, daddy dear. I wrote the flag.'

'Thanks.' Mr. Sheridan took a bite and the sandwich was gone. He took another. 'I suppose you didn't hear of a beastly accident that happened to-day?' he said.

'My dear,' said Mrs. Sheridan, holding up her hand, 'we did. It nearly ruined the party. Laura insisted we should put it off.'

'Oh, mother!' Laura didn't want to be teased about it.

'It was a horrible affair all the same,' said Mr. Sheridan. 'The chap was married too. Lived just below in the lane, and leaves a wife and half a dozen kiddies, so they say.'

An awkward little silence fell. Mrs. Sheridan fidgeted with her cup. Really, it was very tactless of father. . . .

Suddenly she looked up. There on the table were all those sandwiches, cakes, puffs, all uneaten, all going to be wasted. She had one of her brilliant ideas.

'I know,' she said. 'Let's make up a basket. Let's send that poor creature some of this perfectly good food. At any rate, it will be the greatest treat for the children. Don't you agree? And she's sure to have neighbours calling in and so on. What a point to have it all ready prepared. Laura!' She jumped up. 'Get me the big basket out of the stairs cupboard.'

'But, mother, do you really think it's a good idea?' said Laura.

Again, how curious, she seemed to be different from them all. To take scraps from their party. Would the poor woman really like that?

'Of course! What's the matter with you to-day? An hour or two ago you were insisting on us being sympathetic.'

Oh well! Laura ran for the basket. It was filled, it was now heaped by her mother.

'Take it yourself, darling,' said she. 'Run down just as you are. No, wait, take the arum lilies too. People of that class are so impressed by arum lilies.'

'The stems will ruin her lace frock,' said practical Jose.

So they would. Just in time. 'Only the basket, then. And, Laura!'—her mother followed her out of the marquee—'don't on any account—'

'What, mother?'

No, better not put such ideas into the child's head! 'Nothing! Run along.'

It was just growing dusky as Laura shut their garden gates. A big dog ran by like a shadow. The road gleamed white, and down below in the hollow the little cottages were in deep shade. How quiet it seemed after the afternoon. Here she was going down the hill to somewhere where a man lay dead, and she couldn't realise it. Why couldn't she? She stopped a minute. And it seemed to her that kisses, voices, tinkling spoons, laughter, the smell of crushed grass were somehow inside her. She had no room for anything else. How strange! She looked up at the pale sky, and all she thought was, 'Yes, it was the most successful party.'

Now the broad road was crossed. The lane began, smoky and dark. Women in shawls and men's tweed caps hurried by. Men hung over the palings; the children played in the doorways. A low hum came from the mean little cottages. In some of them there was a flicker of light, and a shadow, crab-like, moved across the window. Laura bent her head and hurried on. She wished now she had put on a coat. How her frock shone! And the big hat with the velvet streamer—if only it was another hat! Were the people looking at her? They must be. It was a mistake to have come; she knew all along it was a mistake. Should she go back even now?

No, too late. This was the house. It must be. A dark knot of people stood outside. Beside the gate an old, old woman with a crutch sat in a chair, watching. She had her feet on a newspaper. The voices stopped as Laura drew near. The group parted. It was as though she was expected, as though they had known she was coming here.

Laura was terribly nervous. Tossing the velvet ribbon over her shoulder, she said to a woman standing by, 'Is this Mrs. Scott's house?' and the woman, smiling queerly, said, 'It is, my lass.'

Oh, to be away from this! She actually said, 'Help me, God,' as she walked up the tiny path and knocked. To be away from those staring eyes, or to be covered up in anything, one of those women's shawls even. I'll just leave the basket and go, she decided. I shan't even wait for it to be emptied.

Then the door opened. A little woman in black showed in the gloom.

Laura said, 'Are you Mrs. Scott?' But to her horror the woman answered, 'Walk in, please, miss,' and she was shut in the passage.

'No,' said Laura, 'I don't want to come in. I only want to leave this basket. Mother sent—'

The little woman in the gloomy passage seemed not to have heard her. 'Step this way, please, miss,' she said in an oily voice, and Laura followed her.

She found herself in a wretched little low kitchen, lighted by a smoky lamp. There was a woman sitting before the fire.

'Em,' said the little creature who had let her in. 'Em! It's a young lady.' She turned to Laura. She said meaningly, 'I'm 'er sister, miss. You'll excuse 'er, won't you?'

'Oh, but of course!' said Laura. 'Please, please don't disturb her. I—I only want to leave—'

But at that moment the woman at the fire turned round. Her face, puffed up, red, with swollen eyes and swollen lips, looked terrible. She seemed as though she couldn't understand why Laura was there. What did it mean? Why was this stranger standing in the kitchen with a basket? What was it all about? And the poor face puckered up again.

'All right, my dear,' said the other. 'I'll thenk the young lady.'

And again she began, 'You'll excuse her, miss, I'm sure,' and her face, swollen too, tried an oily smile.

Laura only wanted to get out, to get away. She was back in the passage. The door opened. She walked straight through into the bedroom, where the dead man was lying.

'You'd like a look at 'im, wouldn't you?' said Em's sister, and she brushed past Laura over to the bed. 'Don't be afraid, my lass'—and now her voice sounded fond and sly, and fondly she drew down the sheet—''e looks a picture. There's nothing to show. Come along, my dear.'

Laura came.

There lay a young man, fast asleep—sleeping so soundly, so

226

deeply, that he was far, far away from them both. Oh, so remote, so peaceful. He was dreaming. Never wake him up again. His head was sunk in the pillow, his eyes were closed; they were blind under the closed eyelids. He was given up to his dream. What did garden-parties and baskets and lace frocks matter to him? He was far from all those things. He was wonderful, beautiful. While they were laughing and while the band was playing, this marvel had come to the lane. Happy . . . happy. . . . All is well, said that sleeping face. This is just as it should be. I am content.

But all the same you had to cry, and she couldn't go out of the room without saying something to him. Laura gave a loud childish sob.

'Forgive my hat,' she said.

And this time she didn't wait for Em's sister. She found her way out of the door, down the path past all those dark people. At the corner of the lane she met Laurie.

He stepped out of the shadow. 'Is that you, Laura?'

'Yes.'

'Mother was getting anxious. Was it all right?'

'Yes, quite. Oh, Laurie!' She took his arm, she pressed up against him.

'I say, you're not crying, are you?' asked her brother.

Laura shook her head. She was.

Laurie put his arm round her shoulder. 'Don't cry', he said in his warm, loving voice. 'Was it awful?'

'No,' sobbed Laura. 'It was simply marvellous. But, Laurie—' She stopped, she looked at her brother. 'Isn't life,' she stammered, 'isn't life—' But what life was she couldn't explain. No matter. He quite understood.

'*Isn't* it, darling?' said Laurie.

(1921)

PART THREE

Summer's End

The Voyage

*One day I must write about Grandma at
length, especially of her beauty in her
bath—when she was about sixty. Wiping
herself with the towel. I remember now
how lovely she seemed to me. And her
fine linen, her scent. I have never really
described her yet. Patience! the time will
come.*

The Picton boat was due to leave at half-past eleven. It was a
beautiful night, mild, starry, only when they got out of the cab
and started to walk down the Old Wharf that jutted out into
the harbour, a faint wind blowing off the water ruffled under
Fenella's hat, and she put up her hand to keep it on. It was dark
on the Old Wharf, very dark; the wool sheds, the cattle trucks,
the cranes standing up so high, the little squat railway engine,
all seemed carved out of solid darkness. Here and there on a
rounded wood-pile, that was like the stalk of a huge black
mushroom, there hung a lantern, but it seemed afraid to unfurl
its timid, quivering light in all that blackness; it burned softly,
as if for itself.

Fenella's father pushed on with quick, nervous strides.
Beside him her grandma bustled along in her crackling black
ulster; they went so fast that she had now and again to give an
undignified little skip to keep up with them. As well as her
luggage strapped into a neat sausage, Fenella carried clasped to
her her grandma's umbrella, and the handle, which was a swan's
head, kept giving her shoulder a sharp little peck as if it too
wanted her to hurry. . . . Men, their caps pulled down, their
collars turned up, swung by; a few women all muffled scurried
along; and one tiny boy, only his little black arms and legs

showing out of a white woolly shawl, was jerked along angrily
between his father and mother; he looked like a baby fly that
had fallen into the cream.

Then suddenly, so suddenly that Fenella and her grandma
both leapt, there sounded from behind the largest wool shed,
that had a trail of smoke hanging over it, *Mia-oo-oo-O-O!*

'First whistle,' said her father briefly, and at that moment
they came in sight of the Picton boat. Lying beside the dark
wharf, all strung, all beaded with round golden lights, the
Picton boat looked as if she was more ready to sail among stars
than out into the cold sea. People pressed along the gangway.
First went her grandma, then her father, then Fenella. There
was a high step down on to the deck, and an old sailor in a
jersey standing by gave her his dry, hard hand. They were
there; they stepped out of the way of the hurrying people, and
standing under a little iron stairway that led to the upper deck
they began to say good-bye.

'There, mother, there's your luggage!' said Fenella's father,
giving grandma another strapped-up sausage.

'Thank you, Frank.'

'And you've got your cabin tickets safe?'

'Yes, dear.'

'And your other tickets?'

Grandma felt for them inside her glove and showed him the
tips.

'That's right.'

He sounded stern, but Fenella, eagerly watching him, saw
that he looked tired and sad. *Mia-oo-oo-O-O!* The second
whistle blared just above their heads, and a voice like a cry
shouted, 'Any more for the gangway?'

'You'll give my love to father,' Fenella saw her father's lips
say. And her grandma, very agitated, answered, 'Of course I
will, dear. Go now. You'll be left. Go now, Frank. Go now.'

'It's all right, mother. I've got another three minutes.' To
her surprise Fenella saw her father take off his hat. He clasped
grandma in his arms and pressed her to him. 'God bless you,
mother!' she heard him say.

And grandma put her hand, with the black thread glove that
was worn through on her ring finger, against his cheek, and she
sobbed, 'God bless you, my own brave son!'

This was so awful that Fenella quickly turned her back on

232

them, swallowed once, twice, and frowned terribly at a little green star on a mast head. But she had to turn round again; her father was going.

'Good-bye, Fenella. Be a good girl.' His cold, wet moustache brushed her cheek. But Fenella caught hold of the lapels of his coat.

'How long am I going to stay?' she whispered anxiously. He wouldn't look at her. He shook her off gently, and gently said, 'We'll see about that. Here! Where's your hand?' He pressed something into her palm. 'Here's a shilling in case you should need it.'

A shilling! She must be going away for ever! 'Father!' cried Fenella. But he was gone. He was the last off the ship. The sailors put their shoulders to the gangway. A huge coil of dark rope went flying through the air and fell 'thump' on the wharf. A bell rang; a whistle shrilled. Silently the dark wharf began to slip, to slide, to edge away from them. Now there was a rush of water between. Fenella strained to see with all her might. 'Was that father turning round?'—or waving? —or standing alone? —or walking off by himself? The strip of water grew broader, darker. Now the Picton boat began to swing round steady, pointing out to sea. It was no good looking any longer. There was nothing to be seen but a few lights, the face of the town clock hanging in the air, and more lights, little patches of them, on the dark hills.

The freshening wind tugged at Fenella's skirts; she went back to her grandma. To her relief grandma seemed no longer sad. She had put the two sausages of luggage one on top of the other, and she was sitting on them, her hands folded, her head a little on one side. There was an intent, bright look on her face. Then Fenella saw that her lips were moving and guessed that she was praying. But the old woman gave her a bright nod as if to say the prayer was nearly over. She unclasped her hands, sighed, clasped them again, bent forward, and at last gave herself a soft shake.

'And now, child,' she said, fingering the bow of her bonnet-strings, 'I think we ought to see about our cabins. Keep close to me, and mind you don't slip.'

'Yes, grandma!'

'And be careful the umbrella isn't caught in the stair rail. I saw a beautiful umbrella broken in half like that on my way over.'

233

'Yes, grandma'.

Dark figures of men lounged against the rails. In the glow of their pipes a nose shone out, or the peak of a cap, or a pair of surprised-looking eyebrows. Fenella glanced up. High in the air a little figure, his hands thrust in his short jacket pockets, stood staring out to sea. The ship rocked ever so little and she thought the stars rocked too. And now a pale steward in a linen coat, holding a tray high in the palm of his hand, stepped out of a lighted doorway and skimmed past them. They went through that doorway. Carefully over the high brass-bound step on to the rubber mat and then down such a terribly steep flight of stairs that grandma had to put both feet on each step, and Fenella clutched the clammy brass rail and forgot all about the swan-necked umbrella.

At the bottom grandma stopped; Fenella was rather afraid she was going to pray again. But no, it was only to get out the cabin tickets. They were in the saloon. It was glaring bright and stifling; the air smelled of paint and burnt chop-bones and india-rubber. Fenella wished her grandma would go on, but the old woman was not to be hurried. An immense basket of ham sandwiches caught her eye. She went up to them and touched the top one delicately with her finger.

'How much are the sandwiches?' she asked.

'Tuppence!' bawled a rude steward, slamming down a knife and fork.

Grandma could hardly believe it.

'Twopence *each?*' she asked.

'That's right,' said the steward, and he winked at his companion.

Grandma made a small, astonished face. Then she whispered primly to Fenella, 'What wickedness!' And they sailed out at the further door and along a passage that had cabins on either side. Such a very nice stewardness came to meet them. She was dressed all in blue and her collar and cuffs were fastened with large brass buttons. She seemed to know grandma well.

'Well, Mrs. Crane,' said she, unlocking their washstand. 'We've got you back again. It's not often you give yourself a cabin.'

'No,' said grandma. 'But this time my dear son's thoughtfulness—'

'I hope—' began the stewardess. Then she turned round and

234

took a long, mournful look at grandma's blackness and at Fenella's black coat and skirt, black blouse, and hat with a crape rose.

Grandma nodded. 'It was God's will,' said she.

The stewardess shut her lips and, taking a deep breath, she seemed to expand.

'What I always say is,' she said, as though it was her own discovery, 'sooner or later each of us has to go, and that's a certingty.' She paused. 'Now can I bring you anything, Mrs. Crane? A cup of tea? I know it's no good offering you a little something to keep the cold out.'

Grandma shook her head. 'Nothing, thank you. We've got a few wine biscuits and Fenella has a very nice banana.'

'Then I'll give you a look later on,' said the stewardess; and she went out, shutting the door.

What a very small cabin it was! It was like being shut up in a box with grandma. The dark round eye above the wash-stand gleamed at them dully. Fenella felt shy. She stood against the door, still clasping her luggage and the umbrella. Were they going to get undressed in here? Already her grand-ma had taken off her bonnet, and, rolling up the strings, she fixed each with a pin to the lining before she hung the bonnet up. Her white hair shone like silk; the little bun at the back was covered with a black net. Fenella hardly ever saw her grandma with her head uncovered; she looked strange.

'I shall put on the woollen fascinator your dear mother crocheted for me,' said grandma, and, unstrapping the sausage, she took it out and wound it round her head; the fringe of grey bobbles danced at her eyebrows as she smiled tenderly and mournfully at Fenella. Then she undid her bodice, and some-thing under that, and something else underneath that. Then there seemed a short, sharp tussle, and grandma flushed faintly. Snip! Snap! She had undone her stays. She breathed a sigh of relief and, sitting on the plush couch, she slowly and carefully pulled off her elastic-sided boots and stood them side by side.

By the time Fenella had taken off her coat and skirt and put on her flannel dressing-gown grandma was quite ready.

'Must I take off my boots, grandma? They're lace.'

Grandma gave them a moment's deep consideration. 'You'd feel a great deal more comfortable if you did, child,' said she. She kissed Fenella. 'Don't forget to say your prayers. Our dear

Lord is with us when we are at sea even more than when we are on dry land. And because I am an experienced traveller,' said grandma briskly, 'I shall take the upper berth.'

'But grandma, how ever will you get up there?'

Three little spider-like steps were all Fenella saw. The old woman gave a small silent laugh before she mounted them nimbly, and she peered over the high bunk at the astonished Fenella.

'You didn't think your grandma could do that, did you?' said she. And as she sank back Fenella heard her light laugh again.

The hard square of brown soap would not lather and the water in the bottle was like a kind of blue jelly. How hard it was, too, to turn down those stiff sheets; you simply had to tear your way in. If everything had been different, Fenella might have got the giggles. . . . At last she was inside, and while she lay there panting, there sounded from above a long, soft whispering, as though someone was gently rustling among tissue paper to find something. It was grandma saying her prayers. . . .

A long time passed. Then the stewardess came in; she trod softly and leaned her hand on grandma's bunk.

'We're just entering the Straits,' she said.

'Oh!'

'It's a fine night, but we're rather empty. We may pitch a little.'

And indeed at that moment the Picton boat rose and rose and hung in the air just long enough to give a shiver before she swung down again, and there was the sound of heavy water slapping against her sides. Fenella remembered she had left that swan-necked umbrella standing up on the little couch. If it fell over, would it break? But grandma remembered too, at the same time.

'I wonder if you'd mind, stewardess, laying down my umbrella,' she whispered.

'Not at all, Mrs. Crane.' And the stewardess, coming back to grandma, breathed, 'Your little granddaughter's in such a beautiful sleep.'

'God be praised for that!' said grandma.

'Poor little motherless mite!' said the stewardess. And grandma was still telling the stewardess all about what happened when Fenella fell asleep.

But she hadn't been asleep long enough to dream before she woke up again to see something waving in the air above her head. What was it? What could it be? It was a small grey foot. Now another joined it. They seemed to be feeling about for something; there came a sigh.

'I'm awake, grandma,' said Fenella.

'Oh, dear, am I near the ladder?' asked grandma. 'I thought it was this end.'

'No, grandma, it's the other. I'll put your foot on it. Are we there?' asked Fenella.

'In the harbour,' said grandma. 'We must get up, child. You'd better have a biscuit to steady yourself before you move.'

But Fenella had hopped out of her bunk. The lamp was still burning, but night was over, and it was cold. Peering through that round eye she could see far off some rocks. Now they were scattered over with foam; now a gull flipped by; and now there came a long piece of real land.

'It's land, grandma,' said Fenella, wonderingly, as though they had been at sea for weeks together. She hugged herself; she stood on one leg and rubbed it with the toes of the other foot; she was trembling. Oh, it had all been so sad lately. Was it going to change? But all her grandma said was, 'Make haste, child. I should leave your nice banana for the stewardess as you haven't eaten it.' And Fenella put on her black clothes again and a button sprang off one of her gloves and rolled to where she couldn't reach it. They went up on deck.

But if it had been cold in the cabin, on deck it was like ice. The sun was not up yet, but the stars were dim, and the cold pale sky was the same colour as the cold pale sea. On the land a white mist rose and fell. Now they could see quite plainly dark bush. Even the shapes of the umbrella ferns showed, and those strange silvery withered trees that are like skeletons. . . . Now they could see the landing-stage and some little houses, pale too, clustered together, like shells on the lid of a box. The other passengers tramped up and down, but more slowly than they had the night before, and they looked gloomy.

And now the landing-stage came out to meet them. Slowly it swam towards the Picton boat and a man holding a coil of rope, and a cart with a small drooping horse and another man sitting on the step, came too.

'It's Mr. Penreddy, Fenella, come for us,' said grandma.

She sounded pleased. Her white waxen cheeks were blue with cold, her chin trembled, and she had to keep wiping her eyes and her little pink nose.

'You've got my—'

'Yes, grandma.' Fenella showed it to her.

The rope came flying through the air and 'smack' it fell on to the deck. The gangway was lowered. Again Fenella followed her grandma on to the wharf over to the little cart, and a moment later they were bowling away. The hooves of the little horse drummed over the wooden piles, then sank softly into the sandy road. Not a soul was to be seen; there was not even a feather of smoke. The mist rose and fell and the sea still sounded asleep as slowly it turned on the beach.

'I seen Mr. Crane yestiddy,' said Mr. Penreddy. 'He looked himself then. Missus knocked him up a batch of scones last week.'

And now the little horse pulled up before one of the shell-like houses. They got down. Fenella put her hand on the gate, and the big, trembling dew-drops soaked through her glove-tips. Up a little path of round white pebbles they went, with drenched sleeping flowers on either side. Grandma's delicate white picotees were so heavy with dew that they were fallen, but their sweet smell was part of the cold morning. The blinds were down in the little house; they mounted the steps on to the veranda. A pair of old bluchers was on one side of the door and a large red watering-can on the other.

'Tut! tut! Your grandpa,' said grandma. She turned the handle. Not a sound. She called, 'Walter!' And immediately a deep voice that sounded half stifled called back, 'Is that you, Mary?'

'Wait, dear,' said grandma. 'Go in there.' She pushed Fenella gently into a small dusky sitting-room.

On the table a white cat, that had been folded up like a camel, rose, stretched itself, yawned, and then sprang on to the tips of its toes. Fenella buried one cold little hand in the white, warm fur, and smiled timidly while she stroked and listened to grandma's gentle voice and the rolling tones of grandpa.

A door creaked. 'Come in, dear.' The old woman beckoned, Fenella followed. There, lying to one side of an immense bed, lay grandpa. Just his head with a white tuft and his rosy face and long silver beard showed over the quilt. He was like a very old, wide-awake bird.

238

'Well, my girl!' said grandpa. 'Give us a kiss!' Fenella kissed him. 'Ugh!' said grandpa. 'Her little nose is as cold as a button. What's that she's holding? Her grandma's umbrella?'

Fenella smiled again and crooked the swan neck over the bed-rail. Above the bed there was a big text in a deep black frame:

> Lost! One Golden Hour
> Set with Sixty Diamond Minutes.
> *No* Reward Is Offered
> For It Is GONE FOR EVER!

'Yer grandma painted that,' said grandpa. And he ruffled his white tuft and looked at Fenella so merrily she almost thought he winked at her.

(1921)

Down
the Sounds

If we are ever together down the Pelorus
Sounds come off with me for a whole day—
will you?—and let's just remember.

As the little steamer rounded the point and came into the next
bay, they noticed the flag was flying from Putnam's Pier. That
meant there were passengers to bring off. The Captain swore.
They were half-an-hour late already and he couldn't bear not
to be up to time. But Putnam's flag, cherry-red against the
green bush in this brilliant morning, jigged gaily, to show it
didn't care a flick for the Captain's feelings.

There were three people and an old sheep-dog waiting. One
was a little old woman, nearing seventy perhaps, very spry,
with a piece of lilac in her bonnet and pale lilac strings. She
carried a bundle wrapped in a long shawl, white as a waterfall.
Beside her stood the young parents. He was tall, broad, awkward in a stiff black suit with banana-yellow shoes and a light blue
tie, and she looked soft and formless in a woollen coat; her hat
was like a child's with its wreath of daisies, and she carried a bag
like a child's school-kit, stuffed very full and covered with a cloth.

As the steamer drew near, the old sheep-dog ran forward and
made a sound that was like the beginning of a bark, but he
turned it off into an old dog's cough, as though he had decided
that the little steamer wasn't worth barking about. The coil of
rope was thrown, was looped; the one-plank gangway was
spanned across, and over it tripped the old woman, running
and bridling like a girl of eighteen.

'Thank you, Captain!' said she, giving the Captain a bird-
like, impudent little nod.

240

'That's all right, Mrs. Putnam,' said old Captain Reid, who had known her for the last forty years.

After her came the sheep-dog, then the young woman, looking lost, and she was followed by the young man, who seemed terribly ashamed about something. He kept his head bent, he walked stiff as wood in his creaking shoes, and a long brown hand twisted away, twisted away at his fair moustache.

Old Captain Reid winked broadly at the passengers. He stuffed his hands in his short jacket, drew in a breath as if he was going to sing. 'Morning, Mr. Putnam!' he roared. And the young man straightened himself with an immense effort and shot a terrified glance at the Captain. 'Morning, Cap'n!' he mumbled.

Captain Reid considered him, shaking his head. 'It's all right, my lad,' he said. 'We've all been through it. Jim here'— and he jerked his head at the man at the wheel—'had twins last time, hadn't you, Jim?'

'That's ri', Cap'n,' said Jim, grinning broadly at the passengers. The little steamer quivered, throbbed, started on her way again, while the young man, in an agony, not greeting anyone, creaked off to the bows, and the two women—they were the only women on board—sat themselves down on a green bench against the white deckrail. As soon as they had sat down,

'There, Mother, let me take him!' said the young woman anxiously, quietly. She tossed the kit away.

But Gran didn't want to give him up.

'Now don't you go tiring yourself,' said she. 'He's as nice as can be where he is.'

Torture! The young woman gave a gasp like a sob.

'Give him to me!' she said, and she actually twitched at her mother-in-law's sleeve.

The old woman knew perfectly well what she was feeling. Little channels for laughter showed in her cheeks. 'My goodness gracious me!' she pretended to scold. 'There's impatience for you.' But even while she spoke she swung the baby gently, gently into its mother's arms. 'There now!' said Gran, and she sat up sharp and gave the bow of her bonnet strings a tweak, as though she was glad to have her hands free after all.

It was an exquisite day. It was one of those days so clear, so still, so silent, you almost feel the earth itself has stopped in astonishment at its own beauty.

(1922)

The New Baby

At half-past ten the yacht steamed into the Sound, slowed down. . . . 'Hullo!' said someone. 'We've stopped.' For a moment, and it seemed like a long moment, everybody was silent. They heard the crying of the little waves from the distant beach, the soft moist breath of the large wind came flowing gently over the dark sea. And looking up at the sky, one fancied that those merrily burning stars were telling one another that the yacht had anchored for the night.

Then, 'Come on, girls!' cried the genial old Mayor. And Gertrude Pratt began to bang out *The Honeysuckle and the Bee* on the squat tiny little piano. As the whole party had sung the same song every night for the past three weeks, the noise was considerable, but very pleasant. It was an extraordinary relief after the long dazzling day to lie on deck and put all one's heart into

> I love you dearly, dearly and I
> Want you to love me. . . .

You couldn't say these things. And yet you felt them. At least— the ladies did. Not for anybody in particular but for everybody, for the lamp even, hanging from the deck-awning, for Tanner the steward's hand as it stroked the guitar. Love! Love! there was no escaping it. It was all very well to pretend to be interested in other things, to look through the glasses, to ask the Captain intelligent questions as you stood on the bridge, to admire Mrs. Strutt's marvellous embroidery. . . .

There were exquisite small shells to be found on these beaches, a small greeny-blue kind, coral spirals, and tiny yellow ones like grains of maize.

They asked them questions, had a good look at everything, ate the fruit, or whatever they were offered, and took photographs. If there was a swing—and there was usually an old-fashioned one, hanging from a branch in the orchard—the girls got the men to push them, and they flew, their gossamer veils streaming, while the Mayor sat out on the verandah talking to their host, and the older ladies had a quiet chat somewhere within doors.

'We . . . my wife, that is . . .' But it would not do. He began to smile and it seemed he could not smile . . . simple . . . childish . . . yes. 'As a matter of fact our first kid turned up this morning at half-past three. A fine boy.'

The Mayor stopped and dug his umbrella into the sand. He didn't quite grasp it for the moment. 'You mean—was born?' said he. . .

'That's it,' said the other, nodding.

'Great Scott!' said the Mayor, and he turned back and called his wife. 'Mother! they've got a new baby!'

The flowers in the garden *look like it*. So do the little wet shells on the beach. So does the house. All seems to breathe freshness, peace. I especially see those shells—so naive-looking.

'Take them!' he said gently, and bending down he ruffled the leaves and began to gather the fruit.

'Stop! Stop!' she said, shocked. 'You're cutting them all. You'll have none on the bush.'

'Why not?' he said simply. 'You're welcome!'

And they came away thinking 'What a life!' All very well to land there for an hour or two on a glorious morning, but imagine being stuck there, month in, year in, year out—with nothing to look at but the sea, with for one's greatest excitement—getting fresh ferns for the fireplace! 'Christ! what a life!' thought the men, pacing up and down the deck waiting for the lunch-bell, and 'My dear, just imagine it!' thought the ladies, powdering their noses in the flat cabin mirrors. And lunch in the bright saloon, with the port-holes open and the stewards flying to and fro in their linen jackets, always seemed particularly good afterwards.

(1921–22)

243

Weak Heart

The daughter of the watch-smith. Her piano-playing. Her weak heart. . . . Oh, that tree at the corner of May Street! I forgot it until this moment. It was dark and hung over the street like a great shadow.

Although it sounded all the year round, although it rang out sometimes as early as half-past six in the morning, sometimes as late as half-past ten at night, it was in the spring, when Bengel's violet patch just inside the gate was blue with flowers, that that piano . . . made the passers-by not only stop talking, but slow down, pause, look suddenly—if they were men—grave, even stern, and if they were women—dreamy, even sorrowful.

Tarana Street was beautiful in the spring; there was not a single house without its garden and trees and a plot of grass big enough to be called 'the lawn.' Over the low painted fences, you could see, as you ran by, whose daffys were out, whose wild snowdrop border was over and who had the biggest hyacinths, so pink and white, the colour of coconut ice. But nobody had violets that grew, that smelled in the spring sun like Bengel's. Did they really smell like that? Or did you shut your eyes and lean over the fence because of Edie Bengel's piano?

A little wind ruffles among the leaves like a joyful hand looking for the finest flowers; and the piano sounds gay, tender, laughing. Now a cloud, like a swan, flies across the sun, the violets shine cold, like water, and a sudden questioning cry rings from Edie Bengel's piano.

. . . Ah, if life must pass so quickly, why is the breath of these flowers so sweet? What is the meaning of this feeling of longing, of sweet trouble—of flying joy? Good-bye! Farewell! The

244

young bees lie half awake on the slender dandelions, silver are the pink-tipped arrowy petals of the daisies; the new grass shakes in the light. Everything is beginning again, marvellous as ever, heavenly fair. 'Let me stay! Let me stay!' pleads Edie Bengel's piano.

It is the afternoon, sunny and still. The blinds are down in the front to save the carpets, but upstairs the slats are open and in the golden light little Mrs. Bengel is feeling under her bed for the square bonnet box. She is flushed. She feels timid, excited, like a girl. And now the tissue paper is parted, her best bonnet, the one trimmed with a jet butterfly, which reposes on top, is lifted out and solemnly blown upon.

Dipping down to the glass she tries it with fingers that tremble. She twitches her dolman round her slender shoulder, clasps her purse and before leaving the bedroom kneels down a moment to ask God's blessing on her 'goings out.' And as she kneels there quivering, she is rather like a butterfly herself, fanning her wings before her Lord. When the door is open the sound of the piano coming up through the silent house is almost frightening, so bold, so defiant, so reckless it rolls under Edie's fingers. And just for a moment the thought comes to Mrs. Bengel and is gone again, that there is a stranger with Edie in the drawing-room, but a fantastic person, out of a book, a— a—villain. It's very absurd. She flits across the hall, turns the door handle and confronts her flushed daughter. Edie's hands drop from the keys. She squeeees them between her knees, her head is bent, her curls are fallen forward. She gazes at her mother with brilliant eyes. There is something painful in that glance, something very strange. It is dusky in the drawing-room, the top of the piano is open. Edie has been playing from memory; it's as though the air still tingles.

'I'm going, dear,' said Mrs. Bengel softly, so softly it is like a sigh.

'Yes, Mother,' came from Edie.

'I don't expect I shall be long.'

Mrs. Bengel lingers. She would very much like just a word of sympathy, of understanding, even from Edie, to cheer her on her way.

But Edie murmurs, 'I'll put the kettle on in half an hour.'

'Do, dear!' Mrs. Bengel grasped at that even. A nervous little smile touched her lips. 'I expect I shall want my tea.'

245

But to that Edie makes no reply; she frowns, she stretches out a hand, quickly unscrews one of the piano candlesticks, lifts off a pink china ring and screws all tight again. The ring has been rattling. As the front door bangs softly after her mother Edie and the piano seem to plunge together into deep dark water, into waves that flow over both, relentless. She plays on desperately until her nose is white and her heart beats. It is her way of getting over her nervousness and her way too of praying. Would they accept her? Would she be allowed to go? Was it possible that in a week's time she would be one of Miss Farmer's girls, wearing a red and blue hat-band, running up the broad steps leading to the big grey painted house that buzzed, that hummed as you went by? Their pew in Church faced Miss Farmer's boarders. Would she at last know the names of the girls she had looked at so often? The pretty pale one with red hair, the dark one with a fringe, the fair one who held Miss Farmer's hand during the sermon? . . . But after all . . .

It was Edie's fourteenth birthday. Her father gave her a silver brooch with a bar of music, two crotchets, two quavers and a minim headed by a very twisted treble clef. Her mother gave her blue satin gloves and two boxes for gloves and handkerchiefs, hand-painted the glove box with a sprig of gold roses tying up the capital G and the handkerchief box with a marvellously lifelike butterfly quivering on the capital H. From the aunts in . . .

There was a tree at the corner of Tarana Street and May Street. It grew so close to the pavement that the heavy boughs stretched over, and on that part of the pavement there was always a fine sifting of minute twigs.

But in the dusk, lovers parading came into its shade as into a tent. There, however long they had been together, they greeted each other again with long kisses, with embraces that were sweet torture, agony to bear, agony to end.

Edie never knew that Roddie 'loved' it, Roddie never knew that it meant anything to Edie.

Roddie, spruce, sleek with water, bumped his new bike down

246

the wooden steps, through the gate. He was off for a spin, and looking at that tree, dark in the glow of evening, he felt the tree was watching him. He wanted to do marvels, to astonish, to shock, to amaze it.

Roddie had a complete new outfit for the occasion. A black serge suit, a black tie, a straw hat so white it was almost silver, a dazzling white straw hat with a broad black band. Attached to the hat there was a thick guard that somehow reminded one of a fishing line and the little clasp on the brim was like a fly. . . . He stood at the graveside, his legs apart, his hands loosely clasped, and watched Edie being lowered into the grave—as a half-grown boy watches anything, a man at work, or a bicycle accident, or a chap cleaning a spring-carriage wheel—but suddenly as the men drew back he gave a violent start, turned, muttered something to his father and dashed away, so fast that people looked positively frightened, through the cemetery, down the avenue of dripping clay banks into Tarana Road, and started pelting for home. His suit was very tight and hot. It was like a dream. He kept his head down and his fists clenched, he couldn't look up, nothing could have made him look higher than the tops of the fences—What was he thinking of as he pressed along? On, on until the gate was reached, up the steps, in at the front door, through the hall, up to the drawing-room.

'Edie!' called Roddie. 'Edie, old girl!'

And he gave a low strange squawk and cried 'Edie!' and stared across at Edie's piano.

But cold, solemn, as if frozen, heavily the piano stared back at Roddie. Then it answered, but on its own behalf, on behalf of the house and the violet patch, the garden, the velvet tree at the corner of May Street, and all that was delightful: 'There is nobody here of that name, young man!'

(1921)

Taking
the Veil

It took me about three hours to write finally. But I had been thinking over the décor and so on for weeks—nay, months, I believe. I can't say how thankful I am to have been born in N.Z., to know Wellington as I do, and to have it to range about in. Writing about the convent seemed so natural. I suppose I have not been in the grounds more than twice. But it is one of the places that remain as vivid as ever.

It seemed impossible that anyone should be unhappy on such a beautiful morning. Nobody was, decided Edna, except herself. The windows were flung wide in the houses. From within there came the sound of pianos, little hands chased after each other and ran away from each other, practising scales. The trees fluttered in the sunny gardens, all bright with spring flowers. Street boys whistled, a little dog barked; people passed by, walking so lightly, so swiftly, they looked as though they wanted to break into a run. Now she actually saw in the distance a parasol, peach-coloured, the first parasol of the year.

Perhaps even Edna did not look quite as unhappy as she felt. It is not easy to look tragic at eighteen, when you are extremely pretty, with the cheeks and lips and shining eyes of perfect

248

health. Above all, when you are wearing a French blue frock and your new spring hat trimmed with cornflowers. True, she carried under her arm a book bound in horrid black leather. Perhaps the book provided a gloomy note, but only by accident; it was the ordinary Library binding. For Edna had made going to the Library an excuse for getting out of the house to think, to realise what had happened, to decide somehow what was to be done now.

An awful thing had happened. Quite suddenly, at the theatre last night, when she and Jimmy were seated side by side in the dress-circle, without a moment's warning—in fact, she had just finished a chocolate almond and passed the box to him again—she had fallen in love with an actor. But—fallen—in—love....

The feeling was unlike anything she had ever imagined before. It wasn't in the least pleasant. It was hardly thrilling. Unless you can call the most dreadful sensation of hopeless misery, despair, agony and wretchedness, thrilling. Combined with the certainty that if that actor met her on the pavement after, while Jimmy was fetching their cab, she would follow him to the ends of the earth, at a nod, at a sign, without giving another thought to Jimmy or her father and mother or her happy home and countless friends again....

The play had begun fairly cheerfully. That was at the chocolate almond stage. Then the hero had gone blind. Terrible moment! Edna had cried so much she had to borrow Jimmy's folded, smooth-feeling handkerchief as well. Not that crying mattered. Whole rows were in tears. Even the men blew their noses with a loud trumpeting noise and tried to peer at the programme instead of looking at the stage. Jimmy, most mercifully dry-eyed—for what would she have done without his handkerchief?—squeezed her free hand, and whispered 'Cheer up, darling girl!' And it was then she had taken a last chocolate almond to please him and passed the box again. Then there had been the ghastly scene with the hero alone on the stage in a deserted room at twilight, with a band playing outside and the sound of cheering coming from the street. He had tried—ah! how painfully, how pitifully!—to grope his way to the window. He had succeeded at last. There he stood holding the curtain while one beam of light, just one beam, shone full on his raised sightless face, and the band faded away into the distance....

249

It was—really, it was absolutely—oh, the most—it was simply—in fact, from that moment Edna knew that life could never be the same. She drew her hand away from Jimmy's, leaned back, and shut the chocolate box for ever. This at last was love!

Edna and Jimmy were engaged. She had had her hair up for a year and a half; they had been publicly engaged for a year. But they had known they were going to marry each other ever since they walked in the Botanical Gardens with their nurses, and sat on the grass with a wine biscuit and a piece of barley-sugar each for their tea. It was so much an accepted thing that Edna had worn a wonderfully good imitation of an engagement-ring out of a cracker all the time she was at school. And up till now they had been devoted to each other.

But now it was over. It was so completely over that Edna found it difficult to believe that Jimmy did not realise it too. She smiled wisely, sadly, as she turned into the gardens of the Convent of the Sacred Heart and mounted the path that led through them to Hill Street. How much better to know it now than to wait until after they were married! Now it was possible that Jimmy would get over it. No, it was no use deceiving herself; he would never get over it! His life was wrecked, was ruined; that was inevitable. But he was young. . . . Time, people always said. Time might make a little, just a little difference. In forty years when he was an old man, he might be able to think of her calmly—perhaps. But she, —what did the future hold for her?

Edna had reached the top of the path. There under a new-leafed tree, hung with little bunches of white flowers, she sat down on a green bench and looked over the Convent flower-beds. In the one nearest to her there grew tender stocks, with a border of blue, shell-like pansies, with at one corner a clump of creamy freesias, their light spears of green criss-crossed over the flowers. The Convent pigeons were tumbling high in the air, and she could hear the voice of Sister Agnes who was giving a singing lesson. *Ah-me*, sounded the deep tones of the nun, and *Ah-me*, they were echoed. . . .

If she did not marry Jimmy, of course she would marry nobody. The man she was in love with, the famous actor—Edna had far too much common-sense not to realise that would never be. It was very odd. She didn't even want it to be. Her love was too intense for that. It had to be endured, silently; it had to torment her. It was, she supposed, simply that kind of love.

'But, Edna!' cried Jimmy. 'Can you never change? Can I never hope again?'

Oh, what sorrow to have to say it, but it must be said. 'No, Jimmy, I will never change.'

Edna bowed her head; and a little flower fell on her lap, and the voice of Sister Agnes cried suddenly *Ah-no*, and the echo came, *Ah-no*. . . .

At that moment the future was revealed. Edna saw it all. She was astonished; it took her breath away at first. But after all, what could be more natural? She would go into a convent. . . . Her father and mother do everything to dissuade her, in vain. As for Jimmy, his state of mind hardly bears thinking about. Why can't they understand? How can they add to her suffering like this? The world is cruel, terribly cruel! After a last scene when she gives away her jewellery and so on to her best friends—she so calm, they so broken-hearted—into a convent she goes. No, one moment. The very evening of her going is the actor's last evening at Port Willin. He receives by a strange messenger a box. It is full of white flowers. But there is no name, no card. Nothing? Yes, under the roses, wrapped in a white handkerchief, Edna's last photograph with, written underneath,

The world forgetting, by the world forgot.

Edna sat very still under the trees; she clasped the black book in her fingers as though it were her missal. She takes the name of Sister Angela. Snip! Snip! All her lovely hair is cut off. Will she be allowed to send one curl to Jimmy? It is contrived somehow. And in a blue gown with a white headband Sister Angela goes from the convent to the chapel, from the chapel to the convent with something unearthly in her look, in her sorrowful eyes, and in the gentle smile with which they greet the little children who run to her. A saint! She hears it whispered as she paces the chill, wax-smelling corridors. A saint! And visitors to the chapel are told of the nun whose voice is heard above the other voices, of her youth, her beauty, of her tragic, tragic love. 'There is a man in this town whose life is ruined. . ..'

A big bee, a golden furry fellow, crept into a freesia, and the delicate flower leaned over, swung, shook; and when the bee flew away it fluttered still as though it were laughing. Happy, careless flower!

Sister Angela looked at it and said, 'Now it is winter.' One night, lying in her icy cell, she hears a cry. Some stray animal is out there in the garden, a kitten or a lamb or—well, whatever little animal might be there. Up rises the sleepless nun. All in white, shivering but fearless, she goes and brings it in. But next morning, when the bell rings for matins, she is found tossing in high fever . . . in delirium . . . and she never recovers. In three days all is over. The service has been said in the chapel, and she is buried in the corner of the cemetery reserved for the nuns, where there are plain little crosses of wood. Rest in Peace, Sister Angela. . . .

Now it is evening. Two old people leaning on each other come slowly to the grave and kneel down sobbing, 'Our daughter! Our only daughter!' Now there comes another. He is all in black; he comes slowly. But when he is there and lifts his black hat, Edna sees to her horror his hair is snow-white. Jimmy! Too late, too late! The tears are running down his face; he is crying *now*. Too late, too late! The wind shakes the leafless trees in the churchyard. He gives one awful bitter cry.

Edna's black book fell with a thud to the garden path. She jumped up, her heart beating. My darling! No, it's not too late. It's all been a mistake, a terrible dream. Oh, that white hair! How could she have done it? She has not done it. Oh, heavens! Oh, what happiness! She is free, young, and nobody knows her secret. Everything is still possible for her and Jimmy. The house they have planned may still be built, the little solemn boy with his hands behind his back watching them plant the standard roses may still be born. His baby sister . . . But when Edna got as far as his baby sister, she stretched out her arms as though the little love came flying through the air to her, and gazing at the garden, at the white sprays on the tree, at those darling pigeons blue against the blue, and the Convent with its narrow windows, she realised that now at last for the first time in her life—she had never imagined any feeling like it before—she knew what it was to be in love, but—in—love!

(1922)

The Scholarship

He was just in time. They were pulling down the blind in the Post Office when he burst in, pushing his way through the swing-doors with a kind of extravagant breast-stroke, and: 'I can still send a telegram, can't I?' he cried to snappy little Miss Smythe, who rapped out: 'If it's very important you may. *Not* otherwise!'

'Oh, it is important, frightfully!' said he, giving her such a radiant unexpected beam that it shook two faded old banners into her cheeks. But he did not notice. He wrote in his beautiful flowing hand which even in that blissful moment he couldn't help admiring: *Got it arrive by morning boat to-morrow cheers*, and pushed it under the netting.

'It will be off to-night, won't it?' he asked, counting out a whole handful of pennies.

'Yes, I'll send it now,' said she, and her dry little pencil hopped over the form. 'Is the last word cheese?'

'Oh, no!' Again that beam lighting up the dingy little woman; even her Kruger-sovereign brooch seemed to glow with it. 'It's cheers,—three cheers, you know. Musical cheers— no, that's wrong.'

He was out again and swinging along the street (about two foot up in the air), swinging along the street that he'd never seen before. Glorious place! Such happy, splendid people hurrying home, their faces and hands a deep pink colour in the sunset light. Native women, big, dark and bright like dahlias, lolling on the benches outside the Grand Hotel. The carts and waggons, even the immense two-horse cabs went spanking by as though every horse's head was turned towards home. And then —the shops—fruit shops, a flare of gold—fish shops, a blaze of silver! As for the smell coming off the flower jars that the florist was spraying before he carried them inside for the night—it really knocked you over! That hand, too, hovering in the

253

jeweller's window—taking out the little boxes and trays. Just a hand—so mysterious, so beautiful! To whom could it belong? And then a rolling navvy bumped into him and said: 'Sorry, my lad!'

'My lad!' He wanted to fling his arms round the chap for it.

Although there was everything to be done he couldn't go home yet. He must walk this off a bit, he must climb a hill. Well, that wasn't difficult. The whole place was nothing but hills.

So he chose the steepest, and up and up he went, getting warm, then getting his second wind and simply floating on it to the very top—to a white painted rail against which he leaned and looked over.

For the first time, yes, positively for the first time, he saw the town below him—the red-roofed houses set in plumy, waving gardens, the absurd little city-quarter, 'built in American style', the wharves, the tarred wharf-sheds, and behind these black masses two cranes, that looked somehow, from this distance, like two gigantic pairs of scissors, stuck on end. And then the deep, brimming harbour, shaped like a crater, in a curving brim of hills, just broken in the jagged place to let the big ships through.

For a moment, while he looked, it lay all bathed in brightness—so clear—he could have counted the camellias on the trees—and then, without warning, it was dark, quite dark, and lights began to appear, flowering in the soft hollows like sea-anemones.

His eyelids smarted. His throat ached; he could have wept. He could have flung out his arms, and cried: 'Oh, my darling, darling little town!' And all because he was going to leave it in a week's time—because he was off to Europe and God knows—if he'd ever see it again!

But instead of the fling he took a deep breath and in that breath he discovered how hungry he was. He was starving—quite faint with it. Marching down the hill his knees shook like an old woman's.

Down and down he went. There was nobody about now because it was supper-time. But the lighted houses in their plumy gardens were full of life; they could not hold so much. It broke from them, in voices and laughter, and scattered over the flowers and trees.

'Children! Children! come in at once!' called a woman. And 'Oh, Mother!' answered the children.

Ah, how well he understood what they were feeling, poor little beggars! It was no time at all since he and Isobel had answered just like that.

The garden gate was clammy and cold. As he walked up the path a bough of syringa brushed his face, wetting his cheeks and lips. And he smiled, with a strange little shiver of delight; he felt that the plant was playing with him. . . .

Two oblong pieces of light lay on the grass below the french windows of the dining-room. He leapt on to the verandah and looked in. There he saw his brother-in-law, Kenneth, sitting at the table eating, with a book propped up against a glass jug.

'Hullo—old boy!' said Henry.

'Hullo!' said Kenneth, and he stared at Henry in the solemn absurd way that Henry loved. 'You're late. Had supper?'

'Good God—no!' Henry came in and began wiping the dew and the pollen off his cheeks.

'Been crying?' asked Kenneth. 'Big boy hit you?'

'Yes,' said Henry.

'Lamb?' Kenneth's glance wandered over the table. Finally he took a water biscuit, broke it in half, put one half in his book for a marker and began to carve. And Henry stood beside him, looking at the glorified table.

It was an immense relief to have his hand on Kenneth's shoulder. It rested him. But what was there so lovable about that little tuft of hair that always stood up and wouldn't lie down on the top of Kenneth's head? It was such a part of his personality. Whatever he said—there it stood—waving away. Henry gave the shoulder a hard squeeze. 'I can imagine Isobel marrying him for that,' he thought.

'Stir the mint sauce well,' said Kenneth. 'All what Maisie calls "the nice grittay part" is at the bottom.' Henry sat down, stirred and stirred and pushed the mint sauce away. He leaned back in his chair and tried not to smile, tried to carry it off, frowned at his plate and then said: 'Oh, I heard this afternoon I've got that Scholarship.' He couldn't resist it; he had to look up at Kenneth who didn't give a sign, but rubbed the side of his nose in a way he had.

'Well,' he said finally, 'I knew you would. It was inevitable.'
Henry gulped.

'Have a drink!' Kenneth pushed the glass jug across.
'Don't swallow the cherries. The stones disembody, settle in the
appendix, fertilize and send out shoots which have, sooner or
later, to be snipped off. When do you sail?'

'A week from to-morrow.'

Kenneth was silent. Then he opened his book and ate the
book-marker.

'This is all about whales,' he explained, blowing off the
crumbs.

'It's extraordinarily unpleasant. I shouldn't advise anyone
to read it. There's a description of sharks, too,—how when
they are attacked—in the middle of the fight—they switch
round and eat their own entrails—Sickening! . . . I suppose you
wired Isobel.'

'Yes, I'm going over to her by the morning boat. You know
I promised, if this came off, that we'd spend our last week
together.'

'But what about packing—or aren't you going to take
anything? Just a change of socks and a rook rifle?'

'I'm going to do all that to-night,' said Henry. And then he
smiled a blissful, childish smile, 'I couldn't *sleep*, you know,'
and reached over for the salad.

'Look out for the cowcumber,' said Kenneth. 'It sticks to the
side of the vessel by some curious process—of suction, I believe.
Well—I'm coming across to the Bay to-morrow afternoon. It's
Saturday—you remember—or *don't* remember. We'll have the
week-end together.'

'That will be frightfully——' began Henry.

'Only I wish to God,' Kenneth went on, 'that I wasn't
reading this book. I'll never be able to bathe again. The sea is
simply teeming with horrors.' He got up and filled his pipe.
'Don't hurry. I'm going to smoke on the verandah.'

But Henry couldn't be left alone. Besides, he wasn't hungry
after all. He chose a big orange and followed after.

They walked into the warm velvet dark and into another
world. Kenneth stood with his hands in his pockets looking
over the garden—at all those shapes and shadows built up in
the air. As he stared they seemed to move gently, flowing
together under a rolling wave.

'Those gardens under the sea,' he murmured, 'must be the very devil!'

Henry sat on the verandah edge, eating his orange and looking at the clematis flowers. Wide open—dazzling they lay as if waiting in rapture for the moon. It was strange how frightfully they added to his excitement. He began to quiver all over. He thought, absurdly, 'The top of my head feels just like one of those flowers,' and a hundred miles away Kenneth murmured:

'Well, I'm glad it's you who are going and not me. I've no desire at all to rush into this affair they call Life. No, my job is to hide in a doorway, or squeeze under a porch until it is all over—only issuing forth—if I must issue forth—with Isobel for my Supreme Umbrella or Maisie for my small, coming-on, emergency umbrella—or "sunnyshade" as she calls it. That's the reason why I'm in favour of having large numbers of children—that they may be a kind of tent to me in my old age. . . .'

Henry went off to his packing. He got into his pyjamas just for the sake of coolness, for of course he wasn't going to bed.

But by one o'clock everything was done and his feet were cold, so he just sat up in bed and decided to smoke until it was time to get up. After one cigarette he lay down on his side, curled up, one hand under his cheek, thinking. He felt himself smiling down to his very toes. Yes, every little toe, now that it was warm, had a basking smile on it. And this was so ridiculous that he began to laugh, cuddling down, burying his face in the pillow. And away the little boat floated. . . .

He woke, but did not move. Warm and solemn he lay, with wide open troubled eyes, pouting a little, almost frowning for one long moment. In that long moment he sprang out of bed, bathed, dressed, reached the wharf, boarded the ferry boat, crossed the harbour and was waving—waving to Isobel and Maisie who stood there, waiting for him on the pier. A tall young sailor, standing near him, threw a coil of tarred rope and it fell in a long loop, over a landing post. . . . Beautifully done. . . . And all this moment (vision) was so clear and bright and tiny, he might with his flesh and pout and solemn eyes have been a baby watching a-bubble.

'I'm there—I'm there. Why do I have to start and do it all so slowly all over again?' But as he thought he moved and the

257

bubble vanished and was forgotten, He sat up in bed smiling, pulling down his pyjama sleeves.

(1917–18)

PART FOUR

Winter

Cassandra

As Gertie the parlour-maid passed through the green-baize door that led from the kitchen regions, she nearly dropped the tray of dinner silver she was carrying. For there, beyond the stairs, in the very middle of the big dim hall stood Miss Cassandra—Mrs. Brook—wearing a little black hat with a thick black veil, a long black cape, and clasping her hands as if she was praying. Oh, she did give Gertie a turn—coming on her so sudden, and all in black, too, and standing there so strange. But immediately she saw Gertie, Miss Cassandra came to life, darted forward and said in her sweet husky voice—the servants loved Miss Cassandra's—Mrs. Brook's—voice: 'Oh, good evening, Gertie. Where is Mother?'

'Good evening, Miss—Ma'am. In her room. She must have just about finished dressing.'

'Is Father with her?' asked Cassandra, putting her hand on the banister.

'No, Miss. It's Wednesday. One of his late nights, you know.'

'Oh, yes, I forgot.' Then Cassandra said quickly: 'Where are the others?'

'Miss Jinnie's in the drawing-room and Mr. Jack's in his dark-room.'

'Thank you, Gertie. Then I'll run up.'

And run she did—skimmed rather, like a bird.

She knocked at the big cream-panelled door and turned the glass handle.

'Mother, it's me. Can I come in?'

'Cassandra!' cried her mother. 'Do, darling. Of course. What a surprise! What a strange hour!'

Mrs. Sheridan sat at the dressing-table, clasping her pearls. As she spoke, she settled them, and drew down her daughter's little dark head and kissed her. The black veil only came to

261

Cassandra's nose. Her mother noticed that her lips were hot, and through the thick mesh her eyes looked dark, enormous. But that meant nothing with Cassandra. The child had been to a concert, or she'd been reading, or star-gazing simply, or tracking down a crying kitten. Anything threw Cassandra into a fever.

'Do you know how late it is, my child?' she said tenderly. 'It's just on dinner-time. And I thought Richard only got back to-day.'

'Yes, he did,' said Cassandra. 'This afternoon.' She gave a little gasp.

'Then why didn't you . . .?' Her mother broke off. 'But before we begin talking, darling . . . You'll stay to dinner, of course. I'll just let cook know. She'll be so *furious* if I don't.' And she moved towards the bell beside the fireplace before Cassandra stopped her.

'No, Mother, don't! I'm not stopping to dinner. I don't want any dinner.' Suddenly she threw back her cape and with that gesture she seemed to reveal all her excitement and agitation. 'I've only come to speak to you—to tell you something. Because I must—I simply *must*'—and here Cassandra clasped her hands as she had in the hall below—'confide in somebody.'

'My precious child, don't be so tragic!' said her mother. 'You're frightening me. You're not going to have a baby, are you? Because I'm no good at that kind of thing. What is it? And don't begin crying if you can help it. It's so exhausting!'

She was too late. Cassandra had begun. Pressing her little handkerchief to her eyes, she sobbed. 'I can't talk in this room. I'm afraid we'll be interrupted. Come into my old room, Mother!' And away she sped down the passage into her bedroom that was next to the nursery.

The door of the cold, dim little room was shut behind them. Cassandra almost sprang upon her mother.

'Mother!' she cried. 'I've been betrayed. I've been wickedly, cruelly, deceived. Richard's been false to me. But *so* false!' cried Cassandra, walking away from Mrs. Sheridan and shaking her little fist at the ceiling. 'But *so* false! So utterly, abominably false!'

'Child! What are you saying?' cried Mrs. Sheridan. She really was taken aback by this. 'It can't be true. Richard—of all people! How? When? With whom?'

Instead of replying Cassandra ran back to her mother and, half-shutting her eyes, smiling like an actress, she declaimed in low passionate tones: 'Dearest, you love me—*still*? Ah, my dear one,' pleaded Cassandra, flinging out her hand to her astonished mother. 'Don't forget to end each of our daily letters with "Yes, I love you still" as well as "Bless you", and don't forget'— here Cassandra raised her hand—'do listen to this bit, Mother,' she implored—as though her mother was not listening—'that though I bask, I gloat in the fact that I so perfectly understand your silence, I have a jigsaw of longing to hear you speak. . . .'

After this extraordinary oration Cassandra simply stared at her mother. Mrs. Sheridan really thought the child had become unbalanced.

'But what does it *mean*?' she said. 'Did you hear this? Did someone say it to him?'

'No,' said Cassandra. She gave a little wave and almost laughed. 'I found it—and it's a *mild* specimen, my dear—in his collar-bag!'

(1920)

The Stranger

I've been this man, been this woman. I've
stood for hours on the Auckland Wharf. I've
been out in the stream waiting to be
berthed—I've been a seagull hovering at the
stern and a hotel porter whistling through his
teeth.

It seemed to the little crowd on the wharf that she was never
going to move again. There she lay, immense, motionless on
the grey crinkled water, a loop of smoke above her, an immense
flock of gulls screaming and diving after the galley droppings at
the stern. You could just see little couples parading—little flies
walking up and down the dish on the grey crinkled tablecloth.
Other flies clustered and swarmed at the edge. Now there was a
gleam of white on the lower deck—the cook's apron or the
stewardess, perhaps. Now a tiny black spider raced up the
ladder on to the bridge.

In the front of the crowd a strong-looking, middle-aged man,
dressed very well, very snugly in a grey overcoat, grey silk scarf,
thick gloves and dark felt hat, marched up and down twirling
his folded umbrella. He seemed to be the leader of the little
crowd on the wharf and at the same time to keep them together.
He was something between the sheep-dog and the shepherd.

But what a fool—what a fool he had been not to bring any
glasses! There wasn't a pair of glasses between the whole lot of
them.

'Curious thing, Mr. Scott, that none of us thought of glasses.
We might have been able to stir 'em up a bit. We might have
managed a little signalling. *Don't hesitate to land. Natives harmless.*
Or: *A welcome awaits you. All is forgiven.* What? Eh?'

Mr. Hammond's quick, eager glance, so nervous and yet so

friendly and confiding, took in everybody on the wharf, roped in even those old chaps lounging against the gangways. They knew, every man-jack of them, that Mrs. Hammond was on that boat, and he was so tremendously excited it never entered his head not to believe that this marvellous fact meant something to them too. It warmed his heart towards them. They were, he decided, as decent a crowd of people—Those old chaps over by the gangways, too—fine, solid old chaps. What chests—by Jove! And he squared his own, plunged his thick-gloved hands into his pockets, rocked from heel to toe.

'Yes, my wife's been in Europe for the last ten months. On a visit to our eldest girl, who was married last year. I brought her up here, as far as Crawford, myself. So I thought I'd better come and fetch her back. Yes, yes, yes.' The shrewd grey eyes narrowed again and searched anxiously, quickly, the motionless liner. Again his overcoat was unbuttoned. Out came the thin, butter-yellow watch again, and for the twentieth—fiftieth—hundredth time he made the calculation.

'Let me see, now. It was two fifteen when the doctor's launch went off. Two fifteen. It is now exactly twenty-eight minutes past four. That is to say, the doctor's been gone two hours and thirteen minutes. Two hours and thirteen minutes! Whee-ooh!' He gave a queer little half-whistle and snapped his watch to again. 'But I think we should have been told if there was anything up—don't you, Mr. Gaven?'

'Oh yes, Mr. Hammond! I don't think there's anything to—anything to worry about,' said Mr. Gaven, knocking out his pipe against the heel of his shoe. 'At the same time—'

'Quite so! Quite so!' cried Mr. Hammond. 'Dashed annoying!' He paced quickly up and down and came back again to his stand between Mr. and Mrs. Scott and Mr. Gaven. 'It's getting quite dark, too,' and he waved his folded umbrella as though the dusk at least might have had the decency to keep off for a bit. But the dusk came slowly, spreading like a slow stain over the water. Little Jean Scott dragged at her mother's hand.

'I wan' my tea, mammy!' she wailed.

'I expect you do,' said Mr. Hammond. 'I expect all these ladies want their tea.' And his kind, flushed, almost pitiful glance roped them all in again. He wondered whether Janey was having a final cup of tea in the saloon out there. He hoped

265

so; he thought not. It would be just like her not to leave the deck. In that case perhaps the deck steward would bring her up a cup. If he'd been there he'd have got it for her—somehow. And for a moment he was on deck, standing over her, watching her little hand fold round the cup in the way she had, while she drank the only cup of tea to be got on board. . . . But now he was back here, and the Lord only knew when that cursed Captain would stop hanging about in the stream. He took another turn, up and down, up and down. He walked as far as the cab-stand to make sure his driver hadn't disappeared; back he swerved again to the little flock huddled in the shelter of the banana crates. Little Jean Scott was still wanting her tea. Poor little beggar! He wished he had a bit of chocolate on him.

'Here, Jean!' he said. 'Like a lift up?' And easily, gently, he swung the little girl on to a higher barrel. The movement of holding her, steadying her, relieved him wonderfully, lightened his heart.

'Hold on,' he said, keeping an arm round her.

'Oh, don't worry about *Jean*, Mr. Hammond!' said Mrs. Scott.

'That's all right, Mrs. Scott. No trouble. It's a pleasure. Jean's a little pal of mine, aren't you, Jean?'

'Yes, Mr. Hammond,' said Jean, and she ran her finger down the dent of his felt hat.

But suddenly she caught him by the ear and gave a loud scream. 'Lo-ok, Mr. Hammond! She's moving! Look, she's coming in!'

By Jove! So she was. At last! She was slowly, slowly turning round. A bell sounded far over the water and a great spout of steam gushed into the air. The gulls rose; they fluttered away like bits of white paper. And whether that deep throbbing was her engines or his heart Mr. Hammond couldn't say. He had to nerve himself to bear it, whatever it was. At the moment old Captain Johnson, the harbour-master, came striding down the wharf, a leather portfolio under his arm.

'Jean'll be all right,' said Mr. Scott. 'I'll hold her.' He was just in time. Mr. Hammond had forgotten about Jean. He sprang away to greet old Captain Johnson.

'Well, Captain,' the eager, nervous voice rang out again, 'you've taken pity on us at last.'

'It's no good blaming me, Mr. Hammond,' wheezed old Captain Johnson, staring at the liner. 'You got Mrs. Hammond on board, ain't yer?'

'Yes, yes!' said Hammond, and he kept by the harbour-master's side. 'Mrs. Hammond's there. Hul-lo! We shan't be long now!'

With her telephone ring-ringing, the thrum of her screw filling the air, the big liner bore down on them, cutting sharp through the dark water so that big white shavings curled to either side. Hammond and the harbour-master kept in front of the rest. Hammond took off his hat; he raked the decks— they were crammed with passengers; he waved his hat and bawled a loud, strange 'Hul-lo!' across the water, and then turned round and burst out laughing and said something—nothing—to old Captain Johnson.

'Seen her?' asked the harbour-master.

'No, not yet. Steady—wait a bit!' And suddenly, between two great clumsy idiots—'Get out of the way there!' he signed with his umbrella—he saw a hand raised—a white glove shaking a handkerchief. Another moment, and—thank God, thank God!—there she was. There was Janey. There was Mrs. Hammond, yes, yes, yes—standing by the rail and smiling and nodding and waving her handkerchief.

'Well, that's first class—first class! Well, well, well!' He positively stamped. Like lightning he drew out his cigar-case and offered it to old Captain Johnson. 'Have a cigar, Captain! They're pretty good. Have a couple! Here'—and he pressed all the cigars in the case on the harbour-master—'I've a couple of boxes up at the hotel.'

'Thenks, Mr. Hammond!' wheezed old Captain Johnson.

Hammond stuffed the cigar-case back. His hands were shaking, but he'd got hold of himself again. He was able to face Janey. There she was, leaning on the rail, talking to some woman and at the same time watching him, ready for him. It struck him, as the gulf of water closed, how small she looked on that huge ship. His heart was wrung with such a spasm that he could have cried out. How little she looked to have come all that long way and back by herself! Just like her, though. Just like Janey. She had the courage of a—And now the crew had come forward and parted the passengers; they had lowered the rails for the gangways.

The voices on shore and the voices on board flew to greet each other.

'All well?'

'All well.'

'How's mother?'

'Much better.'

'Hullo, Jean!'

'Hillo, Aun' Emily!'

'Had a good voyage?'

'Splendid!'

'Shan't be long now!'

'Not long now.'

The engines stopped. Slowly she edged to the wharf-side.

'Make way there—make way—make way!' And the wharf hands brought the heavy gangways along at a sweeping run. Hammond signed to Janey to stay where she was. The old harbour-master stepped forward; he followed. As to 'ladies first,' or any rot like that, it never entered his head.

'After you, Captain!' he cried genially. And, treading on the old man's heels, he strode up the gangway on to the deck in a bee-line to Janey, and Janey was clasped in his arms.

'Well, well, well! Yes, yes! Here we are at last!' he stammered. It was all he could say. And Janey emerged and her cool little voice—the only voice in the world for him—said, 'Well, darling! Have you been waiting long?'

No; not long. Or, at any rate, it didn't matter. It was over now. But the point was, he had a cab waiting at the end of the wharf. Was she ready to go off? Was her luggage ready? In that case they could cut off sharp with her cabin luggage and let the rest go hang until to-morrow. He bent over her and she looked up with her familiar half-smile. She was just the same. Not a day changed. Just as he'd always known her. She laid her small hand on his sleeve.

'How are the children, John?' she asked.

(Hang the children!) 'Perfectly well. Never better in their lives.'

'Haven't they sent me letters?'

'Yes, yes—of course! I've left them at the hotel for you to digest later on.'

'We can't go quite so fast,' said she. 'I've got people to say good-bye to—and then there's the Captain.' As his face fell she gave his arm a small understanding squeeze. 'If the Captain comes off the bridge I want you to thank him for having looked after your wife so beautifully.' Well, he'd got her. If she wanted another ten minutes—As he gave way she was surrounded. The whole first-class seemed to want to say good-bye to Janey.

'Good-bye, *dear* Mrs. Hammond! And next time you're in Sydney I'll *expect* you.'

'Darling Mrs. Hammond! You won't forget to write to me, will you?'

'Well, Mrs. Hammond, what this boat would have been without you!'

It was as plain as a pikestaff that she was by far the most popular woman on board. And she took it all—just as usual. Absolutely composed. Just her little self—just Janey all over; standing there with her veil thrown back. Hammond never noticed what his wife had on. It was all the same to him whatever she wore. But to-day he did notice that she wore a black 'costume'—didn't they call it?—with white frills, trimmings he supposed they were, at the neck and sleeves. All this while Janey handed him round.

'John, dear!' And then: 'I want to introduce you to—'

Finally they did escape, and she led the way to her stateroom. To follow Janey down the passage that she knew so well—that was so strange to him; to part the green curtains after her and to step into the cabin that had been hers gave him exquisite happiness. But—confound it!—the stewardess was there on the floor, strapping up the rugs.

'That's the last, Mrs. Hammond,' said the stewardess, rising and pulling down her cuffs.

He was introduced again, and then Janey and the stewardess disappeared into the passage. He heard whisperings. She was getting the tipping business over, he supposed. He sat down on the striped sofa and took his hat off. There were the rugs she had taken with her; they looked good as new. All her luggage looked fresh, perfect. The labels were written in her beautiful little clear hand—'Mrs. John Hammond.'

'Mrs. John Hammond!' He gave a long sigh of content and leaned back, crossing his arms. The strain was over. He felt he could have sat there for ever sighing his relief—the relief at being rid of that horrible tug, pull, grip on his heart. The danger was over. That was the feeling. They were on dry land again.

But at that moment Janey's head came round the corner.

'Darling—do you mind? I just want to go and say good-bye to the doctor.'

Hammond started up. 'I'll come with you.'

'No, no!' she said. 'Don't bother. I'd rather not. I'll not be a minute.'

And before he could answer she was gone. He had half a mind to run after her; but instead he sat down again.

Would she really not be long? What was the time now? Out came the watch; he stared at nothing. That was rather queer of Janey, wasn't it? Why couldn't she have told the stewardess to say good-bye for her? Why did she have to go chasing after the ship's doctor? She could have sent a note from the hotel even if the affair had been urgent. Urgent? Did it—could it mean that she had been ill on the voyage— she was keeping something from him? That was it! He seized his hat. He was going off to find that fellow and to wring the truth out of him at all costs. He thought he'd noticed just something. She was just a touch too calm—too steady. From the very first moment—

The curtains rang. Janey was back. He jumped to his feet.

'Janey, have you been ill on this voyage? You have!'

'Ill?' Her airy little voice mocked him. She stepped over the rugs, came up close, touched his breast, and looked up at him.

'Darling,' she said, 'don't frighten me. Of course I haven't! Whatever makes you think I have? Do I look ill?'

But Hammond didn't see her. He only felt that she was looking at him and that there was no need to worry about anything. She was here to look after things. It was all right. Everything was.

The gentle pressure of her hand was so calming that he put his over hers to hold it there. And she said:

'Stand still. I want to look at you. I haven't seen you yet. You've had your beard beautifully trimmed, and you look— younger, I think, and decidedly thinner! Bachelor life agrees with you.'

'Agrees with me!' He groaned for love and caught her close again. And again, as always, he had the feeling he was holding

something that never was quite his—his. Something too
delicate, too precious, that would fly away once he let go.

'For God's sake let's get off to the hotel so that we can be
by ourselves!' And he rang the bell hard for someone to look
sharp with the luggage.

.   .   .   .   .   .

Walking down the wharf together she took his arm. He had
her on his arm again. And the difference it made to get into the
cab after Janey—to throw the red-and-yellow striped blanket
round them both—to tell the driver to hurry because neither
of them had had any tea. No more going without his tea or
pouring out his own. She was back. He turned to her, squeezed
her hand, and said gently, teasingly, in the 'special' voice he
had for her: 'Glad to be home again, dearie?' She smiled;
she didn't even bother to answer, but gently she drew his hand
away as they came to the brighter streets.

'We've got the best room in the hotel,' he said. 'I wouldn't
be put off with another. And I asked the chambermaid to put
in a bit of a fire in case you felt chilly. She's a nice, attentive
girl. And I thought now we were here we wouldn't bother to
go home to-morrow, but spend the day looking round and leave
the morning after. Does that suit you? there's no hurry, is
there? The children will have you soon enough. . . . I thought a
day's sight-seeing might make a nice break in your journey—
eh, Janey?'

'Have you taken the tickets for the day after?' she asked.

'I should think I have!' He unbuttoned his overcoat and
took out his bulging pocket-book. 'Here we are! I reserved a
first-class carriage to Salisbury. There it is—"Mr. *and* Mrs.
John Hammond." I thought we might as well do ourselves
comfortably, and we don't want other people butting in, do
we? But if you'd like to stop here a bit longer—?'

'Oh no!' said Janey quickly. 'Not for the world! The day
after to-morrow, then. And the children—'

But they had reached the hotel. The manager was standing
in the broad, brilliantly lighted porch. He came down to greet
them. A porter ran from the hall for their boxes.

'Well, Mr. Arnold, here's Mrs. Hammond at last!'

The manager led them through the hall himself and pressed

271

the elevator-bell. Hammond knew there were business pals of his sitting at the little hall tables having a drink before dinner. But he wasn't going to risk interruption; he looked neither to the right nor the left. They could think what they pleased. If they didn't understand, the more fools they—and he stepped out of the lift, unlocked the door of their room and shepherded Janey in. The door shut. Now, at last, they were alone together. He turned up the light. The curtains were drawn; the fire blazed. He flung his hat on to the huge bed and went towards her.

But—would you believe it!—again they were interrupted. This time it was the porter with the luggage. He made two journeys of it, leaving the door open in between, taking his time, whistling through his teeth in the corridor. Hammond paced up and down the room, tearing off his gloves, tearing off his scarf. Finally he flung his overcoat on to the bedside.

At last the fool was gone. The door clicked. Now they *were* alone. Said Hammond: 'I feel I'll never have you to myself again. These cursed people! Janey'—and he bent his flushed, eager gaze upon her—'let's have dinner up here. If we go down to the restaurant we'll be interrupted, and then there's the confounded music' (the music he'd praised so highly, applauded so loudly last night!). 'We shan't be able to hear each other speak. Let's have something up here in front of the fire. It's too late for tea. I'll order a little supper, shall I? How does the idea strike you?'

'Do, darling!' said Janey. 'And while you're away—the children's letters—'

'Oh, later on will do!' said Hammond.

'But then we'd get it over,' said Janey. 'And I'd first have time to—'

'Oh, I needn't go down!' explained Hammond. 'I'll just ring and give the order . . . you don't want to send me away, do you?'

Janey shook her head and smiled.

'But you're thinking of something else. You're worrying about something,' said Hammond. 'What is it? Come and sit here—come and sit on my knee before the fire.'

'I'll just unpin my hat,' said Janey, and she went over to the dressing-table. 'A-ah!' She gave a little cry.

'What is it?'

272

'Nothing, darling. I've just found the children's letters. That's all right! They will keep. No hurry now!' She turned to him, clasping them. She tucked them into her frilled blouse. She cried quickly, gaily: 'Oh, how typical this dressing-table is of you!'

'Why? What's the matter with it?' said Hammond.

'If it were floating in eternity I should say "John!" ' laughed Janey, staring at the big bottle of hair tonic, the wicker bottle of eau-de-Cologne, the two hairbrushes and a dozen new collars tied with pink tape. 'Is this all your luggage?'

'Hang my luggage!' said Hammond; but all the same he liked being laughed at by Janey. 'Let's talk. Let's get down to things. Tell me'—and as Janey perched on his knees he leaned back and drew her into the deep, ugly chair—'tell me you're really glad to be back, Janey.'

'Yes, darling, I am glad,' she said.

But just as when he embraced her he felt she would fly away, so Hammond never knew—never knew for dead certain that she was as glad as he was. How could he know? Would he ever know? Would he always have this craving—this pang like hunger, somehow, to make Janey so much part of him that there wasn't any of her to escape? He wanted to blot out everybody, everything. He wished now he'd turned off the light. That might have brought her nearer. And now those letters from the children rustled in her blouse. He could have chucked them into the fire.

'Janey,' he whispered.

'Yes, dear?' She lay on his breast, but so lightly, so remotely. Their breathing rose and fell together.

'Janey!'

'What is it?'

'Turn to me,' he whispered. A slow deep flush, flowed into his forehead. 'Kiss me, Janey! You kiss me!'

It seemed to him there was a tiny pause—but long enough for him to suffer torture—before her lips touched his, firmly, lightly—kissing them as she always kissed him, as though the kiss—how could he describe it?—confirmed what they were saying, signed the contract. But that wasn't what he wanted; that wasn't at all what he thirsted for. He felt suddenly, horribly tired.

'If you knew,' he said, opening his eyes, 'what it's been like—

waiting to-day. I thought the boat never would come in. There we were, hanging about. What kept you so long?.'

She made no answer. She was looking away from him at the fire. The flames hurried—hurried over the coals, flickered, fell.

'Not asleep, are you?' said Hammond, and he jumped her up and down.

'No,' she said. And then: 'Don't do that, dear. No I was thinking. As a matter of fact,' she said, 'one of the passengers died last night—a man. That's what held us up. We brought him in—I mean, he wasn't buried at sea. So, of course, the ship's doctor and the shore doctor—'

'What was it?' asked Hammond uneasily. He hated to hear of death. He hated this to have happened. It was, in some queer way, as though he and Janey had met a funeral on their way to the hotel.

'Oh, it wasn't anything in the least infectious!' said Janey. She was speaking scarcely above her breath. 'It was *heart*.' A pause. 'Poor fellow!' she said. 'Quite young.' And she watched the fire flicker and fall. 'He died in my arms,' said Janey.

The blow was so sudden that Hammond thought he would faint. He couldn't move; he couldn't breathe. He felt all his strength flowing—flowing into the big dark chair, and the big dark chair held him fast, gripped him, forced him to bear it.

'What?' he said dully. 'What's that you say?'

'The end was quite peaceful,' said the small voice. 'He just'—and Hammond saw her lift her gentle hand—'breathed his life away at the end.' And her hand fell.

'Who—else was there?' Hammond managed to ask.

'Nobody. I was alone with him.'

Ah, my God, what was she saying! What was she doing to him! This would kill him! And all the while she spoke:

'I saw the change coming and I sent the steward for the doctor, but the doctor was too late. He couldn't have done anything, anyway.'

'But—why *you*, why *you*?' moaned Hammond.

At that Janey turned quickly, quickly searched his face.

'You don't *mind*, John, do you?' she asked. 'You don't— It's nothing to do with you and me.'

Somehow or other he managed to shake some sort of smile at her. Somehow or other he stammered: 'No—go—on, go on! I want you to tell me.'

'But, John darling—'

'Tell me, Janey!'

'There's nothing to tell,' she said, wondering. 'He was one of the first-class passengers. I saw he was very ill when he came on board. . . . But he seemed to be so much better until yesterday. He had a severe attack in the afternoon—excitement—nervousness, I think, about arriving. And after that he never recovered.'

'But why didn't the stewardess—'

'Oh, my dear—the stewardess!' said Janey. 'What would he have felt? And besides . . . he might have wanted to leave a message . . . to—'

'Didn't he?' muttered Hammond. 'Didn't he say anything?'

'No, darling, not a word!' She shook her head softly. 'All the time I was with him he was too weak . . . he was too weak even to move a finger. . . .'

Janey was silent. But her words, so light, so soft, so chill, seemed to hover in the air, to rain into his breast like snow.

The fire had gone red. Now it fell in with a sharp sound and the room was colder. Cold crept up his arms. The room was huge, immense, glittering. It filled his whole world. There was the great blind bed, with his coat flung across it like some headless man saying his prayers. There was the luggage, ready to be carried away again, anywhere, tossed into trains, carted on to boats.

. . . 'He was too weak. He was too weak to move a finger.' And yet he died in Janey's arms. She—who'd never—never once in all these years—never on one single solitary occasion—

No; he mustn't think of it. Madness lay in thinking of it. No, he wouldn't face it. He couldn't stand it. It was too much to bear!

And now Janey touched his tie with her fingers. She pinched the edges of the tie together.

'You're not—sorry I told you, John darling? It hasn't made you sad? It hasn't spoilt our evening—our being alone together?'

But at that he had to hide his face. He put his face into her bosom and his arms enfolded her.

Spoilt their evening! Spoilt their being alone together! They would never be alone together again.

(1920)

Six
Years After

A long typical boat dream. I was, as usual,
going to N.Z.

It was not the afternoon to be on deck—on the contrary, it was exactly the afternoon when there is no snugger place than a warm cabin, a warm bunk. Tucked up with a rug, a hot-water bottle and a piping hot cup of tea she would not have minded the weather in the least. But he—hated cabins, hated to be inside anywhere more than was absolutely necessary. He had a passion for keeping, as he called it, above board, especially when he was travelling. And it wasn't surprising, considering the enormous amount of time he spent cooped up in the office. So, when he rushed away from her as soon as they got on board and came back five minutes later to say he had secured two deck-chairs on the lee side and the steward was undoing the rugs, her voice through the high sealskin collar murmured 'Good'; and because he was looking at her, she smiled with bright eyes and blinked quickly, as if to say, 'Yes, perfectly all right—absolutely.' And she meant it.

'Then we'd better—' said he, and he tucked her hand inside his arm and began to rush her off to where their chairs stood. But she just had time to breathe, 'Not so fast, Daddy, please,' when he remembered too and slowed down.

Strange! They had been married twenty-eight years, and it was still an effort to him, each time, to adapt his pace to hers.

'Not cold, are you?' he asked, glancing sideways at her. Her little nose, geranium pink above the dark fur, was answer enough. But she thrust her free hand into the velvet pocket of her jacket and murmured gaily, 'I shall be glad of my rug.'

He pressed her tighter to his side—a quick, nervous pressure. He knew, of course, that she ought to be down in the cabin, he knew that it was no afternoon for her to be sitting on deck, in this cold and raw mist, lee side or no lee side, rugs or no rugs, and he realised how she must be hating it. But he had come to believe that it really was easier for her to make these sacrifices than it was for him. Take their present case, for instance. If he had gone down to the cabin with her, he would have been miserable the whole time, and he couldn't have helped showing it. At any rate, she would have found him out. Whereas, having made up her mind to fall in with his ideas, he would have betted anybody she would even go so far as to enjoy the experience. Not because she was without personality of her own. Good Lord! She was absolutely brimming with it. But because ... but here his thoughts always stopped. Here they always felt the need of a cigar, as it were. And, looking at the cigar-tip, his fine blue eyes narrowed. It was a law of marriage, he supposed. ... All the same, he always felt guilty when he asked these sacrifices of her. That was what the quick pressure meant. His being said to her being: 'You do understand, don't you?' and there was an answering tremor of her fingers, 'I *understand*.'

Certainly the steward—good little chap—had done all in his power to make them comfortable. He had put up their chairs in whatever warmth there was and out of the smell. She did hope he would be tipped adequately. It was on occasions like these (and her life seemed to be full of such occasions) that she wished that it was the woman who controlled the purse.

'Thank you, steward. That will do beautifully.'

'Why are stewards so often delicate-looking?' she wondered, as her feet were tucked under. 'This poor little chap looks as though he'd got a chest, and yet one would have thought ... the sea air ...'

The button of the pigskin purse was undone. The tray was tilted. She saw sixpences, shillings, half-crowns.

'I should give him five shillings,' she decided, 'and tell him to buy himself a good nourishing—'

He was given a shilling, and he touched his cap and seemed genuinely grateful.

Well, it might have been worse. It might have been sixpence. It might, indeed. For at that moment Father turned towards her and said, half apologetically, stuffing the purse back, 'I gave him a shilling. I think it was worth it, don't you?'

'Oh, quite! Every bit!' said she.

It is extraordinary how peaceful it feels on a little steamer once the bustle of leaving port is over. In a quarter of an hour one might have been at sea for days. There is something almost touching, childish, in the way people submit themselves to the new conditions. They go to bed in the early afternoon, they shut their eyes and 'it's night' like little children who turn the table upside down and cover themselves with the table-cloth. And those who remain on deck—they seem to be always the same, those few hardened men travellers—pause, light their pipes, stamp softly, gaze out to sea, and their voices are subdued as they walk up and down. The long-legged little girl chases after the red-cheeked boy, but soon both are captured; and the old sailor, swinging an unlighted lantern, passes and disappears. . . .

He lay back, the rug up to his chin, and she saw he was breathing deeply. Sea air! If anyone believed in sea air it was he. He had the strongest faith in its tonic qualities. But the great thing was, according to him, to fill the lungs with it the moment you came on board. Otherwise, the sheer strength of it was enough to give you a chill. . . .

She gave a small chuckle, and he turned to her quickly. 'What is it?'

'It's your cap,' she said. 'I never can get used to you in a cap. You look such a thorough burglar.'

'Well, what the deuce am I to wear?' He shot up one grey eyebrow and wrinkled his nose. 'It's a very good cap, too. Very fine specimen of its kind. It's got a very rich white satin lining.' He paused. He declaimed, as he had hundreds of times before at this stage, 'Rich and rare were the gems she wore.'

But she was thinking he really was childishly proud of the white satin lining. He would like to have taken off his cap and made her feel it. 'Feel the quality!' How often had she rubbed between finger and thumb his coat, his shirt cuff, tie, sock, linen handkerchief, while he said that.

She slipped down more deeply into her chair.

And the little steamer pressed on, pitching gently, over the grey, unbroken, gently moving water, that was veiled with slanting rain.

Far out, as though idly, listlessly, gulls were flying. Now they settled on the waves, now they beat up into the rainy air and shone against the pale sky like the lights within a pearl. They looked cold and lonely. How lonely it will be when we have passed by, she thought. There will be nothing but the waves and those birds and rain falling.

She gazed through the rust-spotted railing along which big drops trembled, until suddenly she shut her lids. It was as if a warning voice inside her had said, 'Don't look!'

'No, I won't,' she decided. 'It's too depressing, much too depressing.'

But, immediately, she opened her eyes and looked again. Lonely birds, water lifting, white pale sky—how were they changed?

And it seemed to her there was a presence far out there, between the sky and the water; someone very desolate and longing watched them pass and cried as if to stop them—but cried to her alone.

'Mother!'

'Don't leave me,' sounded in the cry. 'Don't forget me! You are forgetting me, you know you are!' And it was as though from her own breast there came the sound of childish weeping.

'My son—my precious child—it isn't true!'

Sh! How was it possible that she was sitting there on that quiet steamer beside Father and at the same time she was hushing and holding a little slender boy—so pale—who had just waked out of a dreadful dream?

'I dreamed I was in a wood—somewhere far away from everybody—and I was lying down and a great blackberry vine grew over me. And I called and called to you—and you wouldn't come—you wouldn't come—so I had to lie there for ever.'

What a terrible dream! He had always had terrible dreams. How often, years ago, when he was small, she had made some excuse and escaped from their friends in the dining-room or the drawing-room to come to the foot of the stairs and listen. 'Mother!' And when he was asleep, his dream had journeyed

279

with her back into the circle of lamplight; it had taken its place there like a ghost. And now—

Far more often—at all times—in all places—like now, for instance—she never settled down, she was never off her guard for a moment but she heard him. He wanted her. 'I am coming as fast as I can! As fast as I can!' But the dark stairs have no ending, and the worst dream of all—the one that is always the same—goes for ever and ever uncomforted.

This is anguish! How is it to be borne? Still, it is not the idea of her suffering which is unbearable—it is his. Can one do nothing for the dead? And for a long time the answer had been—Nothing!

... But softly without a sound the dark curtain has rolled down. There is no more to come. That is the end of the play. But it.can't end like that—so suddenly. There must be more. No, it's cold, it's still. There is nothing to be gained by waiting.

But—did he go back again? Or, when the war was over, did he come home for good? Surely, he will marry—later on— not for several years. Surely, one day I shall remember his wedding and my first grandchild—a beautiful dark-haired boy born in the early morning—a lovely morning—spring!

'Oh, Mother, it's not fair to me to put these ideas into my head! Stop, Mother, stop! When I think of all I have missed, I can't bear it.'

'I can't bear it!' She sits up breathing the words and tosses the dark rug away. It is colder than ever, and now the dusk is falling, falling like ash upon the pallid water.

And the little steamer, growing determined, throbbed on, pressed on, as if at the end of the journey there waited . . .

(1922)

280

An Ideal
Family

That evening for the first time in his life, as he pressed through
the swing-door and descended the three broad steps to the
pavement, old Mr. Neave felt he was too old for the spring.
Spring—warm, eager, restless—was there, waiting for him in
the golden light, ready in front of everybody to run up, to
blow in his white beard, to drag sweetly on his arm. And
he couldn't meet her, no; he couldn't square up once more
and stride off, jaunty as a young man. He was tired and,
although the late sun was still shining, curiously cold, with
a numbed feeling all over. Quite suddenly he hadn't the
energy, he hadn't the heart to stand this gaiety and bright movement any longer; it confused him. He wanted to stand still,
to wave it away with his stick, to say, 'Be off with you!'
Suddenly it was a terrible effort to greet as usual—tipping his
wide-awake with his stick—all the people whom he knew, the
friends, acquaintances, shopkeepers, postmen, drivers. But
the gay glance that went with the gesture, the kindly twinkle
that seemed to say, 'I'm a match and more for any of you'—
that old Mr. Neave could not manage at all. He stumped along,
lifting his knees high as if he were walking through air that had
somehow grown heavy and solid like water. And the home-
ward-going crowd hurried by, the trams clanked, the light carts
clattered, the big swinging cabs bowled along with that reckless,
defiant indifference that one knows only in dreams. . . .

It had been a day like other days at the office. Nothing
special had happened. Harold hadn't come back from lunch
until close on four. Where had he been? What had he been up to?
He wasn't going to let his father know. Old Mr. Neave had
happened to be in the vestibule, saying good-bye to a caller,

when Harold sauntered in, perfectly turned out as usual, cool, suave, smiling that peculiar little half-smile that women found so fascinating.

Ah, Harold was too handsome, too handsome by far; that had been the trouble all along. No man had a right to such eyes, such lashes and such lips; it was uncanny. As for his mother, his sisters, and the servants, it was not too much to say they made a young god of him; they worshipped Harold, they forgave him everything; and he had needed some forgiving ever since the time when he was thirteen and he had stolen his mother's purse, taken the money, and hidden the purse in the cook's bedroom. Old Mr. Neave struck sharply with his stick upon the pavement edge. But it wasn't only his family who spoiled Harold, he reflected, it was everybody; he had only to look and to smile and down they went before him. So perhaps it wasn't to be wondered at that he expected the office to carry on the tradition. H'm, h'm! But it couldn't be done. No business—not even a successful, established, big paying concern —could be played with. A man had either to put his whole heart and soul into it, or it went all to pieces before his eyes. . . .

And then Charlotte and the girls were always at him to make the whole thing over to Harold, to retire, and to spend his time enjoying himself. Enjoying himself! Old Mr. Neave stopped dead under a group of ancient cabbage palms outside the Government buildings. Enjoying himself! The wind of evening shook the dark leaves to a thin airy cackle. Sitting at home, twiddling his thumbs, conscious all the while that his life's work was slipping away, dissolving, disappearing through Harold's fine fingers, while Harold smiled. . . .

'Why will you be so unreasonable, father? There's absolutely no need for you to go to the office. It only makes it very awkward for us when people persist in saying how tired you're looking. Here's this huge house and garden. Surely you could be happy in—in—appreciating it for a change. Or you could take up some hobby.'

And Lola the baby had chimed in loftily, 'All men ought to have hobbies. It makes life impossible if they haven't.'

Well, well! He couldn't help a grim smile as painfully he began to climb the hill that led into Harcourt Avenue. Where would Lola and her sisters and Charlotte be if he'd gone in for hobbies, he'd like to know? Hobbies couldn't pay for the town house and the seaside bungalow, and their horses, and their golf, and the sixty-guinea gramophone in the music-room for them to dance to. Not that he grudged them these things. No, they were smart, good-looking girls, and Charlotte was a re-markable woman; it was natural for them to be in the swim. As a matter of fact, no other house in the town was as popular as theirs; no other family entertained so much. And how many times old Mr. Neave, pushing the cigar-box across the smoking-room table, had listened to praises of his wife, his girls, of himself even.

'You're an ideal family, sir, an ideal family. It's like some-thing one reads about or sees on the stage.'

'That's all right, my boy,' old Mr. Neave would reply. 'Try one of those; I think you'll like them. And if you care to smoke in the garden, you'll find the girls on the lawn, I dare say.'

That was why the girls had never married, so people said. They could have married anybody. But they had too good a time at home. They were too happy together, the girls and Charlotte. H'm, h'm! Well, well! Perhaps so. . . .

By this time he had walked the length of fashionable Harcourt Avenue; he had reached the corner house, their house. The carriage gates were pushed back; there were fresh marks of wheels on the drive. And then he faced the big white-painted house, with its wide-open windows, its tulle curtains floating outwards, its blue jars of hyacinths on the broad sills. On either side of the carriage porch their hydrangeas—famous in the town—were coming into flower; the pinkish, bluish masses of flower lay like light among the spreading leaves. And, somehow, it seemed to old Mr. Neave that the house and the flowers, and even the fresh marks on the drive, were saying, 'There is young life here. There are girls—'

The hall, as always, was dusky with wraps, parasols, gloves piled on the oak chests. From the music-room sounded the piano, quick, loud and impatient. Through the drawing-room door that was ajar voices floated.

'And were there ices?' came from Charlotte. Then the creak, creak of her rocker.

'Ices!' cried Ethel. 'My dear mother, you never saw such ices. Only two kinds. And one a common little strawberry shop ice, in a sopping wet frill.'

'The food altogether was too appalling,' came from Marion.

'Still, it's rather early for ices,' said Charlotte easily.

'But why, if one has them at all . . .' began Ethel.

'Oh, quite so, darling,' crooned Charlotte.

Suddenly the music-room door opened and Lola dashed out. She started, she nearly screamed, at the sight of old Mr. Neave.

'Gracious, father! What a fright you gave me! Have you just come home? Why isn't Charles here to help you off with your coat?'

Her cheeks were crimson from playing, her eyes glittered, the hair fell over her forehead; and she breathed as though she had come running through the dark and was frightened. Old Mr. Neave stared at his youngest daughter; he felt he had never seen her before. So that was Lola, was it? But she seemed to have forgotten her father; it was not for him that she was waiting there. Now she put the tip of her crumpled hand-kerchief between her teeth and tugged at it angrily. The telephone rang. A-ah! Lola gave a cry like a sob and dashed past him. The door of the telephone-room slammed, and at the same moment Charlotte called, 'Is that you, father?'

'You're tired again,' said Charlotte reproachfully, and she stopped the rocker and offered him her warm plum-like cheek. Bright-haired Ethel pecked his beard; Marion's lips brushed his ear.

'Did you walk back, father?' asked Charlotte.

'Yes, I walked home,' said old Mr. Neave, and he sank into one of the immense drawing-room chairs.

'But why didn't you take a cab?' said Ethel. 'There are hundreds of cabs about at that time.'

'My dear Ethel,' cried Marion, 'if father prefers to tire himself out, I really don't see what business of ours it is to interfere.'

'Children, children!' coaxed Charlotte.

But Marion wouldn't be stopped. 'No, mother, you spoil father, and it's not right. You ought to be stricter with him. He's very naughty.' She laughed her hard, bright laugh and patted her hair in a mirror. Strange! When she was a little girl she had such a soft, hesitating voice; she had even stuttered, and now, whatever she said—even if it was only 'Jam, please, father'—it rang out as though she were on the stage.

284

'Did Harold leave the office before you, dear?' asked Charlotte, beginning to rock again.

'I'm not sure,' said old Mr. Neave. 'I'm not sure. I didn't see him after four o'clock.'

'He said—' began Charlotte.

But at that moment Ethel, who was twitching over the leaves of some paper or other, ran to her mother and sank down beside her chair.

'There, you see,' she cried. 'That's what I mean, mummy. Yellow, with touches of silver. Don't you agree?'

'Give it to me, love,' said Charlotte. She fumbled for her tortoise-shell spectacles and put them on, gave the page a little dab with her plump, small fingers, and pursed up her lips. 'Very sweet!' she crooned vaguely; she looked at Ethel over her spectacles. 'But I shouldn't have the train.'

'Not the train!' wailed Ethel tragically. 'But the train's the whole point.'

'Here, mother, let me decide.' Marion snatched the paper playfully from Charlotte. 'I agree with mother,' she cried triumphantly. 'The train overweights it.'

Old Mr. Neave, forgotten, sank into the broad lap of his chair, and, dozing, heard them as though he dreamed. There was no doubt about it, he was tired out; he had lost his hold. Even Charlotte and the girls were too much for him to-night. They were too ... too ... But all his drowsing brain could think of was—too *rich* for him. And somewhere at the back of everything he was watching a little withered ancient man climbing up endless flights of stairs. Who was he?

'I shan't dress to-night,' he muttered.

'What do you say, father?'

'Eh, what, what?' Old Mr. Neave woke with a start and stared across at them. 'I shan't dress to-night,' he repeated.

'But, father, we've got Lucile coming, and Henry Davenport, and Mrs. Teddie Walker.'

'It will look so *very* out of the picture.'

'Don't you feel well, dear?'

'You needn't make any effort. What is Charles *for*?'

'But if you're really not up to it,' Charlotte wavered.

'Very well! Very well!' Old Mr. Neave got up and went to join that little old climbing fellow just as far as his dressing-room. . . .

There young Charles was waiting for him. Carefully, as though everything depended on it, he was tucking a towel round the hot-water can. Young Charles had been a favourite of his ever since as a little red-faced boy he had come into the house to look after the fires. Old Mr. Neave lowered himself into the cane lounge by the window, stretched out his legs, and made his little evening joke, 'Dress him up, Charles!' And Charles, breathing intensely and frowning, bent forward to take the pin out of his tie.

H'm, h'm! Well, well! It was pleasant by the open window, very pleasant—a fine mild evening. They were cutting the grass on the tennis-court below; he heard the soft churr of the mower. Soon the girls would begin their tennis parties again. And at the thought he seemed to hear Marion's voice ring out, 'Good for you, partner. . . . Oh, *played*, partner. . . . Oh, *very* nice indeed.' Then Charlotte calling from the veranda, 'Where is Harold?' And Ethel, 'He's certainly not here, mother.' And Charlotte's vague, 'He said—'

Old Mr. Neave sighed, got up, and putting one hand under his beard, he took the comb from young Charles and carefully combed the white beard over. Charles gave him a folded handkerchief, his watch and seals, and spectacle case.

'That will do, my lad.' The door shut, he sank back, he was alone. . . .

And now that little ancient fellow was climbing down endless flights that led to a glittering, gay dining-room. What legs he had! They were like a spider's—thin, withered.

'You're an ideal family, sir, an ideal family.'

But, if that were true, why didn't Charlotte or the girls stop him? Why was he all alone, climbing up and down? Where was Harold? Ah, it was no good expecting anything from Harold. Down, down went the little old spider, and then, to his horror, old Mr. Neave saw him slip past the dining-room and make for the porch, the dark drive, the carriage gates, the office. Stop him, stop him, somebody!

Old Mr. Neave started up. It was dark in his dressing-room; the window shone pale. How long had he been asleep? He listened, and through the big, airy, darkened house there floated far-away voices, far-away sounds. Perhaps, he thought vaguely, he had been asleep for a long time. He'd been for-gotten. What had all this to do with him—this house and

Charlotte, the girls and Harold—what did he know about them? They were strangers to him. Life had passed him by. Charlotte was not his wife. His wife!

... A dark porch, half hidden by a passion-vine, that drooped sorrowful, mournful, as though it understood. Small, warm arms were round his neck. A face, little and pale, lifted to his, and a voice breathed, 'Good-bye, my treasure.'

My treasure! 'Good-bye, my treasure!' Which of them had spoken? Why had they said good-bye? There had been some terrible mistake. *She* was his wife, that little pale girl, and all the rest of his life had been a dream.

Then the door opened, and young Charles, standing in the light, put his hands by his side and shouted like a young soldier, 'Dinner is on the table, sir!'

'I'm coming, I'm coming,' said old Mr. Neave.

(1921)

The Office
Boy

After a succession of idle, or careless, or clumsy, or unwilling
little boys had passed through the office, after horrid little
boys that the typists couldn't bear to come near them—'Stand
further off, please!'—or clumsy young idiots who tripped on
the Boss's doormat every time they came to him with a
message—the appearance of Charlie Parker on the scene was
more than relief, it was hailed with positive pleasure by everybody. His mother was good old Ma Parker, the office cleaner,
whose husband, a chimney sweep, had died in a chimney!
Really—the poor seem to go out of their way to find extraordinary places to die in! Charlie was the eldest of goodness
knows how many little P's. So many, in fact, that the clergyman's wife, who was tired of delivering parcels of flannelette
at the tiny house with the black brush over the gate, said
that she didn't believe Mr. Parker's death had made the
slightest difference to Mrs. Parker. 'I don't believe anything
will stop her. I am sure there has been a new one since I was
there last. I think it has become pure habit and she will go on
and on—eating into the Maternity Bag,' said the clergyman's
wife crossly. 'I confess, my dear, I find you slightly difficult to
follow,' said her husband.

Well, if they were all like Charlie it wasn't greatly to be
wondered at. What trouble would he have given his mother?
He was one of those children who must have been a comfort
ever since he found his legs. At fourteen he was a firm, upstand-
ing little chap—on the slender side, perhaps—but quite a
little man, with bright blue eyes, shining brown hair, good
teeth that showed when he smiled—he was always smiling—
and a fair baby skin that turned crimson when the typists

teased him. But that wasn't all. He was so neat, so careful of his appearance—so—brushed and combed! There was never a speck on his blue serge suit. When you looked at his tie you wanted to smile, you could see how solemnly that knot had been drawn just so. Beams came from his hair and his boots, and his childish hands were a deep pink colour as though he'd just finished drying them.

From his first day at the office Charlie found his place, as though he had been dreaming all his life what he would do when he was an office boy. He changed the blotting paper on the desks, kept the inkpots clean and filled, saw that there were fresh nibs, carried wire baskets of letters from the typists' room to the Boss, to the acting Manager, to Mr. Tonks of the wholesale order department, went to the post office, bought immense quantities of different kinds of stamps, asked the various callers who it was they wished to see, answered the store-room telephone,—and at four o'clock when Miss Hickness, the head typist, had boiled a kettle on the electric heater she was so proud of, he took in the Boss's tea.

A knock at the door.

'Come in!'

Enter Charlie, with the tea-tray, very serious and yet trying not to smile. He walks so straight that his knees rub together and if as much as a saucer clatters, he draws in his breath and frowns. . . .

'Ah, Charlie!' the Boss leans back. 'That my tea?'

'Yes, Sir'—and very carefully the tray is lowered and a pink hand reaches out and ventures to move back a paper or two. Then Charlie stands upright like a soldier on parade, and glaring at the sugar as if he dared it to take wings and fly, he says: 'Have you everything you want, Sir?'

'Yes, I think so, Charlie,' says the Boss, easy and genial.

Charlie turns to go.

'Oh, one moment, Charlie!'

And the little boy turns round and looks full at the Boss, and the Boss looks back into those candid innocent eyes. 'You might—you might tell Miss Walker to come in to me in half an hour.'

'Very good, Sir!' says Charlie. And he is gone. But the Boss pours out his tea and the tea tastes wonderfully good. There is something especially crisp about the biscuits too, and there's no doubt afternoon tea is refreshing—he's noticed it particularly lately. . . .

It was extraordinary the difference one little boy made in the office, ''E couldn't be made more fuss of if 'e was a little dog,' said the storeman. 'It's like 'aving a pet in the 'ouse, that's what it is.'

And he was right. To have someone who was always eager and merry and ready to play. Someone to like you when saying silly things if you wanted to. Someone who—if you did say a kind word—as good as jumped in the air for joy. But why wasn't he spoilt? That was what the typists couldn't understand. But everybody went out of the way to be nice, to be kind to him—when even the Boss made a fad of him why didn't he become an odious little horror?

Mystery. . . . However . . .

One October afternoon, blustery, with a drizzle of rain . . .

. . . Once they're found out—once the taint's discovered— you might as well try and get rid of a touch of the tar-brush.

. . . 'No,' he thought, staring at a drowned leaf that bobbed against the edge of the cup, 'it's no good. It won't work. Charlie must go.'

. . . And now, thinking over Charlie's cleanliness and cheerfulness and good temper, it seemed to him that it had all been acting. An astonishing example in so young a boy of criminal cleverness. What else could it have been? Look how, even after he had been forgiven and the whole thing wiped out, after he'd been allowed to get off scot free . . .

(1921)

290

The Fly

'Y'are very snug in here,' piped old Mr. Woodifield, and he
peered out of the great, green-leather armchair by his friend
the boss's desk as a baby peers out of its pram. His talk was
over; it was time for him to be off. But he did not want to go.
Since he had retired, since his . . . stroke, the wife and the girls
kept him boxed up in the house every day of the week except
Tuesday. On Tuesday he was dressed and brushed and allowed
to cut back to the City for the day. Though what he did there
the wife and girls couldn't imagine. Made a nuisance of himself
to his friends, they supposed. . . . Well, perhaps so. All the
same, we cling to our last pleasures as the tree clings to its last
leaves. So there sat old Woodifield, smoking a cigar and staring
almost greedily at the boss, who rolled in his office chair, stout,
rosy, five years older than he, and still going strong, still at the
helm. It did one good to see him.

Wistfully, admiringly, the old voice added, 'It's snug in here,
upon my word!'

'Yes, it's comfortable enough,' agreed the boss, and he
flipped the *Financial Times* with a paper-knife. As a matter of
fact he was proud of his room; he liked to have it admired,
especially by old Woodifield. It gave him a feeling of deep,
solid satisfaction to be planted there in the midst of it in full
view of that frail old figure in the muffler.

'I've had it done up lately,' he explained, as he had explained for the past—how many?—weeks. 'New carpet,' and
he pointed to the bright red carpet with a pattern of large
white rings. 'New furniture,' and he nodded towards the
massive bookcase and the table with legs like twisted treacle.
'Electric heating!' He waved almost exultantly towards the
five transparent, pearly sausages glowing so softly in the tilted
copper pan.

But he did not draw old Woodifield's attention to the

291

photograph over the table of a grave-looking boy in uniform
standing in one of those spectral photographers' parks with
photographers' storm-clouds behind him. It was not new.
It had been there for over six years.

'There was something I wanted to tell you,' said old Woodifield, and his eyes grew dim remembering. 'Now what was it?
I had it in my mind when I started out this morning.' His
hands began to tremble, and patches of red showed above his
beard.

Poor old chap, he's on his last pins, thought the boss. And,
feeling kindly, he winked at the old man, and said jokingly,
'I tell you what. I've got a little drop of something here that'll
do you good before you go out into the cold again. It's beautiful
stuff. It wouldn't hurt a child.' He took a key off his watch-
chain, unlocked a cupboard below his desk, and drew forth a
dark, squat bottle. 'That's the medicine,' said he. 'And the
man from whom I got it told me on the strict Q.T. it came from
the cellars at Windsor Castle.'

Old Woodifield's mouth fell open at the sight. He couldn't
have looked more surprised if the boss had produced a rabbit.

'It's whisky, ain't it?' he piped feebly.

The boss turned the bottle and lovingly showed him the
label. Whisky it was.

'D'you know,' said he, peering up at the boss wonderingly,
'they won't let me touch it at home.' And he looked as though
he was going to cry.

'Ah, that's where we know a bit more than the ladies,'
cried the boss, swooping across for two tumblers that stood on
the table with the water-bottle, and pouring a generous
finger into each. 'Drink it down. It'll do you good. And don't
put any water with it. It's sacrilege to tamper with stuff like
this. Ah!' He tossed off his, pulled out his handkerchief,
hastily wiped his moustaches, and cocked an eye at old Woodifield, who was rolling his in his chaps.

The old man swallowed, was silent a moment, and then said
faintly, 'It's nutty!'

But it warmed him; it crept into his chill old brain—he
remembered.

'That was it,' he said, heaving himself out of his chair. 'I
thought you'd like to know. The girls were in Belgium last
week having a look at poor Reggie's grave, and they happened

to come across your boy's. They're quite near each other, it seems.'

Old Woodifield paused, but the boss made no reply. Only a quiver in his eyelids showed that he heard.

'The girls were delighted with the way the place is kept,' piped the old voice. 'Beautifully looked after. Couldn't be better if they were at home. You've not been across, have yer?'

'No, no!' For various reasons the boss had not been across.

'There's miles of it,' quavered old Woodifield, 'and it's all as neat as a garden. Flowers growing on all the graves. Nice broad paths.' It was plain from his voice how much he liked a nice broad path.

The pause came again. Then the old man brightened wonderfully.

'D'you know what the hotel made the girls pay for a pot of jam?' he piped. 'Ten francs! Robbery, I call it. It was a little pot, so Gertrude says, no bigger than a half-crown. And she hadn't taken more than a spoonful when they charged her ten francs. Gertrude brought the pot away with her to teach 'em a lesson. Quite right, too; it's trading on our feelings. They think because we're over there having a look round we're ready to pay anything. That's what it is.' And he turned towards the door.

'Quite right, quite right!' cried the boss, though what was quite right he hadn't the least idea. He came round by his desk, followed the shuffling footsteps to the door, and saw the old fellow out. Woodifield was gone.

For a long moment the boss stayed, staring at nothing, while the grey-haired office messenger, watching him, dodged in and out of his cubby-hole like a dog that expects to be taken for a run. Then: 'I'll see nobody for half an hour, Macey,' said the boss. 'Understand? Nobody at all.'

'Very good, sir.'

The door shut, the firm heavy steps recrossed the bright carpet, the fat body plumped down in the spring chair, and leaning forward, the boss covered his face with his hands. He wanted, he intended, he had arranged to weep. . . .

It had been a terrible shock to him when old Woodifield sprang that remark upon him about the boy's grave. It was exactly as though the earth had opened and he had seen the boy lying there with Woodifield's girls staring down at him. For it was strange. Although over six years had passed away, the boss never thought of the boy except as lying unchanged, unblemished in his uniform, asleep for ever. 'My son!' groaned the boss. But no tears came yet. In the past, in the first months and even years after the boy's death, he had only to say those words to be overcome by such grief that nothing short of a violent fit of weeping could relieve him. Time, he had declared then, he had told everybody, could make no difference. Other men perhaps might recover, might live their loss down, but not he. How was it possible? His boy was an only son. Ever since his birth the boss had worked at building up this business for him; it had no other meaning if it was not for the boy. Life itself had come to have no other meaning. How on earth could he have slaved, denied himself, kept going all those years without the promise for ever before him of the boy's stepping into his shoes and carrying on where he left off?

And that promise had been so near being fulfilled. The boy had been in the office learning the ropes for a year before the war. Every morning they had started off together; they had come back by the same train. And what congratulations he had received as the boy's father! No wonder; he had taken to it marvellously. As to his popularity with the staff, every man jack of them down to old Macey couldn't make enough of the boy. And he wasn't in the least spoilt. No, he was just his bright natural self, with the right word for everybody, with that boyish look and his habit of saying, 'Simply splendid!'

But all that was over and done with as though it never had been. The day had come when Macey had handed him the telegram that brought the whole place crashing about his head. 'Deeply regret to inform you . . .' And he had left the office a broken man, with his life in ruins.

Six years ago, six years. . . . How quickly time passed! It might have happened yesterday. The boss took his hands from his face; he was puzzled. Something seemed to be wrong with him. He wasn't feeling as he wanted to feel. He decided to get up and have a look at the boy's photograph. But it wasn't a favourite photograph of his; the expression was unnatural. It was cold, even stern-looking. The boy had never looked like that.

At that moment the boss noticed that a fly had fallen into his broad inkpot, and was trying feebly but desperately to clamber out again. Help! help! said those struggling legs. But the sides of the inkpot were wet and slippery; it fell back again and began to swim. The boss took up a pen, picked the fly out of the ink, and shook it on to a piece of blotting-paper. For a fraction of a second it lay still on the dark patch that oozed round it. Then the front legs waved, took hold, and, pulling its small, sodden body up, it began the immense task of cleaning the ink from its wings. Over and under, over and under, went a leg along a wing as the stone goes over and under the scythe. Then there was a pause, while the fly, seeming to stand on the tips of its toes, tried to expand first one wing and then the other. It succeeded at last, and, sitting down, it began, like a minute cat, to clean its face. Now one could imagine that the little front legs rubbed against each other lightly, joyfully. The horrible danger was over; it had escaped; it was ready for life again.

But just then the boss had an idea. He plunged his pen back into the ink, leaned his thick wrist on the blotting-paper, and as the fly tried its wings down came a great heavy blot. What would it make of that? What indeed! The little beggar seemed absolutely cowed, stunned, and afraid to move because of what would happen next. But then, as if painfully, it dragged itself forward. The front legs waved, caught hold, and, more slowly this time, the task began from the beginning.

He's a plucky little devil, thought the boss, and he felt a real admiration for the fly's courage. That was the way to tackle things; that was the right spirit. Never say die; it was only a question of . . . But the fly had again finished its laborious task, and the boss had just time to refill his pen, to shake fair and square on the new-cleaned body yet another dark drop. What about it this time? A painful moment of suspense followed. But behold, the front legs were again waving; the boss felt a rush of relief. He leaned over the fly and said to it tenderly, 'You artful little b . . .' And he actually had the brilliant notion of breathing on it to help the drying process. All the same, there was something timid and weak about its efforts now, and the boss decided that this time should be the last, as he dipped the pen deep into the inkpot.

It was. The last blot fell on the soaked blotting-paper, and the draggled fly lay in it and did not stir. The back legs were stuck to the body; the front legs were not to be seen.

'Come on,' said the boss. 'Look sharp!' And he stirred it with his pen—in vain. Nothing happened or was likely to happen. The fly was dead.

The boss lifted the corpse on the end of the paper-knife and flung it into the waste-paper basket. But such a grinding feeling of wretchedness seized him that he felt positively frightened. He started forward and pressed the bell for Macey.

'Bring me some fresh blotting-paper,' he said sternly, 'and look sharp about it.' And while the old dog padded away he fell to wondering what it was he had been thinking about before. What was it? It was . . . He took out his handkerchief and passed it inside his collar. For the life of him he could not remember.

(1922)

PART FIVE

Scenes from Colonial Life

Old Tar

Old Tar must have begun building his house when he was about five years old. Every Sunday morning after church his father and he, hand in hand, went for a bit of a stroll while Mother got dinner, up the new road, through a barbed-wire fence, and on to the great green shoulders of Makra Hill. There they sat down on the blowing grass and pink 'fairy trumpets' or on the white and yellow daisies and dandelions, and while his father had a chew of tobacco, Old Tar (who was very young Tar indeed then) sat quiet and strained his little panting chest against his tight Sunday clothes. Far below, the sea ran with a crashing laugh up Makra beach and slipped back again, stealthy, quiet, and gathered together and came again, biting over the rocks and swallowing the sand. They could snuff it in their nostrils and taste it on their lips. There was nothing to be seen to left or right of them but other hill-tops bounded by dark, high masses of bush. Behind them there was the new road leading to Wadesville, and a further drop to the township, Karori; but all that was hidden, and might have been the length of days away. 'By gum!' the old man would mutter, lifting his worn head. 'It's a durn fine place . . . it's a place to shake yer lungs out in—yer know, boy, my Pap bought this from the Maoris—he did. Ye-es! Got it off Ole Puhui for a "suit of clothes an' a lookin'-glass of yer Granmaw's." My stars! He had an eye! Larst thing the ole man says to me was— "James," 'e says, "don't you be muckin' about with that bit of land top of Makra Hill. Don't you sell it. 'And it on," 'e says, "to you an' yours." ' 'Wot d'you mean?' asked the little boy one day, sitting, his legs straight out, making finger gloves of the fairy trumpets. 'Why, wot I mean is—when I'm put away it'll be yours. See?' 'Wot—all this?' cried the little boy, frightened, clutching the hill, as though he expected it to jump away with him on its back, like a great green camel.

299

'All this!' echoed the father, solemn. 'All yours—once you're through the fence.' Nothing more was said until dinner. He sat with his bib round his neck, drinking tinned soup with Worcester sauce. 'Pop,' he said, 'I'm goin' to build an 'ouse on my hill. Big as . . .' and he stretched his arms wide.

Tar was an only child. His father was fifty when he was born, and his mother forty-three. They were strict, upright people, owners of the Wadesville general store and post office. They did brisk business, and every Saturday night Tar helped his father fasten the wooden shutter on which was printed 'Closed in God's name. Those whom the Lord loveth He chasteneth.' He was brought up so severely that his animal spirits never bubbled at all, and he lived in a sober manner, behind his mother's skirts and his father's counter. The first thing that he remembered was that Sunday morning when his father told him Makra Hill would be his, and the telling took such strange hold of him that there was no room in his mind for anything else. All his plans and plots, all his games and dreams were of what he would do when he had it, and of the fine house he'd build. Sometimes it would be bigger than Government House in Wellington, with its hundred bedrooms and fine red carpets, with palm trees growing out of them, and other times it would be a little house, just room enough to hold him and 'something to set'. Then it would be a farm with all animals on it—even white pigs. At fourteen his father put him behind the counter—a little, pale, freckled boy, with a flop of black hair falling into his eyebrows. After the shop was shut he'd pull off his apron and get a hunk of bread and jam and be off at a run, not stopping to take breath or to look this side or that until he reached the windy hill with the brimming sea below. Every stone of the hill he thought he knew; every pocket and cranny he marched over, lord and master. Swelled up with pride he'd dig with his heel: 'I'll have me front door here, and the rain tanks here, under the balcony scuppers.' And on winter nights in the iron chapel when the rain beat with a million hammers on the roof and walls, and the preacher with a stuck-out beard boomed, 'An' the mountains shall skip like r-rams and the little hills like young sheep,' something jumped in Tar, like a flare in the dark. He saw himself running away from the place and through the fence on the top of it. And the Day of Judgement was come and the hill leaping. . . .

When Tar was twenty his mother died. She was chopping up a candle-box in the backyard, and suddenly the tomahawk fell from her hand and she dropped. Just like that. Not a word. He thought quick, 'If it'd been Pop I'd have had my hill—here,' and hid away the money she left him and began to save every penny for the house. He married at thirty a quiet girl who bossed him. And the business grew and grew, and by-and-by they were well off. They had to add a room now and again at the back of the shop for the children. 'Oh, why can't you build a nice place somewhere, Father?' the wife used to scold. 'You wait, my girl,' said Tar, his eyes suddenly fierce. At last, when he was fifty, and his father ninety-five, the old man stretched out, creaked his bones, and died. That was on a Sunday night. Monday morning, Old Tar hitched the buggy and drove off to Karori, like a man drunk or to his wedding-feast. He wore his best black suit, he cut at the trees as he passed, and greeted people with a grin and a chuckle, and stopped at the builder's. 'Look 'ere, Mr. Stubbs. Will you come back with me? There's a piece of ground I want to show you. I've decided to build.' Not until they were half-way home he remembered to tell Stubbs the old man had gone.

All Wadesville and Karori watched the building of Tar's house. Parties drove up to see it, and picnicked on the piles of yellow, sweet-smelling wood. The store brimmed over with customers, and Mrs. Tar, in black, with her troop of black alpaca children, turned into a fine lady, and talked of nothing but the hinconvenience she'd suffered living in the shop for the sake of her 'usband's father and his sentimentalness. Old Tar, after one day's burst of excitement, kept his grim joy to himself. But he was mad inside, so hot that he felt all the hard years in him melting away. He spent half the day with the workmen, and a great big barn began to grow out of the scooped and jagged hole dug in the side of the hill. It grew quickly. The stairs were up. The flooring was done upstairs. He could creep up at evening to the front room and look through the window-hole at the sea. He would go up and take a lantern and walk from room to room, silent as a cat, feeding his delight. . . . And at last it was finished. Old Tar's house, painted white with green 'pickings', reared up ready at the top of the hill. 'We'll make a party an' all go up this evening,' said his wife, 'an' have a fair look'. 'No you don't,' said Old Tar.

'I got to be there. Business. Measuring. I got to have my 'ead quiet. You kin go termorrow.' She shrugged and obeyed. Tar left the shop early. The setting sun was drawing from the earth the strong, sweet scents of day. There was no wind; just a breeze rippled over the grass and shook the manuka flowers, like tiny white stars down the yellow clay banks of the new road. He walked slowly. No need to get through the fence —the fence was down and carted away. Heavy ruts were carved in the side of the hill, and there was a path to the front door strewn already with a load of white shells. The big white house, with all its hollow eyes, glared at Old Tar.

'It's big,' he thought, and he said as though he prayed, 'Oh, Lord, it is big!' The builders had left the key under the verandah. He felt and found it, and let himself in. At first the house was very still, then it creaked a little, and he heard a tap drip. It smelt strongly of paint and varnish and fine ripe wood. A pencil ray of sun shone across the stairs. As he watched, it shifted and disappeared. The sun had set. Old Tar, tip-toe in his creaking boots, walked through his dream, up and down, in and out, prying like a woman, conscious as a lover, wondering and touching things, and knocking them with his knuckles to hear how thick they sounded. At last he felt a bit tired. He sat down on the stairs. It had begun to grow dusky. The shadows of the door lay across the front hall, sharp and long. He took off his hard hat and leaned his head with the boyish flop of hair against the stair-rail. In the quiet he heard the sea beat, beat up, and then he heard the wind, very slow, snuffling round the house like a lonely dog. 'Ooh Hee! Oooh Hee!' it sounded. 'A rare, sad noise,' thought Old Tar, shaking his head to it. 'Sounds as if it'd lost something an' couldn't find it again.' 'Lost for evermore,' and the sad words fell into his quiet heart and started strange, uneasy ripples. Sitting by himself like that, he felt queer and frightened, somehow. 'Ooh Hee! Ooh Hee!' sounded the wind, rattling the window sashes. ''Tain't like it used to sound up here,' he thought. ''Tain't like it was in the old man's time.' 'Shake out yer lungs, me lad,' he heard old Pop say. Clear as a dream Old Tar saw his Pop and himself sitting where the house stood now, he with the pink, sticky flowers in his fingers, the hill shining and the sea shining below. And then, like a man in a dream, he took off his boots, and stole down into the hall, out of the house. It was getting darker

302

every minute. Thin clouds flew over an ashen sky. The grass between his feet, Old Tar stepped back from the house and looked up at it. He saw in the dusky light the pits the workmen had dug in his hill. He saw the great trampled patches the timber piles had made, and he saw, between him and the sea, the white house perched, the big white nest for his wife and her brood on the top of his hill. As though he saw it for the first time. Old Tar muttered in a strange voice, 'Wot's it doing there—wot's it for?' and 'Oh, Lord, wot 'ave I done—wot 'ave I done, Lord?' A long time Old Tar stood there, while the dark sifted over him and the house paled and stretched up to the sky. His feet seemed to freeze into the cold grass of the hill, and dark thoughts flew across his mind, like clouds, never quiet, never breaking.

(1913)

The Wrong House

'Two purl—two plain—woolinfrontoftheneedle—and knit two together.' Like an old song, like a song that she had sung so often that only to breathe was to sing it, she murmured the knitting pattern. Another vest was nearly finished for the mission parcel.

'It's your vests, Mrs. Bean, that are so acceptable. Look at these poor little mites without a shred!' And the churchwoman showed her a photograph of repulsive little black objects with bellies shaped like lemons. . . .

'Two purl—two plain.' Down dropped the knitting on to her lap; she gave a great long sigh, stared in front of her for a moment and then picked the knitting up and began again. What did she think about when she sighed like that? Nothing. It was a habit. She was always sighing. On the stairs, particularly, as she went up and down, she stopped, holding her dress up with one hand, the other hand on the banister, staring at the steps—sighing.

'Woolinfrontoftheneedle. . . .' She sat at the dining-room window facing the street. It was a bitter autumn day; the wind ran in the street like a thin dog; the houses opposite looked as though they had been cut out with a pair of ugly steel scissors and pasted on to the grey paper sky. There was not a soul to be seen.

'Knit two together!' The clock struck three. Only three? It seemed dusk already; dusk came floating into the room, heavy, powdery dusk settling on the furniture, filming over the mirror. Now the kitchen clock struck three—two minutes late—for *this* was the clock to go by and *not* the kitchen clock. She was alone in the house. Dollicas was out shopping; she had been gone since a quarter to two. Really, she got slower and

304

slower! What did she *do* with the time? One cannot spend more than a certain time buying a chicken. . . . And oh, that habit of hers of dropping the stove-rings when she made up the fire! And she set her lips, as she had set her lips for the past thirty-five years, at that habit of Dollicas'.

There came a faint noise from the street, a noise of horses' hooves. She leaned further out to see. Good gracious! It was a funeral. First the glass coach, rolling along briskly with the gleaming, varnished coffin inside (but no wreaths), with three men in front and two standing at the back, then some carriages, some with black horses, some with brown. The dust came bowling up the road, half hiding the procession. She scanned the houses opposite to see which had the blinds down. What horrible-looking men, too! laughing and joking. One leaned over to one side and blew his nose with his black glove— horrible! She gathered up the knitting, hiding her hands in it. Dollicas surely would have known. . . . There, they were passing. . . . It was the other end. . . .

What was this? What was happening? What could it mean? Help, God! Her old heart leaped like a fish and then fell as the glass coach drew up outside her door, as the outside men scrambled down from the front, swung off the back, and the tallest of them, with a glance of surprise at the windows, came quickly, stealthily, up the garden path.

'No!' she groaned. But yes, the blow fell, and for the moment it struck her down. She gasped, a great cold shiver went through her, and stayed in her hands and knees. She saw the man withdraw a step, and again—that puzzled glance at the blinds —and then—

'No!' she groaned, and stumbling, catching hold of things, she managed to get to the door before the blow fell again. She opened it, her chin trembled, her teeth clacked; somehow or other she brought out, 'The wrong house!'

Oh! he was shocked. As she stepped back she saw behind him the black hats clustered at the gate. 'The wrong 'ouse!' he muttered. She could only nod. She was shutting the door again when he fished out of the tail of his coat a black, brass-bound notebook and swiftly opened it. 'No. 20 Shuttleworth Crescent?'

'S—street! Crescent round the corner.' Her hand lifted to point, but shook and fell.

He was taking off his hat as she shut the door and leaned

against it, whimpering in the dusky hall, 'Go away! Go away!'

Clockety-clock-clock. Cluk! Cluk! Clockety-clock-cluk! sounded from outside, and then a faint *Cluk! Cluk!* and then silence. They were gone. They were out of sight. But still she stayed leaning against the door, staring into the hall, staring at the hall-stand that was like a great lobster with hat-pegs for feelers. But she thought of nothing; she did not even think of what had happened. It was as if she had fallen into a cave whose walls were darkness. . . .

She came to herself with a deep inward shock, hearing the gate bang and quick, short steps crunching the gravel; it was Dollicas hurrying round to the back door. Dollicas must not find her there; and wavering, wavering like a candle-flame, back she went into the dining-room to her seat by the window.

Dollicas was in the kitchen. *Klang!* went one of the iron rings into the fender. Then her voice, 'I'm just putting on the tea-kettle, 'm.' Since they had been alone she had got into the way of shouting from one room to another. The old woman coughed to steady herself. 'Please bring in the lamp,' she cried.

'The lamp!' Dollicas came across the passage and stood in the doorway. 'Why, it's only just on four, 'm.'

'Never mind,' said Mrs. Bean dully. 'Bring it in!' And a moment later the elderly maid appeared, carrying the gentle lamp in both hands. Her broad soft face had the look it always had when she carried anything, as though she walked in her sleep. She set it down on the table, lowered the wick, raised it, and then lowered it again. The she straightened up and looked across at her mistress.

'Why, 'm, whatever's that you're treading on?'

It was the mission vest.

'T't! T't!' As Dollicas picked it up she thought, 'The old lady has been asleep. She's not awake yet.' Indeed the old lady looked glazed and dazed, and when she took up the knitting she drew out a needle of stitches and began to unwind what she had done.

'Don't forget the mace,' she said. Her voice sounded thin and dry. She was thinking of the chicken for that night's supper. And Dollicas understood and answered, 'It's a lovely young bird!' as she pulled down the blind before going back to her kitchen. . . .

(1920)

Second Violin

A February morning, windy, cold, with chill-looking clouds hurrying over a pale sky and chill snowdrops for sale in the grey streets. People look small and shrunken as they flit by; they look scared as if they were trying to hide inside their coats from something big and brutal. The shop doors are closed, the awnings are furled, and the policemen at the crossings are lead policemen. Huge empty vans shake past with a hollow sound; and there is a smell of soot and wet stone staircases, a raw, grimy smell. . . .

Flinging her small scarf over her shoulder again, clasping her violin, Miss Bray darts along to orchestra practice. She is conscious of her cold hands, her cold nose and her colder feet. She can't feel her toes at all. Her feet are just little slabs of cold, all of a piece, like the feet of china dolls. Winter is a terrible time for thin people—terrible! Why should it hound them down, fasten on them, worry them so? Why not, for a change, take a nip, take a snap at the fat ones who wouldn't notice? But no! It is sleek, warm, cat-like summer that makes the fat ones' life a misery. Winter is all for bones. . . .

Threading her way, like a needle, in and out and along, went Miss Bray, and she thought of nothing but the cold. She had just come out of her kitchen, which was pleasantly snug in the morning, with her gas-fire going for her breakfast and the window closed. She had just drunk three large cups of really boiling tea. Surely, they ought to have warmed her. One always read in books of people going on their way warmed and invigorated by even one cup. And she had had three! How she loved her tea! She was getting fonder and fonder of it. Stirring the cup, Miss Bray looked down. A little fond smile parted her lips, and she breathed tenderly, 'I love my tea.'

But all the same, in spite of the books, it didn't keep her warm. Cold! Cold! And now as she turned the corner she took such a gulp of damp, cold air that her eyes filled. *Yi-yi-yi*, a little dog yelped; he looked as though he'd been hurt. She hadn't time to look round, but that high, sharp yelping soothed her, was a comfort even. She could have made just that sound herself.

And here was the Academy. Miss Bray pressed with all her might against the stiff, sulky door, squeezed through into the vestibule hung with pallid notices and concert programmes, and stumbled up the dusty stairs and along the passage to the dressing-room. Through the open door there came such shrill loud laughter, such high, indifferent voices that it sounded like a play going on in there. It was hard to believe people were not laughing and talking like that . . . on purpose. 'Excuse me —pardon—sorry,' said Miss Bray, nudging her way in and looking quickly round the dingy little room. Her two friends had not yet come.

The First Violins were there; a dreamy, broad-faced girl leaned against her 'cello; two Violas sat on a bench, bent over a music book, and the Harp, a small grey little person, who only came occasionally, leaned against a bench and looked for her pocket in her underskirt. . . .

'I've a run of three twice, ducky,' said Ma, 'a pair of queens make eight, and one for his nob makes nine.'

With an awful hollow groan Alexander, curling his little finger high, pegged nine for Ma. And 'Wait now, wait now,' said she, and her quick short little hands snatched at the other cards. 'My crib, young man!' She spread them out, leaned back, twitched her shawl, put her head on one side. 'H'm, not so bad! A flush of four and a pair!'

'Betrayed! Betrayed!' moaned Alexander, bowing his dark head over the cribbage board, 'and by a woo-man.' He sighed deeply, shuffled the cards and said to Ma, 'Cut for me, my love!'

Although, of course, he was only having his joke like all professional young gentlemen, something in the tone in which he said 'my love!' gave Ma quite a turn. Her lips trembled as she cut the cards, she felt a sudden pang as she watched those long slim fingers dealing.

Ma and Alexander were playing cribbage in the basement kitchen of number 9 Bolton Street. It was late, it was on eleven, and Sunday night, too—shocking! They sat at the kitchen table that was covered with a worn art serge cloth spotted with candle grease. On one corner of it stood three glasses, three spoons, a saucer of sugar lumps and a bottle of gin. The stove was still alight and the lid of the kettle had just begun to lift, cautiously, stealthily, as though there was someone inside who wanted to have a peep and pop back again. On the horse-hair sofa against the wall by the door the owner of the third glass lay asleep, gently snoring. Perhaps because he had his back to them, perhaps because his feet poked out from the short overcoat covering him, he looked forlorn, pathetic and the long, fair hair covering his collar looked forlorn and pathetic, too.

'Well, well,' said Ma, sighing as she put out two cards and arranged the others in a fan, 'such is life. I little thought when I saw the last of you this morning that we'd be playing a game together to-night.'

'The caprice of destiny,' murmured Alexander. But, as a matter of fact, it was no joking matter. By some infernal mischance that morning he and Rinaldo had missed the train that all the company travelled by. That was bad enough. But being Sunday, there was no other train until midnight, and as they had a full rehearsal at 10 o'clock on Monday it meant going by that, or getting what the company called the beetroot. But God! what a day it had been. They had left the luggage at the station and come back to Ma's, back to Alexander's frowsy bedroom with the bed unmade and water standing about. Rinaldo had spent the whole day sitting on the side of the bed swinging his leg, dropping ash on the floor and saying, 'I wonder what made us lose that train. Strange we should have lost it. I bet the others are wondering what made us lose it, too.' And Alexander had stayed by the window gazing into the small garden that was so black with grime even the old lean cat who came and scraped seemed revolted by it, too. It was only after Ma had seen the last of her Sunday visitors . . .

(1921)

309

Honesty

There was an expression Rupert Henderson was very fond of
using: 'If you want my *honest* opinion. . . .' He had an honest
opinion on every subject under the sun, and nothing short of a
passion for delivering it. But Archie Cullen's pet phrase was 'I
cannot *honestly* say. . . .' Which meant that he had not really
made up his mind. He had not really made up his mind on any
subject whatsoever. Why? Because he could not. He was unlike
other men. He was minus something—or was it plus? No
matter. He was not in the least proud of the fact. It depressed
him—one might go so far as to say—terribly at times.

Rupert and Archie lived together. That is to say, Archie
lived in Rupert's rooms. Oh, he paid his share, his half in
everything; the arrangement was a purely, strictly business
arrangement. But perhaps it was because Rupert had invited
Archie that Archie remained always—his guest. They each
had a bedroom—there was a common sitting-room and a
largish bathroom which Rupert used as a dressing-room as
well. The first morning after his arrival Archie had left his
sponge in the bathroom, and a moment after there was a knock
at his door and Rupert said, kindly but firmly, 'Your sponge,
I fancy.' The first evening Archie had brought his tobacco jar
into the sitting-room and placed it on a corner of the mantelpiece. Rupert was reading the newspaper. It was a round
china jar, the surface painted and roughened to represent a sea-
urchin. On the lid was a spray of china seaweed with two
berries for a knob. Archie was excessively fond of it. But
after dinner, when Rupert took out his pipe and pouch, he
suddenly fixed his eyes on this object, blew through his moustaches, gasped, and said in a wondering, astonished voice, 'I say!
Is that yours or Mrs. Head's?' Mrs. Head was their landlady.

'It's mine,' said Archie, and he blushed and smiled just a trifle timidly.

'I *say!*' said Rupert again—this time very meaningly.

'Would you rather I . . .' said Archie, and he moved in his chair to get up.

'No, no! Certainly not! On no account!' answered Rupert, and he actually raised his hand. 'But perhaps'—and here he smiled at Archie and gazed about him—'perhaps we might find some spot for it that was a trifle less conspicuous.'

The spot was not decided on, however, and Archie nipped his sole personal possession into his bedroom as soon as Rupert was out of the way.

But it was chiefly at meals that the attitude of host and guest was most marked. For instance, on each separate occasion, even before they sat down, Rupert said, 'Would you mind cutting the bread, Archie?' Had he not made such a point of it, it is possible that Archie in a moment of abstractedness might have grasped the bread knife. . . . An unpleasant thought! Again, Archie was never allowed to serve. Even at breakfast, the hot dishes and the tea, both were dispensed by Rupert. True, he had half apologised about the tea; he seemed to feel the necessity of some slight explanation, there.

'I'm rather a fad about my tea,' said he. 'Some people, females especially, pour in the milk first. Fatal habit, for more reasons than one. In my opinion, the cup should be filled just *so* and the tea then coloured. Sugar, Archie?'

'Oh, please,' said Archie, almost bowing over the table. Rupert was so very impressive.

'But I suppose,' said his friend, 'you don't notice any of these little things?'

And Archie answered vaguely, stirring: 'No, I don't suppose I do.'

Rupert sat down and unfolded his napkin.

'It would be very inconsistent with your character and disposition,' said he genially, 'if you did! Kidneys and bacon? Scrambled eggs? Either? Both? Which?'

Poor Archie hated scrambled eggs, but, alas! he was practically certain that scrambled eggs were expected of him too. This 'psychological awareness,' as Rupert called it, which existed between them might after a time make things a trifle difficult. He felt a little abject as he murmured, 'Eggs, please.'

And he saw by Rupert's expression that he had chosen right.
Rupert helped him to eggs largely.

II

Psychological awareness . . . perhaps it was that which explained their intimacy. One might have been tempted to say
it was a case of mutual fascination. But whereas Archie's reply
to the suggestion would have been a slow 'Poss-ibly!' Rupert
would have flouted it at once.

'Fascination! The word's preposterous in this connection.
What on earth would there be in Cullen to fascinate me even
if I was in the habit of being fascinated by my fellow creatures;
which I certainly am not. No, I'll own I am deeply interested.
I confess my belief is, I understand him better than anybody
else. And if you want my honest opinion, I am certain that my
—my—h'm—influence over—sympathy for—him—call it what
you like, is all to the good. There is a psychological awareness.
. . . Moreover, as a companion, instinctively I find him
extremely agreeable. He stimulates some part of my mind
which is less active without him. But fascination—wide of the
mark, my dear—wide!'

But supposing one remained unconvinced? Supposing one
still played with the idea. Wasn't it possible to see Rupert and
Archie as the python and the rabbit keeping house together?
Rupert that handsome, well-fed python with his moustaches,
his glare, his habit of uncoiling before the fire and swaying
against the mantelpiece, pipe and pouch in hand. And Archie,
soft, hunched, timid, sitting in the lesser arm-chair, there and
not there, flicking back into the darkness at a word but
emerging again at a look—with sudden wholly unexpected
starts of playfulness (instantly suppressed by the python). Of
course, there was no question of anything so crude and dreadful
as the rabbit being eaten by his housemate. Nevertheless, it
was a strange fact, after a typical evening the one looked immensely swelled, benign and refreshed, and the other, pale,
small and exhausted. . . . And more often than not Rupert's
final comment was—ominous this—as he doused his whisky
with soda:

'This has been very absorbing, Archie.' And Archie gasped out, 'Oh, *very!*'

III

Archie Cullen was a journalist and the son of a journalist. He had no private money, no influential connections, scarcely any friends. His father had been one of those weak, disappointed, unsuccessful men who see in their sons a weapon for themselves. He would get his own back on life through Archie. Archie would show them the stuff he—his father was made of. Just you wait till my son comes along! This, though highly consoling to Mr. Cullen *père*, was terribly poor fun for Archie. At two and a half his infant nose was put to the grindstone and even on Sundays it was not taken off. Then his father took him out walking and improved the occasion by making him spell the shop signs, count the yachts racing in the harbour, divide them by four and multiply the result by three.

But the experiment was an amazing success. Archie turned away from the distractions of life, shut his ears, folded his feet, sat over the table with his book, and when the holidays came he didn't like them; they made him uneasy; so he went on reading for himself. He was a model boy. On prize-giving days his father accompanied him to school, carried the great wad of stiff books home for him and, flinging them on the dining-room table, he surveyed them with an exultant smile. My prizes! The little sacrifice stared at them, too, through his spectacles as other little boys stared at puddings. He ought, of course, at this juncture to have been rescued by a doting mother who, though cowed herself, rose on the . . .

(1921)

313

Daphne

I had been in Port Willin six months when I decided to give a
one-man show. Not that I was particularly keen, but little
Field, the picture-shop man, had just started a gallery and he
wanted me—begged me, rather—to kick off for him. He was a
decent little chap; I hadn't the heart to refuse. And, besides, as
it happened, I had a good deal of stuff that I felt it would be
rather fun to palm off on any one who was fool enough to buy
it. So with these high aims I had the cards printed, the pictures
framed in plain white frames, and God knows how many cups
and saucers ordered for the Private View.

What was I doing in Port Willin? Oh well—why not? I'll
own it does sound an unlikely spot, but when you are an impermanent movable, as I am, it's just those unlikely spots that
have a trick of holding you. I arrived, intending to stay a week
and go on to Fiji. But I had letters to one or two people, and
the morning of my arrival, hanging over the side of the ship
while we were waiting in the stream, with nothing on earth to
do but stare, I took an extraordinary fancy to the shape—to
the look of the place.

It's a small town, you know, planted at the edge of a fine
deep harbour like a lake. Behind it, on either side, there are
hills. The houses are built of light painted wood. They have
iron roofs coloured red. And there are big dark plumy trees
massed together, breaking up those light shapes, giving a depth
—warmth—making a composition of it well worth looking
at. . . . Well, we needn't go into that—But it had me that
fine morning. And the first days after my arrival, walking, or
driving out in one of the big swinging, rocking cabs, I took an
equal fancy to the people.

Not to quite all of them. The men left me cold. Yes, I
must say, colonial men are not the brightest specimens. But
I never struck a place where the average of female attractive-

314

ness was so high. You can't help noticing it, for a peculiarity of Port Willin is the number of its teashops and the vast quantity of tea absorbed by its inhabitants. Not tea only—sandwiches, cream cakes, ices, fruit salad with fresh pine-apples. From eleven o'clock in the morning you meet with couples and groups of girls and young married women hurrying off to their first tea. It was a real eleven o'clock function. Even the business men knocked off and went to a café. And the same thing happened in the afternoon. From four until half-past six the streets were gay as a garden. Which reminds me, it was early spring when I arrived and the town smelled of moist earth and the first flowers. In fact, wherever one went one got a strong whiff, like the whiff of violets in a wood, which was enough in itself to make one feel like lingering. . . .

There was a theatre too, a big bare building plastered over with red and blue bills which gave it an oriental look in that blue air, and a touring company was playing 'San Toy.' I went my first evening. I found it, for some reason, fearfully exciting. The inside smelled of gas, of glue and burnt paper. Whistling draughts cut along the corridors—a strong wind among the orchestra kept the palms trembling, and now and again the curtain blew out and there was a glimpse of a pair of large feet walking rapidly away. But what women! What girls in muslin dresses with velvet sashes and little caps edged with swansdown! In the intervals long ripples of laughter sounded from the stalls, from the dress-circle. And I leaned against a pillar that looked as though it was made of wedding-cake icing—and fell in love with whole rows at a time. . . .

Then I presented my letters, I was asked out to dine, and I met these charmers in their own homes. That decided it. They were something I had never known before—so gay, so friendly, so impressed with the idea of one's being an artist! It was rather like finding oneself in the playground of an extremely attractive girls' school.

I painted the Premier's daughter, a dark beauty, against a tree hung with long, bell-like flowers as white as wax. I painted a girl with a pigtail curled up on a white sofa playing with a pale-red fan . . . and a little blonde in a black jacket with pearl grey gloves. . . . I painted like fury.

I'm fond of women. As a matter of fact I'm a great deal more at my ease with women than I am with men. Because I've cultivated them, I suppose. You see, it's like this with me. I've always had enough money to live on, and the consequence is I have never had to mix with people more than I wished. And I've equally always had—well, I suppose you might call it—a passion for painting. Painting is far and away the most important thing in life—as I see it. But—my work's my own affair. It's the separate compartment which is me. No strangers allowed in. I haven't the smallest desire to explain what it is I'm after—or to hear other men. If people like my work I'm pleased. If they don't—well, If I was a shrugging person, I'd shrug. This sounds arrogant. It isn't; I know my limitations. But the truth about oneself always sounds arrogant, as no doubt you've observed.

But women—well, I can only speak for myself—I find the presence of women, the consciousness of women, an absolute necessity. I know they are considered a distraction, that the very Big Pots seal themselves in their hives to keep away. All I can say is work without women would be to me like dancing without music or food without wine or a sailing boat without a breeze. They just give me that . . . what is it? Stimulus is not enough; inspiration is far too much. That—well, if I knew what it is, I should have solved a bigger problem than my own! And problems aren't in my line.

I expected a mob at my Private View, and I got it, too. . . . What I hadn't reckoned on was that there would be no men. It was one thing to ask a painter fellow to knock you up something to the tune of fifty guineas or so, but it was quite another to make an ass of yourself staring. The Port Willin men would as soon have gazed into shops. True, when you came to Europe, you visited the galleries, but then you shop-gazed too. It didn't matter what you did in Europe. You could walk about for a week without being recognised.

So there were little Field and I absolutely alone among all that loveliness; it frightened him out of his life, but I didn't mind, I though it rather fun, especially as the sightseers didn't hesitate to find my pictures amusing. I'm by no means an out-and-out modern, as they say; people like violins and landscapes of telegraph poles leave me cold. But Port Willin is still trying to swallow Rossetti, and Hope by Watts is looked upon as very advanced. It was natural my pictures should surprise them. The fat old Lady Mayoress became quite hysterical. She drew me over to one drawing; she patted my arm with her fan.

'I don't wonder you drew her slipping out,' she gurgled. 'And how depressed she looks! The poor dear never could have sat down in it. It's much too small. There ought to be a little cake of Pears' Soap on the floor.' And overcome by her own joke, she flopped on the little double bench that ran down the middle of the room, and even her fan seemed to laugh.

At that moment two girls passed in front of us. One I knew, a big fair girl called May Pollock, pulled her companion by the sleeve. 'Daphne!' she said. 'Daphne!' And the other turned towards her, then towards us, smiled and was born, christened part of my world from that moment.

'Daphne!' Her quick, beautiful smile answered. . . .

Saturday morning was gloriously fine. When I woke up and saw the sun streaming over the polished floor I felt like a little boy who has been promised a picnic. It was all I could do not to telephone Daphne. Was she feeling the same? It seemed somehow such a terrific lark that we should be going off together like this, just with a couple of rucksacks and our bathing suits. I thought of other week-ends, the preparation, the emotional tension, the amount of managing they'd needed. But I couldn't really think of them; I couldn't be bothered, they belonged to another life. . . .

It seemed to me suddenly so preposterous that two people should be as happy as we were and not be happier. Here we were, alone, miles away from everybody, free as air, and in love with each other. I looked again at Daphne, at her slender shoulders, her throat, her bosom, and, passionately in love, I decided, with fervour: Wouldn't it be rather absurd, then, to behave like a couple of children? Wouldn't she even, in spite of all she had said, be disappointed if we did? . . .

And I went off at a tremendous pace, not because I thought she'd run after me, but I did think she might call, or I might look round. . . .

It was one of those still, hushed days when the sea and the

sky seem to melt into one another, and it is long before the moisture dries on the leaves and grasses. One of those days when the sea smells strong and there are gulls standing in a row on the sand. The smoke from our wood fire hung in the air and the smoke of my pipe mingled with it. I caught myself staring at nothing. I felt dull and angry. I couldn't get over the ridiculous affair. You see, my *amour propre* was wounded.

Monday morning was grey, cloudy, one of those mornings peculiar to the seaside when everything, the sea most of all, seems exhausted and sullen. There had been a very high tide, the road was wet—on the beach there stood a long line of sickly-looking gulls. . . .

When we got on board she sat down on one of the green benches and, muttering something about a pipe, I walked quickly away. It was intolerable that we should still be together after what had happened. It was indecent. I only asked—I only longed for one thing—to be free of this still, unsmiling and pitiful—that was the worst of it—creature who had been my playful Daphne.

For answer I telephoned her at once and asked if I might come and see her that evening. Her voice sounded grave, unlike the voice I remembered, and she seemed to deliberate. There was a long pause before she said, 'Yes—perhaps that would be best.'

'Then I shall come at half-past six.'

'Very well.'

And we went into a room full of flowers and very large art photographs of the Harbour by Night, A Misty Day, Moonrise over the Water, and I know I wondered if she admired them.

'Why did you send me that letter?'

'Oh, but I had to,' said Daphne. 'I meant every word of it. I only let you come to-night to . . . No, I know I shall disappoint you. I'm wiser than you are for all your experience. I shan't be able to live up to it. I'm not the person for you. Really I'm not!' . . .

(1921)

318

A Married Man's Story

I

It is evening. Supper is over. We have left the small, cold dining-room, we have come back to the sitting-room where there is a fire. All is as usual. I am sitting at my writing-table which is placed across a corner so that I am behind it, as it were, and facing the room. The lamp with the green shade is alight; I have before me two large books of reference, both open, a pile of papers. . . . All the paraphernalia, in fact, of an extremely occupied man. My wife, with her little boy on her lap, is in a low chair before the fire. She is about to put him to bed before she clears away the dishes and piles them up in the kitchen for the servant girl tomorrow morning. But the warmth, the quiet, and the sleepy baby, have made her dreamy. One of his red woollen boots is off, one is on. She sits, bent forward, clasping the little bare foot, staring into the glow, and as the fire quickens, falls, flares again, her shadow—an immense *Mother and Child*—is here and gone again upon the wall. . . .

Outside it is raining. I like to think of that cold drenched window behind the blind, and beyond, the dark bushes in the garden, their broad leaves bright with rain, and beyond the fence, the gleaming road with the two hoarse little gutters singing against each other, and the wavering reflections of the lamps, like fishes' tails. While I am here, I am there, lifting my face to the dim sky, and it seems to me it must be raining all over the world—that the whole earth is drenched, is sounding with a soft, quick patter or hard, steady drumming, or gurgling and something that is like sobbing and laughing mingled together, and that light, playful splashing that is of water falling

319

into still lakes and flowing rivers. And all at one and the same moment I am arriving in a strange city, slipping under the hood of the cab while the driver whips the cover off the breathing horse, running from shelter to shelter, dodging someone, swerving by someone else. I am conscious of tall houses, their doors and shutters sealed against the night, of dripping balconies and sodden flower-pots. I am brushing through deserted gardens and falling into moist smelling summer-houses (you know how soft and almost crumbling the wood of a summer-house is in the rain); I am standing on the dark quayside giving my ticket into the wet, red hand of the old sailor in an oilskin. How strong the sea smells! How loudly the tied-up boats knock against one another! I am crossing the wet stackyard, hooded in an old sack, carrying a lantern, while the house-dog, like a soaking doormat, springs, shakes himself over me. And now I am walking along a deserted road—it is impossible to miss the puddles, and the trees are stirring—stirring.

But one could go on with such a catalogue for ever—on and on—until one lifted the single arum lily leaf and discovered the tiny snails clinging, until one counted . . . and what then? Aren't those just the signs, the traces of my feeling? The bright green streaks made by someone who walks over the dewy grass? Not the feeling itself. And as I think that a mournful, glorious voice begins to sing in my bosom. Yes, perhaps that is nearer what I mean. What a voice! What power! What velvety softness! Marvellous!

Suddenly my wife turns round quickly. She knows—how long has she known?—that I am not 'working.' It is strange that with her full, open gaze she should smile so timidly— and that she should say in such a hesitating voice, 'What are you thinking?'

I smile and draw two fingers across my forehead in the way I have. 'Nothing,' I answer softly.

At that she stirs and, still trying not to make it sound important, she says, 'Oh, but you must have been thinking of something!'

Then I really meet her gaze, meet it fully, and I fancy her face quivers. Will she never grow accustomed to these simple —one might say—everyday little lies? Will she never learn not to expose herself—or to build up defences?

'Truly, I was thinking of nothing.'

There! I seem to see it dart at her. She turns away, pulls the other red sock off the baby, sits him up, and begins to unbutton him behind. I wonder if that little soft rolling bundle sees anything, feels anything? Now she turns him over on her knee, and in this light, his soft arms and legs waving, he is extraordinarily like a young crab. A queer thing is I can't connect him with my wife and myself—I've never accepted him as ours. Each time when I come into the hall and see the perambulator I catch myself thinking: 'H'm, someone has brought a baby!' Or, when his crying wakes me at night, I feel inclined to blame my wife for having brought the baby in from outside. The truth is, that though one might suspect her of strong maternal feelings, my wife doesn't seem to me the type of woman who bears children in her own body. There's an immense difference! Where is that . . . animal ease and playfulness, that quick kissing and cuddling one has been taught to expect of young mothers? She hasn't a sign of it. I believe that when she ties its bonnet she feels like an aunt and not a mother. But of course I may be wrong; she may be passionately devoted. . . . I don't think so. At any rate, isn't it a trifle indecent to feel like this about one's own wife? Indecent or not, one has these feelings. And one other thing. How can I reasonably expect my wife, *a broken-hearted woman*, to spend her time tossing the baby? But that is beside the mark. She never even began to toss when her heart was whole.

And now she has carried the baby to bed. I hear her soft, deliberate steps moving between the dining-room and the kitchen, there and back again, to the tune of the clattering dishes. And now all is quiet. What is happening now? Oh, I know just as surely as if I'd gone to see—she is standing in the middle of the kitchen facing the rainy window. Her head is bent, with one finger she is tracing something—nothing—on the table. It is cold in the kitchen; the gas jumps; the tap drips; it's a forlorn picture. And nobody is going to come behind her, to take her in his arms, to kiss her soft hair, to lead her to the fire and to rub her hands warm again. Nobody is going to call her or to wonder what she is doing out there. And she knows it. And yet, being a woman, deep down, deep down, she really does expect the miracle to happen; she really could embrace that dark, dark deceit, rather than live—like this.

II

To live like this. . . . I write those words very carefully, very beautifully. For some reason I feel inclined to sign them, or to write underneath—Trying a New Pen. But, seriously, isn't it staggering to think what may be contained in one innocent-looking little phrase? It tempts me—it tempts me terribly. Scene: The supper-table. My wife has just handed me my tea. I stir it, lift the spoon, idly chase and then carefully capture a speck of tea-leaf, and having brought it ashore, I murmur, quite gently, 'How long shall we continue to live—like—this?' And immediately there is that famous 'blinding flash and deafening roar. Huge pieces of débris (I must say I like débris) are flung into the air . . . and when the dark clouds of smoke have drifted away . . .' But this will never happen; I shall never know it. It will be found upon me 'intact,' as they say. 'Open my heart and you will see . . .'

Why? Ah, there you have me! There is the most difficult question of all to answer. Why do people stay together? Putting aside 'for the sake of the children,' and 'the habit of years' and 'economic reasons' as lawyers' nonsense—it's not much more—if one really does try to find out why it is that people don't leave each other, one discovers a mystery. It is because they can't; they are bound. And nobody on earth knows what are the bonds that bind them except those two. Am I being obscure? Well, the thing itself isn't so frightfully crystal clear, is it? Let me put it like this. Supposing you are taken, absolutely, first into his confidence and then into hers. Supposing you know all there is to know about the situation. And having given it not only your deepest sympathy but your most honest impartial criticism, you declare, very calmly (but not without the slightest suggestion of relish—for there is— I swear there is—in the very best of us—something that leaps up and cries 'A-ahh!' for joy at the thought of destroying), 'Well, my opinion is that you two people ought to part. You'll do no earthly good together. Indeed, it seems to me, it's the duty of either to set the other free.' What happens then? He —and she—agree. It is their conviction too. You are only saying what they have been thinking all last night. And away they go to act on your advice, immediately. . . . And the next time you hear of them they are still together. You see—you've

322

reckoned without the unknown quantity—which is their secret relation to each other—and that they can't disclose even if they want to. Thus far you may tell and no further. Oh, don't misunderstand me! It need not necessarily have anything to do with their sleeping together. . . . But this brings me to a thought I've often half entertained. Which is that human beings, as we know them, don't choose each other at all. It is the owner, the second self inhabiting them, who makes the choice for his own particular purposes, and—this may sound absurdly far-fetched—it's the second self in the other which responds. Dimly—dimly—or so it has seemed to me—we realise this, at any rate to the extent that we realise the hopelessness of trying to escape. So that, what it all amounts to is—if the impermanent selves of my wife and me are happy—*tant mieux pour nous*—if miserable—*tant pis*. . . . But I don't know, I don't know. And it may be that it's something entirely individual in me—this sensation (yes, it is even a sensation) of how extraordinarily *shell-like* we are as we are—little creatures, peering out of the sentry-box at the gate, ogling through our glass case at the entry, wan little servants, who never can say for certain, even, if the master is out or in. . . .

The door opens . . . My wife. She says, 'I am going to bed.'

And I look up vaguely, and vaguely say, 'You are going to bed.'

'Yes.' A tiny pause. 'Don't forget—will you?—to turn out the gas in the hall.'

And again I repeat, 'The gas in the hall.'

There was a time—the time before—when this habit of mine —it really has become a habit now—it wasn't one then—was one of our sweetest jokes together. It began, of course, when on several occasions I really was deeply engaged and I didn't hear. I emerged only to see her shaking her head and laughing at me, 'You haven't heard a word!'

'No. What did you say?'

Why should she think that so funny and charming? she did—it delighted her. 'Oh, my darling, it's so like you! It's so—so—' And I knew she loved me for it. I knew she positively looked forward to coming in and disturbing me, and so— as one does—I played up. I was guaranteed to be wrapped away every evening at 10.30 p.m. But now? For some reason I feel it would be crude to stop my performance. It's simplest to play on. But what is she waiting for to-night? Why doesn't she go? Why prolong this? She is going. No, her hand on the door-knob, she turns round again, and she says in the most curious, small, breathless voice, 'You're not cold?'

Oh, it's not fair to be as pathetic as that! That was simply damnable. I shuddered all over before I managed to bring out a slow 'No-o!' while my left hand ruffles the reference pages.

She is gone; she will not come back again to-night. It is not only I who recognise that—the room changes too. It relaxes, like an old actor. Slowly the mask is rubbed off; the look of strained attention changes to an air of heavy, sullen brooding. Every line, every fold breathes fatigue. The mirror is quenched; the ash whitens; only my sly lamp burns on. . . . But what a cynical indifference to me it all shows! Or should I perhaps be flattered? No, we understand each other. You know those stories of little children who are suckled by wolves and accepted by the tribe, and how for ever after they move freely among their fleet, grey brothers? Something like that has happened to me. But wait! That about the wolves won't do. Curious! Before I wrote it down, while it was still in my head, I was delighted with it. It seemed to express, and more, to suggest, just what I wanted to say. But written, I can smell the falseness immediately and the . . . source of the smell is in that word fleet. Don't you agree? Fleet, grey brothers! 'Fleet.' A word I never use. When I wrote 'wolves' it skimmed across my mind like a shadow and I couldn't resist it. Tell me! Tell me! Why is it so difficult to write simply—and not simply only but *sotto voce*, if you know what I mean? That is how I long to write. No fine effects—no bravura. But just the plain truth, as only a liar can tell it.

III

I light a cigarette, lean back, inhale deeply—and find myself wondering if my wife is asleep. Or is she lying in her cold bed, staring into the dark, with those trustful, bewildered eyes? Her eyes are like the eyes of a cow that is being driven along a road. 'Why am I being driven—what harm have I done?' But I really am not responsible for that look; it's her natural expression. One day, when she was turning out a cupboard, she found a little old photograph of herself, taken when she was a girl at school. In her confirmation dress, she explained. And there were the eyes, even then. I remember saying to her, 'Did you always look so sad?' Leaning over my shoulder, she laughed lightly, 'Do I look sad? I think it's just . . . me.' And she waited for me to say something about it. But I was marvelling at her courage at having shown it to me at all. It was a hideous photograph! And I wondered again if she realised how plain she was, and comforted herself with the idea that people who loved each other didn't criticise but accepted everything, or if she really rather liked her appearance and expected me to say something complimentary.

Oh, that was base of me! How could I have forgotten all the numberless times when I have known her turn away to avoid the light, press her face into my shoulders. And, above all, how could I have forgotten the afternoon of our wedding-day when we sat on the green bench in the Botanical Gardens and listened to the band; how, in an interval between two pieces, she suddenly turned to me and said in the voice in which one says, 'Do you think the grass is damp?' or 'Do you think it's time for tea?' . . . 'Tell me, do you think physical beauty is so very important?' I don't like to think how often she had rehearsed that question. And do you know what I answered? At that moment, as if at my command, there came a great gush of hard, bright sound from the band, and I managed to shout above it cheerfully, 'I didn't hear what you said.' Devilish! Wasn't it? Perhaps not wholly. She looked like the poor patient who hears the surgeon say, 'It will certainly be necessary to perform the operation—but not now!'

IV

But all this conveys the impression that my wife and I were never really happy together. Not true! Not true! We were marvellously, radiantly happy. We were a model couple. If you had seen us together, any time, any place, if you had followed us, tracked us down, spied, taken us off our guard, you still would have been forced to confess, 'I have never seen a more ideally suited pair.' Until last autumn.

But really to explain what happened then I should have to go back and back—I should have to dwindle until my two hands clutched the banisters, the stair-rail was higher than my head, and I peered through to watch my father padding softly up and down. There were coloured windows on the landings. As he came up, first his bald head was scarlet, then it was yellow. How frightened I was! And when they put me to bed, it was to dream that we were living inside one of my father's big coloured bottles. For he was a chemist. I was born nine years after my parents were married. I was an only child, and the effort to produce even me—small, withered bud I must have been—sapped all my mother's strength. She never left her room again. Bed, sofa, window, she moved between the three. Well I can see her, on the window days, sitting, her cheek in her hand, staring out. Her room looked over the street. Opposite there was a wall plastered with advertisements for travelling shows and circuses and so on. I stand beside her, and we gaze at the slim lady in a red dress hitting a dark gentleman over the head with her parasol, or at the tiger peering through the jungle while the clown, close by, balances a bottle on his nose, or at a little golden-haired girl sitting on the knee of an old black man in a broad cotton hat. . . . She says nothing. On sofa days there is a flannel dressing-gown that I loathe and a cushion that keeps on slipping off the hard sofa. I pick it up. It has flowers and writing sewn on. I ask what the writing says, and she whispers, 'Sweet Repose!' In bed her fingers plait, in tight little plaits, the fringe of the quilt and her lips are thin. And that is all there is of my mother, except the last queer 'episode' that comes later.

My father . . . Curled up in the corner on the lid of a round box that held sponges, I stared at my father so long, it's as though his image, cut off at the waist by the counter, has remained solid in my memory, Perfectly bald, polished head, shaped like a thin egg, creased, creamy cheeks, little bags under the eyes, large pale ears like handles. His manner was discreet, sly, faintly amused and tinged with impudence. Long before I could appreciate it I knew the mixture . . . I even used to copy him in my corner, bending forward, with a small reproduction of his faint sneer. In the evening his customers were, chiefly,

young women; some of them came in every day for his famous
fivepenny pick-me-up. Their gaudy looks, their voices, their
free ways fascinated me. I longed to be my father, handing
them across the counter the little glass of bluish stuff they tossed
off so greedily. God knows what it was made of. Years after
I drank some, just to see what it tasted like, and I felt as though
someone had given me a terrific blow on the head; I felt
stunned.

One of those evenings I remember vividly. It was cold; it
must have been autumn, for the flaring gas was lighted after my
tea. I sat in my corner and my father was mixing something;
the shop was empty. Suddenly the bell jangled and a young
woman rushed in, crying so loud, sobbing so hard, that it didn't
sound real. She wore a green cape trimmed with fur and a hat
with cherries dangling. My father came from behind the screen.
But she couldn't stop herself at first. She stood in the middle
of the shop and wrung her hands and moaned; I've never
heard such crying since. Presently she managed to gasp out,
'Give me a pick-me-up!' Then she drew a long breath,
trembled away from him and quavered, 'I've had *bad news*!'
And in the flaring gaslight I saw the whole side of her face was
puffed up and purple; her lip was cut and her eyelid looked as
though it was gummed fast over the wet eye. My father pushed
the glass across the counter, and she took the purse out of her
stocking and paid him. But she couldn't drink; clutching the
glass, she stared in front of her as if she could not believe what
she saw. Each time she put her head back the tears spurted out
again. Finally she put the glass down. It was no use. Holding
the cape with one hand, she ran in the same way out of the shop
again. My father gave no sign. But long after she had gone
I crouched in my corner, and when I think back it's as though
I felt my whole body vibrating—'So that's what it is outside,'
I thought. 'That's what it's like out there.'

V

Do you remember your childhood? I am always coming
across these marvellous accounts by writers who declare that
they remember 'everything.' I certainly don't. The dark

stretches, the blanks, are much bigger than the bright glimpses. I seem to have spent most of my time like a plant in a cupboard. Now and again, when the sun shone, a careless hand thrust me out on to the window-sill, and a careless hand whipped me in again—and that was all. But what happened in the darkness— I wonder? Did one grow? Pale stem . . . timid leaves . . .white reluctant bud. No wonder I was hated at school. Even the masters shrank from me. I somehow knew that my soft, hesi- tating voice disgusted them. I knew, too, how they turned away from my shocked, staring eyes. I was small and thin and I smelled of the shop; my nickname was Gregory Powder. School was a tin building, stuck on the raw hillside. There were dark red streaks like blood in the oozing clay banks of the playground. I hide in the dark passage, where the coats hang, and am discovered there by one of the masters. 'What are you doing there in the dark?' His terrible voice kills me; I die before his eyes. I am standing in a ring of thrust-out heads; some are grinning, some look greedy, some are spitting. And it is always cold. Big crushed-up clouds press across the sky; the rusty water in the school tank is frozen; the bell sounds numb. One day they put a dead bird in my overcoat pocket. I found it just when I reached home. Oh, what a strange flutter there was at my heart when I drew out that terribly soft, cold little body, with the legs thin as pins and the claws wrung. I sat on the back door step in the yard and put the bird in my cap. The feathers round the neck looked wet and there was a tiny tuft just above the closed eyes that stood up too. How tightly the beak was shut! I could not see the mark where it was divided. I stretched out one wing and touched the soft, secret down underneath; I tried to make the claws curl round my little finger. But I didn't feel sorry for it—no! I wondered. The smoke from our kitchen chimney poured downwards, and flakes of soot floated—soft, light in the air. Through a big crack in the cement yard a poor-looking plant with dull, reddish flowers had pushed its way. I looked at the dead bird again. . . . And that is the first time that I remember singing— rather . . . listening to a silent voice inside a little cage that was me.

VI

But what has all this to do with my married happiness? How can all this affect my wife and me? Why—to tell what happened last autumn—do I run all this way back into the Past? The Past—what is the Past? I might say the star-shaped flake of soot on a leaf of the poor-looking plant, and the bird lying on the quilted lining of my cap, and my father's pestle and my mother's cushion belong to it. But that is not to say they are any less mine than they were when I looked upon them with my very eyes and touched them with these fingers. No, they are more—they are a living part of me. Who am I, in fact, as I sit here at this table, but my own past? If I deny that, I am nothing. And if I were to try to divide my life into childhood, youth, early manhood and so on, it would be a kind of affectation; I should know I was doing it just because of the pleasantly important sensation it gives one to rule lines and to use green ink for childhood, red for the next stage, and purple for the period of adolescence. For, one thing I have learnt, one thing I do believe is, Nothing Happens Suddenly. Yes, that is my religion, I suppose.

My mother's death, for instance. Is it more distant from me to-day than it was then? It is just as close, as strange, as puzzling, and, in spite of all the countless times I have recalled the circumstances, I know no more now than I did then, whether I dreamed them, or whether they really occurred. It happened when I was thirteen and I slept in a little strip of a room on what was called the half-landing. One night I woke up with a start to see my mother, in her nightgown, without even the hated flannel dressing-gown, sitting on my bed. But the strange thing which frightened me was, she wasn't looking at me. Her head was bent; the short, thin trail of hair lay between her shoulders; her hands were pressed between her knees and my bed shook; she was shivering. It was the first time I had ever seen her out of her own room. I said, or I think I said, 'Is that you, Mother?' And as she turned round, I saw in the moonlight how queer she looked. Her face looked small—quite different. She looked like one of the boys at the school baths, who sits on a step, shivering just like that, and wants to go in and yet is frightened.

'Are you awake?' she said. Her eyes opened; I think she

smiled. She leaned towards me. 'I've been poisoned,' she whispered. 'Your father's poisoned me.' And she nodded. Then, before I could say a word, she was gone; I thought I heard the door shut. I sat quite still, I couldn't move, I think I expected something else to happen. For a long time I listened for something; there wasn't a sound. The candle was by my bed, but I was too frightened to stretch out my hand for the matches. But even while I wondered what I ought to do, even while my heart thumped—everything became confused. I lay down and pulled the blankets round me. I fell asleep, and the next morning my mother was found dead of failure of the heart.

Did that visit happen? Was it a dream? Why did she come to tell me? Or why, if she came, did she go away so quickly? And her expression—so joyous under the frightened look—was that real? I believed it fully the afternoon of the funeral, when I saw my father dressed up for his part, hat and all. That tall hat so gleaming black and round was like a cork covered with black sealing-wax, and the rest of my father was awfully like a bottle, with his face for the label—*Deadly Poison*. It flashed into my mind as I stood opposite him in the hall. And Deadly Poison, or old D.P., was my private name for him from that day.

VII

Late, it grows late. I love the night. I love to feel the tide of darkness rising slowly and slowly washing, turning over and over, lifting, floating, all that lies strewn upon the dark beach, all that lies hid in rocky hollows. I love, I love this strange feeling of drifting—whither? After my mother's death I hated to go to bed. I used to sit on the window-sill, folded up, and watch the sky. It seemed to me the moon moved much faster than the sun. And one big, bright green star I chose for my own. My star! But I never thought of it beckoning to me or twinkling merrily for my sake. Cruel, indifferent, splendid—it burned in the airy night. No matter—it was mine! But, growing close up against the window, there was a creeper with small, bunched-up pink and purple flowers. These did know me. These, when I touched them at night, welcomed my fingers; the little tendrils, so weak, so delicate, knew I would not hurt them. When the wind moved the leaves I felt I understood their shaking. When I came to the window, it seemed to me the flowers said among themselves, 'The boy is here.'

As the months passed there was often a light in my father's room below. And I heard voices and laughter. 'He's got some woman with him,' I thought. But it meant nothing to me. Then the gay voice, the sound of the laughter, gave me the idea it was one of the girls who used to come to the shop in the evenings—and gradually I began to imagine which girl it was. It was the dark one in the red coat and skirt who once had given me a penny. A merry face stooped over me—warm breath tickled my neck—there were little beads of black on her long lashes, and when she opened her arms to kiss me there came a marvellous wave of scent! Yes, that was the one.

Time passed, and I forgot the moon and my green star and my shy creeper—I came to the window to wait for the light in my father's window, to listen for the laughing voice, until one night I dozed and I dreamed she came again—again she drew me to her, something soft, scented, warm and merry hung over me like a cloud. But when I tried to see, her eyes only mocked me, her red lips opened and she hissed, 'Little sneak! Little sneak!' But not as if she were angry,—as if she understood, and her smile somehow was like a rat—hateful!

The night after, I lighted the candle and sat down at the table instead. By and by, as the flame steadied, there was a small lake of liquid wax, surrounded by a white, smooth wall. I took a pin and made little holes in this wall and then sealed them up faster than the wax could escape. After a time I fancied the candle flame joined in the game; it leapt up, quivered, wagged; it even seemed to laugh. But while I played with the candle and smiled and broke off the tiny white peaks of wax that rose above the wall and floated them on my lake, a feeling of awful dreariness fastened on me—yes, that's the word. It crept up from my knees to my thighs, into my arms; I ached all over with misery. And I felt so strangely that I couldn't move. Something bound me there by the table—I couldn't even let the pin drop that I held between my finger and thumb. For a moment I came to a stop, as it were.

Then the shrivelled case of the bud split and fell, the plant in the cupboard came into flower. 'Who am I?' I thought.

331

'What is all this?' And I looked at my room, at the broken bust of the man called Hahnemann on top of the cupboard, at my little bed with the pillow like an envelope. I saw it all, but not as I had seen before. . . . Everything lived, everything. But that was not all. I was equally alive and—it's the only way I can express it—the barriers were down between us—I had come into my own world!

VIII

The barriers were down. I had been all my life a little outcast; but until that moment no one had 'accepted' me; I had lain in the cupboard—or the cave forlorn. But now I was taken, I was accepted, claimed. I did not consciously turn away from the world of the human beings; I had never known it; but I from that night did beyond words consciously turn towards my silent brothers. . . .

(1918)

Ole Underwood

Down the windy hill stalked Ole Underwood. He carried a black umbrella in one hand, in the other a red and white spotted handkerchief knotted into a lump. He wore a black peaked cap like a pilot; gold rings gleamed in his ears and his little eyes snapped like two sparks. Like two sparks they glowed in the smoulder of his bearded face. On one side of the hill grew a forest of pines from the road right down to the sea. On the other side short tufted grass and little bushes of white manuka flower. The pine trees roared like waves in their topmost branches, their stems creaked like the timber of ships; in the windy air flew the white manuka flower. 'Ah-k!' shouted Ole Underwood, shaking his umbrella at the wind bearing down upon him, beating him, half strangling him with his black cape. 'Ah-k!' shouted the wind a hundred times as loud, and filled his mouth and nostrils with dust. Something inside Ole Underwood's breast beat like a hammer. One, two—one, two— never stopping, never changing. He couldn't do anything. It wasn't loud. No, it didn't make a noise—only a thud. One, two—one, two—like someone beating on an iron in a prison, someone in a secret place—bang—bang—bang—trying to get free. Do what he would, fumble at his coat, throw his arms about, spit, swear, he couldn't stop the noise. Stop! Stop! Stop! Stop! Ole Underwood began to shuffle and run.

Away below, the sea heaving against the stone walls, and the little town just out of its reach close packed together, the better to face the grey water. And up on the other side of the hill the prison with high red walls. Over all bulged the grey sky with black web-like clouds streaming.

Ole Underwood slackened his pace as he neared the town, and when he came to the first house he flourished his umbrella like a herald's staff and threw out his chest, his head glancing quickly from right to left. They were ugly little houses leading

into the town, built of wood—two windows and a door, a
stumpy veranda and a green mat of grass before. Under one
veranda yellow hens huddled out of the wind. 'Shoo!' shouted
Ole Underwood, and laughed to see them fly, and laughed
again at the woman who came to the door and shook a red,
soapy fist at him. A little girl stood in another yard untwisting
some rags from a clothes-line. When she saw Ole Underwood
she let the clothes-prop fall and rushed screaming to the door,
beating it screaming 'Mumma—Mumma!' That started the
hammer in Ole Underwood's heart. Mum-ma— Mum-ma!
He saw an old face with a trembling chin and grey hair
nodding out of the window as they dragged him past. Mumma
—Mum-ma! He looked up at the big red prison perched on the
hill and he pulled a face as if he wanted to cry.

At the corner in front of the pub some carts were pulled up,
some men sat in the porch of the pub drinking and talking.
Ole Underwood wanted a drink. He slouched into the bar.
It was half full of old and young men in big coats and top-boots
with stock-whips in their hands. Behind the counter a big girl
with red hair pulled the beer handles and cheeked the men.
Ole Underwood sneaked to one side, like a cat. Nobody looked
at him, only the men looked at each other, one or two of them
nudged. The girl nodded and winked at the fellow she was
serving. He took some money out of his knotted handkerchief
and slipped it on to the counter. His hand shook. He didn't
speak. The girl took no notice; she served everybody, went
on with her talk, and then as if by accident shoved a mug
towards him. A great big jar of red pinks stood on the bar
counter. Ole Underwood stared at them as he drank and
frowned at them. Red—red—red—red! beat the hammer.
It was very warm in the bar and quiet as a pond, except for the
talk and the girl. She kept on laughing. Ha! Ha! That was
what the men liked to see, for she threw back her head and her
great breasts lifted and shook to her laughter.

In one corner sat a stranger. He pointed at Ole Underwood.
'Cracked!' said one of the men. 'When he was a young fellow,
thirty years ago, a man 'ere done in 'is woman, and 'e foun'
out an' killed 'er. Got twenty years in quod up on the 'ill.
Came out cracked.'

'Oo done 'er in?' asked the man.

'Dunno. 'E dunno, nor nobody. 'E was a sailor till 'e marrid 'er. Cracked!' The man spat and smeared the spittle on the floor, shrugging his shoulders. "E's 'armless enough.'

Ole Underwood heard; he did not turn, but he shot out an old claw and crushed up the red pinks. 'Uh-Uh! Yo ole beast! Uh! You ole swine!' screamed the girl, leaning across the counter and banging him with a tin jug. 'Get art! Get art! Don' you never come 'ere no more!' Somebody kicked him: he scuttled like a rat.

He walked past the Chinamen's shops. The fruit and vegetables were all piled up against the windows. Bits of wooden cases, straw and old newspapers were strewn over the pavement. A woman flounced out of a shop and slushed a pail of slops over his feet. He peered in at the windows, at the Chinamen sitting in little groups on old barrels playing cards. They made him smile. He looked and looked, pressing his face against the glass and sniggering. They sat still with their long pigtails bound round their heads and their faces yellow as lemons. Some of them had knives in their belts, and one old man sat by himself on the floor plaiting his long crooked toes together. The Chinamen didn't mind Ole Underwood. When they saw him they nodded. He went to the door of a shop and cautiously opened it. In rushed the wind with him, scattering the cards. 'Ya-Ya! Ya-Ya!' screamed the Chinamen, and Ole Underwood rushed off, the hammer beating quick and hard. Ya-Ya! He turned a corner out of sight. He thought he heard one of the Chinks after him, and he slipped into a timber-yard. There he lay panting. . . .

Close by him, under another stack, there was a heap of yellow shavings. As he watched them they moved and a little grey cat unfolded herself and came out waving her tail. She trod delicately over to Ole Underwood and rubbed against his sleeve. The hammer in Ole Underwood's heart beat madly. It pounded up into his throat, and then it seemed to half stop and beat very, very faintly. 'Kit! Kit! Kit!' That was what she used to call the little cat he brought her off the ship—'Kit! Kit! Kit!'—and stoop down with the saucer in her hands. 'Ah! my God! my Lord!' Ole Underwood sat up and took the kitten in his arms and rocked to and fro, crushing it against his face. It was warm and soft, and it mewed faintly. He buried his eyes in its fur. My God! My Lord! He tucked the little cat in his coat and stole out of the woodyard and slouched down

335

towards the wharves. As he came near the sea, Ole Under-wood's nostrils expanded. The mad wind smelled of tar and ropes and slime and salt. He crossed the railway line, he crept behind the wharf-sheds and along a little cinder path that threaded through a patch of rank fennel to some stone drain-pipes carrying the sewage into the sea. And he stared up at the wharves and at the ships with flags flying, and suddenly the old, old lust swept over Ole Underwood. 'I will! I will! I will!' he muttered.

He tore the little cat out of his coat and swung it by its tail and flung it out to the sewer opening. The hammer beat loud and strong. He tossed his head, he was young again. He walked on to the wharves, past the wool-bales, past the loungers and the loafers to the extreme end of the wharves. The sea sucked against the wharf-poles as though it drank something from the land. One ship was loading wool. He heard a crane rattle and the shriek of a whistle. So he came to the little ship lying by herself with a bit of a plank for a gangway, and no sign of anybody—anybody at all. Ole Underwood looked once back at the town, at the prison perched like a red bird, at the black webby clouds trailing. Then he went up the gangway and on to the slippery deck. He grinned, and rolled in his walk, carrying high in his hand the red and white handkerchief. His ship! Mine! Mine! Mine! beat the hammer. There was a door latched open on the lee-side, labelled 'State-room.' He peered in. A man lay sleeping on a bunk—his bunk—a great big man in a seaman's coat with a long, fair beard and hair on the red pillow. And looking down upon him from the wall there shone her picture—his woman's picture—smiling and smiling at the big sleeping man.

(1912)

The Woman at the Store

All that day the heat was terrible. The wind blew close to the ground; it rooted among the tussock grass, slithered along the road, so that the white pumice dust swirled in our faces, settled and sifted over us and was like a dry skin itching for growth on our bodies. The horses stumbled along, coughing and chuffing. The pack-horse was sick—with a big open sore rubbed under the belly. Now and again she stopped short, threw back her head, looked at us as though she were going to cry, and whinnied. Hundreds of larks shrilled; the sky was slate colour, and the sound of the larks reminded me of slate pencils scraping over its surface. There was nothing to be seen but wave after wave of tussock grass, patched with purple orchids and manuka bushes covered with thick spider webs.

Jo rode ahead. He wore a blue galatea shirt, corduroy trousers and riding boots. A white handkerchief, spotted with red—it looked as though his nose had been bleeding on it— was knotted round his throat. Wisps of white hair straggled from under his wideawake—his moustache and eyebrows were equally white—he slouched in the saddle—grunting. Not once that day had he sung

> 'I don't care, for don't you see,
> My wife's mother was in front of me!'

It was the first day we had been without it for a month, and now there seemed something uncanny in his silence. Jim rode beside me, white as a clown; his black eyes glittered and he kept shooting out his tongue and moistening his lips. He was dressed in a Jaeger vest and a pair of blue duck trousers, fastened round the waist with a plaited leather belt. We had hardly spoken since dawn. At noon we had lunched off fly biscuits and apricots by the side of a swampy creek.

'My stomach feels like the crop of a hen, said Jo. 'Now then, Jim, you're the bright boy of the party—where's this 'ere store you kep' on talking about. "Oh yes," you says, "I know a fine store, with a paddock for the horses and a creek runnin' through, owned by a friend of mine who'll give yer a bottle of whisky before 'e shakes hands with yer." I'd like ter see that place—merely as a matter of curiosity—not that I'd ever doubt yer word—as yer know very well—*but* . . .'

Jim laughed. 'Don't forget there's a woman too, Jo, with blue eyes and yellow hair, who'll promise you something else before she shakes hands with you. Put that in your pipe and smoke it.'

'The heat's making you balmy,' said Jo. But he dug his knees into the horse. We shambled on. I half fell asleep and had a sort of uneasy dream that the horses were not moving forward at all—then that I was on a rocking-horse, and my old mother was scolding me for raising such a fearful dust from the drawing-room carpet. 'You've entirely worn off the pattern of the carpet,' I heard her saying, and she gave the reins a tug. I snivelled and woke to find Jim leaning over me, maliciously smiling.

'That was a case of all but,' said he. 'I just caught you. What's up? Been bye-bye?'

'No!' I raised my head. 'Thank the Lord we're arriving somewhere.'

We were on the brow of the hill, and below us there was a whare roofed with corrugated iron. It stood in a garden, rather far back from the road—a big paddock opposite, and a creek and a clump of young willow trees. A thin line of blue smoke stood up straight from the chimney of the whare; and as I looked a woman came out, followed by a child and a sheepdog —the woman carrying what appeared to me a black stick. She made gestures at us. The horses put on a final spurt, Jo took off his wideawake, shouted, threw out his chest, and began singing 'I don't care, for don't you see . . .' The sun pushed through the pale clouds and shed a vivid light over the scene. It gleamed on the woman's yellow hair, over her flapping pinafore and the rifle she was carrying. The child hid behind her, and the yellow dog, a mangy beast, scuttled back into the whare, his tail between his legs. We drew rein and dismounted.

'Hallo,' screamed the woman. 'I thought you was three 'awks. My kid comes runnin' in ter me. "Mumma," says she, "there's three brown things comin' over the 'ill," says she. An' I comes out smart, I can tell yer. "They'll be 'awks," I says to her. Oh, the 'awks about 'ere, yer wouldn't believe.'

The 'kid' gave us the benefit of one eye from behind the woman's pinafore—then retired again.

'Where's your old man?' asked Jim.

The woman blinked rapidly, screwing up her face.

'Away shearin'. Bin away a month. I suppose ye're not goin' to stop, are yer? There's a storm comin' up.'

'You bet we are,' said Jo. 'So you're on your lonely, missus?'

She stood, pleating the frills of her pinafore, and glancing from one to the other of us, like a hungry bird. I smiled at the thought of how Jim had pulled Jo's leg about her. Certainly her eyes were blue, and what hair she had was yellow, but ugly. She was a figure of fun. Looking at her, you felt there was nothing but sticks and wires under that pinafore—her front teeth were knocked out, she had red, pulpy hands and she wore on her feet a pair of dirty Bluchers.

'I'll go and turn out the horses,' said Jim. 'Got any embrocation? Poi's rubbed herself to hell!'

"Arf a mo!' The woman stood silent a moment, her nostrils expanding as she breathed. Then she shouted violently, 'I'd rather you didn't stop. . . . You *can't*, and there's the end of it. I don't let out that paddock any more. You'll have to go on; I ain't got nothing!'

'Well, I'm blest!' said Jo heavily. He pulled me aside. 'Gone a bit off 'er dot,' he whispered. 'Too much alone, *you know*,' very significantly. 'Turn the sympathetic tap on 'er, she'll come round all right.'

But there was no need—she had come round by herself.

'Stop if yer like!' she muttered, shrugging her shoulders. To me—'I'll give yer the embrocation if yer come along.'

'Right-o, I'll take it down to them.' We walked together up the garden path. It was planted on both sides with cabbages. They smelled like stale dish-water. Of flowers there were double poppies and sweet-williams. One little patch was divided off by pawa shells—presumably it belonged to the child—for she ran from her mother and began to grub in it with a broken clothes-peg. The yellow dog lay across the doorstep, biting fleas; the woman kicked him away.

'Gar-r, get away, you beast . . . the place ain't tidy. I 'aven't 'ad time ter fix things to-day—been ironing. Come right in.'

It was a large room, the walls plastered with old pages of English periodicals. Queen Victoria's Jubilee appeared to be the most recent number. A table with an ironing board and wash-tub on it, some wooden forms, a black horsehair sofa and some broken cane chairs pushed against the walls. The mantelpiece above the stove was draped in pink paper, further ornamented with dried grasses and ferns and a coloured print of Richard Seddon. There were four doors—one, judging from the smell, led into the 'Store,' one on to the 'backyard,' through a third I saw the bedroom. Flies buzzed in circles round the ceiling, and treacle papers and bundles of dried clover were pinned to the window curtains.

I was alone in the room; she had gone into the store for the embrocation. I heard her stamping about and muttering to herself: 'I got some, now where did I put that bottle? . . . It's behind the pickles . . . no, it ain't.' I cleared a place on the table and sat there, swinging my legs. Down in the paddock I could hear Jo singing and the sound of hammer strokes as Jim drove in the tent pegs. It was sunset. There is no twilight in our New Zealand days, but a curious half-hour when everything appears grotesque—it frightens—as though the savage spirit of the country walked abroad and sneered at what it saw. Sitting alone in the hideous room I grew afraid. The woman next door was a long time finding that stuff. What was she doing in there? Once I thought I heard her bang her hands down on the counter, and once she half moaned, turning it into a cough and clearing her throat. I wanted to shout 'Buck up!' but I kept silent.

'Good Lord, what a life!' I thought. 'Imagine being here day in, day out, with that rat of a child and a mangy dog. Imagine bothering about ironing. *Mad*, of course she's mad! Wonder how long she's been here—wonder if I could get her to talk.'

At that moment she poked her head round the door.

'Wot was it yer wanted?' she asked.

'Embrocation.'

340

'Oh, I forgot. I got it, it was in front of the pickle jars.'

She handed me the bottle.

'My, you do look tired, you do! Shall I knock yer up a few scones for supper! There's some tongue in the store, too, and I'll cook yer a cabbage if you fancy it.'

'Right-o.' I smiled at her. 'Come down to the paddock and bring the kid for tea.'

She shook her head, pursing up her mouth.

'Oh no. I don't fancy it. I'll send the kid down with the things and a billy of milk. Shall I knock up a few extry scones to take with yer ter-morrow?'

'Thanks.'

She came and stood by the door.

'How old is the kid?'

'Six—come next Christmas. I 'ad a bit of trouble with 'er one way an' another. I 'adn't any milk till a month after she was born and she sickened like a cow.'

'She's not like you—takes after her father?' Just as the woman had shouted her refusal at us before, she shouted at me then.

'No, she don't! She's the dead spit of me. Any fool could see that. Come on in now, Else, you stop messing in the dirt.'

I met Jo climbing over the paddock fence.

'What's the old bitch got in the store?' he asked.

'Don't know—didn't look.'

'Well, of all the fools. Jim's slanging you. What have you been doing all the time?'

'She couldn't find this stuff. Oh, my shakes, you are smart!'

Jo had washed, combed his wet hair in a line across his forehead, and buttoned a coat over his shirt. He grinned.

Jim snatched the embrocation from me. I went to the end of the paddock where the willows grew and bathed in the creek. The water was clear and soft as oil. Along the edges held by the grass and rushes white foam tumbled and bubbled. I lay in the water and looked up at the trees that were still a moment, then quivered lightly and again were still. The air smelt of rain. I forgot about the woman and the kid until I came back to the tent. Jim lay by the fire watching the billy boil.

I asked where Jo was, and if the kid had brought our supper.

'Pooh,' said Jim, rolling over and looking up at the sky.

'Didn't you see how Jo had been titivating? He said to me before he went up to the whare, 'Dang it! she'll look better by night light—at any rate, my buck, she's female flesh!'

'You had Jo about her looks—you had me too.'

'No—look here. I can't make it out. It's four years since I came past this way and I stopped here two days. The husband was a pal of mine once, down the West Coast—a fine, big chap, with a voice on him like a trombone. She'd been barmaid down the Coast—as pretty as a wax doll. The coach used to come this way then once a fortnight, that was before they opened the railway up Napier way, and she had no end of a time! Told me once in a confidential moment that she knew one hundred and twenty-five different ways of kissing!'

'Oh, go on, Jim! She isn't the same woman!'

''Course she is. . . . I can't make it out. What I think is the old man's cleared out and left her: that's all my eye about shearing. Sweet life! The only people who come through now are Maoris and sundowners!'

Through the dark we saw the gleam of the kid's pinafore. She trailed over to us with a basket in her hand, the milk billy in the other. I unpacked the basket, the child standing by.

'Come over here,' said Jim, snapping his fingers at her.

She went, the lamp from the inside of the tent cast a bright light over her. A mean, undersized brat, with whitish hair and weak eyes. She stood, legs wide apart and her stomach protruding.

'What do you do all day?' asked Jim.

She scraped out one ear with her little finger, looked at the result and said, 'Draw.'

'Huh! What do you draw? Leave your ears alone!'

'Pictures.'

'What on?'

'Bits of butter paper an' a pencil of my Mumma's.'

'Boh! What a lot of words at one time!' Jim rolled his eyes at her. 'Baa-lambs and moo-cows?'

'No, everything. I'll draw all of you when you're gone, and your horses and the tent, and that one'—she pointed to me—with no clothes on in the creek. I looked at her where she couldn't see me from.'

'Thanks very much. How ripping of you,' said Jim. 'Where's Dad?'

The kid pouted. 'I won't tell you because I don't like yer face!' She started operations on the other ear.

'Here,' I said. 'Take the basket, get along home and tell the other man supper's ready.'

'I don't want to.'

'I'll give you a box on the ear if you don't,' said Jim savagely.

'Hie! I'll tell Mumma. I'll tell Mumma.' The kid fled.

We ate until we were full, and had arrived at the smoke stage before Jo came back, very flushed and jaunty, a whisky bottle in his hand.

''Ave a drink—you two!' he shouted, carrying off matters with a high hand. ''Ere, shove along the cups.'

'One hundred and twenty-five different ways,' I murmured to Jim.

'What's that? Oh! stow it!' said Jo. 'Why 'ave you always got your knife into me? You gas like a kid at a Sunday School beano. She wants us to go there to-night and have a comfortable chat. I'—he waved his hand airily—'I got 'er round.'

'Trust you for that,' laughed Jim. 'But did she tell you where the old man's got to?'

Jo looked up. 'Shearing! You 'eard 'er, you fool!'

The woman had fixed up the room, even to a light bouquet of sweet-williams on the table. She and I sat one side of the table, Jo and Jim the other. An oil lamp was set between us, the whisky bottle and glasses, and a jug of water. The kid knelt against one of the forms, drawing on butter paper; I wondered, grimly, if she was attempting the creek episode. But Jo had been right about night time. The woman's hair was tumbled—two red spots burned in her cheeks—her eyes shone—and we knew that they were kissing feet under the table. She had changed the blue pinafore for a white calico dressing-jacket and a black skirt—the kid was decorated to the extent of a blue sateen hair ribbon. In the stifling room, with the flies buzzing against the ceiling and dropping on to the table, we got slowly drunk.

'Now listen to me,' shouted the woman, banging her fist on the table. 'It's six years since I was married, and four miscarriages. I says to 'im, I says, what do you think I'm doin' up 'ere? If you was back at the Coast I'd 'ave you lynched for child murder. Over and over I tells 'im—you've broken my spirit and spoiled my looks, and wot for—that's wot I'm driving at.' She clutched her head with her hands and stared round at us. Speaking rapidly, 'Oh, some days—an' months of them—I 'ear them two words knockin' inside me all the time—"Wot for!" but sometimes I'll be cooking the spuds an' I lifts the lid off to give 'em a prong and I 'ears, quite suddin again, "Wot for!" Oh! I don't mean only the spuds and the kid—I mean—I mean', she hiccoughed—'you know what I mean, Mr. Jo.'

'I know,' said Jo, scratching his head.

'Trouble with me is,' she leaned across the table, 'he left me too much alone. When the coach stopped coming, sometimes he'd go away days, sometimes he'd go away weeks, and leave me ter look after the store. Back 'e'd come—pleased as Punch. "Oh, 'allo," 'e'd say. "'Ow are you gettin' on? Come and give us a kiss." Sometimes I'd turn a bit nasty, and then 'e'd go off again, and if I took it all right, 'e'd wait till 'e could twist me round 'is finger, then 'e'd say, "Well, so long, I'm off", and do you think I could keep 'im?—not me!'

'Mumma,' bleated the kid, 'I made a picture of them on the 'ill, an' you an' me an' the dog down below.'

'Shut your mouth!' said the woman.

A vivid flash of lightning played over the room—we heard the mutter of thunder.

'Good thing that's broke loose,' said Jo. 'I've 'ad it in me 'ead for three days.'

'Where's your old man now?' asked Jim slowly.

The woman blubbered and dropped her head on to the table. 'Jim, 'e's gone shearin' and left me alone again,' she wailed.

"'Ere, look out for the glasses,' said Jo. 'Cheer-o, 'ave another drop. No good cryin' over spilt 'usbands! You, Jim, you blasted cuckoo!'

'Mr. Jo,' said the woman, drying her eyes on her jacket frill, 'you're a gent, an' if I was a secret woman I'd place any confidence in your 'ands. I don't mind if I do 'ave a glass on that.'

Every moment the lightning grew more vivid and the thunder sounded nearer. Jim and I were silent—the kid never moved from her bench. She poked her tongue out and blew on her paper as she drew.

'It's the loneliness,' said the woman, addressing Jo—he

made sheep's eyes at her—'and bein' shut up 'ere like a broody
'en.' He reached his hand across the table and held hers, and
though the position looked most uncomfortable when they
wanted to pass the water and whisky, their hands stuck together
as though glued. I pushed back my chair and went over to the
kid, who immediately sat flat down on her artistic achievements
and made a face at me.

'You're not to look,' said she.

'Oh, come on, don't be nasty!' Jim came over to us, and
we were just drunk enough to wheedle the kid into showing us.
And those drawings of hers were extraordinary and repulsively
vulgar. The creations of a lunatic with a lunatic's cleverness.
There was no doubt about it, the kid's mind was diseased.
While she showed them to us, she worked herself up into a
mad excitement, laughing and trembling, and shooting out her
arms.

'Mumma,' she yelled. 'Now I'm going to draw them what
you told me I never was to—now I am.'

The woman rushed from the table and beat the child's head
with the flat of her hand.

'I'll smack you with yer clothes turned up if yer dare say
that again,' she bawled.

Jo was too drunk to notice, but Jim caught her by the arm.
The kid did not utter a cry. She drifted over to the window and
began picking flies from the treacle paper.

We returned to the table—Jim and I sitting one side, the
woman and Jo, touching shoulders, the other. We listened to
the thunder, saying stupidly, 'That was a near one,' 'There it
goes again,' and Jo, at a heavy hit, 'Now we're off,' 'Steady
on the brake,' until rain began to fall, sharp as cannon shot on
the iron roof.

'You'd better doss here for the night,' said the woman.

'That's right,' assented Jo, evidently in the know about this
move.

'Bring up yer things from the tent. You two can doss in the
store along with the kid—she's used to sleep in there and won't
mind you.'

'Oh, Mumma, I never did,' interrupted the kid.

'Shut yer lies! An' Mr. Jo can 'ave this room.'

It sounded a ridiculous arrangement, but it was useless to
attempt to cross them, they were too far gone. While the

woman sketched the plan of action, Jo sat, abnormally solemn and red, his eyes bulging, and pulling at his moustache.

'Give us a lantern,' said Jim, 'I'll go down to the paddock.' We two went together. Rain whipped in our faces, the land was light as though a bush fire was raging. We behaved like two children let loose in the thick of an adventure, laughed and shouted to each other, and came back to the whare to find the kid already bedded in the counter of the store. The woman brought us a lamp. Jo took his bundle from Jim, the door was shut.

'Good night all,' shouted Jo.

Jim and I sat on two sacks of potatoes. For the life of us we could not stop laughing. Strings of onions and half-hams dangled from the ceiling—wherever we looked there were advertisements for 'Camp Coffee' and tinned meats. We pointed at them, tried to read them aloud—overcome with laughter and hiccoughs. The kid in the counter stared at us. She threw off her blanket and scrambled to the floor, where she stood in her grey flannel night-gown rubbing one leg against the other. We paid no attention to her.

'Wot are you laughing at?' she said uneasily.

'You!' shouted Jim. 'The red tribe of you, my child.'

She flew into a rage and beat herself with her hands. 'I won't be laughed at, you curs—you.' He swooped down upon the child and swung her on to the counter.

'Go to sleep, Miss Smarty—or make a drawing—here's a pencil—you can use Mumma's account book.'

Through the rain we heard Jo creak over the boarding of the next room—the sound of a door being opened—then shut to.

'It's the loneliness,' whispered Jim.

'One hundred and twenty-five different ways—alas! my poor brother!'

The kid tore out a page and flung it at me.

'There you are,' she said. 'Now I done it ter spite Mumma for shutting me up 'ere with you two. I done the one she told me I never ought to. I done the one she told me she'd shoot me if I did. Don't care! Don't care!'

The kid had drawn the picture of the woman shooting at a man with a rook rifle and then digging a hole to bury him in.

She jumped off the counter and squirmed about on the floor biting her nails.

Jim and I sat till dawn with the drawing beside us. The rain ceased, the little kid fell asleep, breathing loudly. We got up, stole out of the whare, down into the paddock. White clouds floated over a pink sky—a chill wind blew; the air smelled of wet grass. Just as we swung into the saddle Jo came out of the whare—he motioned to us to ride on.

'I'll pick you up later,' he shouted.

A bend in the road, and the whole place disappeared.

(1911)

Millie

Millie stood leaning against the veranda until the men were out of sight. When they were far down the road Willie Cox turned round on his horse and waved. But she didn't wave back. She nodded her head a little and made a grimace. Not a bad young fellow, Willie Cox, but a bit too free and easy for her taste. Oh, my word! It was hot. Enough to fry your hair!

Millie put her handkerchief over her head and shaded her eyes with her hand. In the same distance along the dusty road she could see the horses, like brown spots dancing up and down, and when she looked away from them and over the burnt paddocks she could see them still—just before her eyes, jumping like mosquitoes. It was half-past two in the afternoon. The sun hung in the faded blue sky like a burning mirror, and away beyond the paddocks the blue mountains quivered and leapt like the sea.

Sid wouldn't be back until half-past ten. He had ridden over to the township with four of the boys to help hunt down the young fellow who'd murdered Mr. Williamson. Such a dreadful thing! And Mrs. Williamson left all alone with all those kids. Funny! she couldn't think of Mr. Williamson being dead! He was such a one for a joke. Always having a lark. Willie Cox said they found him in the barn, shot bang through the head, and the young English 'johnny' who'd been on the station learning farming—disappeared. Funny! she couldn't think of anyone shooting Mr. Williamson, and him so popular and all. My word! when they caught that young man! Well, you couldn't be sorry for a young fellow like that. As Sid said, if he wasn't strung up where would they all be? A man like that doesn't stop at one go. There was blood all over the barn. And Willie Cox said he was that knocked out he picked a cigarette up out of the blood and smoked it. My word! he must have been half dotty.

Millie went back into the kitchen. She put some ashes on the stove and sprinkled them with water. Languidly, the sweat pouring down her face, and dropping off her nose and chin, she cleared away the dinner, and going into the bedroom, stared at herself in the fly-specked mirror, and wiped her face and neck with a towel. She didn't know what was the matter with herself that afternoon. She could have a good cry—just for nothing—and then change her blouse and have a good cup of tea. Yes, she felt like that!

She flopped down on the side of the bed and stared at the coloured print on the wall opposite, *Garden Party at Windsor Castle*. In the foreground emerald lawns planted with immense oak trees, and in their grateful shade a muddle of ladies and gentlemen and parasols and little tables. The background was filled with the towers of Windsor Castle, flying three Union Jacks, and in the middle of the picture the old Queen, like a tea-cosy with a head on top of it. 'I wonder if it really looked like that.' Millie stared at the flowery ladies, who simpered back at her. 'I wouldn't care for that sort of thing. Too much side. What with the Queen an' one thing an' another.'

Over the packing-case dressing-table there was a large photograph of her and Sid, taken on their wedding day. Nice picture that—if you *do* like. She was sitting down in a basket chair, in her cream cashmere and satin ribbons, and Sid, standing with one hand on her shoulder, looking at her bouquet. And behind them there were some fern trees and a waterfall, and Mount Cook in the distance, covered with snow. She had almost forgotten her wedding day; time did pass so, and if you hadn't anyone to talk things over with, they soon dropped out of your mind. 'I wunner why we never had no kids. . . .' She shrugged her shoulders—gave it up. 'Well, *I've* never missed them. I wouldn't be surprised if Sid had, though. He's softer than me.'

And then she sat quiet, thinking of nothing at all, her red swollen hands rolled in her apron, her feet stuck out in front of her, her little head with the thick screw of dark hair drooped on her chest. *Tick-tick* went the kitchen clock, the ashes clinked in the grate, and the venetian blind knocked against the kitchen window. Quite suddenly Millie felt frightened. A queer trembling started inside her—in her stomach—and then spread all over to her knees and hands. 'There's somebody about.'

She tiptoed to the door and peered into the kitchen. Nobody there; the veranda doors were closed, the blinds were down, and in the dusky light the white face of the clock shone, and the furniture seemed to bulge and breathe . . . and listen, too. The clock—the ashes—and the venetian—and then again—something else, like steps in the back yard. 'Go an' see what it is, Millie Evans.'

She darted to the back door, opened it, and at the same moment someone ducked behind the wood pile. 'Who's that?' she cried, in a loud bold voice. 'Come out o' that! I seen yer. I know where y'are. I got my gun. Come out from behind of that wood stack!' She was not frightened any more. She was furiously angry. Her heart banged like a drum. 'I'll teach you to play tricks with a woman,' she yelled, and she took a gun from the kitchen corner, and dashed down the veranda steps, across the glaring yard to the other side of the wood stack. A young man lay there, on his stomach, one arm across his face. 'Get up! You're shamming!' Still holding the gun she kicked him in the shoulders. He gave no sign. 'Oh, my God, I believe he's dead.' She knelt down, seized hold of him, and turned him over on his back. He rolled like a sack. She crouched back on her haunches, staring; her lips and nostrils fluttered with horror.

He was not much more than a boy, with fair hair and a growth of fair down on his lips and chin. His eyes were open, rolled up, showing the whites, and his face was patched with dust caked with sweat. He wore a cotton shirt and trousers, with sandshoes on his feet. One of the trousers was stuck to his leg with a patch of dark blood. 'I *can't*,' said Millie, and then, 'You've got to.' She bent over and felt his heart. 'Wait a minute,' she stammered, 'wait a minute,' and she ran into the house for brandy and a pail of water. 'What are you going to do, Millie Evans? Oh, I don't know. I never seen anyone in a dead faint before.' She knelt down, put her arm under the boy's head and poured some brandy between his lips. It spilled down both sides of his mouth. She dipped a corner of her apron in the water and wiped his face and his hair and his throat, with fingers that trembled. Under the dust and sweat his face gleamed, white as her apron, and thin, and puckered in little lines. A strange dreadful feeling gripped Millie Evans' bosom— some seed that had never flourished there, unfolded and struck

350

deep roots and burst into painful leaf. 'Are yer coming round? Feeling all right again?' The boy breathed sharply, half choked, his eyelids quivered, and he moved his head from side to side. 'You're better,' said Millie, smoothing his hair. 'Feeling fine now again, ain't yer?' The pain in her bosom half suffocated her. 'It's no good you crying, Millie Evans. You got to keep your head.' Quite suddenly he sat up and leaned against the wood pile, away from her, staring on the ground. 'There now!' cried Millie Evans, in a strange, shaking voice.

The boy turned and looked at her, still not speaking, but his eyes were so full of pain and terror that she had to shut her teeth and clench her hands to stop from crying. After a long pause he said, in the little voice of a child talking in his sleep, 'I'm hungry.' His lips quivered. She scrambled to her feet and stood over him. 'You come right into the house and have a sit-down meal,' she said. 'Can you walk?' 'Yes,' he whispered, and swaying he followed her across the glaring yard to the veranda. At the bottom step he paused, looking at her again. 'I'm not coming in,' he said. He sat on the veranda step in the little pool of shade that lay round the house. Millie watched him. 'When did yer last 'ave anythink to eat?' He shook his head. She cut a chunk off the greasy corned beef and a round of bread plastered with butter; but when she brought it he was standing up, glancing round him, and paid no attention to the plate of food. 'When are they coming back?' he stammered.

At that moment she knew. She stood, holding the plate, staring. He was Harrison. He was the English johnny who'd killed Mr. Williamson. 'I know who you are,' she said, very slowly, 'yer can't fox me. That's who you are. I must have been blind in me two eyes not to 'ave known from the first.' He made a movement with his hands as though that was all nothing. 'When are they coming back?' And she meant to say, 'Any minute. They're on their way now.' Instead she said to the dreadful, frightened face, 'Not till 'arf-past ten.' He sat down, leaning against one of the veranda poles. His face broke up into little quivers. He shut his eyes, and tears streamed down his cheeks. 'Nothing but a kid. An' all them fellows after 'im. 'E don't stand any more of a chance than a kid would.' 'Try a bit of beef,' said Millie. 'It's the food you want. Somethink to steady your stomach.' She moved across the veranda and sat down beside him, the plate on her

351

knees. ''Ere—try a bit.' She broke the bread and butter into little pieces, and she thought. 'They won't ketch him. Not if I can 'elp it. Men is all beasts. I don't care wot 'e's done, or wot 'e 'asn't done. See 'im through, Millie Evans. 'E's nothink but a sick kid.'

.   .   .   .   .   .

Millie lay on her back, her eyes wide open, listening. Sid turned over, hunched the quilt round his shoulders, muttered 'Good night, ole girl.' She heard Willie Cox and the other chap drop their clothes on to the kitchen floor, and then their voices, and Willie Cox saying, 'Lie down, Gumboil. Lie down, yer little devil,' to his dog. The house dropped quiet. She lay and listened. Little pulses tapped in her body, listening, too. It was hot. She was frightened to move because of Sid. ''E must get off. 'E must. I don't care anythink about justice an' all that rot they've bin spoutin' to-night,' she thought savagely. ''Ow are yer to know what anythink's like till yer *do* know. It's all rot.' She strained to the silence. He ought to be moving. . . . Before there was a sound from outside, Willie Cox's Gumboil got up and padded sharply across the kitchen floor and sniffed at the back door. Terror started up in Millie. 'What's that dog doing? Uh! What a fool that young fellow is with a dog 'anging about. Why don't 'e lie down an' sleep.' The dog stopped, but she knew it was listening.

Suddenly, with a sound that made her cry out in horror the dog started barking and rushing to and fro. 'What's that? What's up?' Sid flung out of bed. 'It ain't nothink. It's only Gumboil. Sid, Sid!' She clutched his arm, but he shook her off. 'My Christ, there's somethink up. My God!' Sid flung into his trousers. Willie Cox opened the back door. Gumboil in a fury darted out into the yard, round the corner of the house. 'Sid, there's someone in the paddock,' roared the other chap. 'What is it—what's that?' Sid dashed out on to the front veranda. ''Ere, Millie, take the lantin. Willie, some skunk's got 'old of one of the 'orses.' The three men bolted out of the house, and at the same moment Millie saw Harrison dash across the pad-dock on Sid's horse and down the road. 'Millie, bring that blasted lantin.' She ran in her bare feet, her night-dress flicking her legs. They were after him in a flash. And at the sight of

Harrison in the distance, and the three men hot after, a strange mad joy smothered everything else. She rushed into the road—she laughed and shrieked and danced in the dust, jigging the lantern. 'A—ah! Arter 'im, Sid! A—a—a—h! Ketch him, Willie. Go it! Go it! A—ah, Sid! Shoot 'im down. Shoot 'im!'

(1913)

The Canary

*I have just finished a story with a canary
for the hero, and almost feel I have lived
in a cage and pecked a piece of chickweed
myself.*

You see that big nail to the right of the front door? I can
scarcely look at it even now and yet I could not bear to take it
out. I should like to think it was there always even after my
time. I sometimes hear the next people saying, 'There must
have been a cage hanging from there.' And it comforts me; I
feel he is not quite forgotten.

. . . You cannot imagine how wonderfully he sang. It was
not like the singing of other canaries. And that isn't just my
fancy. Often, from the window, I used to see people stop at
the gate to listen, or they would lean over the fence by the
mock-orange for quite a long time—carried away. I suppose
it sounds absurd to you—it wouldn't if you had heard him—
but it really seemed to me that he sang whole songs with a
beginning and an end to them.

For instance, when I'd finished the house in the afternoon,
and changed my blouse and brought my sewing on to the
veranda here, he used to hop, hop, hop from one perch to
another, tap against the bars as if to attract my attention, sip a
little water just as a professional singer might, and then break
into a song so exquisite that I had to put my needle down to
listen to him. I can't describe it; I wish I could. But it was
always the same, every afternoon, and I felt that I understood
every note of it.

. . . I loved him. How I loved him! Perhaps it does not
matter so very much what it is one loves in this world. But
love something one must. Of course there was always my

354

little house and the garden, but for some reason they were never enough. Flowers respond wonderfully, but they don't sympathise. Then I loved the evening star. Does that sound foolish? I used to go into the backyard, after sunset, and wait for it until it shone above the dark gum tree. I used to whisper, 'There you are, my darling.' And just in that first moment it seemed to be shining for me alone. It seemed to understand this . . . something which is like longing, and yet it is not longing. Or regret—it is more like regret. And yet regret for what? I have much to be thankful for.

. . . But after he came into my life I forgot the evening star; I did not need it any more. But it was strange. When the Chinaman who came to the door with birds to sell held him up in his tiny cage, and instead of fluttering, fluttering, like the poor little goldfinches, he gave a faint, small chirp, I found myself saying, just as I had said to the star over the gum tree, 'There you are, my darling.' From that moment he was mine.

. . . It surprises me even now to remember how he and I shared each other's lives. The moment I came down in the morning and took the cloth off his cage he greeted me with a drowsy little note. I knew it meant 'Missus! Missus!' Then I hung him on the nail outside while I got my three young men their breakfasts, and I never brought him in until we had the house to ourselves again. Then when the washing-up was done, it was quite a little entertainment. I spread a newspaper over a corner of the table, and when I put the cage on it he used to beat with his wings despairingly, as if he didn't know what was coming. 'You're a regular little actor,' I used to scold him. I scraped the tray, dusted it with fresh sand, filled his seed and water tins, tucked a piece of chickweed and half a chilli between the bars. And I am perfectly certain he understood and appreciated every item of this little performance. You see by nature he was exquisitely neat. There was never a speck on his perch. And you'd only to see him enjoy his bath to realise he had a real small passion for cleanliness. His bath was put in last. And the moment it was in he positively leapt into it. First he fluttered one wing, then the other, then he ducked his head and dabbled his breast feathers. Drops of water were scattered all over the kitchen, but still he would not get out. I used to say to him, 'Now that's quite enough. You're only showing off.' And at last out he hopped and, standing on one leg, he began to

peck himself dry. Finally he gave a shake, a flick, a twitter and
he lifted his throat—Oh, I can hardly bear to recall it. I was
always cleaning the knives at the time. And it almost seemed
to me the knives sang too, as I rubbed them bright on the
board.

. . . Company, you see—that was what he was. Perfect
company. If you have lived alone you will realise how precious
that is. Of course there were my three young men who came in
to supper every evening, and sometimes they stayed in the
dining-room afterwards reading the paper. But I could not
expect them to be interested in the little things that made my
day. Why should they be? I was nothing to them. In fact, I
overheard them one evening talking about me on the stairs as
'the Scarecrow.' No matter. It doesn't matter. Not in the least.
I quite understand. They are young. Why should I mind? But
I remember feeling so especially thankful that I was not quite
alone that evening. I told him, after they had gone out. I said,
'Do you know what they call Missus?' And he put his head on
one side and looked at me with his little bright eye until I could
not help laughing. It seemed to amuse him.

. . . Have you kept birds? If you haven't all this must sound,
perhaps, exaggerated. People have the idea that birds are
heartless, cold little creatures, not like dogs or cats. My washerwoman used to say on Mondays when she wondered why I
didn't keep 'a nice fox-terrier,' 'There's no comfort, Miss, in
a canary.' Untrue. Dreadfully untrue. I remember one night.
I had had a very awful dream—dreams can be dreadfully
cruel—even after I had woken up I could not get over it. So
I put on my dressing-gown and went down to the kitchen for a
glass of water. It was a winter night and raining hard. I suppose I was still half asleep, but through the kitchen window,
that hadn't a blind, it seemed to me the dark was staring in,
spying. And suddenly I felt it was unbearable that I had no one
to whom I could say 'I've had such a dreadful dream,' or—or
'Hide me from the dark.' I even covered my face for a minute.
And then there came a little 'Sweet! Sweet!' His cage was on
the table, and the cloth had slipped so that a chink of light
shone through. 'Sweet, Sweet!' said the darling little fellow
again, softly, as much as to say, 'I'm here, Missus! I'm here!'
That was so beautifully comforting that I nearly cried.

. . . And now he's gone. I shall never have another bird,

another pet of any kind. How could I? When I found him, lying on his back, with his eye dim and his claws wrung, when I realised that never again should I hear my darling sing, something seemed to die in me. My heart felt hollow, as if it was his cage. I shall get over it. Of course. I must. One can get over anything in time. And people always say I have a cheerful disposition. They are quite right. I thank my God I have.

. . . All the same, without being morbid, and giving way to —to memories and so on, I must confess that there does seem to me something sad in life. It is hard to say what it is. I don't mean the sorrow that we all know, like illness and poverty and death. No, it is something different. It is there, deep down, deep down, part of one, like one's breathing. However hard I work and tire myself I have only to stop to know it is there, waiting. I often wonder if everybody feels the same. One can never know. But isn't it extraordinary that under his sweet, joyful little singing it was just this—sadness?—Ah, what is it? —that I heard.

(1922)

NOTES AND SOURCES

Where no other source is indicated, stories are reprinted from the three collections published by Katherine Mansfield in her life-time (*In a German Pension*, 1911; *Bliss*, 1920; *The Garden-Party*, 1922) and the two posthumous collections made by J. Middleton Murry (*The Doves' Nest*, 1923; *Something Childish*, 1924). These five collections were reprinted, without alteration other than continuous pagination, in a single volume, *Collected Stories of Katherine Mansfield*, 1945. For other frequently cited references, the following abbreviations are used:

A.T.L. Alexander Turnbull Library, Wellington; which holds a large collection of Mansfield notebooks and manuscripts

Berkman S. Berkman, *Katherine Mansfield*, 1951

Journal, 1954 *Journal of Katherine Mansfield*, 1954

Journal, 1927 *Journal of Katherine Mansfield*, 1927

K.M. Katherine Mansfield

Letters, 1951 *Letters to John Middleton Murry 1913–22*, 1951

Letters, 1928 *Letters of Katherine Mansfield*, 2 vols., 1928

Scrapbook *The Scrapbook of Katherine Mansfield*, 1939

T.L.R. *Turnbull Library Record*, Wellington (periodical)

p. ix *The longer I live* . . . *Letters*, 1928, ii, p. 199.

p. xi *I am the little Colonial* . . . *Journal*, 1954, p. 157.

p. xiv *I want to write recollections of my own country* . . . *Journal*, 1954, p. 93.

p. xvi *Father at the last was wonderfully dear to me* . . . *Letters*, 1951, p. 387.

p. xviii *I have a passion for technique* . . . *Letters*, 1928, ii, p. 92.

p. xviii *I choose not only the length of every sentence* . . . *Letters*, 1928, ii, p. 88.

p. xix *I want to write a kind of long elegy* . . . *Journal*, 1954, p. 94.

p. 1 Part I SPRING: The Burnells. In this section, the 'heroine', Kezia, is a young child. The action moves from the original family home at 11 Tinakori Road ('A Birthday') to Chesney Wold, the house Harold Beauchamp acquired in Karori ('Prelude'; 'The Doll's House'; 'About Pat'), to a holiday house on the far side of Wellington Harbour ('At the Bay'), and back to Wellington.

p. 3 *My literary career began* . . . *Journal*, 1954, p. 252.

p. 3 'Enna Blake': *The High School Reporter* (Wellington Girls'

High School), 1898. It is printed as by 'Kathleen Beauchamp, aged nine years' and is followed by the prophetic note 'This story, written by one of the girls who have lately entered the school, shows promise of great merit.'

p. 5 'An Unfinished Memory': *Journal*, 1927 pp. 45–7. This journal entry (of 14 February 1916) written after Chummie's death is K.M.'s fullest 'statement of intention' of the family chronicle.

p. 7 'A Recollection of Childhood': *Journal*, 1927, pp. 48–52. Most of what Murry printed in both editions of the *Journal* and in the *Scrapbook* was assembled from notebooks and papers now held in A.T.L. An examination of these has revealed that Murry took very considerable editorial liberties with his material (see Ian A. Gordon, *Katherine Mansfield*, 1971 revised edition, pp. 29–32). He added titles (as here) and not infrequently mis-read a piece of fiction as a 'diary' entry. This 'recollection' is as much fiction as personal memory.

p. 10 'A Bad Idea': included by Murry (as an unfinished story) in *The Doves' Nest*. The theme of young husband/sick—probably pregnant—wife and the Wellington references ('tram'; the strong wind; 'tea'; (i.e. the New Zealand evening meal); the cows on the road) place it in the same 'fictional chronology' as the following story 'A Birthday', but the 'hero' is very different. For the real theme, see note on 'Cassandra', p. 336.

p. 13 'A Birthday': published as a 'German' story in *In a German Pension*, but the specific local references (the 'iron suspension bridge'; the 'fennel' in the 'gully'; the 'ferns'; the strong wind; the 'sea'; notably the 'dining-room looked over the breakwater of the harbour') clearly identify the scene as K.M.'s birthplace at 11 Tinakori Road. Recent motorway construction has destroyed some features, though the 'public-house at the corner' still remains.

p. 23 'How Pearl Button was Kidnapped': the 'dark women' are not (as has been suggested) gypsies, but New Zealand Maoris—they carry a 'flax basket of ferns' and one wears 'a green ornament round her neck' (i.e. a Maori greenstone 'tiki') and the men have 'feather mats round their shoulders'. A photograph, taken on the 1907 camping trip (see Introduction) shows K.M. with a group of Maoris so dressed. K.M. has projected the 1907 memory further back into her childhood. The title is ironic. Pearl Button is not 'kidnapped', but liberated, from the House of Boxes.

p. 27 'About Pat': *Scrapbook*, 1919, pp. 1–5. A 'Karori' sketch written when K.M. was in her London school and one of several published in the school's journal *Queen's College Magazine*.

p. 30   *I try to make family life so gorgeous* . . . Letter to A. E. Rice, January, 1921, printed in *Adam International Review*, no. 300, p. 93, London, 1965.

p. 30   'Prelude': This climactic story, which established K.M.'s full involvement with her Wellington/family chronicle theme, occupied her for a long time. It was begun as 'The Aloe' early in 1915, re-written (after Chummie's death) in December 1915 and in 1916, reshaped in its present form in the summer of 1917, and first published as a little hand-printed quarto in 1918 by Leonard and Virginia Woolf at the Hogarth Press.

The central scenes are set in the house and garden of Chesney Wold, in Karori, a suburb which is now part of Wellington but which in 1893 (the year of the Beauchamps' move) was an outlying village, approachable only by 'steep hills . . . bushy valleys . . . wide shallow rivers'. Literally and metaphorically, the Burnells/Beauchamps move into another world.

p. 73   'The Doll's House': The scene is the same as in 'Prelude'; the Burnell children are older and at school.

p. 81   'New Dresses': The grandmother 'Mrs. Carsfield' is the 'Mrs. Fairfield' of other stories. These names play on two family names—'Beauchamp' (i.e. 'Fairfield') and 'Mansfield'. In the *Rhythm* (1912) version, the family is Binzer and 'German'.

p. 93   *'Do you remember, Katie?' I hear his voice* . . . *Journal*, 1954, pp. 89–90. Chummie's arrival in England revived memories that flooded back to both. He was six years younger than K.M., but her reunion with a grown-up brother—now in every sense her 'contemporary'—strongly colours this section. Fictional brother and sister are always portrayed as equals and coevals.

p. 93   'Evening': *Journal*, 1954, pp. 83–5. They 'remember'.

p. 96   'The Apple-Tree': originally published as 'Autumn I' in *The Signature*, October 4, 1915. 'Bogey' is (here and elsewhere in K.M.) Chummie, but she also uses the name for Murry (sometimes differentiating him as 'dark Bogey'). Setting: the 'Prelude' garden with the 'lily-lawn' of the latter 'Garden-Party' house.

p. 100   *Don't think I underestimate* . . . *Letters*, 1928, ii, p. 96.

p. 100   'The Little Girl': the recurring child/father theme.

p. 105   'That Woman': *Scrapbook*, pp. 39–41. This title is probably Murry's.

p. 107   *I shall tackle something different* . . . *Journal*, 1954, p. 257.

p. 107   *It took me nearly a month to 'recover' from* At the Bay . . . *Journal*, 1954, p. 267.

p. 107 'At the Bay'; the setting is the Eastbourne/Day's Bay/ Muritai shore of Wellington Harbour, where Beauchamp rented summer quarters in the 1890's. Business-men could travel daily to work by the 'coach' (actually a horse-drawn bus) to the ferry wharf and so across the harbour to Wellington. Women and children were left to a long—timeless—summer's day. For a detailed discussion of the topography, with excellent photographs, see *T.L.R.*, November 1968, pp. 19–23; April 1969, pp. 15–21.

p. 143 'Rose Eagle': *Journal*, 1954, pp. 117–18. The 'hot December day' is an indication of a mid-summer New Zealand setting.

p. 145 'Aunt Fan': *Journal*, 1954, pp. 311–13. The 'D.I.C.' was (and is) a Wellington departmental store. The manuscript (in A.T.L.) has no title, which was supplied by Murry from one of K.M.'s lists of titles.

p. 147 'A Man and his Dog': a relatively late (1921) addition to the 'Prelude'/'The Doll's House' Karori group of stories. 'Chesney Flat' (i.e. Karori) is derived from the name of the Beauchamp 'Prelude' house, Chesney Wold.

p. 150 'Sixpence': written at Montana in 1921, when K.M. had contracted to write regularly for *The Sphere*, which published it in August. K.M. excluded this variation on the father/child theme from *The Garden-Party* of 1922 because she considered it 'sentimental' (see *Collected Stories*, p. 532).

p. 156 'The Skerritt Girl': *Journal*, 1954, pp. 264–6. A story fragment with Susannah/Kezia in childhood. The title is likely to be Murry's since 'Miss Skerritt', with her 'blue-black hairpin', is to Susannah one of the alien adults, not a 'girl'. C. P. Skerrett, a Wellington lawyer, was a neighbour of the Beauchamps in Thorndon.

p. 158 'Susannah': an unfinished variation on the child/father theme, with memories of a Wellington 'exhibition' at the 'recreation ground' at Basin Reserve.

p. 161 Part II SUMMER: The 'Burnells' have become the 'Sheridans'. The family move to a grander house in the Thorndon area of Wellington, though some of their neighbours are anything but grand. The children leave childhood and face the discoveries of adolescence.

p. 163 'Spring in Tyrrell Street': *Scrapbook*, 1939, p. 218. A brief sketch of 'Tyrrell Street' (i.e. Tinakori Road), the setting of the 'Garden-Party' house, which was number 75.

p. 164 'Sisters': *Journal*, 1954, pp. 308–9. Setting same as the previous, linked by the image of the 'butcher's cart'.

p. 166 'Saunders Lane': *Journal*, 1927, pp. 56–7. This description was written in 1916. The contrast between the life of Saunder's Lane and of 75 Tinakori Road was to become the concluding theme of 'The Garden-Party', written five years later. Little George Street, off Tinakori Road, was popularly known as 'Saunders Lane' from the name of a contractor who lived nearby. There had been a fatal accident at the corner of 'Hawke Street' (Hawkestone Street).

p. 167 'Kezia and Tui': *Scrapbook*, 1939, pp. 41–48. A manuscript version is in the A.T.L. (MS papers 119, no. 11) in which the grandmother is called 'Mrs. Preston' and Kezia is called 'Rachael' or 'Ray'. It contains no annotations by Murry. In general, where he alters a text, he gives no indication of this in the printed version, but scrupulously annotates the *manuscript* with a pencil note indicating what he has done. Since there is no annotation, it is possible he printed this story from a fair copy, in which K.M. had already dropped the thin disguise of 'Rachael' and 'Mrs. Preston' for the recognisable 'Kezia' and 'Mrs. Fairfield'.

When the Beauchamps left Karori, the girls moved from the village school ('The Doll's House') to Wellington Girls' High School and then to Miss Swainson's private school in Fitzherbert Terrace, where K.M. became friendly with a Maori classmate, Maata. She is to some extent the model for 'Tui', but the story is an amalgam of several elements, including the Maoris in 'How Pearl Button was Kidnapped' and even a suggestion of the halfcaste family (see 'Saunders Lane') who lived near the Beauchamps . . . note the 'weedy garden' and Tui's displeasure at her mother's 'piggy little house'. The 'real' Maata was sent by her parents to finish her education in Paris and London, where she resumed contact with K.M.

p. 172 'Maata': *Scrapbook*, 1939, pp. 26–7. This is the only fragment published of what K.M. planned as a long story with a Maori 'princess' as a heroine. She is a variant of Kezia. Further fragments of this planned but uncompleted story exist. There are two short pieces among the A.T.L. manuscripts; and a further portion was purchased at the Middleton Murry sale in London in 1957 for a buyer who has not responded to appeals for information made by the Turnbull Library. The reassembly of the full 'Maata' is at present not possible.

p. 174 'A Dream': *Journal*, 1927, pp. 106–7.

p. 175 *I dreamed a short story last night* . . . *Letters*, 1928, i, p. 127.

p. 175 'Sun and Moon': Berkman (p. 106) finds this story 'fanciful'. It is, in fact, a firm extension of the family chronicle in its period of lavish entertainment in the Garden-Party house at 75 Tinakori Road, the children younger and seen through the eyes of 'invisible' K.M./Laura. Structure and theme anticipate 'The Garden-Party': preparation, excitement, joy, then the grief for something 'broken—broken'.

p. 182 *Oh Chummie! Put your arms around me . . . Journal*, 1954, pp. 96–7.

p. 182 'The Wind Blows': originally published as 'Autumn II' in *The Signature*, October 18, 1915. The brother/sister pair are now Matilda/Bogey—note that K.M. on occasion used 'Matilda Berry' as a nom-de-plume. One of K.M.'s finest evocations of Wellington, which she included in her collection *Bliss*, so giving it her own imprimatur. The closing scene (the departure from Wellington wharf by ship) is re-echoed in 'The Scholarship'.

p. 187 'Love-Lies-Bleeding': *Scrapbook*, 1939, pp. 65–73. In spite of the 'German' surnames and christian names, the story is set in Wellington and is part of the 'Sheridan' series. 'Eichelbaum' is a memory of the late Siegfried Eichelbaum, LL.B., one of K.M.'s dancing partners in 1907; the nuns collect for an orphanage at 'Lyall Bay'—a Wellington suburb. The whereabouts of the manuscript are unknown. It is not in A.T.L. Murry may have misread K.M.'s handwriting. She probably wrote not 'Muffi' but 'Mutti' (the Bavarian diminutive for 'Mutter' i.e. 'Mother'). For 'Rudi' cf. 'Roddy' (i.e. Chummie).

p. 193 'Sewing Class': *Journal*, 1954, pp. 114–17.

p. 196 'The Dressmaker': *Journal*, 1954, pp. 299–30. A few slight corrections have been made, from the A.T.L. manuscript.

p. 198 'A Dance': *Journal*, 1954, pp. 209–10. Laura/Laurie/Grandmother. K.M. and her sisters returned from London to Wellington, December 1906. During 1907 K.M. went to various dances; but Chummie was twelve years old and her grandmother was dead. The scene, based on telescoped memories, is fiction, not a reconstruction of actual events.

p. 199 'Her First Ball': the heroine Leila (like K.M. in 1907) is eighteen. Her cousins, the three Sheridan girls and their brother Laurie (old enough to be a partner, with new white gloves) at the ball. Again, fiction, not a record of actual events, but the Wellington scene sharply remembered—balls in 1907 took place in the 'drill hall' in Maginnity Street.

p. 206 *The light should fall on the figure of Mrs. Sheridan . . . Journal*

1954, pp. 324–5. K.M. recalls in precise detail the topography of the area of the 'Garden-Party' house.

p. 206 'The Sheridans': *Scrapbook*, 1939, pp. 219-24. An evocation of the entire 'family'.

p. 209 *This isn't bad . . . I wish I could go back to N.Z. for a year*: *Scrapbook*, 1939, p. 184. K.M.'s comment on the story following.

p. 209 'By Moonlight': *Scrapbook*, 1939, pp. 180–4. A continuation of 'The Sheridans', though the two servants are given 'foreign' names, Zaidee and Hans. The manuscript is A.T.L. Mansfield notebook no. 25. K.M. wrote 'shavings of pineapple-outside'. Murry noted in pencil on the manuscript: 'I altered to "rind".' Some other minor corrections have been incorporated from the manuscript.

p. 213 *I am sitting in my own room thinking of Mother . . . Journal*, 1954, p. 154.

p. 213 *I thought of the Burnells . . . much better the Sheridans . . . Journal*, 1954, p. 313.

p. 213 'The Garden-Party': This famous story pulls together and rounds off all the scenes, the characters, and the themes of the whole second section. The children are no longer children, but young adults, facing 'the diversity of life and how we try to fit in everything, Death included' (*Letters*, 1928, ii, p. 196).

p. 229 Part III SUMMER'S END: In this section, childhood is left behind. Even where childhood is evoked, in memories of holidays across Cook Strait to Picton and the (Marlborough) Sounds (as in 'The Voyage') it is shadowed by adult experience. For the young, it is a time for decision ('Taking the Veil'; 'The Scholarship'), leaving the family behind.

p. 231 *One day I must write about Grandma . . . Journal*, 1954, p. 289.

p. 231 'The Voyage': Grandmother, granddaughter; the shadow of the dead mother.

p. 240 *If we are ever together down the Pelorus Sounds ... Letters*, 1928, ii, p. 143.

p. 240 'Down the Sounds': *Journal*, 1954, pp. 304–6. 'Kit' is a small hand-bag (from Maori *kete*: bag woven from strands of flax).

p. 242 'The New Baby': *Journal*, 1954, pp. 309–11. To the visitors, the holiday place of childhood looks idyllic, but 'imagine being stuck there, month in—year in, year out ... Christ! what a life!' The summer of childhood is over.

p. 244 *The daughter of the watchsmith . . . Journal*, 1954, p. 214. K.M. (1920) planning the story following, which was not begun till over a year later. The 'great shadow' is emblematic of this whole section.

p. 244 'Weak Heart': Setting 'Tarana Street' (i.e. Tinakori Road, which is intersected by May Street). The theme of this unfinished story is the death of young hopes.

p. 248 *It took me about 3 hours . . . Journal*, 1954, p. 290. This is a key passage for the understanding of K.M.'s Wellington scenes. Her visual memory never failed her.

p. 248 'Taking the Veil': The setting is Wellington ('Port Willin'), in the gardens of the Hill Street Convent, which was a short distance from the 'Garden-Party' house. The heroine (like K.M. in 1907) is eighteen, day-dreaming of leaving family and friends. It is, like the following story, a symbolic leave-taking.

p. 253 'The Scholarship': Murry printed this, as an unfinished story, in *Scrapbook*, 1939, pp. 93–100. He was unaware that he had already printed its conclusion (in the 1927 edition of the *Journal*, pp. 77–8) as a 'journal' entry to which he supplied a title 'A Good Day'. Murry, as has been noted, sometimes cannot distinguish between K.M.'s personal 'journal' entries and the short sections of fiction which she wrote up in her notebooks. The final paragraphs of the story (beginning 'He woke, but did not move . . .') have here been re-united, to present the story complete.

Henry wins a scholarship that will take him to Europe. He climbs the 'steepest' hill of the hilly town of Wellington (Tinakori Hill, which overlooks the 'Garden-Party' house) and surveys his 'darling little town' and its harbour. In his imagination he is already aboard the ship for 'this affair called Life'—'I'm there—I'm there'. The story is K.M.'s farewell to Wellington and to childhood.

p. 259 Part IV WINTER: In this final section of the family chronicle, the children have all grown up. Kezia has become the married and disillusioned Cassandra. Father and mother grow older and apart ('The Stranger') and in the end there is only the cold memory of the dead ('Six Years After'; 'The Fly'; 'The Canary').

p. 261 'Cassandra': *Scrapbook*, 1939, pp. 157–61. The resentment in this story is associated with K.M.'s suspicions of Murry, recorded in a notebook begun 27 December, 1920 (A.T.L. Mansfield notebook no. 35). This notebook was not used in the 1927 edition of the *Journal* but some of its entries were later dispersed among *Scrapbook* 1939, pp. 161–2 and *Journal*, 1954, p. 228, pp. 229–30, pp. 232–3.

K.M. makes a 'Sheridan' family story out of her distrust.

p. 264 *I've been this man. been this woman . . . Letters*, 1928, ii, p. 72.

p. 264 'The Stranger': The jealousies of middle-age. The story was completed in November 1920 and reflects the mood of 'Cassandra', which was written at the same time—the theme of distrust. She projects it to the Sheridans, now (as they age) the Hammonds.

p. 276 *A long typical boat dream . . . Journal*, 1954, p. 281. A 'boat-dream', involving a return to New Zealand, is frequently recorded in K.M.'s diaries and notebooks.

p. 276 'Six Years After': Chummie was killed on 7 October 1915. In October 1921 K.M. began a notebook (A.T.L. Mansfield notebook no. 41) which contains two lists of 'story' outlines, including the following: 'N.Z. Six Years After: A wife and husband aboard a steamer. They see someone who reminds them'. The resultant story appears elsewhere in the notebook. It is a chilling evocation of middle-aged wife, husband, dead son.

p. 281 'An Ideal Family': An evocation of what might have been. The scene is recognisably the magnificent Beauchamp house at the corner of Fitzherbert Terrace (altered to 'fashionable Harcourt Avenue') to which K.M. returned in 1906. Father has grown old. The son has taken his place in the business—significantly, the son's name is 'Harold'—he has taken over both name and business. The title is ironic: the old man is finished, swept aside by the girls, and the story concludes with the 'spider' (death), the creeping insect image that will be repeated in 'The Fly'.

p. 288 'The Office Boy': *Scrapbook*, 1939, pp. 227–31. K.M. abandoned this unfinished story with the note 'It is a silly story'. Instinctively, she must have recognised that she was blending two incompatible worlds—the banker/father/Boss and the boy (who is the son of 'old Ma Parker'). But the figure of the Boss remained in her mind and became the centre of the next great story.

p. 291 'The Fly': The slight local references ('the City'; 'Windsor Castle'; 'the *Financial Times*') imply a London setting, but 'old Mr. Woodifield' and 'the boss' are both aspects of the Burnell/ Sheridan/Hammond/Neave figure and this remarkable story of father and dead son ('over six years had passed away') is a fitting close to the family chronicle—'what it was he had been thinking about.' The dead are in the end forgotten. But see 'The Canary' in the next section.

p. 297 Part V: SCENES FROM COLONIAL LIFE. It is significant that (with one exception) these stories are either early or uncompleted. They lack the sense of commitment of the family chronicle. The exception is 'The Canary', which—apart from its overt theme—belongs in many ways to the previous section.

p. 299 'Old Tar': an early story, printed in the *Westminster Gazette*, 25 October, 1913, but never before collected. Setting is Karori. Makara Hill (the local pronunciation is 'Makra') overlooks the Beauchamp house, Chesney Wold.

p. 304 'The Wrong House': set in Wellington.

p. 307 'Second Violin': one manuscript draft indicates an 'English' setting but 'Bolton Street' is Wellington. The story was abandoned, perhaps because of this inherent confusion.

p. 310 'Honesty': incomplete; setting partly Wellington.

p. 314 'Daphne': the text was derived by Murry from a series of pieces in a notebook written 1921–2 (A.T.L. Mansfield notebook no. 31). It is a 'Wellington' story ('Port Willin' or 'Wellinborough' in the manuscript) but the point of view is that of a satirical 'outsider' and is completely at variance with the deeply-felt family chronicle. It was probably started to fulfil her 1921 contract with *The Sphere* but abandoned. Compare for tone the 1921 *Sphere* story 'Marriage a la Mode'.

p. 319 'A Married Man's Story': Much of this uncompleted story is not localised, but the childhood scenes in the fifth section are set in New Zealand—the 'oozing clay banks' and the 'rusty water in the school tank' belong to the Karori period.

p. 333 'Ole Underwood': an early (1912) Wellington story. It is a 'dark' version of 'The Scholarship'—Wellington is a prison and the only escape is the wharves and the ships with the flag flying.

p. 337 'The Woman at the Store': an early (1911) thriller based on K.M.'s memories of the 1907 camping trips through the isolated settlements of the New Zealand backblocks. 'Good Lord, what a life . . . day in, day out . . .' Cf. 'The New Baby' (note, p. 365).

p. 348 'Millie': an early New Zealand thriller (1913) written for *The Blue Review*.

p. 354 *I have just finished a story with a canary for a hero . . . Letters*, 1928, ii, p. 225. K.M. to her father.

p. 354 'The Canary': completed 7 July 1922. In an affectionate letter to her father written at Sierre on 9 July (from which the above comment is derived) she wrote 'I too wish that I were taking a trip home with you'. 'The Canary' is the last story K.M. wrote. It is unobtrusively but firmly set in Wellington. Beauchamp had arrived in London in late June. He wrote K.M. three letters in rapid succession to Sierre, and thoughts of her family filled her mind, resulting in 'The Canary', her final elegy to Chummie. It carries unconscious echoes of what she had earlier written—the lonely woman in 'The

Canary' looking at the evening star 'after sunset' and whispering 'There you are, my darling' recalls K.M.'s *Journal* entry on Chummie in 1916 'You, my little sun of it, are set'. Like 'The Fly', another elegy on her dead brother, 'The Canary' is full of symbolism of which even the author was unaware.